BENEATH THE SKIN

KYLA STONE

PAPER MOON PRESS

Copyright © 2016 by Kyla Stone

All rights reserved.

No part of this book may be reproduced in any form or by any electronic or mechanical means, including information storage and retrieval systems, without written permission from the author, except for the use of brief quotations in a book review.

This book is a work of fiction. Any references to historical events, real people, or real places are used fictitiously. Other names, characters, places, and events are products of the author's imagination, and any resemblances to actual events or places or persons, living or dead, is entirely coincidental.

Printed in the United States of America

Cover design by Clarissa Yeo

First Printing December, 2016

Paper Moon Press

Atlanta, Georgia

ISBN: 978-1-945410-02-4

Created with Vellum

*To my mother, who courageously fought her own battle and won,
freeing herself and her children from the cycle of abuse.
Thank you for saving us.*

There are wounds
that never show on the body
that are deeper and more hurtful
than anything that bleeds.
-Laurel K. Hamilton

ONE

For half a second, I allow myself to believe I'll get away with it. That for once, something will go right in my stupid, sucky life. I guess hope springs eternal, even for a diehard cynic. Until now, anyway.

"Sidney Shaw, please come to the principal's office." The intercom hiccups with static. "Sidney Shaw, you are needed immediately in the principal's office."

My heart jolts in my chest. The whole AP Spanish III class stops mid-verb conjugation and turns to stare at me. I stuff my book and papers into my backpack as Mr. Primero orders everyone to refocus.

I walk through the empty halls to the principal's office, my stomach curdling with dread. The only sounds are the rustle and murmur of voices behind closed classroom doors and my sneakers scuffing the worn floor.

The secretary buzzes me through the locked door into the office suite. She's in her twenties, but wears old-lady glasses. She peers at me over her cat-eye frames like she knows everything, as if she's already formulating the gossip she's going to spread in the teacher's lounge during her next coffee break.

"Have a seat, Miss Shaw." She pops her gum and gestures at the parallel waiting room sofas covered in some swirly floral pattern from the nineties. A frizzy-haired freshman curls up on one of the couches, her face an unfortunate shade of green.

I sit down on the cushion closest to the principal's office. I'm twitchy, jumpy. My fists clench and unclench on my lap.

I can hear voices through the wooden door. Apparently, the meeting started without me.

"Honestly, I don't know that another suspension is even going to get through to her," the high-pitched voice of the principal, Mrs. Rittenburg, says from the other side of the door.

"Clearly, something must be done," says the vice-principal, Mr. Adeyemi, in his deep baritone.

There's a new voice. Muffled, edgy, irate. "I've had enough! That girl is a menace to society. The seriousness of this offense warrants an arrest. I want her expelled."

Mrs. Rittenburg clears her throat. "Yes, Mr. Cole. We'll take your concern under advisement. Rest assured, we *will* take appropriate disciplinary action."

I stare at my rings. Red splotches fleck the cheap metal and plastic. My knuckles still sting. It hurt more than I thought it would, the shock waves traveling all the way up my arm. And the sound of it, the soft squelch of my fist hitting flesh. I wince.

I try not to think about expulsion, a possibility that grows stronger with every passing moment. I've had plenty of detentions and a few suspensions over my high school career, but it will be some kind of record to get expelled less than two weeks into my senior year.

Frank will go nuclear if I get expelled. He'll do more than that. Acid coats the back of my throat. I swallow hard.

My knee starts shaking. You can't exactly put expulsion on your college applications. And I can't stay here in this pathetic Podunk town full of cornfields and morons. I can't.

There's a pause in the ranting through the door. I can barely hear a fourth voice. I tilt my head without overtly looking like I'm listening.

". . . calm down for a second."

"Calm down for a second?" Mr. Cole bellows.

". . . heat of the moment . . . overreacting . . . look at this from another angle."

The fourth voice belongs to the guidance counselor, Dr. Yang. I've had weekly appointments with him since October of junior year, when I decided to take a stand for feminism. I may have flipped off the P.E. teacher for forcing me to wear my too-short and too-tight uniform. I may have also suggested Coach Taylor was a pervert for insisting on required activewear that showcased the adolescent female form. While I've been stuck with Dr. Yang for a year, I'm also allowed to wear my uniform sweatpants permanently.

I don't think I'm getting my way this time. My knee shakes harder. Green-faced girl opens her eyes, glares at me for a second, then flips on her side and turns her back.

Dr. Yang is still talking. I've missed a large chunk of it. ". . . gifted student . . . shame to lose . . ."

"How dare you!" Mr. Cole cuts in. "What about the malicious assault of my son?"

". . . not technically on school grounds . . . extenuating circumstances."

"You've got to be kidding me!"

Mrs. Rittenburg says something too softly for me to hear, something about "your responsibility."

Mr. Cole slams open the door and storms out. It's been four years since I last saw him, since I hung out with his stepdaughter and my ex-best friend, Jasmine Cole. He looks at me and curls his upper lip in a snarl of rage, but he keeps on walking.

Mrs. Rittenburg calls me in. She stands behind her massive desk, all five feet and two inches of her, hands fisted on her hips. Vice Principal Adeyemi towers next to her.

"Sidney, I'm sure we don't need to tell you how upset Mr. Cole is," Mrs. Rittenburg proceeds to lecture me, her voice grating my ears. "We have a zero-tolerance bullying policy. Do you understand? You need to seriously consider your future, young lady."

"Yes, ma'am," I nod, acting concerned and adequately contrite. My pulse pounds in my ears. The lights are too bright. I'm dizzy and sick to my stomach.

Then it comes.

They're not going to expel me.

Relief floods through me, almost enough to wash the nausea away. Almost.

I murmur "Yes, ma'am" whenever the principal pauses, keeping my gaze glued to the faded orange carpet. If I let myself meet her gaze, she'll realize I'm not sorry. I'm not sorry at all.

Dr. Yang taps my shoulder. "My office. Now."

I follow him out of the principal's office and down the hall without speaking. The counseling office is small and crowded with a laminate desk, some puke-green file cabinets, and a bulletin board stuffed with inspirational clichés like "Genius is 10% inspiration and 90% perspiration" and "Everyone is a Winner." There's a photo on his desk of a pretty Asian lady with a wide, laughing smile.

I sink into the navy La-Z-Boy across from his desk and cross my arms over my chest. "That guy has a major case of male PMS. Am I right?"

Dr. Yang clears his throat and smooths his slightly rumpled gray suit. He's Korean and somewhere north of forty, the first strands of gray threading through the black hair combed across his forehead. He rests his elbows on his desk and steeples his fingers under his chin. One finger taps against his jaw. "Are you ready to talk?"

"What for?"

"You do realize you're teetering on the edge, don't you?" He pauses as if I'm supposed to reply. "You were almost expelled today. Mr. Cole wanted to file an assault report. He still might."

My breath hitches in my throat. "Yeah, I got that."

He adjusts his glasses, squinting at me like he's trying to analyze some foreign object for the first time. "Sidney. What in the world were you thinking, beating up a twelve-year-old boy?"

"I didn't beat him up. We were clearing up a misunderstanding."

"You still have blood on your rings!"

I glance down at my hands, surprised he's noticed. "Okay, fine. I might have hit him."

"Whatever for?"

"I'm pretty sure he's a demon's spawn out to steal the souls of the impressionable young students of Brokewater Elementary."

"And I'm pretty sure he's not. Try again."

I twirl my plastic ring with the blue flower around my middle finger. "Okay, fine. He's an alien in child-form sent to earth to gather intelligence on us. He must be destroyed before the mothership returns."

"Sidney, I'm on your side. When are you going to start believing that?"

I snort. No one's on my side. I'm on my own. Always have been, always will be. "I couldn't help myself. He has a punchable face."

Dr. Yang's finger keeps tapping his jaw. "What do you have to lose by telling me the truth?"

That one gets me. I don't have anything to lose. And Dr. Yang saved my ass just now, whether I want to admit it or not. He's been trying to save me for over a year. The fact that I'm beyond saving hasn't registered on his radar yet. "Okay, fine. Look, this isn't some adorable little kid we're talking about here, okay? That prick is a sociopath in training. He torments my little brother constantly."

Every day since school started two weeks ago, eight-year-old Aaron has come home with red finger marks on his arms, bruised knees, rips in his shirt, and tiny pinpricks in his skin from the sharp jab of a mechanical pencil. Yesterday, a deep purple bruise pooled around his right eye.

He finally admitted the bully was Jackson Cole, Jasmine's younger brother. When he spoke Jackson's name, something cold and dark slithered into my brain. There was no way in hell I was letting another Cole mess with this family. Not again.

"Okay." Dr. Yang nods emphatically. "I think I get it, but there are other ways to handle bullying."

"You don't understand. Aaron is … different. He can't defend himself. Someone has to." I tried to get Aaron to stand up for himself, but he couldn't. He's weak, soft in all the wrong places. He never fights back. Never. The world stomps all over him, and he just lets it happen. He's going to be someone's prey his entire life. I can't let that happen. I won't. He's good—innocent and pure in a way no one else is. I want him to stay that way.

"If bullying is an issue, one of your parents should contact the teacher or the elementary school administration."

I snort again. In what fantasy world would that ever happen? Ma and Frank don't even put food on the table half the time. They're either drunk or fighting or gone. It's my job to protect my brothers. No one else will. "Are you serious right now?"

He sighs. "I do realize your parents aren't the most . . . reliable, but you can't just—"

"I had to take care of it myself, okay?"

And I did take care of it, just like I'd promised Aaron. The thought of Jasmine Cole's brother hurting him burned like a white flame in the center of my skull. I needed to make sure Jackson regretted ever messing with my family, just like I made Jasmine regret messing with me.

I skipped first period this morning and waited at the bus stop on the corner of Elm and Broadview in the only upscale neighborhood in Brokewater. Jackson rode the 709 bus, the same one Jasmine used to take before her step-daddy bought her a new Camaro in junior year. A few younger kids milled around on the sidewalk, untucking their designer T-shirts and kicking at stray pebbles with their $80 shoes.

Jackson Cole slouched up to the bus stop in skater jeans and an over-sized orange shirt emblazoned, "Skate. Eat. Repeat." He high-fived a couple of lookalike twerps. Before he could do anything else, I was on him.

I spun him around and got right up in his face. His eyes widened.

"Look, you ferret-faced little monster. I'm going to say this once, and only once. You lay a hand on Aaron, or even look at him sideways, and I will come after you with a chainsaw and chop off those fancy shoes of yours. We clear?"

His surprise faded quickly. "Get your hands off me. My dad's a lawyer."

"That's a big fat lie. I happen to know he's a dentist. And a lousy one at that. Stay away from Aaron."

"And what if I don't?" He tossed his head, a fringe of highlighted blonde hair falling into his eyes.

I'd planned on just scaring some sense into him, not actually hurting him. But anger zapped through me like an electrical current. I couldn't help myself. I grabbed his shoulders and shook him. "Don't test me. I will rip your insides out and feed your entrails to you, piece by piece. Do you hear me? Leave. Him. Alone."

"Get off me!"

I gritted my teeth. Where was the shy kid who used to spy on me and Jasmine through her bedroom door, who used to do cannon-balls into the pool right next to our lounge chairs? I pushed the images out of my mind. That boy was long gone.

The bus pulled up next to us. He glared at me in disgust. "That gay prick gets everything he's got coming to him."

That's when I punched Jackson Cole right in his smug little face.

He dropped to the pavement, grabbing his nose with both hands, blood spurting between his fingers. The rest of the kids stared at me in shock, like I'd just transformed into a wild grizzly bear before their very eyes. The bus driver yelled, "Hey! Hey, you! Get back here!"

I walked away, knuckles stinging. A fat, satisfied grin spread across my face.

I grin again, just thinking about it.

"Sidney, you have to understand," Dr. Yang says. "One more situation involving violence, and we're beyond expulsion. We'll be having a conversation about arrest warrants and police records. Scratch that. *You'll* be having the conversation—or worse—with cops, lawyers, and judges. Do you understand?"

"Yes." And I do. Dread scrabbles up and down my spine. My knee starts shaking again, and I push it down with my hands. "Can I go now?"

Dr. Yang watches me for a long moment. "Sidney, your potential, your obvious intelligence—no one wants to see that go to waste. Your PSAT scores were quite good. You could easily get into a decent college. It would make us all very happy to see you pursue your higher education."

I roll my eyes. "Well, if it'll make you happy, I'll definitely consider it."

"You have to turn things around, clean up your record. This is your senior year."

I know he's right, and I hate that about him. How often he's right, and I'm in the wrong. "Okay, fine. Whatever. I got it."

"And your Phys Ed grade. You have to bring it up. You already have a D in badminton. And it's only the second week of classes. Really?"

"Coach Taylor hates me."

"Haven't you given him good reason? I'm not sure why you signed up for another class with him when Coach Puglisi offers alternative P.E. classes."

"Because I'm not a Zumba girl, okay? Can you really see me in a ponytail and spandex? And I'm pretty sure Pilates would kill me." I'm also a glutton for punishment, apparently. "Can I go now?"

"No. Not yet. Did you hear the part about being suspended? You looked like you were doing your zoning out thing in Mrs. Rittenburg's office."

He surprises me again. I debate whether to admit it or not, but there's no harm in coming clean now. I shrug. "I might have missed a few things."

Dr. Yang nods. He looks tired. "One: three-day suspension. Two: a letter of apology to Jackson Cole. Three: twice-a-week counseling sessions."

Heat flushes through me. "Why should I apologize to a bully? No thanks. I'll pass."

"You can always choose expulsion."

I feel the walls closing in. I cannot be expelled. Not now, when it's finally senior year and escape is within sight, the red blinking EXIT sign that is graduation. And not when I know how Frank will react, what he'll do. My mouth goes dry. I hate every word of what I'm about to say. I hate this feeling of capitulation, of defeat, of letting the bad guys win. "Okay, fine. I'll write the stupid letter, but only under official protest. But why more counseling sessions? You know how much I love these weekly gab fests with you, but they interfere with my studies. It's my senior year, as you so graciously reminded me."

Dr. Yang writes something on a notepad. "We're going to try something a little different. Group counseling."

"That sounds horrifying. What is it?"

"You will continue to meet with me on Fridays during your free period at 10 a.m. But we're adding a session on Tuesdays at 9:30 a.m. You and at least one other student will meet with me as part of a small group therapy session."

I stare at him suspiciously. This really does sound horrifying. "Who?"

"Arianna Torrès, for one."

I laugh out loud. He's got to be joking. "No way."

"Yes."

"What the hell do I have in common with Miss Beauty Queen? Is she in grief therapy because she broke a nail?"

"We'll discuss things further at our next meeting. Your suspension is effective immediately. Counting today, tomorrow, and Monday, you'll be back just in time for Tuesday's session."

"Look, Doc. There's no way. I can't—"

He stands up and walks around his desk. He opens the office door. "You can, and you will. I happen to have faith in you, Sidney Shaw."

"Damn it all to hell." I spit the words out.

Arianna Torrès is one of the most popular girls in school, a firmly entrenched member of Jasmine Cole's platinum-haired Bitch Squad. She's on the student council, plays the flute, and worse, she's one of those goody-two-shoe Christians who meet at the flagpole to pray and plaster "Good Clean Fun Bible Study" posters all over the school every month.

Panic lurches through me, like Dr. Yang's just told me I'll be locked in a cage with a prowling tiger for an hour every week.

"Please take care of yourself," he says pleasantly. If there's one thing I know about Dr. Yang, it's that he's solid as a rock once his mind's made up. There's no getting through to him.

I grab my backpack and stomp out of his office. I tried to help Aaron and things got more than a little out of control. As usual, all I've done is make things worse. How much worse, I'm afraid to even think about.

TWO

All around me, students are laughing, shrieking, slamming locker doors, dropping binders and notebooks into backpacks and messenger bags, shoving each other, hugging and flirting. They move like some huge, mindless organism. I ignore them all.

I grab *King Lear,* my English notebook, and my Spanish III workbook out of my locker and shove them into my backpack. At least I can get some actual homework done during this ridiculous suspension. I shut my locker and turn around, nearly slamming into Jasmine freakin' Cole.

"You bitch!" Jasmine's formerly frizzy, mouse-brown hair is dyed ice blonde and falls sleekly down her back. She's wearing a white peasant shirt that skims her belly and perfectly frayed skinny jeans. I can barely see the girl I used to know through her contoured blush, heavy cat-eye liner, and spiky layers of mascara.

My hands curl at my sides, my muscles tensing. "Looks like someone forgot to take her happy pills this morning."

A small crowd forms a ring around me, with Jasmine right in the center. On her left is Margot Hunter, the ultimate Queen Bee of Brokewater High. Margot is tall and slim, perpetually tanned, with honey-blonde locks tumbling down her back in big, bombshell curls.

Though she looks like a cheerleader, she's into drama and musicals, and lands the starring role in every school play. The teachers worship her. She's charming on the surface, but nasty in an underhanded, passive, unprovable way. Tearing girls apart is as much a pastime for Margot Hunter as painting her nails.

Jasmine steps into my personal space. "You beat the crap out of my baby brother!"

Peyton Daugherty and Isabel Gutierrez press in around us.

"Ugh. What a lard-ass," Peyton says with a sniff, flipping her burgundy, chin-length hair.

"If you were any bigger, you'd have moons orbiting you," Isabel says. She and Peyton are both cheerleaders and rally girls. They bounce into classrooms and remind everyone of this rally or that football game, don't forget to cheer your heart out and gulp down the school spirit Kool-Aid.

What they don't understand, what they'll never understand, is that I don't care about the weight they seem to find so revolting. I wear my fat like armor. It's my shield and my weapon, a barricade against their puny barbs and useless arrows. They can't touch me. I'll bulldoze them to the ground.

"You're mental, you know that?" Jasmine jabs her finger at me.

I slap it away. "And your brother's a douchebag. He got what he had coming to him. If only someone would sucker-punch your whole family, you'd all be better off."

Margot puts her hand on Jasmine's arm. "She thinks she can hit a little kid and get away with it. Doesn't she know we strictly enforce anti-bullying polices?" Margot's voice is calm and silky.

Her thing is talking about the unpopular girls like they aren't even here, like they're not even worth acknowledging. Either that, or they suddenly get disreputable reputations. They're sluts. They hooked up with the entire football team. They're cheaters, liars, freaks, backstabbing losers. The rumors spread through the hallways and classrooms like poison gas. You breathe it in, and supposition, rumor, hearsay, and innuendo harden into concrete truth in your lungs.

I know. She did it to me.

"You might want to step off that pedestal," I snap. "It's starting to crack under your weight."

Jasmine's upper lip curls. "Why am I even surprised? You've always been a freak."

Pain splinters inside me. I can't help it. Out of all of them, she's the only one who can hurt me, whose words still slice to the bone. I pretend I don't care. I pretend I'm invincible. I clench my teeth and push out everything but my anger. "It must be hard to use your entire vocabulary in one pathetic sentence."

Jasmine glances at Margot, then steps closer. "Are you even for real right now?"

"Get out of my face. Your breath stinks so bad I don't know whether to offer you gum or toilet paper."

Someone in the group snorts. Jasmine's eyes narrow to slits. "You think this is funny? My dad says you belong in jail."

"I think it's freaking hilarious. Now get out of my way." I glance past the ring of faces. Behind them, Arianna Torrès stands in the hallway, staring at me, one hand pressed against her stomach. Her perfect face is closed, unreadable.

Does she already know about the stupid therapy group? Is she repulsed by the thought of being stuck with a loser like me?

Why should I care? I don't. I don't give a rat's ass about her. I glare at her, and she ducks her head and keeps walking.

"Jazzy, make her apologize to you." Margot's voice is syrupy-sweet.

"I'd rather boil myself alive in a vat of oil, *Jazzy*."

"That can be arranged." Isabel crosses her arms over her chest.

Eli Kusuma strolls up with Nyah McNally, a stunning black girl and a card-carrying member of Margot's squad. She glares at me from beneath a lush cloud of caramel-colored hair.

Eli slings his arm around Margot's shoulders. He's the captain of Brokewater High's loser football team, the Wildcats. Eli is one of those human specimens of nearly perfect dimensions. He has a strong, wide jaw, gorgeous amber eyes, and his body looks like it's been chiseled from granite.

"Hey, ladies." He flicks a strand of shaggy brown-black hair out of his eyes and flashes a megawatt grin. He's shallow and vain and oh so popular, but he's never been mean to me.

I turn to him. "Why do you hang out with these mentally deficient Barbie dolls?"

"Um, hello?" Nyah says, tossing her hair. "Because we're hot."

Eli just grins and shrugs at me, like he can't help himself.

"Jazzy, make her apologize before she regrets it," Margot says.

"You aren't pretty enough to be this stupid," I say. "Get the hell out of my way."

Margot's face hardens. Her eyes go dark and furious. She's used to girls withering beneath her gaze. She's not used to this, to me, and she's royally pissed.

She's not the only one. My pulse pounds against my skull. I want to claw their self-satisfied, judgmental eyes out with my fingernails. I would try it, too, if *expulsion* wasn't scrawled in red ink across my brain. "I'm warning you. Move or I'll go nuclear on your ass."

Jasmine hesitates. Her gaze flicks to Margot. "Let's go. I need a shower after being around this disease-infested slut."

They're going to leave. I should shut the hell up, but I can't help myself. "You need more than a shower to get rid of your diseases."

Jasmine's face blooms bright red. "You're a psycho-bitch. Just like your mother."

Anger mixes with the pain twisting my stomach. I blink back hot, stinging tears. I will not let them see me cry. "And you're a festering ass-wart, just like your brother."

I push past her before I completely lose it. The bell rings, and the rest of the crowd falls away, letting me through.

"Skank!" Margot mock-coughs.

"We're not done here!" Jasmine yells after me.

But I'm out of there before I start throwing punches. I want nothing more than to slap the smugness right off their shiny, starved faces. My eyes burn. My heart stutters in my chest. Dark, painful emotions threaten to boil right out of my skin.

I know what I need to do, what I have to do.

THREE

I bang open the front doors and make a hard left off the parking lot, following the rusted, rundown fence that rings the school property. There's a gutted section wide enough to scoot through just past the parking lot, hidden by a row of trees.

The ground around the fence hole is littered with cigarette butts, wrappers, and other bits of trash. A thick band of trees screen smokers and dopers from any teachers peering out classroom windows. Nobody's hanging out here today.

Once I'm past the fence, I shove through the tangle of underbrush and maneuver around the black ash, red maple, and white cedar trees to get to the river. Officially, it's Brokewater Creek, but it's so wide and deep most people just call it a river. It empties into Lake Michigan about 30 miles west of our tiny town of Brokewater, Michigan, population 3026, plus 99 cornfields.

The river is the only thing I like about this place. There are several deep spots out by the bridge where people gather in the warmer months to get drunk, stoned, and hook up. Sometimes they dare each other to swim out to the massive rock in the center of the river. I used to show up there sometimes, back in seventh and eighth grade, before everything went to hell. Now, I just want to be left alone.

The rushing sound of the river pulses in my ears. It feels alive, like some huge, twisting snake that might swallow me whole. Above the trees, a few clouds straggle across the sun. The heat and humidity suck energy right out of the air. I feel heavier with every step, my legs like blocks of cement.

I make my way along the riverbank for several minutes until I come to a large rock jutting out into the river. It's big enough for a half-dozen people to sit on, but this is my rock, my sanctuary.

I sit down and shrug off my backpack. The heat of the stone seeps through my jeans. Insects trill in the heavy stillness. A huge red maple arches over me, shading me from the sun with its reddish, hand-shaped leaves.

My blood buzzes, my skin hot and tingling. Anger and pain and need collide in my mind, crashing like thunder, ricocheting against my skull. I pull out the plastic baggy containing a fresh razor, several folded tissues, and a few Band-Aids. I roll up my pant leg and push down my sock. The tender spots below and above my ankle are laddered with raised white lumps and fresh cuts.

Only this can untangle the dark snarl of emotions inside me. Only this pain can sharpen my focus. Only this can drown out the roar inside my own head.

I tilt the razor against an old scar just above my right ankle. The scar is an inch long, thick and bunched like a white worm. I press until I see the bloom of red, then slowly drag the edge over the damaged skin. I welcome the pain, seek it, search it out beneath my skin. My heartbeat slows. The noise fades away. Sweet, languid relief melts through me.

A black, white-spotted Baltimore butterfly flutters out over the water, its wings flashing in the sunlight. Sometimes I see monarchs or the yellow-brown of a checkerspot hovering over a bush. The sight of one always makes my heart ache, my body filling with a cold, hollow emptiness.

I make another cut, watch the tiny chasm open in my skin, and let my mind drift back. Back to the time before the world tilted off its axis, back to eighth grade, when Jasmine Cole was still my best friend.

She talked too loud and too much, and she snorted like a horse when she laughed. She had glasses and braces and was the only kid I knew with an actual microscope in her house.

Back then, Jasmine was one of those rare people who seemed to know exactly how her life would turn out ahead of time. She loved bugs and science and wanted to study butterflies, to become a lepidopterist like her father, a science professor at Notre Dame who died when she was a toddler.

One side of her walk-in closet was stuffed with clothes; the other side was lined with shelves containing her father's old supplies: spreading boards, glass-topped specimen boxes, insect pins, envelopes, tiny forceps, glass and wood containers, a long-handled net, and the killing jars on the top shelf her mother wouldn't let her touch.

The walls of Jasmine's bedroom were covered with framed displays of butterflies, their jewel-toned wings splayed and tacked to display boards with tiny metal pins. Some she'd paid for or received as gifts; others, she'd caught herself.

Sometimes I went with her on her expeditions, lugging around her supplies in a canvas tote bag while she searched for the flowers that lured her prey. I still remember their satiny, iridescent wings, their names like a whispered promise on my lips: Painted Lady, White Admiral, Mourning Cloak, Dreamy Duskywing, Fluted Swallowtail, Glass Winged Skipper.

She collected caterpillars in mason jars filled with sticks and leaves. She studied them as they attached to branches and formed their mummy-like shell, the chrysalis. She called them larvae, which always made me think of maggots.

I would sit on her bed and draw while she worked. I could never kill the butterflies like she could. I drew them instead. I filled up notebook after notebook with wood nymphs and monarchs, admirals and hairstreaks, swallowtails and sulphurs, and my favorites, the blues.

"Do you know how the caterpillar makes its transformation?" she asked me once. She leaned over her desk, intent as she thrust a pin through the butterfly's thorax, then used paper strips to hold open the fragile orange wings without tearing the membranes.

I sat on her bed with my legs crossed, lightly sketching the shape of a large Morpho Blue, its huge, iridescent wings spread in midflight. I shaded in the mid-tones with my charcoal stick, slowly bringing out the depth of shadow and light. "Not really," I said, because I knew she was dying to tell me.

"It has to eat its own body. Gross, right? It releases these enzymes that digest itself and dissolve nearly all of its tissues. Look, I'll show you."

She pulled a chrysalis attached to a small stick out of one of her jars and grabbed a knife. I watched as she carefully sliced open the filmy skin, revealing an oozing caterpillar soup. "That's disgusting."

"I know, right? But check this out. There are still groups of organized cells in all that goo. They contain everything the butterfly needs to develop the wings, antennae, legs, eyes, and anything else she needs to survive. She basically annihilates herself and then rebuilds herself into something completely new."

I listened to Jasmine talk, her words spinning their own cocoon around us. I used my paper stumps to blend and blend until the individual pencil strokes were indistinguishable, until the butterfly looked poised to lift off the page.

"There's this study," Jasmine said excitedly. "The researchers discovered the butterflies retain memories from their experiences as a caterpillar, in spite of almost complete cellular disintegration during the metamorphosis. How cool is that?"

But that was shortly before Jasmine underwent her own metamorphosis. During the summer between eighth and ninth grade, she traded the glasses for contacts and the braces for a blazing white smile. Her mother took her to a salon and bought her a straightening iron, and her mouse-brown frizz transformed into silky white-blonde tresses cascading down her back like a Pantene commercial.

But it was the popular girls who made her transformation complete. Margot Hunter adopted Jasmine into her Bitch Squad. Plus, Jasmine's step-dad has one of the only in-ground pools in the whole town, sealing her fate. Jasmine shucked her science nerd persona like a caterpillar's collapsing flesh. And unlike her butterflies, she didn't seem to retain any memories of her former life, or former friends.

I make another cut, sucking in my breath from the sharp sting. I wipe the blood away with a tissue and watch the red bloom again. My heart aches. My whole body aches. I take a deep breath, blinking back the tears.

Jasmine knew I did this. She knew the things that happened at home. Some of them. In a moment of idiotic weakness, I told her. I don't know why. It's only the cutting that brings relief. Only this that calms the frenetic flutter-flap of my heart.

I thought telling her might change something. It did, but not in any way that mattered.

I can still hear the words ringing in my ears from the day I put my tray down next to hers at the lunch table. Margot and the others were already sitting, but there was an empty space on the end next to Jasmine. Jasmine wore clothes I'd never seen before: a tight, sparkly tank top that hugged her chest, frayed short-shorts, and wedge heels. She glared at me. "You don't belong here, you emo, self-mutilating freak."

I sat there like she'd slapped me, my mouth frozen in a half-smile, my brain unable to process the horror unfolding right in front of me.

Two of the girls covered their mouths with their hands.

Margot's eyes widened. "What?"

"Oh, yeah." Jasmine said it like it was nothing, like it was old news. "She slices up her legs with a razor every night. She belongs in a wacko-house or something."

"With cushioned walls." Margot's lips curled in disgust as she stared at me.

"Go sign yourself in," Jasmine said. But she wasn't looking at me anymore. She was looking at Margot. "You stink like the trailer pigsty you live in."

I felt like my chest was about to explode. Pain vibrated through me, radiating into every cell of my being. I felt brittle, hollow, like I might crack wide open and my guts would come spilling out right onto the cafeteria table. I forced myself to my feet, my legs trembling, the heat of humiliation flushing my face. The pain was too much. It was like holding hot burning coals in my bare hands. I felt my skin catch fire, my bones.

I reached out and tipped over her tray of food, spilling ravioli and red tomato sauce all over her lap. I walked out of the cafeteria to the sound of a tableful of squealing, shrieking girls. I walked with my head held high, but inside, my heart was shrinking, shriveling up into a hard, black pit.

You can't give any part of yourself to anyone. They'll just use it to break you.

I stare at the reflection of the trees rippling on the surface of the water. A robin chirps from a branch somewhere above me. The memories are still like weeping wounds, four years later.

Now it's the beginning of senior year, and I don't care about any of them. I don't care about anything. Escape is less than a year away.

My mind slides away from the darkness. The stinging cuts focus my attention. The pain drowns out the shrieking in my head, dulls the ache pulsing beneath my ribs. I use my last tissue and press it against my ankle until the blood stops seeping. I dab the new cuts with a bit of Neosporin and slap on a Band-Aid.

I check my phone. I've completely lost track of time. It's already after three.

I have to get to my after-school job at Bill's Bar and Grill, where I bus tables. It's depressing, mind-numbing work, but it's also my lifeline.

To escape this hellhole, I figure I need six grand in savings. Three months' rent in advance for an apartment, since I don't have much credit, plus the security deposit. Then savings for a start on utilities, food, gas, and car payments. Not to mention college tuition left over after a butt-load of school loans. Bill's will also provide a steady employment history, which I'll also need. So I work every day, and as many hours as I can.

My future is still a hazy, nebulous idea in my head. When I try to imagine it, I can't.

I know I have to get there, but when I think past this year, my future is blank. A boiling black cloud rears up in my path. I can't see through it or around it.

But the money—the $1876.42 in my bank account—that's real. And it's going to get me out. Right now, that's all that matters.

I shove my things into my backpack and head back to the hell that is my life.

FOUR

After my shift at Bill's, I have to stop for groceries. Because Ma's account is overdrawn, again—I have to pay with my own money. Forty-four bucks down the drain.

By the time I get home, my stomach is growling, and my frustration levels are creeping higher and higher. I'll never make my goal when I'm the one paying for crap.

I grit my teeth and sweep my arm across the counter, clearing off several old newspapers and three empty beer cans. I put down the brown paper bags and start unloading the groceries: off-brand Corn Chex cereal, cans of sliced pineapples, Ramen noodles, and a jug of milk. I toss the leftover change on the counter. It's all that's left of my tips from the night.

Ma's nowhere in sight. I'm guessing she's passed out in her bedroom, as usual. And Frank—he's been gone for weeks. It's all on me: making dinner for the boys, cleaning up, doing laundry, bedtime routines, and then homework, if I can manage to stay awake that long.

I try not to look at the state of the house: the shabby furniture, the scummy counters, the cabinet door half-swinging off its hinges, dirt gathering in the corners. It doesn't matter how much I scrub; nothing ever looks clean.

Waning sunlight spills across the worn kitchen table. My little brothers sit across from each other: eight-year-old Aaron slanting forward over a drawing pad, small shoulders hunched so tightly his neck is barely visible; eleven-year-old Frankie leaning back in his chair, arms crossed, a cigarette sagging from his lips.

I slam the orange juice against the counter. "What the hell do you think you're doing?"

"Nothin'." Frankie bites into the cigarette.

Hot anger flares through me. I rip the cigarette out of Frankie's mouth. "You're smoking now?"

Frankie barely flinches. "Who cares? Screw you, Sid-*Ney.*" He says the last part of my name in a whiny singsong, dragging out the *ney*. He's been calling me Sid-*Ney* since he was three, when he would toddle after me with Ratty Bunny, his favorite stuffed animal clutched in his little fists, his swollen face wet with tears and snot. He'd cry for me to pick him up and take him away from the screaming and shouting and the sounds of ashtrays and liquor bottles being thrown against walls. Back when he was still soft and trusting, before he'd started turning into Frank.

"It's poison." I struggle to keep my voice even.

"Who cares?" Frankie stares at me, returning the same flinty gaze. His eyes are cobalt twins of mine, his short, spiky hair the same shiny blue-black as mine. But where I'm bulky and solid, he's long and lean, like Frank.

My gaze slides away first. I stub out the cigarette in an empty glass stacked on the counter and start unpacking the grocery bags. He's too damn young. Somebody needs to tell him; somebody in this house has to at least act like a parental figure. "I care. You're not ready for that kind of stuff."

"Okay, Ma." Frankie rolls his eyes.

"I'm serious. You want to get suspended again?" Of course, I don't tell him I've just been suspended myself. He'll go straight to Ma, and I'm planning on keeping this whole debacle my little secret. Frank's gone and Ma's so out of it, she won't even know the difference.

He just shrugs. "Who cares?"

I hate the words even as they spill out of my mouth. "You know what Frank will say."

"Dad doesn't care." But his voice loses some of its fight. We all know Frank cares. A lot. Good grades are the one thing he gives a flying crap about when it comes to his kids.

I finish putting the groceries away. I crush the paper bags into two balls and toss them in the trashcan under the sink. Both the trashcan and the sink are overflowing. The dishwasher is broken. Again. I'll have to do all the dishes by hand.

I turn around just as Frankie kicks Aaron's shin beneath the table. Aaron shrinks into himself, ducking his head. Where Frankie is tough and hard, Aaron is soft. Even his features are pliant: his cheeks doughy, his nose flat, his eyes wide apart and slanted down at the corners, as if they're beginning to melt into the rest of his face. Frankie and I inherited the delicate, fine-boned features of our father, but Aaron looks like our mother.

A tangle of emotions unspools inside me. I want to protect him, to keep him safe from anyone who would hurt him, but I can't. I can't even protect him from the people who live in this house.

He has to learn to do it himself. He has to learn how to be strong. "Stand up for yourself, Aaron."

"He doesn't dare," Frankie says. "Aaron's *afraid.* Wussy Aaron wouldn't know what to do if a *girl* attacked him."

Aaron huddles over the drawing pad, his messy curls falling across his face. Frankie leans across the table and snatches it.

"Table's real interesting to look at, isn't it?" Frankie throws the pad on the floor.

Aaron grips the pencil he's holding with whitened knuckles. He doesn't say anything, doesn't do anything. He just takes it.

"Stop it, Frankie. Leave him alone." Fear for Aaron tightens my throat. I give him back his drawing pad and rub his back in slow circles, like I used to do when he was a baby. "It's okay. You're okay. Look, you can't keep letting people bully you around, alright? Not even Frankie. You have to stand up for yourself."

He nods.

"Jackson Cole mess with you today?"

Aaron looks up, tears trembling in his eyelashes. "No. He wasn't at school. Did you do what you promised?"

"I pinkie-swore, didn't I? Don't worry. I took care of it. He won't bother you anymore."

Aaron wipes the snot dripping from his nose with his shirtsleeve. The enormous grin he gives me makes it all worth it. I would do the same thing a hundred times over, no matter the consequences.

I turn on the faucet and start the dishes. I've barely scrubbed the first pan when Aaron yelps.

I whirl around and grab Frankie's arm. "Did you kick him again? What'd I just tell you?"

"Screw you, Sid-*Ney*!"

"Shut up! You want to wake up Ma?"

Tears spark at the corners of his eyes. "You're hurting me!"

I realize how hard I'm gripping his arm and let go, but not fast enough. Four red half-moons appear on Frankie's upper arm. Guilt stabs me, a razor-sharp blade sliding right between my ribs. I just screwed up. Again. "I'm sorry. I didn't mean it. Frankie, I—"

"Sidney!" Ma stands in a puddle of sunlight in the kitchen doorway, her nightgown stretched tight across her plump body. Her brown hair is stringy and slick against her neck. Her face is swollen, her eyes glassy, unfocused. "What's all this racket? I thought I told you to keep quiet."

My fists curl and uncurl at my sides. The anger drains out of me, and suddenly I'm very, very tired. "You should go back to bed now, Ma. You know you're not feeling good."

I don't want the boys seeing her like this. I take Ma's arm and lead her through the narrow hallway back to her bedroom. She smells like sweat and alcohol.

"Are you hurting those boys?"

"No! I mean, it was an accident. I just—I'm sorry." I have to be better.

I have to control this anger that's consuming me from the inside. I can't let it touch them. It's my job to take care of them, to protect them. No one else does.

"All I asked was for some peace and quiet." Her voice slurs. She lies down, and I roll the covers over her doughy legs. "Can't you even do that right?"

I wince. I try not to let her get to me, but the words still sting. They always do. "I'm trying, Ma. Okay?"

Used tissues, bottles of Advil and Tylenol, and half-empty glasses of beer litter the nightstand. The TV is on, as always. I pick up the beer glasses, balancing them in my arms to keep from spilling them.

I remember Ma's laughter, from a long time ago. Remember sitting next to her at the kitchen table, drawing while she did her needlework art projects or knit me a scarf out of wooly yarn she let me pick out myself. The memories are from so long ago that they're gray around the edges.

"You think your dad will be home tonight?" She looks up at me hopefully, as if my answer can make her wish come true.

"I don't know." I edge toward the door, stepping around several piles of dirty clothes. I hate the smell of this room, soured with sweat and alcohol and something else, something dank and unwashed. "You know Frank. He comes, he goes."

"He's been gone for weeks already. I text him and he never answers. And don't you go calling him Frank. You know better. You and your smart mouth."

I stand in the doorway and stare at the slight hump in her belly. "You shouldn't drink, Ma. You're pregnant."

Ma's gaze fixes on the TV. "As soon as your father comes home, I'll stop. A couple of drinks are fine. Everyone does it. Frank knows how lonely I get when he's gone."

"Whatever you say. Look, I spent all of my tip money today on groceries. The electric bill and the water bill are due at the end of the week." I say the words slowly, with a patience I don't feel. I want to shake her right out of her stupor.

"Your father will bring money when he comes back."

"Who knows when that will be? He always skips town and leaves us with nothing." He disappears, Ma takes to her bed, and I'm the one left with everything else: the bills, the boys, the cooking and cleaning. Even so, Frank gone is always better than Frank here, with his temper and his ashtray breath and his leering gaze.

She scowls. "Look at you, always talking bad about him. Are you trying to make me more upset?"

"No. I'm trying to tell you we're broke."

"Then we'll call Aunt Ellie. Ellie's rich. Well, rich enough." She coughs and wipes her mouth on her nightgown. "Her house has more bathrooms than we have bedrooms. She could give us some, she could, but she never does . . . the self-righteous old hag. She always did think she was better than us."

Aunt Ellen lives somewhere in Ohio. I haven't seen her or spoken to her in years. She practically disowned my mother when she married Frank, as did the rest of that side of the family. There were one or two strained get-togethers. I remember running around a brown grass lawn with a couple of much older cousins. I remember skinning my knee.

Ma takes a swig from a flask she's hidden somewhere in the bed beside her.

"You're going to hurt the baby." I say it louder this time.

Ma just ignores me. "We'll be fine. Frank will come home. He always does."

I sigh. Trying to reason with her is pointless. "Are you hungry? You want dinner?"

She pinches the flab on her arm. "Stop trying to make me fat. It pisses Frank off."

"Suit yourself. Good night, Ma," I say, though it's only 7:00 p.m. I go back to the kitchen and put the beer glasses on the counter, since there's no room in the sink. The boys are gone, probably hiding out in their room. There's a loaf of Wonder Bread, a jar of peanut butter, and two empty cans of sliced pineapple on the kitchen table. They made their own sandwiches, a favorite concoction I first created for them years ago.

They know when to leave someone alone in this family. Neither of them will bother me tonight. I grab the crunchy peanut butter jar and head for my room. My bedroom is on the other side of the living room, separated from all the other bedrooms. Frank insisted I have that room when I turned thirteen, said girls needed their privacy. Yeah, right. I need Frank's privacy like I need a shot in the head.

I close the door to my bedroom and flop on the bed. I keep my Strathmore drawing pads, charcoal sticks, Prismacolor colored pencils, kneaded erasers, pastels, and blending stumps in the nightstand drawer. My pencils are artist quality, a rare gift from Frank for my eighth-grade graduation. Their pigment is as smooth and saturated as oil paint.

My art wall is next to my closet. Most of the drawings in cheap plastic frames are of butterflies, a few of my brothers, or landscapes of places I've never been. When I ran out of frames, I taped my drawings directly to the wall. I like to look at the butterflies, the rich, dappled colors, the sleek shape of their wings lifted in flight.

My stomach growls. I open the lid to the peanut butter and gouge out a large chunk. It sticks to my finger like a giant slug. I lick it off and do it again. And again. I eat until I am stuffed, past stuffed, until I'm bloated and a little sick. But the pit inside me never fills. When the jar is half-empty, I screw the lid back on and put it on the nightstand.

Pain gathers behind my eyes. I need relief. I'm desperate for it. I dig beneath my mattress for my baggie of razors and bundle of tissues and lean back against the wall. The blade glints in the twilight slanting through the curtains. I yank off my jeans. A dizzying parade of wounds decorate the soft white expanse of my upper thighs. Fresh red slashes crisscross the white lines of scar tissue.

I never cut my wrists. That's the coward's way out. If I ever do it, it won't be like this. I'll use Frank's gun, the big Glock .22 he tucks beneath the mattress he sometimes shares with Ma. My father and I are the same this way; we keep our most sacred things beneath us when we sleep.

I make three new cuts, horizontal and lined up next to each other, each about an inch long. One for me, one for Frankie, and one for Aaron. They're my brothers. They're my responsibility.

Frankie's cut is deeper than the others. I press the blade hard, until the sharp sting equals my guilt. Shame washes over me. I don't want to be that girl, the one who hurts what she loves.

I'll do better tomorrow, make it up to him somehow. I'll be more patient. I'm just so tired. And he's so hard, so angry. He's too much like me.

It's after ten when I finish. I press my leg with an old washcloth until it stops bleeding to keep any seeping blood off the sheets. I pull on the boxers and oversized T-shirt I use as pajamas.

My fingers twitch. There's still something I need to do. I open my nightstand drawer and get out my sketch pad and graphite pencil. I draw a cartoon of Ratty Bunny. Ratty Bunny was just Bunny when it was mine, an adorable white stuffed rabbit with black button eyes and the softest fur I'd ever felt. When Frankie was born, I gave Bunny to him. And when Aaron came three and a half years later, Frankie passed on the tradition.

Aaron still sleeps with it every single night. Now the fur is matted and dingy, with one button eye hanging loose. The stuffing started drifting out of a rip in the paw. One day, Ma asked, "Why do you want that old ratty bunny?" But Aaron cried, so she sewed it up with pink thread during one of her good days. And now we call it Ratty Bunny.

In my drawing, Ratty Bunny has enormous, cartoony eyes. He's wearing a cape that swirls heroically behind him. He stands on a stick figure lying on the ground, his little paws raised in triumph. I always make Ratty Bunny the hero who comes riding in on a magnificent steed or swooping down Superman-style to save the day. I tear off the page and fold it into a triangle, the only half-assed origami trick I actually learned back in some middle school art class.

A honey-colored buffet stands in the narrow hallway between the bathroom and the boys' room, too bulky to fit in our tiny kitchen. It takes up too much space, and looms out of the dark to stub toes or scrape shins and hips during middle-of-the-night bathroom trips. The drawers are full of junk no one ever uses. Except for this.

I tuck the paper triangle into the front left corner of the left drawer. This is our message center, when we need to share the things we can't say aloud in this house. I draw Ratty Bunny cartoons for Aaron. I used to leave funny-shaped rocks for Frankie. He liked to glue googly eyes to them, add a silly mouth with permanent marker, and stack them up on the top of his dresser. He doesn't do that anymore.

Before I climb into my own bed, I check on Ma. She's passed out, snoring loudly, the nub of a cigarette smoldering between her fingers. I take it out of her hand and grind it out in her empty water glass. Then I go back to my room.

Headlights from passing cars make strange designs slip and slide across the walls. I watch the alarm clock's green numbers blink from 11:59 to 12:00 a.m.

The hours pass, and I cannot sleep. The weight of the darkness, the ceiling, the house, the sky splattered with spiky stars—I feel them like a heaviness, like iron in my bones.

A heaviness that will not go away.

FIVE

The metal bars of the chair press into my back. Fat droplets of rain slap against the windows of the unused classroom Dr. Yang utilizes for his so-called group therapy sessions. A dozen chairs and desks are stacked against the far wall below the bulletin board still tacked with yellowed prom queen nominations and a cafeteria schedule from two years ago. My stomach rumbles.

I sit closest to the wall of gray windows and the rusted radiator beneath them. It's raining so hard I can barely see the tree line fifty feet past the school. I can't see the river at all.

Dr. Yang keeps glancing at his watch. "She'll be here shortly."

And I tried so hard to be late. Damn.

My eyelids are heavy, and I just want to sleep this whole day away. I spent my three days of suspension scouring the house, catching up on homework, and taking extra shifts at Bill's Bar and Grill.

I made enough to pay the electric bill, at least until it's due again next month. I had to take another fifty bucks from my account for the water bill. The bills together added up to over two hundred dollars I could have added to my escape funds. Sometimes it feels like I'm moving backward.

Ma was so checked out she didn't even realize I was supposed to be in school. I took her cell phone while she slept and deleted the message from the office informing her of my suspension. I intercepted the letter in the mail, too. It's about time something worked out in my favor. Not much else does.

The classroom door opens, and Arianna Torrès floats in.

My hands curl into fists on my lap. "How nice of you to grace us with your presence."

Arianna's cheeks flush. She is extremely thin. She's wearing khaki-colored skinny pants and an oversized pink cashmere sweater that brings out the tawny bronze of her skin and the hazel flecks in her dark eyes. Her thick black waves spill down her back. She has a pixie-doll face, with a button nose and full lips. Her only imperfection is the tiny constellation of pimples dotting her forehead.

"I'm so sorry," she says breathlessly. "AP French went over and—"

I sigh loud enough to break off her words.

"Arianna, this is Sidney Shaw. Sidney, this is Arianna Torrès. I think a small group session will really help to … open things up."

"Where's the rest of the group?" I ask.

Dr. Yang furrows his brow. "We may have a few other students join us in the future. For now, however, we'll start with you two. It'll be good for everyone to get out of their comfort zones a little. Why don't you introduce yourselves? Sidney?"

"Well, like the good Doc just said, my name is Sidney. I've been forced here because I killed three cats and drank their blood."

Arianna raises her eyebrows.

"All right, it was five cats. And two dogs. But I didn't drink the dogs' blood. Tasted funny."

Arianna folds her right leg over her left and smooths the wrinkles in her pants. She looks imploringly at Dr. Yang.

Dr. Yang clears his throat and does his steepling fingers thing under his chin. "Let's start with Arianna, then. Maybe if Sidney sees how it is done, she will be more inclined to cooperate."

Arianna sits up straighter, her tiny, birdlike hands folded on her lap. "I'm senior class secretary. I'm on the honor roll. I'm in band—"

I snort. "Go on, continue, please. I'm a big fan of band."

"I play the flute. First chair. Uh, I live over on Broadview; that's across the bridge. Oh, and since everyone always asks, my parents are Colombian, but they both lived here in the states almost their whole lives. They never taught me Spanish, so don't ask me to help with your homework. And my eyes are naturally this color, not contacts."

I stare at Dr. Yang, trying to beam my disgust and sense of indignity into his brain. Can't he see how awful this is? This is a horrible idea.

"Do you think you could talk about why you're here?" Dr. Yang asks her.

"Oh, please do," I say. "I want so badly to hear what terrible atrocities you must have endured to earn your spot in this exclusive therapy group."

Arianna smooths her hair with both hands. She's so skinny her bones seem to poke out of her paper-thin skin. "I wake up most mornings and feel sad, like there's this heavy weight dragging me down."

"And why is that?" Dr. Yang asks in his shrink-voice.

"I don't know." She bites at her nails. Her nails on both hands are bitten down to the quick, the skin red and raw.

"Well, that's why we're here. To figure it out together." Dr. Yang flashes me one of his looks. "Are you ready to talk yet, Sidney?"

"I've been talking ever since I got here."

Dr. Yang frowns at me. I stare back at him. He's the one who dragged me here. I never signed up for this or agreed to do anything other than show up. Besides, every time I look at Arianna, I see Jasmine. I see everything I've lost. My heart contracts. I don't want to be here. I don't want to think about any of this. "When I was three, my parents gave me away to a circus. I was made to sit on my head for six hours every day and pretend I was a mutant."

Arianna looks like she just swallowed something distasteful. Dr. Yang only sighs. "Group sessions will not work if we don't cooperate and speak honestly with each other."

The familiar churn starts in my gut, a roaring, out-of-control feeling that washes everything else away. "Does that 'we' include you? Have you told us all about you? Are you in a band? Do you eat cats?"

Dr. Yang frowns. "No and no. Sidney, are you ready to be a contributing member of this group?"

"Of course not. There's no way I'm telling anything to Miss Beauty Queen over here. I thought the whole point was to put me with a damaged individual like myself."

"She is like you."

"No, she's a spoiled rich girl with too much time on her hands."

"I resent that statement." Arianna's voice is soft. "You are mistaken on so many levels. But I realize you have a lot of anger issues, and cutting other people down probably makes you feel better."

I don't even feel the pain any more. I'm just pissed. "Anger issues?" I lean forward, my upper lip curling. "What are you, an aspiring Freudian? You pretending to be mentally deranged so you can study a psycho like a zoo animal?"

"No, of course not. I am only trying to say I think I understand—"

"You don't understand anything." I cut her off. "Don't even try."

Dr. Yang clears his throat. "The first rule we need here is respect. Everybody has the right to say what they need to say, and the other person needs to respect that, even if they don't agree with what's being said. Sidney, you are walking a very fine line here. I don't think you want to be dismissed from this group, do you?"

My mouth tightens. He has me, and he knows it. I cannot get expelled. I have to be here, no matter how much I despise this whole debacle. I have no choice. It hurts to say it. "No."

"Okay, then. Why don't you tell us the real reason why you're here?"

"I have an 'anger issue'. I tend to hurt people who piss me off."

"Then why are we in this group together?" Arianna frowns at Dr. Yang. "Isn't her problem pretty unrelated to mine?"

"Not quite. Sidney?"

He's going to make me say it. I hate him even more than usual. It doesn't matter that everyone already knows, thanks to Jasmine Cole. It doesn't matter that it's scrawled on the gym bathroom wall, along with a few other choice epitaphs.

I don't want to give her anything. But they're both staring at me. He's not going to let me out of this claustrophobic room until I say it. "I cut. I'm a vampire. I have to get blood somehow. Biting people is frowned upon these days."

"I do that, too," she says in a hesitant voice. "Cut."

My stomach twists in iron knots. Where do these perfect girls get off, acting like they have any problems deeper than finding a boyfriend or surviving bad hair days? It makes me sick. It makes me want to punch her in her perfectly-shaped nose. That would give her some problems. "Congratulations. Would you like a trophy? We're handing out awards for 'most tragically disturbed.'"

Arianna looks stricken, like she's even more desperate to escape than I am.

"I realize it will take a while to open up, but I believe it will happen, if given time," Dr. Yang says. "This is why we will continue to meet and talk though our issues. Each of you holds the power to heal both yourselves and each other."

I roll my eyes. "Sorry to burst your bubble, but I doubt we're gonna be besties, Doc."

"I like to think of this journey as climbing a mountain," Dr. Yang continues, unperturbed. "When you're at the foot of the mountain, it's terrifying just to look up. It's so high and looming, and it feels impossible. You feel terrified, not brave, but you decide to do it anyway, because it's worth doing. So you act brave, even though you don't feel it yet, and you take a step. And you act brave again and again and again. Pretty soon, you find out you aren't just acting anymore. You are brave. You just need to keep going, day after day, until you stop and look back and discover you've traveled further and higher than you ever thought possible. And the view; the view is breathtaking."

"That's quite poetic, Doc. Maybe you're in the wrong line of work."

"I'll be your facilitator, but the real work is up to you. As for you, Sidney, my patience is finite. Remember that."

I sigh. "Whatever. Doc."

He drones on, but I'm just watching the minute hands tick by on the clock on the wall. "Isn't it time to go yet?"

Dr. Yang looks at his watch. "Yes. I think we'll break for today. But first, I have something for you both." He pulls something out of his desk. Two things, actually. He stands up and hands one to Arianna, then to me.

It's a small, suede book. A diary. And it's bubblegum pink. Gross. "Why don't you just add the unicorns and sparkles while you're at it, Doc? Just to complete our humiliation."

"My six-year-old niece helped pick them out," Dr. Yang said placidly. "I think they're nice."

"So do I," Arianna says in her disgustingly pert and perfect voice.

"Of course you do," I growl and hold the book with the tips of my fingers. "What is it for?"

"It's a journal," Dr. Yang says. "I would like you to write your truths inside it. I'm going to be giving you some tasks, some challenges to work through. You can write your responses in there. You can add anything else you'd like—your thoughts, ideas, and feelings—and those will be private, unless you want to share them."

"I don't."

Dr. Yang ignores me. "For your first assignment, please write down three things that make you angry."

"Only three?" I quip. "I can think of about fifty right frickin' now."

"Three is all," Dr. Yang says in his infuriatingly calm voice. "Three things that make you angry, and three ways you usually deal with that anger. Remember to come back next Tuesday, same time, same empty classroom." He gives me a sharp look. "I expect you both here."

I'm out of the classroom and nearly to my locker by the time the bell rings. I consider tossing the journal in the trash, but my brain reminds me what'll happen if I'm expelled, so I shove it into my backpack instead. What a ridiculous bucket-load of crap. Dr. Yang is a sham. So is picture-perfect Arianna and the whole damn thing. Diary-keeping, my ass.

I slam the locker shut with a satisfying clang just as my stomach grumbles. I missed breakfast. Getting the boys ready for the bus every morning doesn't leave much time for anything but a granola bar on the way out.

I swing by the cafeteria to get a bag of Reese's Pieces from the vending machine. I almost always get Reese's Pieces or a package of peanut butter cups for a snack or lunch. I go to the river, the school library, or sit in the car to eat. It's cheaper than buying lunch in the cafeteria, and it keeps me from having to spend one more minute than I have to with these moronic asshats.

I have Miss Pierre's AP Classic Literature next, the only half-interesting class at Brokewater High. You can barely see the river from her classroom, so I don't bother sitting by the windows.

Miss Pierre likes class discussions. She wants us to talk about race, class, sexism, imperialism, greed, and whatever other themes she can squeeze out of the all-white, all-male canon of books we have to wade through in high school. Actually, though, I do like Shakespeare. The sentences are like puzzles; you have to concentrate, focus. You have to work at it to figure out the real meaning.

"Good morning, class," Miss Pierre greets us from the front of the room. She's only in her forties, her light brown skin still unlined, but her hair is completely silver. She leaves it natural and curly to her chin, giving her an air of easy sophistication. "We have a new student today."

Everyone looks around for the new kid, but they all seem to be looking at me. No, they're looking a bit askance. The new kid is sitting directly to my left.

He's Asian, with olive-toned skin, warm brown eyes glittering with mischief, and tufts of black hair sticking up all over his head, as if he rolled out of bed without bothering to glance in a mirror. He's wearing an orange and black plaid shirt over jeans.

He smiles and gives a little wave. Someone snickers.

Miss Pierre is wise enough not to put him on the spot by making him say anything. "Please make sure to help him feel welcome today, as I'm sure you will. Now let's move on. In act three, scenes four through five, which you should have read last night, Shakespeare challenges us with the idea of madness. Lear descends into madness as he wanders the heath in the storm. I'd like to spend some time discussing the purpose of Lear's madness. Is there ever a purpose in madness? How does Shakespeare use it to spur change in his characters?"

While Miss Pierre talks, the new boy turns to me and actually sticks out his hand. "I'm Lucas Kusuma."

I ignore his hand. "Lucas Kusuma as in Eli Kusuma?"

"He's my cousin. I'm staying with him for a while. I know, little family resemblance, right?"

I just stare at him.

"Our dads are Indonesian. My mom's Chinese-American, and Eli's mom is from Argentina. He takes after her." He shrugs. "People keep asking why we don't look alike."

He's related to Eli Kusuma, boyfriend of Margot Hunter, friend of Jasmine Cole. That's all I need to know.

Lucas's hand is still suspended in midair between us. "And you are?"

"That was not an invitation for a conversation." I open my book and face the front.

"But what's your name?" he whispers, like I didn't just shut him down.

Other people are still twisting around in their seats, their mouths contorted in disgust behind their hands. They're staring at his face, at the cystic acne dotting his forehead and jawline.

A thread of red anger knots itself in my stomach. So what? Why do they judge everything, hate everyone who's even a little bit different? They're all so small-minded and vile and awful; I despise every single one of them. Right now, I despise Lucas just as much, but it's got nothing to do with the state of his skin.

I have no interest in talking to anybody. Everyone here knows already, and they pretty much leave me alone, except for the Bitch Squad. I especially have no interest in speaking to a Kusuma. Like, ever.

"Pssst," he hisses.

"Piss off."

"Just tell me your name."

"You're poisoning my air with your presence. Go away."

He shrugs, the corner of his mouth lifting. "Somebody's a moody monkey."

"What's that supposed to mean?"

"Sidney Shaw, is there something you'd like to share with the class?" Miss Pierre stares at me from the front of the classroom.

My neck flushes with heat. I clear my throat. "No, ma'am."

For the rest of class, I slump in my seat, killing time. I barely hear a word. Finally the bell rings.

Something bright catches my eye. Against my better judgment, I glance over at Lucas. He's playing with something on his desk. It's a bright pink, sparkly lighter with a rhinestone skull on both sides.

I stand and shoulder my backpack as the classroom erupts in noise and movement around me. Margot and her crew will have a field day with that. And there are worse bullies than her. And the poor new kid is already marked because of his skin.

I sigh and lean down. "Put that away or they'll call you a queer. I don't give a crap whether you are, but they sure as hell will."

He starts to give me a lopsided grin, but I'm already stomping out the door.

"See you later, Sidney Shaw," he calls cheerily.

I don't know what he's so pleased about. It's unnerving as hell.

SIX

The next day is pretty much a repeat of the day before. In Classic Lit, Lucas Kusuma tries to talk to me again. This time, I don't even respond. I stare straight ahead, pretending to be enthralled in the class discussion.

Halfway through class, he passes me a note. A literal paper note, like we're in middle school. When he leans close, I catch the smell of spearmint gum and a little too much cologne, which has a woodsy, dense scent that reminds me of the trees along the riverbank—oak and maple, pine and willow.

I crumple the note and drop it on the floor without looking at him. He tries again, and I push the little folded paper off my desk with my forearm. What is it with this guy not getting the hint?

When the bell rings, I grab my stuff and get out of there.

"Hey, Sidney!" I recognize his voice behind me, but I keep walking.

I head to the cafeteria to grab a bag of Reese's Pieces. I've just torn open the bag and tossed a handful in my mouth when I see Jasmine, Margot, and their squad sauntering down the hall, straight toward me. Arianna's with them, not at the front of the pack, but trailing a bit to the side.

They all have their glittery iPhones in their hands, texting while simultaneously chatting and walking. They don't have to worry about running into anyone; the crowd parts before them.

Arianna sees me first. She gives a small shake of her head. But it's too late. Jasmine's heavily made-up face contorts into a sneer. "How are you even still here? I thought they'd have locked you in a cage by now."

My heart drops into my stomach. I lift my chin. "No such luck."

She eyes me up and down. "Nice outfit. It looks like someone poured you into it and forgot to say when. Don't you ever get tired of eating?"

I pop a handful of candy into my mouth and chew loudly. "Nope. Don't you ever get tired of being a greasy piece of human garbage? Maybe if you ate some of that makeup, you'd be pretty on the inside."

"You're the trashy freak."

"See? You just confirmed my hypothesis."

Margot rests her manicured fingers on Jasmine's arm. "Ignore her, Jazzy. Keep walking."

As I pass by them, Margot kicks my ankle with one of her spiked three-inch heels. I go down hard, landing on my hands and knees. The rest of my Reese's Pieces scatter across the floor.

A few people laugh.

"Oopsies." Margot's voice drips with saccharine sweetness. "It's a wonder how some people make it through the day."

My mind goes red. They want to fight? I'll give them a fight. Let's see how arrogant they are with broken noses and black eyes marring their perfect faces.

Before I can scramble to my feet, someone grabs my arm and hoists me up. Lucas. He's so close I could count his eyelashes. I flinch and try to shake him off, but he holds on.

"Don't," he says in a low voice. "It's not worth it."

"She's not worth it." Margot tosses her hair over her shoulder.

Jasmine slits her eyes. "Don't waste your breath. She's just a fat freak. A nobody."

Lucas's grip on my arm tightens, like he knows exactly what I'm about to do. His fingers are strong and warm. I feel the heat of his palm against my skin.

I hate it, but he's right. I can't. I can't let myself go. I can't get expelled. I make myself breathe deeply, one, two, three times. And it's enough. The pounding red in front of my eyes slowly fades.

Margot and Jasmine flounce down the hall. Students part and move around us, either ignoring us completely or throwing us contemptuous glances. Lockers slam and a stampede of footsteps head for class, the lunchroom, or the front door.

I yank my arm free. I can still feel his handprint. I expect to see a mark, but there's none.

My cheeks redden. I hate that he saw them get the best of me. I hate that he—or anyone—saw me on my knees, beaten. Shame and humiliation burn through me. "Don't touch me. Ever. What part of 'leave me alone' do you not understand?"

He smiles that awful lopsided grin again. "Come to lunch with me."

My stomach clenches. There's no way. No. Freaking. Way. I don't have a clue what he wants from me, but I'm not stupid enough to fall for whatever game he's playing. He's part of the Bitch Squad by association. That's all I need to know. "That's about as likely as a blizzard in July."

"Well—this is Michigan. Isn't this place known for temperamental weather?"

"I'm leaving. Go away." I turn on my heels and head the other way. I duck into the bathroom and lean against the sink without glancing in the mirror. I don't want to look.

A minute later, the bathroom door opens. Jasmine Cole walks in, still focused on her phone.

My stomach turns itself inside out. "You following me now? Don't tell me you have some weird obsession with listening to me pee?"

Surprise flits across her face before her features settle into a sneer. "Hell no." Jasmine pulls a tube of lipstick from the pocket of her purple skinny pants and peers at herself in the mirror. She slits her eyes. "You're really something else, you know that?"

A fissure opens up inside me. Painful memories lodge in my brain like splinters. Jasmine with her loud, honking laugh and constant chatter that could almost fill up all the empty spots inside me, who could make me feel normal through the force of her exuberant will alone.

I remember that summer after eighth grade, when I biked to her house almost every day. Only a mile away and her neat, tree-lined neighborhood felt like another planet. Her house was always clean and bright. It was like being transported into a happy-ending movie, where her mother made us crunchy cucumber sandwiches. We lounged in her pool until we were sun-crisped, or sprawled on her bed, me sketching in my notebooks, her concentrating on pinning her butterfly wings.

We haven't spoken in years.

"What's your deal?" She glances at me in the mirror's reflection.

"I could ask you the exact same thing. You're the one who unleashed your attack dog on me."

She rolls her eyes. "What? You mean Margot? You brought that on yourself. You think nobody's going to care if you punch an innocent sixth grader?"

"Innocent? What're you smoking? You always hated him anyway."

Something like bewilderment passes across her face, like she's completely forgotten I used to know all her secrets. She clears her throat. "Whatever. That's so not even the point."

She applies a fresh layer of matte salmon-pink lipstick and presses her lips into a pout. I look for something I recognize, some part of her that still exists from before. She has the same thin, flat eyebrows, the divot in the center of her nose from a gymnastics accident in fifth grade, the same squinty green eyes. She's a different girl now. "What happened to you?"

She straightens. "Nothing happened to me. Hello? People change."

I want to believe it was Margot who stole her from me, but the reality is we were already pulling away from each other that summer after eighth grade. She didn't understand why I stopped laughing. Why I started inhaling food like it was air, more and more, as much as I could force into my bloated stomach, why I needed an armor of fat to shield me. Most of all, she didn't understand why I cut.

I remember the look on her face when I first risked showing her. We were lounging in chairs beside her pool. My hands trembled as I slid up the hem of my swim shorts. I needed her to see me. I needed to show her what was happening inside me, my bones splintering into shards.

But I couldn't speak the words. I could only show her, desperate for her to understand, desperate for her to see the pain I wrote on my skin was only the surface, only the beginning of a dark terror I couldn't begin to describe.

Her expression when she saw my legs was a mix of confusion, shock, and revulsion. She leapt to her feet like I'd turned into a cockroach. "My mom wants me to finish up some chores" was all she'd said as she wrapped herself in a saffron towel.

We never spoke of it again. That was the last time I was ever invited over to her house. Within a few months, we were barely speaking. By Christmas, we were strangers.

I blink back the memory with hot, stinging eyes. "We both changed."

She stares at me in the mirror, like maybe she's remembering, too. "Yeah, I guess we did."

An immense loneliness fills me. For years, I've kept myself numb. Made myself believe I didn't care. But with her this close, wrinkling her nose like she used to do whenever she was confused or irritated—I can't keep the pain out. I hate her and I miss her at the same time. "It doesn't have to be like this."

"I don't know what you're talking about."

"Your brother bullied Aaron," I say, my voice trembling. "That's why I did it. Remember Aaron? The scruffy little kid who ate crayons all the time? He's eight now."

She blinks. "That doesn't change anything."

"Jackson gave him a black eye."

She adjusts her creamy off-the-shoulder sweater. "I don't care, okay? That's not my problem."

I wince. What did I expect? Nothing's going to change between us.

We're enemies now, and we always will be. "Just tell your attack dog to leave me the hell alone."

"In case you haven't noticed, Margot does what she wants."

"Trust me, I've noticed. You should watch your back. Getting close to that one is like cuddling with a rattlesnake."

"She's not that bad." But she blinks again, her gaze sliding away in the mirror.

"Yeah, right." I swallow hard. "If you think that, you really are an idiot. Everyone's entitled to be stupid, but you're abusing the privilege."

Something shifts in Jasmine's face, like a door closing. "I almost feel sorry for you. Almost. You nearly broke Jackson's nose. My mom *cried*. You're just—you're a psycho, a freak. You deserve whatever you've got coming to you." She turns and flounces out of the bathroom.

I stand there, the sound of my heartbeat echoing off the tile walls. The pain burns through me. I want to be numb, want a heart carved in stone.

Instead, I feel like someone's pressed a lit cigarette to my skin.

SEVEN

In AP Government, I sit in the back, in the seat closest to the bank of windows. You can't see the river through the trees until the leaves drop in November. A few of the red maples are beginning to turn, their leaves blushing reddish-pink.

"As we prepare for our test on Friday, let us contemplate our economic relations with foreign nations, including NAFTA, tariffs, foreign aid and sanctions," Mr. Cross drones. He's an ancient guy in his sixties who slicks his three remaining strands of hair over his gleaming scalp, still wears three-piece suits to work, and should have retired five years ago. He literally just reads from the textbook, and his gravelly, monotone voice puts half the class into an after-lunch stupor. Some people play Candy Crack on their phones beneath their desks. Others are flat-out napping with their heads resting on their folded arms.

"I hope you have already noted the date in your syllabus, but our collaborative ten-page issue analysis paper is due in only a few short weeks, people." He always says "we" and "us," like he isn't exempt from the piles of homework drivel he divvies out.

"But I've got a test in Chemistry!" someone moans.

Mr. Cross ignores the complaints and drones on.

I doodle around the edges of my notebook. I sketch a Silvery Blue, forming her antennae, the curl of her proboscis, the folded praying mantis-look of her segmented legs. Then the thorax, the abdomen, and the wings, the branched veins, the transparent membranes shingled with tiny, flat scales.

Though I don't have my colored pencils, I imagine the shining powder-blue of its wings. I darken the black outline along the outer margin of its forewings and hindwings. I crosshatch the dark areas with my pencil, digging harder and harder until the paper rips.

"I understand not everyone has chosen a partner yet," Mr. Cross says. "It would behoove us to do so post-haste. There are twenty-four students exactly, and I have the same sign-up sheet on my desk that's been sitting here for the last week. Sign up before you leave class today, or I'll be forced to dock grades 10%."

Everyone groans. The noise level quickly reaches a dull roar as people pair up. Three fourths of the class find a partner in five seconds. They grab their backpacks and notebooks and pile out of the classroom, yelling and laughing and pushing each other. I slouch deeper into my seat. There's no way I'm collaborating with any of these douchebags.

The fact that I don't have a choice makes me grind my teeth and imagine destroying things. Taking a chainsaw to Mr. Cross's desk would be a nice start. I rip the drawing out of my notebook. I'm about to crumple it up and throw it in the trash when a shadow falls over my desk.

"That's actually really good." Arianna Torrès hugs her textbook to her chest and eyes me warily. "Like, professional artist good."

"Are you surprised? Were you expecting stick figures from a trailer trash freak? Or maybe sketches of impaled body parts, stabbings, and other disturbing material?"

"Oh, never mind." She starts to walk away. Stops. Turns back around. She chews her lower lip like she wants to say something.

I sigh. "Spit it out."

"Do you need a partner?"

I look at her and I see Jasmine. I remember four years of a loneliness so deep it's like a constant, savage ache in my chest. I can't let myself feel that pain. Whatever this girl's game is, I'm not going to fall for it. Not this time. Not ever again. There's no room inside me for more heartache. "I don't need anything."

"But do you have a partner?"

"What do you think?"

Arianna sighs heavily. By this time, the classroom is empty, except for Mr. Cross slumped at his desk. "Look. This isn't open-heart surgery. My friend Lin-Mae asked me, but I said no."

My head snaps up. She feels sorry for me; that's it. She's doing one of her goody-Christian charity things to get more stars on her crown, or whatever. That's the last thing I need. "I'm not your pity case."

"I know. Of course not. Dr. Yang said we might want to be friends. I thought—" She frowns, and I can tell she already regrets whatever she's trying to do. "But you need a partner."

"Look, I don't have the time or the crayons to explain this to you. I don't want to be your partner. In anything. Ever."

She flinches. "Well, it's too late now. We're the only ones left."

Once again, I don't have a choice. "Whatever. I couldn't care less."

"Is that a yes?"

"Just sign the damn sheet." I scoop up my backpack and head for the door. I'm about to throw the drawing in the trash on the way out when something makes me hesitate. Arianna is right. The drawing is good. I fold it instead, slip it into my pocket, and escape as fast as I can.

EIGHT

After school, I head to my shift at Bill's Bar and Grill. Bill's is a small, red-brick restaurant just off the main thoroughfare into town. It's got about two dozen tables and traffic cone-orange booths with ripped stuffing. The inside walls are brick and decorated with a couple hundred old license plates and framed black-and-white prints of Marilyn Monroe, James Brown, Elvis, James Dean, Nat King Cole, and Ray Charles.

"Hey, Bill," I say as I walk back into the kitchen area. The cook station contains a grill, fry pit, cutting counter, and stainless-steel sinks. The cracked tile floors and stained counters have seen better days.

"What's up, kid?" Bill Beauvais, the owner and manager, simultaneously flips burgers at the grill and chops red peppers on the cutting board. Bill went to MSU with Frank back in the '90s, both on football scholarships. Frank—tall, lean, fast with good hands—played wide receiver. Bill was a linebacker. They both came back home sophomore year. Frank lost his scholarship due to poor grades. Bill tore his ACL clean through. He walks with a slight limp, but he still looks the linebacker part—big and meaty, thick-necked, with huge ham-hands.

"Same old crap," I say, tying on my apron. "How's the afternoon crowd?"

"Slow," Bill says with a sigh. He's Haitian, with a full, bushy beard and long dreads tied back so they don't interfere with his work.

The locals crowd in on the weekends, but it's usually quiet before six on the weekdays. Bill never puts me on weekends or gives me prime hours. He knows he'd lose customers.

When I used to waitress, I may have yelled at a few rude ones, purposefully spilled their drinks, or delayed their orders. That didn't work out so well for the customers or Bill's bottom line, so now I bus tables.

It's nasty work, collecting the dirty plates and dishware, scraping the half-eaten scraps into the industrial trash bins, scrubbing down greasy, sticky tables. I refill drinks, too, and sometimes deliver the dishes to the customers if the waitresses are busy. It's not exactly fun, but I'm grateful. Anybody but Bill would've fired me long ago.

Today is quiet, only a half-dozen customers. I do my work without speaking to anyone else, smiling only when I have to. It keeps my hands and my mind busy. When it's slow, I slip into the cook station and steal battered curly fries or boneless chicken wings from the fryer when no one is looking.

The smell of food is overwhelming. It's on my skin, in my hair. It makes me want to eat everything in sight. I grab a handful of hot fries and shove them into my mouth, swallowing them in three gulps. They burn on the way down.

The bell over the door rings in the front. I grab a paper towel from the hand sink and wipe the grease from my lips. I slip the order pad into my apron pocket and head out.

I stiffen. It's Lucas, the messy-haired new kid. Occasionally Brokewater High students make their way here, but mostly they hang out at Chili's or Delia's Ice Cream Shoppe, or they drive to the beachfront restaurants thirty miles west. Eli Kusuma never comes in. So what is Lucas doing here?

He sits in the corner booth, elbows on the table, the hair on the right side of his head all smooshed and spiking up on the other side, like he's just woken up from an afternoon nap. He's playing with something in his hands.

"Why are you here?" I ask. It comes out sharp.

He looks up at me, the beginnings of a grin puckering his mouth. "I came for the food and the pleasant atmosphere." Behind him, somebody's kid throws a chicken nugget and almost nails him in the head. Someone else blows bubbles in their pop. Lucas grins wider. "What are *you* doing here?"

"I work here." I cross my arms over my chest and glare at him.

"I know."

The hairs on my arms prickle. What the hell is wrong with this guy? "Are you stalking me?"

"No! I told you, I'm here as a customer."

"Fine. Then what do you want?"

"Something to drink?"

I sigh and roll my eyes. "Whatever. You want pop?"

"What's that?"

Is he playing me? Setting me up for some sort of trick? "Don't be thick."

He squints at me. "No. Really. What's pop?"

"Um, hello? A fizzy drink full of sugar that will rot your teeth out."

"Oh. You mean soda. I'll take a Mountain Dew."

"Fine. But it's pop. Nobody's called it soda since the fifties. We don't wear poodle skirts anymore either."

"I'm from Florida, from a town called Bushnell. We call Mountain Dew and Coca Cola and everything else soda." He smiles this big, lopsided grin that makes him look young and earnest. It's almost adorable.

It also makes me want to punch him.

I shrug. "Good for you."

"But if they call it pop here, then pop it is." He rubs whatever he's holding. It's the pink lighter from the other day. He sees me looking. "Thanks for the heads-up, by the way."

I shrug, already regretting it. "Just giving you fair notice."

He furrows his thick, dark eyebrows and stares at the lighter. "Notice taken. It's my mom's."

"Sure it is. If pink sparkles are your thing, you've got bigger problems than I thought." I head to the back before he can say anything else. I grab a straw and a tall glass, fill it at the drinks dispenser, and bring it back to the table. "Here you go."

Lucas is still staring at the lighter. He's not smiling anymore. "My mom gave it to me before I left. She's—she's dying. Stage four breast cancer."

In spite of myself, I feel a prickle of sympathy. "Life sucks."

"That's why my dad shipped me up here. Back home, I'm about as useless as tits on a boar."

That's a good one, but I don't tell him so. I file it away in my brain for future use.

He clears his throat. He drums the lighter on the table and looks up. "So, there's a party in a few weeks, second Friday of October. It's near Silver Beach. Xavier Jones-Gray—do you know him? He's on the football team with Eli. His grandparents own a beach house. They're antique shopping in Muskegon for the weekend or something. Xavier's throwing a huge bonfire shindig. Food, beer, whatever."

"Okay . . ." I know where this conversation is headed, and it's making me itchy and uncomfortable. I've had about enough.

"So . . . do you wanna go with me?"

I freeze. "No."

"Are you sure? It could be fun. Like a date. Or not a date. Whatever. I'm flexible."

I stare at him. My face heats up. It must be a trick. Yet, his eyes seem so sincere, so serious. Some small part of me whispers *what if* . . . I shut the thought down as quickly as it enters my head. No one has asked me out in nearly four years.

I wouldn't say yes anyway. Everyone is just using everybody else. Everyone has an angle. You let someone in, and they betray you the first chance they get. I'm sure as hell not interested in that.

I'm alone. It's what I do, who I am. My heart is a closed fist. It has to be. "Nope. Not my thing."

"Okay, well," Lucas says, raking his hand through his hair and grinning sheepishly, "you sure you don't want to reconsider? I'm excellent company, I promise."

"Whatever you're doing? You need to stop. Don't confuse me with someone who cares." I force myself to walk away before he can react.

An older couple leaves, and I grab my tub to bus their table. The place isn't crowded, but it's busy enough that I can avoid Lucas. Still, I feel his gaze on me as I work.

I nearly break a plate as I slam the dirty dishes into the tub. I toss in the crumpled napkins and half-finished cups. My gaze blurs. I rub the heel of my hand against my eyes with my free hand.

It's a trick anyway, him pretending to be nice to me. Probably something Margot and Jasmine cooked up. I just want to be left the hell alone. It's better this way.

It's almost five p.m. when he finally leaves. I bus his table. He ate the entire mushroom burger he ordered, and the table is free of crumbs and trash. There's a ten tucked under his empty cup. I give it all to the waitress, Brianna. I may need money, but I don't need his pity. Or his pathetic puppy-dog shtick.

His table is my last. I can finally clock out.

"How's your mom, kid?" Bill asks as I strip off my dirty apron. He always calls me "kid," never my name. He's at the stainless steel cutting counter, chopping up the lettuce, tomato, and onions for a Fiesta Chicken Salad.

"Fine," I say, like every time. No one really wants to know.

"Haven't seen her for awhile."

I shrug.

"How's Frank? Haven't seen him either."

When Frank is around, he always gets together with Bill and his drinking buddies every weekend to play poker, get drunk, and relive the glory days. He usually leaves every month or two for a couple of weeks at a time—for odd jobs, short-term factory gigs, or just to get out of dodge.

"He'll be around soon, I'm sure."

He pauses and turns toward me. His dark eyes have that crinkled, concerned look he gets sometimes. "And how are you doing, kid? Things okay at home?"

My body tenses. "Super."

He keeps looking at me, his knife half-raised over the cutting board. "You sure?"

I lick my lips. I never know what to say when he gets like this, but it's not like he really wants to know. He's friends with Frank. Even if I told him everything, he'd just take Frank's side. "Everything's fantastic. Stupendous."

"Alright then. Have yourself a good one, kid."

I nod, finish hanging up my apron, and grab my keys.

The rusty, dented fifteen-year-old Camry I drive is Ma's, but when she has her bad spells, she never leaves the house. Basically, the car is mine. The engine makes a raspy, grunting sound before it sputters to a start, but it still runs.

We only live a mile or so from town, but the trim neighborhoods give way quickly to farms, apple orchards, and old, dilapidated houses tucked into fields and forests along unkempt dirt and gravel roads. The houses on my road are concrete boxes or trailers with sagging porches and scabby lawns.

Our trailer is a quarter mile down the road. It's on two acres, backed by the neighbor's cornfields. It's a doublewide, and it used to be decent, back before everything went to hell. Ma used to put fresh pink-veined geraniums and dainty white and purple petunias in window boxes. She planted ivy, and the vines curl up both sides of the porch posts and straggle along the ceiling. She got Frank to tack on some cornflower blue shutters, and for a while, she painted them fresh every year.

But that summer four years ago, everything changed. Her drinking got worse. She started fading into her stupors for longer and longer. She wouldn't leave the house and barely left her bedroom. She started forgetting how to be Ma. Before, even with Frank's drinking and the fights, it wasn't bad for long.

Now, it's always bad. Now the white siding is dingy and scummy with mold. The wooden shutters are peeling. The flowers are dead. There's a broken board on the second step of the porch. But the ivy is still there, jungle green and full and growing constantly, reaching its tendrils out along the siding. I hope it engulfs the whole trailer someday.

I pull into the weed-infested driveway.

I feel it like a change in the weather, like the stirring in the current alerting the fish a shark is near. It's his mud-crusted black truck, with the naked woman silhouette bumper sticker and the steel balls dangling from the hitch.

Frank is home.

NINE

My fingers grip the steering wheel until my knuckles turn white. I think about peeling out of the driveway and going somewhere else, anywhere else. But there's nowhere to go.

I get out of the car as thunder rumbles in the distance. The air smells electric, singed. I open the front door, my legs like lead, my heart punched into my throat.

He's sitting at the kitchen table with the boys. He bought them model car kits, and the kitchen table is covered with newspaper, glue, and pieces of miniature cars. Aaron kneels on a chair, his elbows on the table, his plump face bright and happy. Frankie is on the other side of Aaron, his eyes squinty and his face scrunched up in concentration as he carefully applies glue to a side mirror.

Frank looks up, his tan skin creasing around his mouth as he smiles. "Sidney! My long-lost daughter. I'd hug you, but I'm a little messy right now." He raises his hands and wiggles fingers dripping with glue. He wipes one hand on Aaron's arm, and Aaron giggles.

"Eww, gross, Daddy!"

"Don't bother," I say. The thought of his hands on me makes me cringe. I spin my rings on my fingers, willing my hands not to tremble.

Frank's eyes cloud, but only for a moment. "Later, then." He turns back to helping Aaron glue on a fender.

"Where's Ma?"

"She's just in the bathroom, but she's in the middle of cooking dinner. Can't you smell it?"

I do now. Chicken and gravy. A pot of rice is on the stove. "So she's having a good day?"

"Every day when Pop's home is a good day. Right, boys?"

The boys nod eagerly. They hope it will be. I pray it will be, not that anything can save us if it isn't.

"Here, like this." Frank guides Aaron's hands as they paste the fender to the back of the little metal car.

I just stand there. A storm of emotions churn inside my chest. Frank is a handsome man, his shiny hair swept back off his forehead, so dark it's almost a blue-black—like mine. His eyes are like mine: the color of blue flame. "Have a seat, baby girl. It's family time." Frank gestures at the chair next to him, his body lean and strong, his every move graceful, echoing his days as the star receiver for the Brokewater High Wildcats.

I feel the involuntary pull, the desire to please this handsome, charismatic man who is my father. If I just sit down and plaster a smile on my face, then it will be real. Maybe I can just step into this charade and believe it, like Frankie and Aaron. Maybe this time will be different.

Except the echo of every other time thrums through my body, my bones. The bitterness wells up, and I can't help myself. "Where were you?"

"When?"

"These past three and a half weeks, when your family barely had money for food."

"I had to work, to get money. Don't I always bring back money? We have plenty now." He wipes his hands on the newspapers and pulls a thick wad of cash out of his jeans pocket. He thumbs through the bills as the boys' eyes go wide.

"How much is that?" Aaron asks.

"Twenty grand, kiddo." Frank's eyes shine. "Your pop is a real winner."

I think about new shoes and backpacks for the boys. Fixing the Camry. A new dishwasher. Paying bills and buying groceries for years. Only it won't last that long. "But where did you go, what did you do?"

He's never specific about where he gets the money. Maybe he goes to the Four Winds casino in New Buffalo, or the Firekeepers in Battle Creek, or as far as the casinos in Detroit. He bets on his card games: blackjack, stud poker, roulette, and baccarat. He gets odd jobs with friends, remodeling a house or digging ditches. Who knows? Maybe he's robbing pharmacies or stealing cars. Nothing would surprise me.

He frowns. "What died and crawled up your ass? Whatever happened to children who respected their parents, who knew when to keep their mouths shut?"

Frankie glares up at me. I'm ruining it. I'll make him mad, and then he'll drink more, and that will be the end of model cars at the kitchen table and Ma making dinner. I run my tongue over my front teeth. I want to scream at him, demand answers from him.

I look at Aaron. He gazes back at me expectantly, a rare light in his brown eyes. And something deflates inside me. They need this happy fiction. I won't be the one that takes it away from them.

"Okay, fine." I edge around the table.

"Where are you going?"

"I have homework. Three papers to write by Friday."

Homework always appeases him. "Good girl. Your grades? Still all A's?"

"Of course." Not really. But give it time, and he'll get drunk enough to forget he ever asked.

He shakes a finger at Frankie. "You see? If your dumbass sister can do it, so can you. What're your grades?"

"All A's," Frankie lies. I don't correct him. Something swells in my heart when I look at Frankie. Somewhere inside that eleven-year-old tough guy is the little boy with the googly-eyed rock people, the love of Bunny, the brave face trying so hard to be strong whenever the shouting got too loud. We comforted each other, back then. Now, there is no one.

"Good. Atta boy!"

I scoot around the table and am almost free, only I'm blocked in the entryway between the kitchen and the living room. It's Ma.

"There you are. Come help me stir the gravy." Ma wipes her hands on her apron. She's washed her hair, pulled the lank strands back in some kind of French twist. She's wearing makeup, the pink discs of blush on her cheeks doing little to mask skin with the pallor of mayonnaise. "Look what your father got for me!" She holds up the ugliest ceramic rooster I've ever seen.

"What is that?"

"It's a cookie jar! See? Gobble, gobble!" She lifts off the turkey's head and neck.

Like anybody's going to bake cookies in this house. She hands me the rooster, and I find a spot for it on the counter next to the back door.

Ma stoops over Frank and plants a kiss on his forehead. He wraps an arm around her, rubs her belly.

"So, what's everybody been up to while I've been working myself to the bone?"

I turn my back on this suddenly picture-perfect family and stir the gravy. Frankie talks about science projects at school, the local skateboarding contest next week he's been practicing for. Aaron drones on about his teachers, art class, making collages with newspapers and macaroni noodles.

"You better watch out with that art stuff; you'll turn into a faggot." Frank's laugh has a hard edge to it.

"Frank." Ma's voice is light, teasing. She flits around the kitchen, pulling garlic bread out of the oven, testing the chicken, drawing glasses down from the shelf, pausing at the table to ruffle Aaron's hair, squeeze Frank's shoulder.

This mother, with the smile plastered on her rouged face, is different from the sickly, sweaty, whimpering woman in the bed when Frank is gone, different from the sniveling, clumsy cow she becomes beneath Frank's rage. My mother is a chameleon; her personality transforms at the drop of Frank's hat.

"Clean up the table, boys," she says. "Dinner will be ready soon."

"And what have you done with yourself, Susie Q?" Frank asks as he helps the boys put the model cars back in their boxes.

"Oh. You know. Cookin', cleanin', taking care of the kids and this baby in my belly."

I clench my jaw. The ache in my bones reminds me. "Like hell you did. I'm the one that cleaned. I made sure the boys had regular meals. I got them up and dressed, got them to school, made sure they took their showers and brushed their teeth. You couldn't get your lazy ass out of bed for three weeks."

Ma looks at me. Her eyes go hard and shiny. "Watch your mouth, girl. We're having a nice, family dinner. Of course I had a nap or two. I'm growing a child."

"Respect your mother," Frank growls, "or I'll smack that sassy tongue right out of you."

I should shut up. I need to shut up. But something inside me is sharp as glass. I can't help myself. "I'm not lying! She didn't leave her room this whole time! She barely even showered. I did everything."

"What'd I tell you, Frank? She's always trying to make me look bad. She's trying to turn you against me."

"That's a lie!"

"Enough!" Frank slams his fist on the kitchen table.

I cringe against the counter. The boys' faces are white with dread.

"Leave your mother alone. You lazy, ungrateful—"

"Frank," Ma breaks in with her sweetest voice. She comes behind him and kneads his shoulders. "Don't let her ruin this. We're celebrating! We're celebrating you."

Frank's gaze pierces me. There's a long, tension-filled moment where we all just wait and see what he'll do next.

He blinks, turns, and smiles at the boys. "Who wants a hundred bucks?"

My brothers cheer. Frank peels off crisp twenty-dollar bills so new, they look fake.

I don't get anything. I don't expect it. They're punishing me for telling the truth. Still, I want that money in my bank account. I need it. Relief, guilt, and dread twist my stomach. I hate Frank here, but at least when he's home, the bills get paid, and I can start saving again.

When the food is ready, I clean up the newspaper, wash the table, and set out the silverware. Frank sits on my right, his presence like radiating heat. I eat in silence and let the conversation roll around me. Frankie and Aaron can barely keep quiet for a moment; they're so eager to tell Frank all the minute details of their small little lives.

I shovel in the rice, the chicken, the corn, the gravy. I taste nothing. Fork to mouth. Fork to mouth. My stomach fills, and I eat more, more, more until I'm about to explode. Ma brings out apple pie and vanilla ice cream, and I eat that too.

I excuse myself as soon as the table is cleared and spend the rest of the evening in my room. Tonight, the cuts are long and deep. I make five of them, pressing the blade hard into the white flesh of my left thigh. It bleeds for over an hour.

TEN

Tuesday comes too soon. I slouch in the hard metal chair in the group therapy classroom, staring out the window and waiting for the next torture session to start. Outside, the leaves on the trees by the river are tipped with marigold and rust.

I'm edgy and restless. Last night's cutting session wasn't enough. The dark thing that makes its home inside me oozes through my veins.

"Well, well," I drawl as Arianna sinks into her chair and tucks her backpack between her legs. She's wearing a silky slip dress, knee-high leather boots, and a jean jacket. She's too perfect for words. "If it isn't our resident Beauty Queen. Deigning to join us today?"

"Sorry. I had to get my—"

"Actually, I don't give a rat's ass."

"Sidney, name-calling and putdowns are inappropriate in this group. We respect each other, remember?" Dr. Yang looks more tired than usual. His shirt is rumpled, and sweat stains are already beginning to show beneath his armpits.

"Whatever, Doc."

Arianna's skin glows even under the classroom's fluorescent lights. She presses her hands against her flat stomach.

"We're both glad you could make it, Arianna. Today, I thought we'd share some fun, non-threatening information about ourselves, such as where we were born, how long we've lived here, what our parents do, etc. Who would like to start?"

Arianna shifts in her seat, crosses her legs. "I guess I'll go. My mom is a general practitioner and has her own office on Walton Rd. My dad is head pastor at Westside Christian Church. He used to be the associate pastor at a megachurch outside of Chicago, but he got tired of being a little fish in a big pond. Here he gets to be a big fish, I guess. We moved here half-way through my freshman year."

"So you buy into all that religion crap?" I ask.

"It's not crap, and yeah, I kinda do. I believe in God."

I shake my head. "How's all that peace and joy working out for you? All your prayers and Friday night Bible studies and the 'Jesus Loves You' flyers you and your little club plaster all over the school like graffiti. From where I'm sitting, being a Jesus freak isn't doing you any favors."

Arianna's mouth tightens. "I'd be happy to explain it to you, if you were actually interested. Having faith doesn't mean your life is perfect."

"But it does mean you aren't supposed to be slashing up your body, the temple of God, right? Isn't that a cardinal sin or something?"

She looks away. "You're thinking of Catholics. And suicide."

"Whatever floats your boat."

"Anyway." She shrugs. "I'm just trying to be normal, I guess."

She reminds me so much of Jasmine it hurts. I grit my teeth. "Do you think cutting is normal? Is that the new 'in' thing you and your besties do to pass the time?"

"No! Of course not. None of them know anything about—anything." Arianna gnaws at her pinkie nail. "Anyway, I thought we were talking about non-threatening subjects?"

"We are," Dr. Yang says. "Let's get back to that, shall we? Arianna, do you have any siblings or pets?"

"I'm an only child. I have a white Persian cat named Cleo."

I make a gagging noise. "Is this torture or therapy?"

Dr. Yang glares at me. "Would you prefer to be somewhere else?"

"Actually, yes. I would *prefer* to be popping chilled grapes on a deserted beach in Hawaii. And yet, I find myself here. Odd how that happens."

"You are free to leave at any time. However, there are consequences for your actions. And your words."

How I'd love to ditch this place right now. But he's right. I can't. I slouch further in my chair and spin my rings around my fingers. Arianna keeps talking and I ignore her. I answer whatever dumb questions he asks me about—my brothers (two) and how long I've lived here (forever) and what hobbies I have (none, unless you count cutting. Dr. Yang does not.)

"What about college choices?" Dr. Yang asks. "Have either of you decided yet?"

Arianna's eyes darken. Her voice goes monotone, like she's sick to death of talking about how privileged she is. "I've signed up for the October SATs. I'm applying for early admission to Notre Dame and Northwestern, definitely. And University of Chicago. U of M is my safety school, obviously."

"Obviously," I echo.

Dr. Yang shoots me a look. "And you, Sidney?"

"No idea."

"It's almost October," Arianna says in a scandalized tone. "Have you at least narrowed down your favorites? Toured a few campuses?"

I snort. Like that's an option for me. I know I have to go to college. It's my only escape, but I'll be paying every dime myself. The idea of my parents taking me on campus tours is laughable. "Maybe next weekend. My mom's gonna fly me out to Yale. We'll have tea with the provost and pick out decorations for my dorm room."

Arianna frowns. "This is serious. This is your *future*."

That black cloud billows up behind my eyes. My future. She says it like senior year is some stairway to heaven, and our nebulous future is the paradise we're aiming for. I can't see it.

I want out more than anybody in this God-forsaken town. But there's that shadowy thought always there, always nibbling at the corners of my mind: I have no future. My escape funds will keep dwindling, drained by the needs of everyone but me. College is just a fantasy, a dream I'll wake up from, another disappointment. There's only this, forever.

"Sidney?" Dr. Yang asks. "Are you with us?"

I blink. They're both staring at me. "What? I said I don't know. Go fret about your chipping nail polish or something else equally important."

"Sidney." Dr. Yang's voice is as calm as always, but his eyes are shooting me a warning.

I force myself to sit up straighter. I cannot be expelled. I know that. I've got to keep it together. I clear my throat. "Okay, yeah. I've looked at a few community colleges in Chicago." It's far, but not so far that I can't check in on my brothers. "I've done some virtual tours or whatever. Happy now?"

"Very." Dr. Yang steeples his fingers beneath his chin. "Okay, let's switch gears a bit. Did you both bring your journal assignments?"

"I spent two hours writing last night," Arianna says as she pulls her pink journal out of the satchel at her feet.

I groan.

"Did you have difficulty with the assignment?" Dr. Yang asks me.

"If you mean difficult in the sense that I don't care for useless, impractical, time-wasting nonsense, then yes."

Dr. Yang's brow furrows. "It can be hard to express real feelings, sometimes. I understand that. Arianna, would you like to go first?"

She opens her journal and smooths out the page. There's a Band-Aid on her left pinkie finger. "Well, I wrote a bunch of stuff. Like, war makes me angry. And little kids going hungry in America. And those terrorists who—"

"This isn't a Beauty Pageant contest," I break in. "Though you'd definitely win."

"Arianna," Dr. Yang says gently. "These are all very real, very terrible things. Do you have anything on your list that's personal to you? Something about the people and situations that directly impact your life?"

Her face blanches. "Um, I don't really get angry."

I snort. "What?"

"Anger is a negative emotion and isn't helpful or productive. I, um, try to focus on the positive."

"That's a big fat load of bullshit."

"That seems uncalled for," Arianna says, her nose wrinkling.

I sit up straighter, fresh anger surging through me. "Everyone gets angry about something. And how the hell does cutting fit into your everything-is-unicorns-and-rainbows positivity shtick?"

Her hands tighten around the journal. "I don't know."

"What makes you angry, Sidney?" Dr. Yang says quietly.

My hands curl into fists on my lap. For a moment, I think about saying nothing. Instead, I blurt, "Everything."

"Would you care to elaborate?"

I tilt my head at Arianna. "Her perfect princess act, for one. Bullies like Jasmine Cole and her snotty little brother for another. People who prey on the weak." I think of Frank. My heart beats harder. I am not weak. I cannot be weak.

"What else?"

But my defenses slide back up. I can't talk about this. About any of it. "I can't stand how the vending machine runs out of Reese's Pieces and it takes them over a week to refill it. I mean, the gall of these people."

Arianna shakes her head. Dr. Yang sighs.

The rest of the session drones on. I barely hear a thing until Dr. Yang clears his throat loudly. "For next week, I'd like you to think about how cutting helps you."

Arianna's eyebrows shoot up to her hairline.

Dr. Yang gives her a small smile. "It is an unhealthy coping mechanism, of course, but it serves a role, a purpose, in your life right now. What is that purpose? Why do you feel that you need it? Please consider that this week and come back with some thoughts."

I have plenty of thoughts. I don't need to write any of them down. I don't need to share them either.

When the bell rings, I'm out of my seat and barreling for the door.

"Sidney, a word please."

I stop reluctantly, already knowing what he's going to say.

After Arianna slips out, he turns to me, his expression grave. "You need to take this seriously, Miss Shaw. I must report your progress to my superiors, and I cannot lie for you. I do not wish to see you expelled, but if you blow off another assignment, I will have no choice but to report it. Do you understand?"

My mouth goes dry. If I get expelled, bye-bye escape to college, no matter how much money I've saved. I'll be stuck in this ass-end of nowhere town. I make myself nod. "Got it."

I bolt from the room. I grab my books from my locker and head to my next class.

I'm in zone-mode: no thinking, no eye contact. Just survive the damn day.

ELEVEN

Officially, I have study hall last period. I usually cram in the rest of my homework so I'm done by the time I have to go to work, then head home to clean and cook and take care of the boys. And Ma. But Frank's home. They've been playing house all week. Happy drinking. It's only a matter of time before happy drinking turns into the other kind.

But today, there's too many people at school I'd rather not run into, so I head to work early. Bill's usually pretty good about my hours. Sometimes I catch him watching me, and there's something sad and pensive in his eyes. I hate it, but he hasn't fired me yet, so I endure it.

"Great timing," Bill says when I get there. "Brianna's kid got sick. She's not gonna be able to cover her shift. I was going to call Jessie, but here you are. Can you handle it?"

I make a face. He wants me to wait the tables. More interaction with the customers. More chances to screw it up. Again. "You trust me?"

His laugh comes from somewhere deep in his gut. "Nope. Not even a little."

I can't help it. He wrings a tight smile out of me. "Okay, then. Glad we're on the same page. I'll try my best not to spit on anybody's food."

He pats my shoulder. "That's all I'm asking for, kid."

I tie on Brianna's apron, make sure I've got my pad and pens with ink, and clock in.

I work for two hours, serving and bussing a few dozen tables. Dr. Yang's lecture is fresh in my mind. I don't dump food in anyone's lap or yell at unruly toddlers. When a kid draws all over the table with her scarlet-colored crayon, I handle it with aplomb.

"I'll take care of this," I say to the parents, who don't seem to care and didn't bother to stop the kid in the first place. I'd rather slap them or maybe spit in their burgers, but I grit my teeth and smile instead. Dr. Yang would be proud. I'm possibly a tiny bit proud of myself, too.

I've made almost sixty bucks in tips when the front bell jingles. Brianna comes in, all smiles and perfect blonde pigtails. Her husband must have come home early to take over the sick-kid duties. Bill gives her a lot of shifts because she can work the bar. Plus, she's perky and bouncy. The old guys love her—unlike me, the sullen, sulky smart-ass.

I jerk off my apron and clock out as soon as I see her car pull into the gravel parking lot. Another car pulls in right behind her—a black, mud-crusted truck. Damn it all to hell.

I watch through the glass front door as Frank, Ma and her swollen belly, and my brothers all topple out of the truck. My gut tightens. Frank comes here a lot when he's home, but it's usually to throw back some beers with the boys after dark. Never with the family. Never when I'm here.

Frank strides through the front door, a huge grin on his face and a Coors already in one hand. "Where's Bill?" he hollers. "Where's the best linebacker the Wildcats ever had?"

Three or four men at the bar spin on their barstools and greet Frank with handshakes and claps on the back. One of them is Hector Gonzales, dressed in his starched blue police uniform. I think he's supposed to be off-duty to drink, but he's not the kind of cop that lets regulations cramp his style. He played football too, a tight end or something, but wasn't good enough to get a scholarship for it. He's one of Frank's main poker buddies.

Bill comes out, and Frank pulls him into a bear hug. They all start in on the '98 state championship, the year the Wildcats nearly went all the way. They can jaw on about their glory days for hours. The more alcohol buzzing through their veins, the more glory to go around.

And they all love Frank. He's loud and fun and can electrify the room. He tells great stories, plays excellent poker, can win a game of pool or darts with one hand tied behind his back, and he always gives credit where credit is due.

Ma waits silently by the door. Aaron and Frankie watch Frank with adoration in their eyes, like it's the greatest thing in the world to be a big shot in a small-town bar with a handful of funny stories about things you did twenty years ago.

"What're you doing here?"

Aaron gives me a small wave and Frankie ignores me. Ma touches my arm. "He and the boys went to the gun range and fired some rounds. You should have seen how wonderful they were."

"Did he take them out of school?" I ask, already annoyed.

Ma pretends I didn't say a word. "Frank wants to take us all out to a nice dinner."

Fan-freaking-tastic. More family time. Like this day hasn't contained enough horror. "Not here, I hope."

Ma shakes her head, a strand of hair falling into her eyes. Her too-bright tangerine lipstick bleeds into the fine lines around her mouth. "Olive Garden. In St. Joe. Afterward, we're getting a new stainless-steel dishwasher from Lowes."

"Well, that's something, at least."

Her face darkens. "Don't ruin tonight with your nasty attitude, young lady. Show some respect."

I sigh, but I shut up.

The whole night, the boys and Frank chatter about the guns they shot and how many targets they hit. Frank loves his guns almost as much as his truck and his beer. Almost. Then Frank tells the boys he picked up the newest PlayStation while they were at school, and they about wriggle out of their seats with excitement. Frank loves playing the hero.

But that's more money we need for bills and food the next time he takes off. More money that's not going to fix the leak in the roof over Aaron's bed or the air conditioner in the Camry. More money that will come out of my bank account when we need groceries, or the next bill comes due. And I'm stuck watching my dream of escape fading further and further away.

It's like he doesn't know or care that when he's gone, we eat peanut butter sandwiches and Ramen noodles, rationing out the food to make it last.

I shove the dark thoughts out of my head. Here, now, we can eat whatever we want. Today, we are rich.

At Olive Garden, we get the usual salad and breadsticks, and Frank orders a bottle of wine. We get whatever drinks we want, even chocolate milk for the boys. *Screw it,* I think, and I order the biggest item on the menu, the Tour of Italy. Frank doesn't bat an eyelash.

Frank's laugh is warm. He rubs Ma's shoulder, and her face glows with pleasure. Frankie and Aaron compete to tell the best stories about school, their classmates, whatever they can think of.

A sick, sour taste lodges in the back of my throat. I hate that I am an outsider in my own family. I resent my brothers' giddiness with a jealousy that makes my eyes burn, makes my heart throb with pain.

I want so badly to join in, to be a part of this bright, shiny picture. But I can't. It's not real.

Frank doesn't ask me questions, and I don't talk. But every time I look up, I catch his gaze on me, crawling over my skin. I recognize that look. I know what's coming. I swallow hard. I eat everything on my plate, slurping up the fettuccine so fast I'm barely chewing, shoveling every bite of food into the black pit opening up inside my gut. My heart thuds against my ribcage so loud I'm sure everyone can hear it.

After Olive Garden, we go to Lowes, and Ma gets to pick out a $900 dishwasher with steam this and sterilize that, all the bells and whistles. Frank and Ma discuss specifications with a skinny college kid in a red Lowes' vest.

I stare at the rows of shiny white and steel appliances until my vision blurs. My head is buzzing, and it's hard to think straight. Frankie pushes Aaron up and down the wide aisles in one of those massive flat carts. He rounds a row of refrigerators too fast and swerves to avoid hitting a middle-aged woman with a toddler in tow. Aaron tumbles off and skids against the concrete.

He bursts into tears and holds his knee, which is already trickling blood. "You stupidhead!" he shrieks at Frankie.

"You're the moron who let go."

"Shut up!" I grab his arm and hoist him to his feet. I dab the scrape with the corner of my shirt. "You're okay, Aaron. You're fine."

But he sees the blood and howls louder.

Frank stomps over. Storm clouds descend over his features. He squats down and puts his face right up into Aaron's. "What the hell is going on here?"

"Frankie d-did it."

"Then stop crying and hit him back. Be a man."

Aaron blanches.

"Hit him!"

Aaron's terrified eyes dart to me and then Frankie. He shakes his head, the tears coming faster.

Frank's face hardens. He's already half-drunk and out of patience. "No son of mine acts like this. Are you a crybaby? A wimpy faggot? What's wrong with you?"

Snot runs down Aaron's lip. His crying turns into harsh, hiccupping sobs.

Frank shakes his head in disgust. "Your mother's turned you soft. Little fag baby."

I cringe at the ugliness of his words. I sense the rage mounting inside of Frank, can feel it thrumming in my own blood like a warning, a time bomb ticking so quietly only I can hear it.

I try to mentally count the glasses of wine he had at dinner. Three? Four? Things aren't looking good. I need to do something, or things are going to go sideways real fast. "I'll take him to the car."

"At least do something useful with yourself. Get him out of my sight."

I grab Aaron's hand and lead him out of the store. It's dark out, the parking lot almost empty. I get Aaron in the truck. I sit next to him and wipe the fresh blood dribbling from his knee. "You have to stop crying. Please."

"I can't!" he says in between sobs. The parking lot street lights reflect through the windows and flicker across his face.

I close my eyes, take a deep breath. My skin is cold and clammy. I'm lightheaded. No matter how I feel, I have to calm him down. I rub circles over his back and speak in my softest voice, the one I used with him when he was a baby. "Take deep breaths. Ready? One, two, three. Good. Take a big one. Let it out slow. It's okay. It's almost stopped bleeding. Calm down."

He takes several ragged breaths. He sniffles and wipes his nose with his arm. "Frankie did it on purpose."

"I know. But you can't cry about everything. You know how he gets." I'm talking about more than Frankie, and Aaron's old enough, has seen enough, to know what I mean. "You've got to toughen up."

"Okay." He sniffs again, his little body shuddering with every breath. "Sidney?"

"What?"

"Am I the word that Pop said? Faggot?"

I bite my lip so hard I taste blood. My hatred for Frank this moment is a towering inferno. "No. Never. There's nothing you could do to make you that word. It's a mean, nasty word that mean and nasty people use to tear someone down and make them feel bad. That's all. Okay?"

"Okay, but people at school say that word to me, too. 'Cause I like pink and sparkly things. 'Cause I cry sometimes. They say I like boys."

I want to beat the snot out of every kid in his school. I don't care how young they are. They're old enough to know better. I want to shake Aaron and tell him he has to be tougher, stronger, harder, but his sweet little face is looking up at me, and I just can't bring myself to do it. "You are good. Just like this. Whatever you want to be is just fine. It doesn't matter if you like boys or pink sparkles or wear purple polka-dotted skirts to school every day. Okay? No one has the right to treat you like crap."

The corners of his mouth tilt into a tiny smile. "Will you hold my hand?"

I lace my fingers through his. They are still so small, so delicate. I swallow hard. "Tonight, you need to stay in your room. Don't come out, okay?"

He nods. I hold his hand all the way home in the crackling silence.

The dread creeps up my throat, strangling my breath.

~

I help Ma get Aaron to bed. I tuck him in with Ratty Bunny and kiss his damp forehead. Once I'm ready for bed, I sketch a quick picture of Ratty Bunny driving the cart, flying through the air in Lowes, shooting low over an aisle full of a hundred different kinds of toilets. I fold the page into a triangle and tuck it into the buffet drawer. It'll make him smile when he checks it in the morning.

Frank installs the dishwasher in the kitchen, with Ma humming and Frank chain-smoking and swearing with increasing volume. Things are normal now, but they won't be for long. I know what's coming. I try to read the assigned chapter from Government. The words keep scrabbling across the page, jumping and leapfrogging until I can't even make out individual sentences anymore.

I take out the stupid pink journal and stare at it, but I can't write anything, not a single word. It has no answers for me, and I have none for it, so why bother?

After a while, the house goes dark. Ma switches off the lights and locks the doors and there's murmuring from down the hallway and then silence. Awhile after that, footsteps pad down the hallway and pause at my door.

My head is full of cotton, and I can feel my body—thick and heavy, sinking through my comforter, sinking through the mattress, then the flimsy green carpeting and the floorboards and then the concrete and the soft dark earth below.

Then he comes in and does what he does, and there are no sounds but breathing. And even if there were, I wouldn't hear them.

I'm far away. I've flapped up and up and out the window to explore wide open skies. This body I loathe isn't mine. It's discarded, dissolved, the larva shrugging off its skin, liquefying its organs, leaving everything —including itself—behind.

TWELVE

Friday morning, I smash myself into Dr. Yang's blue nubby chair, trying to get comfortable. He's talking about something, but I'm only half-listening. I unwrap a Reese's Peanut Butter Cup and offer him one. He shakes his head.

"I can't help you if you refuse to help yourself," Dr. Yang says, spewing out more of his shrink talk. His fingers steeple beneath his chin. There are hollows under his eyes and stubble spattered with gray around his jawline. He looks like he needs more help than I do.

I pop the peanut butter cup in my mouth. I close my eyes as the deliciously sweet taste fills my mouth. "What does that even mean?"

"You know what it means. You've neglected to write your apology letter to Jackson Cole and his family."

"And?"

"It would behoove you to write the letter. It's been weeks. You should know the Cole family is still threatening legal action. I can't protect you from that."

I eat the second peanut butter cup, crush up the wrapper, and toss it in the trash can beside the desk. "Whatever."

"In addition, Coach Taylor informs me you're one point from failing Phys Ed. How do you feel about that?"

More shrink talk. "I feel dandy. Splendiferous. That's a word, right?"

He sighs. "In here, it's safe to talk about your feelings."

My feelings are a boiling vat of poison ready to scorch through my veins and spill into the world like acid, incinerating everything it touches. He'd be shocked and repulsed by the ugliness in me. He'd make one phone call, and they'd drag me kicking and screaming straight to a padded room somewhere, or at least a cell with a big, fat lock.

No one cares. No one wants to see. Some pretend to want to know, but they don't really. No one wants to know about all the ugly things in the world. They don't want to know that the darkest, most despicable acts happen right under their noses, that the real monsters live amongst us. They don't want to know.

I told one person. Once. The summer after eighth grade when my breasts sprouted like tumors and it all went to hell.

I can recall every detail. My mother sitting at the kitchen table in a pool of sunlight, her head bowed over her embroidery. It was the purple vase full of daisies and forget-me-nots, the one she framed and hung by the bathroom in the hallway.

She wove a purple thread on a needle back and forth through the white canvas. She hummed, and her face was flushed. Beads of sweat glistened on her forehead. There was a glass of cranberry-colored wine on the table next to a half-empty bottle.

I sat down at the table, dug a fingernail into one of the dings in the aged, honey-colored wood. Frankie and Aaron were messing around in the front yard, learning to ride the shiny red scooters Frank brought home.

Aaron was only five, but Frank picked out a regular-sized scooter which was far too big for Aaron. He kept falling on the driveway, spitting out cries of frustration and disappointment. Frankie rode circles around him, hooting with delight.

The window air conditioner unit was out again, and Ma had a box fan blowing hot air in her direction. It was August, and the whole house was sweltering.

But I was ice cold, my fingers so numb and limp I could hardly put on my clothes or lift my spoon at breakfast. For two days, I'd been sleepwalking through some kind of nightmare, my mind shrieking and banging against the cage of my skull. But outside my skin, no one could hear, no one could see how I was flayed, turned inside out, flesh raw and bleeding.

Ma was never the most reliable even on her best days, but who else did I have? Mothers were supposed to be the protectors of their children, to shield them from the terrors of the night. At least, that's what they promised in books and movies.

"Ma?"

"Hmmm." Her face was thin, young still. She wore mascara and blush, brightening her pale skin. "Morning, sleepyhead. Make yourself some cereal. I started toast, but it got burned somehow. Must be something wrong with the toaster again."

"Where's Frank?"

"Don't call him that. He's your father. He went to the gun range. Then he's got some meeting with Dan Wallback about a temp manufacturing job in Detroit somewhere."

"So he's leaving again."

Ma shrugged. For a few years, Frank had worked at the used car lot on Broadview for his old high school buddy, Mac Roos. But having a boss never sat well with him, and he'd quit (or gotten fired) the year before. Since then, he'd grab temp jobs at the local factories, help build a shed or fix someone's engine or transmission, whatever he could find. On the weekends, he went out drinking with Bill Beauvais and Hector Gonzales and hit the casinos.

"Ma," I tried again. I rolled the words I needed to say over my tongue. They were bitter, nasty words. Words that would tear a gaping hole right through the fabric of our sun-strewn kitchen. My muscles were rigid. My thoughts banged around inside my head. *There's this thing eating my insides* . . . "I need to tell you something."

"About next school year?" She wove the thread through the canvas, deftly puncturing it with the needle. I watched it punch through, come back up, leaving a slim line of fuchsia that wasn't there before. Even when she was half-drunk, she could still weave the needle like it was nothing. She'd finished a dozen needlepoints over the last few years, pictures of flowers or old farm houses, framing them and hanging them in the hallway or in the living room over the couch.

"Not about school."

"What then?"

I stared at the cigarette still smoldering in Ma's ashtray, watched a thin curl of smoke drift over the table. "It's—it's about Dad. He's been drinking a lot."

"Everyone needs a drink to relax. Your dad works hard to provide for this family."

"That's not it. When he's drunk, he—he does things."

Ma looked at me. "Now, don't you get started on that again. You kids stress him out to no end. With your complaining, your disrespect, your attitude. He's gonna raise you right, whether you like it or not. All good parents discipline their kids."

Outside, Aaron shrieked. Frankie answered with a sharp bark of laughter.

My heart stuttered in my chest. I licked my lips, gripped my own hands beneath the table, my fingernails digging into the flesh of my palms. The shred of pain kept me there, kept me going, kept my butt in the chair. "That's not it, either. The way he looks at me sometimes. Two nights ago, he came into my room and he did something. Ma, he—"

Aaron screamed louder.

Ma stood up so fast she banged into the table. "What's he on about now?"

My head snapped up. "What?"

Her eyes weren't soft and drowsy anymore. They were hard as she stared out the window, not meeting my gaze. "Those boys. Your brother's out there sobbing."

My brain was full of fog. I could barely follow her words. "But I'm trying to tell you—"

"Don't be selfish, Sidney. It can wait. What will I ever do with Frankie?"

"I don't know," I said numbly, staring down at my jean shorts riding high up my legs, the pale expanse of my upper thighs. The straps of my low-cut tank top dug into my shoulders. "But Ma . . ."

She took a long slug of her wine, wiped her mouth with her arm. She shoved the glass down so hard that droplets of red liquid spilled over the sides, staining the edge of her canvas. "Damn it! Now look what they've made me do. Go help him, Sidney. I've gotta take care of this."

She wasn't listening. She didn't care.

I knew I couldn't try again. It had taken all my courage to bring it up once. My nerve failed me, and I ran outside, my eyes burning and blurred with tears. The hatred was a dark, enormous thing. It was a monster birthed deep inside me, a creature slick and trembling, just waiting to break free and destroy everything it could reach. I imagined torching our ugly little trailer, setting fire to the whole town.

Aaron squealed in pain. He sat on the brown grass, clutching his elbow, crying loudly. I covered the space between us in three swift steps. I grabbed his shirt and screamed in his face. "Shut up! Shut up! Shut up!"

I turned and fled. I ran the mile and a half over the asphalt roads shimmering with heat to the school campus. I ran until my sides ached and my vision blurred with sweat. I followed the chain link fence to the back of the property and waded through the underbrush along the riverbank until I reached the rock.

Jasmine and I had found it two years before in sixth grade, when we first grew brave enough to cut classes. She hadn't bothered to come out there in almost a year.

I crouched on the rock and punched it with my fists until my knuckles split open. My insides were a cauldron of dark and ugly things spitting and hissing and raging. I beat the rock and screamed out my despair. There was no one to hear me. There was no one.

Only me. Only the terror and the darkness and everything ugly living inside me.

I clawed at my bare legs with my fingernails. Long, red welts appeared on my skin like magic. Slowly, slowly, the pain brought me back to myself. I wept as I scratched myself, my own self-loathing scraping me raw. But it brought the calm, the cold, sharp relief. The roaring in my ears softened to the dull thudding of my heart. The rattle in my chest slowed to a murmur.

The brown river rushed by beneath my feet, splashing against the rock. I could fill my pockets with stones and slide right in. The water would slip over my head, carrying me down, down, down to the murky bottom. The fish would nibble on my bloated carcass until I was unrecognizable. Until I was nothing but sharp, gleaming bones.

"Sidney? Are you okay?"

I blink up at Dr. Yang, the cool air conditioning pimpling my skin, the nubby fabric of the chair against my bare arms. "I'm fine. Fantastic."

"You went somewhere. Can you tell me what you were thinking about?"

I shake my head, fighting back the emotions I can't let myself feel. I tried to speak it once. My own mother didn't care enough to listen. There's no way I can ever do it again. "I was thinking about how I can't wait until Halloween."

"And why is that?"

I blink back tears. "I've always wanted to skin a black cat and offer it as a sacrifice to Satan, to see if it'll really give me dark powers."

Dr. Yang takes off his glasses and rubs the bridge of his nose. "What were you really thinking?"

After the rock that day, I walked home, scratched and bloodied, drenched in sweat. I dreaded how angry she would be, terrified of what Frank would do once he found out I'd told. But when I dragged open the screen door and went inside, Ma was slicing up watermelon at the counter. The boys sat at the table eating cheese-and-tomato sandwiches.

Frank sat next to them. The table was covered with cleaning rods and rags stained with barrel oil and solvents. His rifle and two shotguns lay on the table, the Glock .22 in parts spread out on a newspaper.

Frank swabbed out the chamber with his cleaning rod. "Hey, you."

Ma smiled her slow, lazy smile. "We've been waiting for you. Get cleaned up and eat with us." She acted like nothing had ever happened, like I hadn't just tried to tell her the fabric of my life had been ripped to pieces.

"Sidney?" Dr. Yang prodded.

"It doesn't matter. Nothing matters."

He writes something down in his notebook. "Do you often feel this way? Like nothing matters?"

"Stop psychoanalyzing me, okay? I'll write your stupid letter."

"You know this is a safe place, Sidney. What you say here stays here."

I roll my eyes. The idea of a safe place sounded fantastic—if it were true. I don't have any safe places, but I'm not going to tell him that.

"How about that journal entry you promised me? Did you write it?"

I slouch further in my seat and spin my rings. Before my session, I'd scribbled a few things, but they were all lies, stupid sarcastic nonsense. Suddenly, I don't want to give it to him. "I've had a rough few days, Doc. Give me until next session, okay? I'll write something."

He nods. "Even if you're unable to talk to me at the moment, you should talk to someone. We all need a friend. I think Arianna is a good choice, but it's up to you."

I glare at him. "I don't need anyone."

"I think it would be very lonely to live like that."

"You have no idea," I mumble.

He raises his eyebrows. "That's an excellent task for you, actually. Take a few risks, Sidney. Trust someone, even with a small thing. Try opening yourself up to something new. People might surprise you."

I need to get out of here. I stand up and shoulder my backpack. "I'll try, Doc. I promise."

"Just tell the truth," he says. "In your journal, in your letter. That's a start."

The truth is this: my soul is a black, repulsive thing. That monster still lives inside me, as ravenous as ever. This dark thing isn't just after me.

It's inside of me.

THIRTEEN

Lucas corners me in Classic Lit. He sits on my desk and folds his lanky arms over his chest. "Come with me to the beach party tomorrow night."

I don't even look at him. "And why would I do that?"

"Because I'm fun, interesting, and a terrific conversationalist."

"I highly doubt it," I say, but I feel the nearness of his body like static electricity.

"Don't tell me you have something better to do."

"I hate parties. Too many idiots crammed into small spaces."

"But this is the beach. There's more space. You can walk as far as you want in either direction." He cocks his head. "We can even go swimming."

"This is Michigan, not Florida. Remember? We try to avoid hypothermia around here."

More students pile into the room. They eye us as they shuffle past.

"Isn't it sad how some people are just born ugly?" Peyton slides into her seat.

"I actually feel sorry for you," Nyah says.

"Really? I don't think about you at all." I need them to go away and leave me alone. I can't stand them, can't stand this place.

A few people snicker. Nyah rolls her eyes.

"Keep rolling your eyes," I mutter. "Maybe someday you'll find a brain back there."

Lucas laughs.

"What's so funny, Pizza Face?" Peyton snaps. "Just shut up."

"Pretty sure it's a free country still," Lucas says in a neutral tone. He turns back to me. "Can I see your phone for a second?"

Dr. Yang's irritatingly calm voice echoes in my ear. I can write this down in that stupid book. But also, something inside me kind of wants to do it. I don't know why; maybe something to do with the clean, woodsy scent of him. Or the sweet earnestness in his eyes. It's annoying and disconcerting. I take the phone—old, dented, but still working—out of my backpack and hand it to him.

The bell rings. We're almost done with the play, but Miss Pierre starts in on the madness of King Lear again. Lucas sits in his own seat, still fiddling with my phone.

A minute later, he hands it back to me. He's entered his phone number under the handle "Lucas, aka Stud Muffin." He also punched in an appointment reminder for Friday night: "Beach with Stud Muffin."

I shake my head, about to delete it, when Miss Pierre clears her throat from the front of the room. "Is that a phone I see in your hands, Sidney Shaw?"

I slip the phone into my backpack. "No, ma'am."

"Good. That's what I want to hear. Now, let's talk about last night's reading. What did you think of Cordelia's response to her sisters?"

The rest of the day blurs. I do my homework. I do my shift at Bill's. I manage to stay away from Jasmine and Margot, except for the times they hurl insults under their breath as they pass me in the hallways and sit behind me in class. But that's nothing.

Thursday night, I eat peanut butter from the jar with a spoon as I scribble an apology letter to Jackson Cole. The first several drafts don't go so well. I finish with "You've raised your son to be a prick and your daughter is a raving bitch from hell." I'm sure Dr. Yang will love it. Friday morning, I slide it beneath his office door.

Everyone's talking about the party tonight, but the sound is like a current flowing around me. I barely hear it. In Classic Lit, Xavier Jones-Gray stands at the door and hands out flyers with directions. He's tall and wiry, with dark brown skin, close-cropped black hair, and a too-wide, too-bright smile. "Oops, almost gave you one," he says as I edge past. "No losers allowed."

My fingers curl at my sides. "I guess you're banned from your own party, then."

"Why do you have to be such a flaming bitch, Shaw?"

"Don't like my sarcasm? Too bad. I don't like your stupid." I give him the finger, just to make sure my point comes through loud and clear.

"Rude much?" Peyton says. I ignore her.

Lucas looks at me hopefully when I sit down. "See you tonight?"

I don't bother to answer. My whole body aches from the tension of keeping it all together. This day can't end soon enough.

In Government, Arianna drops a paper on my desk.

"What's this?"

"An outline of the chapters our paper is based on. Why don't you look at it over the weekend? We can get together on Monday to discuss a thesis topic. Maybe at lunch?"

"That's not going to work for me. Look, I don't do partners. This is how it goes: I'll write the whole freakin' paper, and you'll turn it in with both our names on it and still get your A. Okay?"

Arianna frowns and shakes her head. Her dark hair fans around her face. "That's cheating."

"Did you not hear me correctly? I do the work. You get the grade."

"I'm not going to do that."

"Why the hell not?"

"Because it's wrong, and because I do my own work."

I glare daggers at her, expecting her to melt like putty. But she straightens her shoulders. "I'm not going to bite. Not everyone is out to get you, Sidney." She sighs and points at the paper. "Just read it over the weekend. I'll find you Monday morning."

No one's ever had a problem with this my entire high school career. Now here's perfect little Arianna Torrès, shaking her head because she's a goody-goody Christian, who apparently picks when and where she's gonna act the part. Damn it all to hell.

FOURTEEN

Frank is drunk. I smell it as soon as I step through the front door. My shift at Bill's ended at 7:00, and I'm hungry and cranky. Bill sent me home with a Styrofoam container filled with fried fish strips and tartar sauce. I bolted down two strips in the car.

Frank and Ma are in the living room. Frank lets out a loud, braying laugh. Ma murmurs something I can't quite make out. I have to go past them to get to my bedroom. I drop my keys and the leftovers on the table and edge out into the living room. My gut tightens, my skin prickling. Maybe they won't see me.

Fat chance.

"Sidney!" Frank bellows. "Where you headin', baby girl?" He's got a bottle of Jack Daniels in one hand and an empty cup in the other. His feet are planted wide on the carpet, but his top half sways like a flower in a breeze. He raises the bottle and grins at me. "Want some?"

I press my body against the wall. I'm only ten or so feet from my bedroom door, but it might as well be a thousand. If I run, he'll sense my terror and be on me like a wolf. "You need to go to bed, Frank. Sleep it off."

"Oh, he's just havin' fun." Ma's voice is high and slurred. She's sitting on the edge of the couch, wearing only high heels and her bra and underwear. A long black dress is slung over the back of the couch.

"Mother." I force my voice to stay controlled. "You're having a baby. You can't get drunk when you're pregnant. What are you thinking?"

"We're just celebratin', that's all. I had my ultrasound today. Baby's healthy, just a little small. But that'll make it easier come time for birthing it." She hiccups.

I stare at them, acid creeping up my throat. "Is it a boy or a girl?"

She shrugs. "Dunno yet. Baby wouldn't show us. But it's okay. Frank's gonna pay for another appointment. No yellow baby outfits for this little 'un. Your daddy's still taking me out, though. 'Cept I couldn't get into my dress. Isn't that a hoot? Bought that dress last month two sizes too big, and I'm too fat to fit in it." She laughs again, a high, hysterical laugh, slapping her bare thigh.

I close my eyes. Why should I care about this baby when my mother is so obviously trying to destroy it? I should shut the hell up and escape to my room, but I can't. My stomach is a curdled soup of dread, but I still can't shut my damn mouth. "Who cares about your stupid dress? Do you want your baby deformed? You want to murder it?"

"Hey!" Frank yells, taking an unsteady step toward me. He shakes the bottle, small drops of brown liquid slurping over the top and spilling to the floor. "Shut your mouth or I'll shut it for you! Don't yell at your mother!"

"Then you do it! Someone needs to." I'm making it worse. There's a reason Aaron and Frankie are already squirreled away in their room. The first rule of this house is to know when to get lost. What he does next will be my fault, but the bile is surging up my throat. I'm choking on it. I cannot keep silent. "Neither of you are fit to raise a dog."

Ma's laughter bubbles into tears. She begins to sob. "Don't let her talk to me that way, Frank. You see how terrible she is to me? It's so awful when you're gone. You leave me here all alone with this smart-mouthed little slut."

Every muscle in my body tenses. I'm frozen in place, forced to watch. If I move, his gaze might snag on me next.

"Shut up!" Frank whirls on Ma. His slicked hair is mussed, his eyes red-rimmed.

"You don't love me!" Ma whimpers. "That's why you're always gone. You think I'm fat, don't you? Ellie was right about you. Admit it. You despise everything I've given you, everything I've sacrificed!"

"Stop it!" Frank shakes the bottle at her.

"I'm sorry, I'm sorry." Her gaze fastens on Frank, wide and pleading. "Don't hurt me. I'll stop. I love you, baby. I'll stop . . ."

"Sorry? You make me sick, you stupid cow." Frank looms over Ma. Her hands tremble and flutter about her face, mascara tracking in black smears beneath her eyes.

My veins are ice. I'm barely breathing. A hundred bricks are pressing on my chest, slowly crushing my ribcage. I have to get out of here. They've both forgotten about me, but that can change fast. Frank's in the mood to horrify and humiliate, and I've already seen everything I need to. As long as Frankie and Aaron stay in their room, they should be safe. Forgotten. But I won't be. Not for long.

Carefully, I back out of the living room and head through the kitchen. My elbow bumps into Ma's ugly rooster cookie jar, but I catch it before it falls. I freeze, listening. But there's nothing. I shut the front door softly. The porch light is still switched on from when I came home ten minutes ago. Bugs buzz around the light. The sun is just sinking behind the line of trees across the road.

I sag against the door. I can still hear Ma whimpering, but Frank is silent. His silence is the worst. It's when he's the most dangerous.

I try to stand up, but my legs give out. I hug them to my chest and rest my head on my knees. I can't stay here. But I'm so shaky there's no way I can drive. Besides, my car keys are inside on the kitchen table. I can't go back in there.

My phone beeps. I pull it out of my back pocket. The appointment alarm. The beach party. I close my eyes. Open them slowly. Dr. Yang said to take risks. He said to make friends. And if I don't have stuff to write in his stupid book, I get expelled. And besides, anywhere is better than here.

It's a no-brainer. Still, my stomach tightens with dread.

There are only five numbers in my phone book. Home, Bill's Bar and Grill, Frank, Jasmine's old number, which I never got around to deleting, and now Lucas, aka Stud Muffin. I tap on his name.

He answers on the first ring. "Hey, you."

"I need to know something."

"Shoot."

"Why'd you come to the restaurant?"

"I told you. I like you."

"Why?"

"Because you're full of sunshine and rainbows?"

I choke out a strangled laugh. "No. For real."

He doesn't say anything for a minute. "Can we not do this over the phone?"

I don't speak. I count his breaths. I'm still shaking, like I'm lying on the tracks while a train roars over me. I need him. I hate it, but I do. I need to get out of here. I take a deep breath. "Do you want to pick me up?"

"Hell yes, I do! I haven't left yet. Give me your address."

I rattle it off.

"Pick you up in ten."

I wait for him, rubbing my arms and trying not to shiver. I keep thinking I hear noises in the kitchen, but the front door doesn't open. The seconds tick by. Frank doesn't come for me.

Lucas's Jeep rumbles into the driveway. I jump up and run down to meet it.

"You look great."

I'm in my regular baggy jeans and oversized T-shirt, my hair pulled back in a messy bun. "So does your ride," I say, kicking aside an empty bottle of Mountain Dew and several crumpled Taco Bell wrappers. The seats are frayed, and the dashboard is gouged in several places. It reeks of stale tennis shoes.

"Thanks," he says without a hint of sarcasm.

There's a few minutes of silence as we drive down several roads and turn onto the highway. The beach is a good forty-five minutes away. "So, what do you think of Miss Pierre?" he says finally.

"You mean all her soliloquies on the meaning of madness? She's weird." But in a good way. I do like Miss Pierre, when I'm able to concentrate on what she's saying.

"Yep. She's as nutty as a squirrel's poop. Do you think it's true? That we all have the seed of madness inside us?"

I tug off one of my rings and roll it between my fingers. I'm still tense. It's hard to think straight. I need white space. "Lucas?"

"Yeah?"

"Can we not talk right now?" It comes out sharper than I intend. He's doing me a favor, after all. Arianna's words rattle around my head. *Not everyone is out to get you.* I take a breath. "I'm sorry. I'm just —stressed."

"Sure." I can feel his shrug in the dark. He doesn't sound pissed. For some reason, I'm glad.

"Thanks." I rest my head against the passenger side window and stare out at the rolling farms and scabby forests. We pass through small, tired-looking towns. Xavier's grandparents live a few miles north of the little beachfront town of St. Joe. After a while, we pull into a ritzy neighborhood with McMansions ringed with spotlights in the fancy, manicured shrubbery—showing off even in the dark.

Xavier's grandparents live at the top of a hill. Lucas parks at the bottom of their circular brick driveway, which is already packed with cars. We make our way up toward the house, a slate monstrosity of postmodern lines and edges and huge walls of glass.

A girl in a bouncy string bikini is standing at the corner of the walkway, chomping gum and holding a poster sign with an arrow and the words: "Party this way. Don't enter the house or I'll kill you. -Xavier." The girl tilts her head toward the brick walkway behind her.

We round the corner of the house and skirt the massive patio with a built-in kitchen and grill. A sand path leads down a large dune about 200 yards to the beach. A bonfire flickers, and I can see the movement of bodies, black outlines against the moon-silvered waves.

My stomach clenches. This is a bad idea.

Lucas touches my shoulder.

I flinch. "Don't touch me."

He holds his hands up. "No harm, no foul. I won't touch you, I promise. Unless you ask me to."

I remember the feeling of his warm hand on my arm. My pulse quickens. I turn my face away before he can see my cheeks redden. "Trust me. That's not going to happen."

"Okay." He shrugs. "Ready to go?"

I'm pretty sure this is Dante's ninth circle of hell. But where else am I going to go tonight? "Screw it. Let's go."

We make our way down to the beach, trying not to slip in the sand. I have to grab his arm once for balance. Mercifully, he doesn't make any smart-ass comments.

The bonfire's about a yard across. Several guys from the football team are feeding it from a stack of logs piled beside the keg table. Three yellow kegs dispense beer and who knows what else. A mountain of red plastic cups threatens to tip and spill all over the sand. There's a black Sharpie marker to write your name on your cup.

Below the table, an opened cooler is stuffed with water bottles, iced tea, Monster drinks, and Mountain Dew cans. To the right, another folding table holds a couple of wireless speakers thumping out the latest mind-numbing electronic dance music.

A ring of tiki lamps surrounds the bonfire. Within the ring, groups of people sit in canvas folding chairs or lounge on blankets. The guys wear beach shorts and sandals, and the girls wear only bikini tops and short-shorts or filmy little sundresses. They must be freezing.

"Who invited you here?" Xavier confronts us before we can enter the circle.

"She's my guest," Lucas says.

Xavier pokes his chest. "I was talking to you, too, Pepperoni Head. What do you wash your face with? Fried chicken?"

"Leave him alone," Eli calls from his spot on a blanket close to the fire. "He's with me." He's massaging Margot's bare shoulders. Jasmine stands next to them, holding a cup in each hand and looking like her eyeballs are going to pop from glaring so hard.

"Whatever." Xavier grins. His teeth are really, really white. All that grandparent money to pay for braces and teeth whitening. "I guess we can play connect the dots on your face when we get bored."

Lucas tenses beside me. "Very funny."

Xavier squints at Lucas like he's seeing him for the first time. He sways a bit on his feet. "How come you look different than Eli? Aren't you, like, brothers or something?"

Lucas clenches his jaw. "Cousins. His mom is Argentinian. Not that you really care."

"I do, man. I do. I just mean, I never thought an Asian dude's face could be so red, you know?"

"Look, you jerkwad—" I start.

Lucas interrupts me. "I think we're done here." He sounds calm, but there's a vein throbbing in his neck.

Xavier opens his mouth like he's going to say something else, which he really, really shouldn't. Not if he wants to keep those shiny teeth.

"Come on, man!" Eli says.

"Xavier! Get over here!" Nyah says in a sing-song voice, patting the blanket next to her.

"Whatever, dude." Xavier loses interest and wanders back to his group.

Lucas turns to me. "Don't insult the alligator until after you cross the river."

"What the hell does that mean? Is that some weird Florida slang?"

"It just means it's safer to hold your tongue around certain people."

I dig my sneakers into the sand. "I can't do that. I love sarcasm. It's like punching people in the face, only with words. I mean, I'm not against literally punching people in the face either, if the situation calls for it."

Lucas smiles tightly. "If only closed minds came with closed mouths."

"Exactly. People are idiotic cretins, and I pretty much hate everyone."

"That's what I like about you. You always look on the bright side."

I roll my eyes. "You should fight back, defend yourself from those cotton-brained douchebags."

"It doesn't bother me that much."

"I call BS." I point down at his hands, which are still balled into fists at his sides.

He sighs, unclenching his fists. "Yeah, it sucks rocks. But fighting back just makes things worse. In case you haven't noticed, I'm a skinny nerd. The odds are not in my favor."

"They'll just stomp all over you if you let them."

He runs his hand through his hair, making it stick up even more. "If you don't react like they want, they get bored and go away. I just pretend I don't care. They're not worth a bucket of emu spit anyway."

"Is that how people talk where you're from?"

"Not really. It's just stuff my dad says all the time. It rubs off on you. Look, I don't want this to ruin the night, okay? It's really not a big deal."

"Whatever floats your boat."

"Can I grab you a drink?"

I shift uncomfortably. "I guess. Whatever's in the keg is fine."

I'm still waiting for Lucas when Grayson Myers staggers up to me. He clearly started his own party hours ago. He's built like a bear and is nearly as hairy, with a pelt of wiry hair covering his arms, chest, and legs. "You'd be a dime, baby, if you weren't such a lard-ass."

"And you'd be a human, if you weren't such a Neanderthal."

"I'd still tap that." He says it like he's offering me a compliment. His breath stinks of stale beer. "Right behind that dune. I'll even let you—"

"Get out of my face before you find your balls tied around your neck."

He raises his cup, liquid sloshing over the edge. "Why you gotta be such a tease?"

"Are you not hearing me correctly? I'd rather be gnawed to death by sewer rats than voluntarily touch any of your STD-infested body parts."

"So, you really don't want to . . . ?" he asks, making an obscene hand gesture.

"Sorry, my mom taught me small objects were choking hazards."

He takes a step toward me. "Wait. What'd you just say?"

My muscles tense. My heart jackhammers against my ribs. I'm already planning a knee-jab to Grayson's crotch when Lucas comes up next to me. "Is everything okay?"

Grayson squints. "Who the hell are you?"

"Is he bothering you?" Lucas asks me as he hands me a cup. His voice has a hard edge to it, one I've never heard before.

Just then, Eli leaps up from his blanket. "Let's liven this party up!"

"Look, a distraction!" Lucas points.

Grayson obediently turns his attention to Eli. Eli stands up and drains his cup in three swallows. "In this evening's episode of American Ninja Warrior, we're going to leap a flaming pit of fire without frying our balls!"

A bunch of guys cheer. Grayson raises his fist and yells, "Hurrah!" The girls squeal and make faces.

"Don't be an idiot. That's dangerous." Margot tugs on his arm.

"She needs your balls later!" someone shouts to explosions of laughter.

Eli gives Margot a sloppy kiss. "For later, my dear."

Margot has the decency to blush.

Eli tosses off his shirt, ab muscles rippling. He raises his arms and gallops around the ring. Everyone chants, "Do it! Do it! Do it!"

This is why Eli is so popular. He's not only a golden Adonis in human form, not only the star receiver of the football team and Margot Hunter's boy toy; he's also wild fun at parties.

Lucas and I watch from the outskirts. For a second, I wonder how Lucas feels, suddenly thrust into the glow of popularity and found wanting. He's so close to the glow, to the coveted inner circle, but not in it; tolerated, but not included. Does it bother him? It doesn't seem to, at least, not as far as I can tell.

Eli folds into a gallant bow. Then he shoves his hair out of his eyes, plants his feet in the sand, and runs toward the fire. Lucas goes rigid beside me, nervous for his cousin's safety. But Eli is an athlete. He sails easily over the flames and lands on the other side with a foot to spare. The crowd erupts into cheers.

"Who's next?" he shouts, beating his chest.

A dozen guys leap up, eager to show off their skills.

On the other side of the fire, I see Arianna sitting on a bench of bleached driftwood. It takes me a few seconds to place the guy and two girls sharing the bench with her. It's the Bible club group, the ones always trumpeting their meet-at-the-pole prayer groups and brownie bake sales for the homeless and Friday night Bible study/make-out sessions. Arianna's one of the only girls wearing a one-piece.

She looks up, and her eyes meet mine. I'm the first to look away.

Lucas clears his throat. "You know, with that guy back there. I would have folded him up like a lawn chair. If you'd asked me."

"I didn't need any help."

"Obviously."

"I thought you were all anti-violence."

He shrugs. "I am, but that doesn't mean I'm unwilling to defend a lady's honor."

"I can defend myself, thank you very much. Besides, chivalry is ridiculously outdated."

"Maybe. I still believe in it, though. Wanna walk?" Lucas nods at the water.

I don't know what I'm doing here. I sure as hell don't belong. But Lake Michigan is beautiful. The waves slap the shore and the horizon seems to stretch out forever. I want more of it. Lucas seems so different from the rest, different from the Xaviers and the Graysons of the world. I might actually want to walk with him, crazy as it sounds inside my own head. "Whatever."

We have to pass Margot, Jasmine, and the rest of her crew lounging on their blankets. Margot is telling a story, some epic prank about filling a girl's locker with tampons they'd colored with a red Sharpie.

When the girl opened the locker, the tampons spilled out everywhere, all the guys yelling and leaping away like they were bloody bombs.

They did it to Deirdre McClintock, a shabby girl with too-thick glasses and frizzy hair the color of dishwater. There's a rumor going around that she's a lesbian. I don't care whether she is or isn't, but I know exactly where that rumor originated.

Jasmine laughs so hard she starts snorting. Then her voice breaks, and that loud, honking laugh I haven't heard in four years escapes her mouth. Her eyes bulge in embarrassment. She covers her mouth with her hands.

"You sound like a pig, Jazzy!" Peyton shouts gleefully.

"Like a drunk donkey." Margot shoves Jasmine's arm.

Iron fingers squeeze my heart. I remember that laugh from the time at Delia's Ice Cream Shoppe when we got kicked out for flicking each other with spoons full of frozen yogurt, or the time in seventh grade when she convinced me to skinny dip in her pool. Her parents came home early just as we frantically yanked on our swimsuits, giggling hysterically the whole time. She didn't care how her laugh sounded back then.

The pain is like a small explosion in my chest.

I shouldn't feel it. I won't let myself feel it. I let the anger erase the pain, let it crackle through me and burn everything else away. Instead of bypassing their blanket, I stride right up and kick as hard as I can. A bucket's worth of sand sprays Margot, Jasmine, and Peyton.

"Hey!"

"What the hell?"

They scramble to their feet, their drinks tipping and spilling onto the blanket as they brush out their bikini tops and scrape their hands through their hair.

The side and back of Jasmine's shorts are wet from her overturned beer. "Look what you did!"

"Someone should put that skank out of her misery," Margot says softly.

Adrenaline pumps through my veins. I'm ready to finish this—

right here, right now. "Oh, yeah? 'Cause so far, the best you can do is repeat the same three insults ad nauseum. Ooh, scary. You want me? Come get me. Let's go. Or are you too much of a pussy to actually fight me?"

They all glare at me, but none of them makes a move. "That's what I thought. You're all malignant, lily-livered cowards. Every single one of you. Get out of my sight."

"Let's go," Lucas says, tension in his voice.

"Don't lose your rectal matter," I mutter. "I'm coming."

"No one likes you," Peyton yells at my back as I walk away.

I stick up both of my middle fingers.

Most of the crowd is still focused on Eli, Xavier, and a few others brave enough to leap the fire. No one else stops me as I walk down to the water's edge.

I spin my rings, my fingers trembling. I never feel much during a confrontation. It's afterward my emotions tangle in my gut. It's afterward I think about the before, what it was like when it was me and Jasmine, and no one else mattered. What it was like to have a friend. Pain and loneliness grip my heart and won't let go.

I feel Lucas beside me. "Come on. Let's walk it off."

I almost want to apologize to him. But what for? This is my life. I'm that girl everyone loves to hate. He'll see soon enough there's no point in hanging around someone like me.

We walk along the shoreline. The breeze is chilly away from the fire, nipping at my skin, flinging my hair behind me. The waves roll and crash, the white foam just missing my shoes. The pulse of the water ebbs and flows, ebbs and flows. It's like the river, only so much bigger, grander, like the whole thing could swallow all of this up, make it disappear.

The pressure in my bones lessens. The nasty tangle of anger, hate, and fear slowly unwinds itself. For now.

"I think Miss Pierre is right," I say finally. "There is a sliver of madness in all of us. Depending on what happens to us, we might go mad. Or maybe it happens in pieces, only sometimes. Or maybe some of us use that little sliver of madness, when we need to, to do what has to be done."

Lucas is quiet for a minute. "Maybe some forms of madness can teach us something, give us what we need, like Lear. Unless it grows too big and takes you over. Back in Florida, we were reading Sylvia Plath's *Bell Jar*. Imagine sticking your head in an oven, how committed you'd have to dying to be."

"Or filling your pockets with rocks and wading into a river, a la Virginia Woolf." I imagine the weight of it, the water rising higher and higher with each step, then the choking, can't-breathe sensation when the water fills your nostrils, your mouth, your throat, spills down into the cavities of your lungs. Was she afraid? Did she change her mind when it was already too late?

"Like Hunter S. Thompson, Hemingway, and even Jack London, depending on what you read."

"You've actually read all these people?"

He pauses. "Are you going to think less of me if I haven't?"

"Yes."

He laughs. "Well, there you go. Then I have. I've read *Leaving Las Vegas* three times

and *To the Lighthouse* until even I wanted a room of my own. Just don't ask me what they're actually about, okay?"

I roll my eyes.

Lucas kicks a strand of seaweed. "There's also Kurt Cobain, Robin Williams, Marilyn Monroe."

"You seem to know a lot about suicide."

He pulls his pink lighter out of his back pocket and flicks it open. The flame flickers in the breeze. "My mom's dying of cancer now, but she overdosed on pills when I was twelve."

I glance at him. There's real pain in his voice. Something stirs deep inside me. We both know something about broken mothers.

"She was an actress, or at least, she desperately wanted to be. She did some plays, a few commercials in Orlando when I was young. But the industry wasn't ready for diverse leading ladies back then, I guess. They always cast her as a maid or a waitress. The failure of her career made her a bitter woman. Or so my dad says. Whatever her reasons, she's one of the saddest people I know."

I'm angry on his behalf. "That really sucks."

He nods. "I'm coming to terms with it, in my own way."

I want to call BS again, but I don't. The words stick in my throat. He doesn't want to talk about it. I know exactly how that feels.

"There's a link between creativity and mental illness," Lucas continues. "Creative people feel more, think more. They're more sensitive. Most people try to skim over the painful stuff; artists dwell on it. Dad always says Mom thinks too much. Too much brewing spoils the pot. Or something like that."

We keep walking, and I listen to him talk. He sounds so much like a normal human being, nothing like the shallow jerks that surround us. I haven't had a conversation like this in years. Scratch that. I haven't had a conversation with anyone in years, period. My heart contracts.

A gust of wind kicks up, whipping strands of hair across my face. I shiver.

"You're cold. I mean, it's the middle of October in Michigan. I shouldn't have brought you out here."

"First of all, you didn't 'bring' me anywhere. And second, I'm fine."

"No, it's true. It's colder than a witch's tit in a brass bra out here." He turns around and shields his eyes with his hand, as if that's going to help him see further in the dark. The bonfire is just a glimmer on the horizon.

"I know how to get warm, if you want," he says.

I flinch away from him, my hands already clenching into fists. How stupid was I to think he was any different from the rest of them? He read the words scrawled on the bathroom tile over the boys' john, and now he thinks he's going to get some. He thought wrong. And so did I. I messed up, again. "Screw you, jerkwad. If you think—"

"Hey, hey!" He raises his hands again, the lighter clutched in one hand. "Slow down. I was going to ask you if you wanted to run."

I stare at him stupidly. "Run?"

The corner of his mouth crinkles up. "Yeah, like moving your legs really fast? It raises your core body temperature."

Now I really do feel like an idiot. But also, wildly, stupidly relieved. I let myself breathe again. "Oh. I mean, okay. I thought—"

He waves his hand. "No worries. I run track. That's my thing. At my old school, I won regionals and placed second at state. I even won third in the 1600 meters in the USATF Junior Olympics. I like to run. What about you?"

"I hate running. I almost always skip running laps, and when I do bother to show up, I walk, no matter how much Coach Taylor screams at me."

"That's different. You want to try? You've even got sneakers on already."

"And jeans," I point out.

He just grins, his face silvery in the moonlight. His features are handsome, his dark eyes warm and intense. His gaze sends a shiver through me that has nothing to do with the weather. "I'll go slow."

So we run. Or jog. Or whatever. My feet pound the damp, packed sand. I try to time my breathing with his. But he's long, lanky, and trained. He pulls ahead of me almost immediately, loping across the sand like an antelope, easy, graceful. I keep my eyes trained on his back, but no matter how fast I run, I can't keep up. My side aches. My jeans scratch and rub my fresh-cut thighs with each stride. Still, everything fades away but the night sky studded with stars, the silver waves, the pulse of the tide, and the rhythm of my own ragged breath.

We get back too soon.

I bend over and grab my side, gasping for air.

"Too much?" Lucas asks, jogging back to me. He's not even winded.

I'm fine," I wheeze. "Or, I will be in a minute."

The music is pounding again. Couples are dancing or cuddling on the blankets. Girls are wrapped in cute cardigans or their boyfriends' hoodies. Eli and a bunch of guys are throwing footballs down the beach, yelling and whooping as they tackle each other in the moonlight.

"Wanna go swimming?"

"And freeze to death?"

"Okay, stupid question. That sounded much better in my head." He runs his fingers through his hair, which just makes it stand up more. "To be honest, I'm just trying to find ways to spend more time with you."

I stop. "Whatever for?"

"Because you're special. I like you."

I shake my head. "No one likes me, okay? Not unless they want something. So what exactly do you want? What's your angle?"

His eyebrows shoot up. "I don't have an angle. I just thought you were interesting."

"Well, I'm not."

His smile fades. "I didn't mean to upset you."

I feel the darkness rising up, the hard, spiky part of me that keeps out everyone and everything. "And yet you succeeded."

"I'm just trying to be friendly."

I stare out at the shimmering waves. Guilt stabs me. *Take risks*, Dr. Yang said. Okay, fine. But only because I owe Lucas for the ride. "I didn't mean that," I force out. "Sometimes I'm a jerk."

Lucas shrugs. "No worries. We all have our days."

I hide my relief with a scowl.

Xavier saunters up then, grinning with his glow-in-the-dark teeth. "Helluva party, isn't it, Shaw?"

I stare at him. "It's ass-tastic."

He sways, more than a bit drunk. "Thanks."

"Not a compliment, dude," Lucas says.

Xavier just grunts and turns to Lucas. "Pizza boy!" he crows like they're best buds. "I need your help. We need more sustenance, more thirst-quenchers. There's no way I'm letting any of these losers up in my Nan's house. I trust you, man."

"What do you need?"

"Didn't I just say? There's eight more six-packs in the fridge. Bring 'em down for me. And don't step on the white carpet. Nan'll kill me. Eli! We're ready to grab the drinks!"

Eli lopes over and fist-bumps Lucas' shoulder. "Hey, man. What's up?"

"Not much."

Xavier hands Eli the house keys. "I gotta keep an eye on things down here, if you know what I mean." He winks as Nyah slips under his arm and gives his waist a squeeze.

"Come on," Eli says to Lucas. "Let's get this done."

Lucas glances at me, like he's checking to make sure I'm okay alone. It's kind of sweet, in an awkward sort of way. "I'm good," I say, waving him off.

Lucas flashes me a smile before he and Eli jog up the sand path. I head over to the keg table. I need a drink.

I haven't had to use my social skills—or lack of them—like this in four years. It feels weird and uncomfortable, but I also don't hate it. Which is the most surprising part of all.

FIFTEEN

I'm reaching for a Mountain Dew when something knocks my legs out from under me.

I jerk forward, my head smacking into the table, knocking it over. The yellow jugs tumble onto the sand. I half-fall on the upturned table. One leg bangs hard against the cooler, splattering ice chunks everywhere. Pain judders up my spine, flashes through my knee.

"What a klutz," says an all-too-familiar voice

I scramble to my feet, wipe the sand off my shirt and the front of my jeans, and face Jasmine. She's got Margot, Nyah, Peyton, Xavier, Isabel, and a few others behind her. Icy adrenaline flushes through me. I need to be smart here. I've got no exit, no threat of teachers to stop anything. Too cowardly to face a fair fight, they've rigged the game. They outnumber me six to one.

"It's so unfortunate when certain people choose to show up uninvited," Margot says in her syrupy voice, the one she uses right before she claws your eyes out.

"Get out of my way, you repugnant parasites." My voice catches. Anger sizzles through me, but also fear. And they know it.

Margot's lip curls in a vicious smile. She gets right up in my face. This close, I can see the creases in her makeup, the enlarged pores on her nose. "What do you think, girls? Why's she wasting time with Pizza Face? Does she think he's really going to take her out on a date?"

"Yeah, to an all-you-can-eat buffet!" Peyton giggles.

"There's no accounting for taste," Jasmine says, glancing at Margot.

"Exactly," Margot says. "She's just going to give him what she gives all the guys. Why does she play so hard to get when she's obviously so hard to want?"

My hands clench into fists. "Are you always this stupid or are you making a special effort today? Get out of my face or fight me fair, you hell-bitch." I look past Margo and stare at Jasmine. My anger burns white-hot, hotter than the flames of the bonfire licking the sky. "Why don't you fight your own battles for a change? I'm right here."

Margot sneers. "Let's give her what she wants. Drag her to the ground."

Nyah and Peyton grab my arms. I flail away, but Margot kicks my ankles. I lose my footing in the sand and slam to the ground.

"Take off her shirt. She's a slut. Let's make her look like a slut."

They pin my arms. There are hands on my legs too, pressing me down.

Margot bends over me. "Aww. Look how she insists on making things more difficult than they have to be. Stupid, stupid girl."

The smart thing is to submit to whatever humiliations they have planned, let them get bored with me like cats with a chipmunk. Then they'll let me go, and everything will stay the same. That's what every other cowering, hunch-shouldered freak, nerd, and ugly girl does in this school.

But I'm not them. I'd rather die than let the likes of Margot Hunter get the best of me. Rage blooms inside me and I let it. It crackles through me and explodes into my skull.

I kick as hard as I can and connect with something soft.

Somebody screams. I hope I broke their nose.

I scratch Peyton's shoulder. I jerk my arm out of her grasp and claw out a handful of sand. I hurl it straight at Margot's face. She squeals and stumbles back, wiping furiously at her eyes. "Get her!"

"Grab her wrists!" Nyah yells.

I scream and twist and writhe, but there's too many of them. They clamp me down. And that's it. I've lost.

Helplessness wells up, turning my lungs to lead. The music thumps through my bones. My nerves are frayed, my brain on fire. The shadows of the crowd fall across my face. Everyone is watching, their phones already out, snapping pics and videoing away.

I catch sight of Arianna. She's standing a little behind Xavier's shoulder. Her face is leached of color. Her eyes look panicky. All of her goody two-shoe friends are gaping at the spectacle. I hate her most of all.

"Get her shirt off." Margot scrapes at her eyelids. Someone hands her a water bottle, and she pours water into her eyes. "I swear, if that slut blinded me . . ."

Nyah sits on my stomach. She's breathing hard, her chest heaving.

At least they can't get my shirt off with my arms pinned like this. When they try, I'm gonna claw somebody's eyeballs out. For real.

Xavier hands Nyah something shiny. She flicks it open. A pocket knife.

My eyes widen. I fight harder, jerking and writhing as hard as I can. Hot tears of humiliation and fear burn my eyes.

"What're you waiting for?" Margot snarls. "Do it already!"

Nyah grabs a handful of my T-shirt and rips the knife through it. She flips out the two sides of my shirt like she's flayed me, like it's my internal organs she's displaying to the crowd, and not my faded bra and rolls of soft belly.

"She looks like a beached whale."

"Trash."

"Um, hello? Disgusting."

Goosebumps pimple my stomach in the cold air. Shame engulfs me. My throat burns like it's coated in acid. I'm naked, exposed to all of them. Their contempt and derision pelt me like rocks. Blood pounds in my skull. I want to curl up and die. I want to hurt them as badly as they're hurting me. "Leave me alone!"

"What should we do to teach her a lesson, Jazzy?" Margot asks.

Jasmine chews on her lower lip. Her face looks stretched, distorted. "I don't know."

Margot rolls her eyes. "Where's your brains when we need them?" She picks up something from the sand. It's the black Sharpie from the keg table. "What do you think, Jazzy?"

"I don't know," Jasmine says again.

Margot scowls. "I cannot even freaking believe what a pussy you are." She holds the marker out to Nyah. "Show this ho what she is."

Nyah hesitates.

"Hurry the hell up!" Margot snaps.

Nyah shakes her head. Her eyes are wide. "Maybe we shouldn't—"

"Are you even serious right now? I'll do it myself." Margot pushes Nyah off and grabs the marker.

She straddles me and writes on my stomach. The marker is cold as she presses it into my skin. I can't tell what the word is, but I can guess.

Margot smirks. "That's a good start. But it's not enough." She reaches out and plucks the pocket knife from Nyah's hand. "We need to carve it into her. She's a cutter already. She won't mind a few more scars on her repulsive body. Right, Jazzy?"

"Margot." I recognize Jasmine's voice, trembling and hesitant. "Haven't we done enough? Come on."

Margot whirls on her. "Did I ask for an opinion? No? That's what I thought. Now shut your ugly mouth or go away."

From the back of the crowd, I hear several people mutter, "Let's go."

But the rest, the ones surrounding me, they're drunk and they're rabid. They want a show, and Margot's giving it to them. No one's yelling, or jeering, or making any noise at all. They just stand there and watch, phones up, eyes glassy.

Acid stings the back of my throat. I gag. I try again to wrestle out of their grasp, but I'm held fast. Terror pulses through me.

Margot's face contorts in a skull-like mask in the glow and shadow of the firelight. Her eyes are red. "Hold still or this will be worse," she says in a low, cold voice. She points the knife and holds it against my skin. I suck in my breath, waiting for the pain.

The music stops. Something bangs on one of the tables behind me. A phone rings on speaker. "Hello. This is nine-one-one. What is your emergency?" the tinny voice rings out.

"I'm at the beach house at 9775 Beach Grass Dr. in St. Joe," a girl shouts. "There's an out-of-control party on the beach with underage drinking. Someone's being attacked. Please send the police as fast as you can."

Just like that, the crowd scatters. The hands holding me down disappear. Everybody's making a mad dash for the path leading to their cars. I roll onto my stomach, gasping and choking for air.

"You're dead," Margot says in a voice dripping poison. I hear her footsteps pounding after the rest. It's not until I pull myself to my feet that I realize she wasn't talking to me. Arianna stands twenty feet away, her arms hanging loose at her sides, her cell phone in her right hand.

"You?" I force out. My throat is coated in gravel. Why the hell would a card-carrying member of the Bitch Squad snitch to the police on her own best friends? My mind scrambles to comprehend what's happening. "Why the hell did you just do that?"

She glares at me. Her whole body is shaking. "I couldn't let them. I'm not a monster, no matter what you think."

I shake my head, still not believing this is real.

"I'll wait with you for the police."

"Hell, no. I have to get out of here."

She gives me a sharp look. "That had to be illegal. She basically assaulted you."

I wrap the jagged sides of my shirt around me. "No cops. I can't."

"She crossed a line. You should tell the police."

I just shake my head harder. "No freakin' way. Why are you still standing here? Let's go."

She follows me up the path. We're almost halfway up when Lucas meets us on the way down. "What're you still doing here?"

Lucas makes a gesture with his hands. "I heard the yelling about the cops. I came down to make sure you were all right."

"Does it look like I'm all right?"

He looks at me and then at Arianna. His gaze drifts down to my shirt. "Wait. What just happened?"

"Nothing gets past you, Sherlock."

Sirens wail in the distance.

"I gotta go." Panic grips me. I start running. I run around the house and head down the driveway. I'm past Lucas's car when he catches up to me.

"I'll take you home."

I keep going, breathing hard. "No. I'm not going home. I can't go home. Not like this. Not tonight."

"Then where are you going to go?" he asks, bewildered.

"What do you care?"

"Holy hell, Sidney," Lucas says. "Take it down a notch."

"We're trying to help you," Arianna says as she comes up behind me, holding her side.

I can't breathe and talk anymore. I stop running. I try to hold the two sides of my shirt together, but my whole body's shuddering and my fingers are going numb. Post-traumatic stress or something.

Lucas stares at my shirt. "Who did that to you?"

"Who do you think?"

Something sharp and angry flickers across his face. He yanks off his hoodie and hands it to me.

I tug his sweatshirt over me as fast as I can. "Thanks."

He catches a glimpse of the letters on my stomach and sucks in his breath. "Should you tell the cops?"

"For them to do what? Just humiliate me further and then do jack squat? No thanks."

"Are you sure?"

"Some of them are friends with my dad, okay? Do you know what he'd do to me if he knew I was here?" *If he knew I was here with another guy.* I can't speak those words. The thought of how furious he would be, what he might do . . . Pure terror wrenches through me.

Lucas puts up his hands. "Have it your way, but I'm still not going to leave you here."

Arianna catches up to us, holding her side and gasping. She grabs my arm. "You can sleep at my house. My parents won't even know you're there. Trust me."

Suddenly I'm furious with her. With both of them. I feel naked, exposed. They saw me. They all saw me. Margot and Jasmine humiliated me. Everyone saw it. I pull away from her. "No thanks, Beauty Queen."

"Then where are you going to go?"

The question hangs over the swelling of the sirens.

"It's not like we're herding pandas here," Lucas says. "We need to decide. You've got less than a minute."

"Come with me," Arianna says again.

I've hit a brick wall. I don't have any other options. I have no choice, and they know it. "Fine, okay? Whatever. You win."

"What about your parents? Do you need to call them?" Lucas asks.

I shrug. "They'll have epic hangovers and won't even notice I'm gone until dinnertime tomorrow, if then."

"Then it's settled." Arianna turns to Lucas. "Except, I don't actually have a ride. I came with Jasmine. Can you take us home?"

"Does a cat have nine lives?"

"Huh?"

"That means yes, obviously. Let's go."

Lucas takes us to Arianna's house. She offers to sit in back with me, but I insist I'm fine. She sits in front next to Lucas, but she keeps twisting around to look at me. "Stop it," I hiss at her. "I'm fine."

But the truth is, I'm lightheaded and dizzy. The lights flashing by outside the window leave long streaks across my vision. My eyes burn and every muscle in my body aches. All I want to do is lie down and sleep forever.

But at least I'm not alone.

SIXTEEN

The next morning, I don't crawl out of the nest of comforters and goose-down pillows Arianna made for me until almost noon.

"You okay?" Arianna asks. She's already dressed, with her makeup on and her hair pulled back in a side French braid. She's sitting at her desk with her laptop and her Government textbook opened beside it. She's doing homework. On a Saturday morning.

"I'm spectacular. Splendid. Never better," I say. I feel like crap, a steaming bucket load of it. "What are you doing?"

"I'm finishing up our issues analysis paper."

I raise my eyebrows. "Isn't that cheating? You doing all the work?"

She shrugs. "I'll let you do most of the work next time. It'll even out."

"Whatever floats your boat."

She nods to the phone next to her elbow on the desk. "It fell out of your pocket while you were sleeping. You have some messages."

I snatch it up. "Were you spying on me?"

She glances up at me, her eyes wide. "No, of course not."

I scroll through the messages, all from Lucas, all basically saying the same thing: *R U OK?*

I text back: *Fan-freaking-tastic*. Then: *Thanks.* I yank on my jeans and slip the phone into my back pocket.

I look around. Arianna's room is all white light and pastel pink curtains and fairy lights strung across her four-post bed. "Nice digs."

"It's just a house. Come on, I'll make you breakfast."

She leads me into the kitchen. The living room has plush cream carpets, oriental throw rugs, and cathedral ceilings. The kitchen has slate tile floors, real marble countertops, and sleek white glass cabinets. It looks like something out of a magazine. There aren't even family photos cluttering up the walls or end tables.

"It's a mansion."

"It's way too big for only three people." Arianna gestures for me to sit down at the large island. "I'm not big into all the marble and steel. It's too harsh."

Rich people are all the same. They have no clue how much they have. My body aches when I sit down, reminding me of last night's events.

"How do you feel?"

"Like I have a hangover from Hades, even though I didn't drink a drop." I lift up the sweatshirt from Lucas I'm still wearing and check my stomach. The black letters are about three inches tall and start to the left of my belly button. SLUT. I try not to wince. I won't let her see how much I loathe that word, how it hurts like they actually carved it into my flesh. "They can't even manage to be original. It's like slut, bitch, and whore are the limits of their pathetic vocabulary. Oh wait, sorry. I guess I shouldn't talk trash about your friends."

"They're not my friends," Arianna says softly. "Not anymore, anyway."

Part of me wants to ask her why she did it. But I can't. My tongue won't form those words. "What do you have to eat around here? Please tell me this magnificent kitchen isn't just for looks."

Arianna glances at the time on the microwave. "It's already lunchtime. I could whip up *arepa con quesito,* corn cakes with soft, white cheese, or *huevos pericos?* It's like scrambled eggs with tomatoes and scallions."

"They both sound delicious, but I'm a simple girl. You have peanut butter?"

"Yeah. You want me to make you a sandwich?"

"No sandwich. Just peanut butter and a spoon. I don't need a meal or anything." I don't need to owe her any more than I already do. I'm already trying to figure out how I can make things even again. I hate owing people. I hate the leverage it gives them.

"You sure? I could make some stroganoff, or an Asian salad?"

"What, are you a chef-in-training or something?"

A faint blush colors her cheeks. "Actually, I love to cook." She hands me the peanut butter and a fancy-looking spoon.

The jar is unopened, so I peel off the tab and sink the spoon into the creamy goodness. I'm so hungry. "Seriously? You're so scrawny."

Her hands stray to her stomach. It's so flat it's almost concave. I can see the points of her hip bones through her lavender leggings. "Not really."

I don't say anything. These types of girls are always going on about how fat they are so their friends can jump in with a chorus of "you're so thin and beautiful, blah, blah blah." None of them would know what to do with a real problem.

Arianna pours me a glass of milk. "Make sure you use the coasters. Water marks are evil, according to my neurotic mother."

"Whose mother isn't neurotic?" I say around a mouthful of peanut butter. "And where is your mother? Where's your family?"

Arianna folds her hands around her glass, but doesn't drink it. Shadows ring her eyes. "I'm an only child."

"Your dad's a pastor, right?" I remember fuzzy details from our sessions with Dr. Yang.

"Yeah. He's preaching now, actually. Last night he and my mom led a marriage seminar. Part two was this morning and there's a third session tonight, I think, culminating with his sermon on the sacred marital bond or something on Sunday morning."

"Sounds like perfect parents."

"Not exactly. Do you mind if I make something? I'm feeling kind of jittery. Cooking calms me down."

"I'll eat anything." I slurp a dollop of peanut butter off my finger.

Something furry touches my leg. My heart leaps into my throat. I must jump three feet in the air.

Arianna laughs. "Say hello to Cleo."

A pure white fluffball of a cat winds around my ankles. I reach down and run my fingers through her fur. She looks like she costs more than Ma's car.

Just then, a sleek black BMW rolls up the driveway. Arianna stiffens. "Crap. I thought they wouldn't be back until the afternoon. I apologize in advance."

Arianna's father opens the door and holds it for his wife. "*Hola*, darling," her mother says as she walks in. She's wearing a tan trench coat that falls to her shins, and beneath it, a fitted white pantsuit. Her black hair is short, streaked with auburn highlights, and curled around her ears.

She is thin, thinner than Arianna, if that's even possible, and her features are small and sharp as a bird's. She must have been beautiful once, but now her skin is pulled a little too tight around her eyes, and her eyebrows are too highly arched. They look penciled on.

"*Buenas, mi amor*," her father booms with a slight accent. He takes off his jacket and holds out his arm for his wife. "Introduce us to your friend." He is tall and trim, his hair and mustache almost completely silver.

"Oh, a guest," her mother coos as Arianna gives them each a perfunctory hug. "I am so sorry about the state of this house. I was not expecting visitors." She looks sharply at Arianna.

"*Papà, Mamà*, this is Sidney Shaw."

Her father reaches his arm across the island. He's got a tight, strong handshake. "Nice to meet you. I'm Pastor Torrès. I pastor the church over on Culver Street."

"What a pretty name, Sidney," Mrs. Torrès says.

"Are you a senior as well?" Pastor Torrès asks.

"Yep."

Arianna presses her hands against her stomach. "We were just going up to my room to do some studying."

"Oh, won't you stay and visit awhile?" Her mother shoots another look at Arianna. "Ari so seldom has friends over."

Arianna's face clouds, but her parents don't seem to notice. "How was the seminar?"

Pastor Torrès gives a brilliant white smile. His teeth must be capped. They're too perfect, like a neat row of white dominoes. "It went splendid. The congregation is eating it up. I'll think we'll prevent at least one divorce this weekend, won't we, Paola?"

"Mmm hmm." Mrs. Torrès fingers a gold cross around her neck. She stares in disgust at my jar of peanut butter, nearly a third empty. "Really, girls? Don't you know how fattening peanut butter is? You're planning on fitting into your prom dress, aren't you, Ari? Keep up your self-discipline, or you'll never get rid of that extra fluff on your rear end."

"Yes, *Mamà*," Arianna says in a pinched voice.

"Remember, girls. What you eat in private, you wear in public." She whisks the jar off the table and hands us each something I don't even recognize as food. "Here, have some rice cakes. Eat those, if you must eat between meals. Only forty calories a cake!"

People actually eat these things? It's some kind of disc-shaped wafer, nothing like a cake at all. This isn't food. I'm angry on Arianna's behalf. "Actually," I say, imitating Mrs. Torrès' prim voice. "I've been trying to gain weight."

The woman looks mortified. She'd raise her eyebrows, but they're too high already. She opens her mouth but doesn't say anything.

Pastor Torrès laughs. "Thatta girl. What's your name, again? I like anyone who can render my Paola speechless, if only for a moment. What do your parents do?"

Mrs. Torrès' lips press into a thin line. Her fingers close around the gold cross. She's the butt of a joke, and from the looks of it, she doesn't like comedians.

"I'm a ward of the state," I say, crushing the rice cake between my fingers.

Arianna's parents exchange looks, as if they don't realize I'm staring right at them.

"I'm sorry to hear that," Pastor Torrès says finally. "Well, how about college? You got your applications ready? Started on your essays? Arianna's going to medical school like her momma. She's got her applications almost ready for Northwestern, U of M, Notre Dame."

"She's not going to Notre Dame." Mrs. Torrès waves her hand dismissively. "She'll never get in with those grades. You know Ari; she never pushes herself."

Arianna stares straight ahead, her face expressionless. "I get it, Mom."

Mrs. Torrès tucks a curl into place and turns back to me. "Do you exercise? Exercise really revs your metabolism, you know."

Arianna stands up fast. "Can we please go now? We have lots of studying to do."

"Nice to meet you!" Pastor Torrès calls as we hurry up the stairs. "Come to church with us next week!"

Arianna pauses at the top of the stairs. "I apologized in advance. Remember that. They're awful."

I shrug. "Not that bad."

"Liar. My mother is a jerk."

"I've seen worse." I follow her down the hall to her room. "And what the hell was all that talk about dieting?"

"I couldn't fit into the prom dress she bought me."

I shake my head. I cannot imagine anyone thinking Arianna has more of herself to lose. "Is she like that all the time?"

"Often enough."

I walk around her room, trying not to think about whether Ma or Frank's noticed I'm gone. Everything in Arianna's room is decorated in shades of white and cream. There's not an iota of dust anywhere. A bunch of band and recital ribbons are pinned to a pink corkboard over her dresser, a French antique piece with swirly legs and aged pewter pulls.

A couple of rose-colored stationary pages are also pinned to the corkboard. "Schedule" is scrawled in purple pen. Arianna's got her life charted down to the half-hour with flute practice, homework, Bible study meetings, and an hour's worth of daily exercises, like 50 pushups, 100 stomach crunches, 200 sit-ups, etc. On another sheet, she's broken down the whole week's schedule of tests, quizzes, and homework assignments by due date and estimated time to complete them.

"You really do all this? Like, every day?"

Arianna nods. She stands in front of an expensive-looking full-length mirror. Her fingers spread over her stomach. "Can I tell you something?"

"Sure." I plop back down on the nest of pillows in the center of her room.

"I wake up sad every day. Not just not happy—but sad. Sometimes I'm so sad I'm not sure I'll make it. I'm just so tired. All. The. Time. Then I feel guilty, like I don't deserve to feel this way. And that just makes everything worse. Everyone just tells me to make myself feel better or smile more. I mean, if I could do something about it, I would. But I don't know how."

Why is she telling me this? I've never done a single nice thing for her. Ever. In fact, I'm still pretty much a jerk in our counseling sessions.

I don't want to be a jerk. I owe her. She saved me. Whether I like it or not, it means something. It's like this room, right now, is separate from the rest of the world, is somehow above all the previous rules and hierarchies of high school.

I rest my chin on my knee and stare at her. "You don't look like you're depressed."

"Of course not. You're not the only one adept at hiding things."

She keeps gazing into the mirror, her face impassive. "It always surprises me how the deepest pain—the stuff nobody ever sees—how it doesn't even leave a mark, no scars. Nothing. It didn't seem right. So I made one myself." She lifts her sweater and rolls down the band of her leggings, revealing a savage purple scar arcing across her lower abdomen.

My eyes widen. "That's a terrible-looking scar."

Arianna lowers her sweater. "From you, I'm sure that's a compliment."

"It is."

"What about your Jesus-freak friends? What do they say?"

"My friends from youth group and Bible Study? They all act perfect. If they make mistakes or have doubts, they keep it to themselves. So, no, I haven't told them about it."

"Sounds like they're hypocrites."

She sighs. "Maybe. Some of them. Do you ever go to church?"

I shake my head. "Only when I was little. My mother went through a religious phase." I remember cushioned pews and the pea-green carpet digging into my bare knees when we knelt for prayer, and a choir singing and swirling dresses and a large, firm hand gripping mine. I shake the memory out of my head. "Do you just go to church because of your dad, or because you actually believe that stuff?"

"I believe in God, yes. In spite of all the platitudes and warm fuzzy talk and hypocrites, there is a presence bigger than myself out there. I believe that. I've felt it. My *abuelita* was this really strong woman of faith. She was so kind and loving, and she had peace, even when she was dying. Faith is important. What about you?"

"Honestly? I don't know. If He does exist, is He even the kind of God I would want to believe in? Why is there so much war, pain, and death? Wouldn't a God of love stop all that? Where's the bolt of lightning to strike down terrible people doing terrible things?"

"A God of love allows free will. If He did away with evil, then we wouldn't have a choice. We wouldn't be choosing love."

Cleo wanders up to me and rubs her whiskered chin against my shin. "I don't get it."

"If you had a boyfriend—"

"I don't," I say.

"I didn't say you did. *If* you had a boyfriend, or girlfriend, or whatever, you'd want them to love you for you, right? You would want them to choose to be with you. Because if he was forced into it, the love wouldn't be real. It wouldn't be worth anything."

The cat flops on her back and exposes her belly for me to scratch. "Like a robot. You might as well love a toaster oven."

"Right. Exactly," Arianna says. "Love isn't real if it's forced. Goodness isn't real if there isn't also the option of choosing evil."

"That makes sense."

"So people choose evil," Arianna continues. "They choose hate instead of love, cowardice instead of bravery, cruelty instead of kindness. Love allows them that choice."

"I wonder if people really think about it that way, like they're making a choice. Don't they just do things because it feels good, because they want something, so they'll do whatever they have to do to get it?"

"Everything is a choice, whether you think about it or not." Arianna nibbles on her fingernails. "I thought you hated cats."

I cross my legs, and the cat crawls into my lap, turns herself in circles, and curls into a ball of fluff. "I do. Obviously."

She smiles, but it doesn't reach her eyes. "You want to paint your nails?"

I look at her. It's like I see something in her for the first time. I'm not seeing the Bitch Squad anymore. I don't know why she's choosing to help me. But here I am. And she's treating me like I'm somebody she can trust, like somebody who matters. "You have turquoise?"

Arianna brings over several bottles of polish, a clear topcoat, nail polish remover, and cotton balls. I lean carefully over the cat, who doesn't seem to mind being half-squished. We work silently, and the silence is peaceful, not awkward or tense.

I like the turquoise color. It's a deep, shimmery teal, like the forewings of the Red Spotted Purple, a brush-footed butterfly that's more teal than purple, with bright orange dotting its wings.

"Thanks for letting me talk to you." Arianna paints the top coat on her last toenail. "I haven't talked about this stuff in a long time. It's just not the same talking with Dr. Yang. You know?"

No problem." The warmth of this room is getting to me. I could curl back up in those blankets and let all the stress, the anger, the fear drift away in happy oblivion. I could live here. I cap the turquoise polish and spread my fingers. "What do you talk about with Dr. Yang?"

"The same stuff he has me write about in my journal. Stopping negative self-talk, giving positive affirmations to myself in the mirror, understanding how my perceptions of my body are distorted, if I'm maintaining adequate calorie and energy intake. Boring stuff like that."

"Because you don't eat."

"Something like that."

"Your mom doesn't seem to think you have a problem."

Arianna grimaces. Her hand flutters to her stomach. "It's complicated. My dad wanted me to talk to someone because I wasn't eating much and acted depressed. Dr. Yang talks to me about food and stuff. He called a meeting last year with my parents. It didn't go well. My mom thinks I'm fine. Or actually, she thinks I'm not good enough in any way, shape, or form."

I should say or do something to try to comfort her, but I don't know how. I'm really bad at this kind of stuff. It's been so long since I've had a deep conversation with someone, since someone's shared anything with me. Not since Jasmine, and even then, we never talked about serious stuff. I don't know how I'm supposed to act, what I'm supposed to say. I blow on my nails and try not to think about the guilt digging into me.

"You can trust me, you know. Every time I saw them doing crap to you, I hated it. They're not always like that. Nyah's strong and funny, and Jasmine's really smart, even though she pretends not to be. Even Margot has her moments. She can be fun and crazy.

"Before I hung out with them, some of the guys wouldn't stop harassing me. It's like, because I'm a PK, a preacher's kid, they think it's even funnier to say crap to me, trying to hook up and stuff. But Margot got them off my back."

"She sounds like a real angel," I snap.

"Margot can be terrible, but she can also be—it's hard to explain. It's like she lets you into this inner circle. She's the one who knows all the inside jokes, everybody's secrets. It's like being welcomed into this exclusive world. I don't know. Margot can shine this light on you, make you feel like the most important person in the world. But when she flips the light off, when she decides to turn on you . . ."

"Yeah, I've experienced that soft and squishy side of her. What's her deal?"

Arianna sighs. "I don't really know. Her parents are divorced. Her mom has a high-powered job. Margot doesn't see her much. But none of that justifies what she did."

"That's the truth." People always want a reason for stuff. And most of the time, there is. But there's always that person, the one that enjoys being a bully, who enjoys hurting people. The one who does it for fun. The girl who's beautiful and rich and perfect and bored.

Arianna touches her stomach. "I'm a coward. I never said anything. I was scared. I am scared. But you can trust me."

I shrug, suddenly painfully uncomfortable. I can't trust her. I can't trust anyone. I'm nothing like all her little friends, the Jasmines and the Nyahs of the world.

For someone like me, there's no God who can save me and no one I could ever trust. For someone like me, my own pathetic self is all I have. I can't let a few minutes of escape lull me into complacency. Not with the monster waiting for me at home. Or the one curled up inside me.

But I resist the urge to flee or resort to my usual sarcastic barbs. I don't know what her angle is or what she wants from me, but at this moment, right now, I'm desperate for this feeling, for this slender thread of something good and calm and right.

So I swallow my fear and say the words that are so much harder than they should be. "Thank you."

SEVENTEEN

It's Monday, and one of those typical October days. The leaves are a cacophony of brilliant orange, red, purple and yellow. The colors are stark against the dreary charcoal sky and the rain sliding down the window pane.

Dr. Yang's chair squeaks as he leans back and adjusts his pant leg. He folds his hands over his knee. "Today we're going to talk about what happened this past weekend." He's looking straight at me.

My breath catches in my throat. "What?"

"It's come to the administration's attention that there was an altercation at a party Friday evening. The police were involved to some degree. No one seems to want to talk about it, although a teacher overheard both your names mentioned."

"And the administration wants you to get to the bottom of it?" I ask. "Lucky you."

"Not necessarily. Sidney and Arianna, my job is to ensure your well-being, your safety, and your personal and academic success. That's my priority, but there's nothing I can do for you unless you talk to me."

I stare at my fingernails. They're already chipping. Figures. "Nothing happened."

Arianna looks at me nervously, raising her eyebrows. I shake my head at her.

"Neither of you want to speak? If you talk to me, we can discipline the individuals responsible for . . . whatever happened."

"I doubt it."

His mouth is tight, and his eyes look sad. He could almost make you believe he cares. "Are you sure? I want to help you."

I just stare at him. I'm not a snitch, and I'm not about to start now. That would only make things worse. I'll get revenge on Margot and her crew, but I'll do it my way.

Dr. Yang sighs. He takes off his glasses and rubs the lenses with the sleeve of his shirt. "Alright. As you wish. We'll move on for now. For the last few weeks, we've been talking about the reasons behind our self-harm."

Arianna clears her throat as she opens her journal. "It's a real thing that I can see. It makes the pain inside me real. When I feel numb, it makes me feel something."

"Very good, Arianna. Sidney?"

I glare down at the stupid journal, willing my vision not to go blurry on me. "Let's see. How self-harm promotes health and well-being." I tick off my list with my fingers. "Blood-letting strengthens the immune system. It gives me superpowers. For every cut, I get ten points for Gryffindor. And then there's the whole vampire side of it."

Arianna and Dr. Yang just look at me. I can see the disappointment in their eyes. It makes me feel itchy and uncomfortable.

"Shall I go on?" I say too sharply.

"Yes," Arianna says.

"I think you can do better than that," Dr. Yang says. He doesn't have to mention the expulsion thing. We both know it's the big fat elephant plopped in the middle of the room.

"Fine," I sigh. The words I've written are dark and slanting. Angry. They feel like burrs in my throat. It's hard to say them out loud. "The razor calms me down. When things are all crazy inside me and I feel like I can't deal, it's the one thing that keeps my heart from exploding.

Like for those few minutes, I can make everything go away. I don't know. That sounds stupid."

"No, it doesn't," Arianna says softly. Our gazes meet for a moment. I'm the first one to look away. I hate how exposed this makes me feel, how ugly and vulnerable and ridiculous.

"Is there more you would like to share?" Dr. Yang asks.

I shake my head. I don't say the last thing on my list. *Because I don't have anything else.*

"Fantastic, both of you," Dr. Yang says. "Let's unpack some of this, shall we?"

I try to stay engaged in the rest of the session, but it's hard. Just reading a few lines from that stupid journal makes me feel exhausted and even more irritated with the world.

After the session, Dr. Yang pulls me aside. "I think you're aware that the apology letter you submitted is far from acceptable."

"Personally, I thought it was terrific. Very descriptive."

He frowns, his face tense. "I can finagle a bit of grace for you if you need it. Do you need it?"

I grit my teeth. He wants me to admit I need his help, at least in this. "Fine. I do."

"You made some progress this session. I'm proud of you. Honesty is the first step to climbing up that mountain. However, I need you to turn in a new draft of your apology letter by Friday. That's the latest I can give you."

"It'll be a work of art, I promise."

"Make sure that it is, Sidney."

For the next several days, the whole school buzzes with the beach party drama. The police decided Arianna's phone call was a prank. Still, they gave Xavier's grandparents a noise ordinance violation citation, which got Xavier grounded for a week.

Most of Margot's crew send me triumphant glares. They think

they've won. They didn't finish it, but they beat me enough. And I let them think it. Revenge is a dish best served cold. I'll figure out what I'm going to do when I can think straight again.

In AP Chemistry, the yearbook photographer named Lena McKenna —a girl with a spray of freckles across her face and a mass of wavy red hair—comes up to me. "It wasn't right what they did. It made me sick."

I don't know how to respond, so I click into my default mode: sarcasm. "Well, if it made you sick, I guess it must have been truly horrific."

She cocks her head and gives me a funny look. "What I mean to say is, we all don't think and act like Margot Hunter. Some of us hate her, too."

I don't want her pity. It feels like spiders crawling over my skin. I feel guilty even as I say the words, but I can't stop them. "Great. Maybe you should try doing something about it, then."

Her face blooms red. "Anyway, that's all I wanted to say. I'm sorry." She turns and flees out the classroom door. I watch her go, hating myself all over again for being such a jerkwad. Everything about me is ugly.

In my private session with Dr. Yang on Friday, I hand in my newest version of Jackson Cole's apology letter in a sealed envelope.

Dr. Yang raises his eyebrows. "Would you like me to read it now or later?"

"Definitely later. It's a work of art, just like I promised." I smile sweetly. I'm not lying. The letter is nothing but an excellent, extremely detailed, extremely anatomically correct close-up drawing of a banded woolly caterpillar's anus.

I would've done a butterfly, but unfortunately, they don't eat—only drink nectar—so they don't poop. I'm sure Dr. Yang will enjoy it. He must have a sense of humor somewhere beneath that unflappable façade.

We spend most of the time talking about how classes are going, and Dr. Yang admonishes me again about the importance of college applications. "Your SAT is scheduled for next Saturday. Try to study beforehand. Have you decided on a major?"

"I want to be a rodeo clown."

He just looks at me.

"How about underwater basket-weaving? Is that a thing?"

He shuffles some papers on his desk. "You have some time to decide while you finish your generals. But I want to know if you're okay, Sidney. You have circles under your eyes. You don't look good."

I haven't been sleeping much. I keep waking in the middle of the night, straining for sounds. I've had nightmares, dark dreams about the beach, and other things. I keep thinking about Arianna trudging through the hallways, ostracized, enduring Margot's taunts and insults because of me. Because of what she did for me.

I hate it. I hate that I even care. I'm plagued with guilt. My mind keeps spinning in angry, guilty, confused circles. But I can't say any of that.

So I say nothing at all and escape as fast as I can.

EIGHTEEN

After school, I'm twenty minutes into my shift when Frank pulls into the restaurant parking lot. I stop mid-movement, hovering over an empty table, my hands stuffed with crumpled napkins.

Cold sweat prickles my skin. What the heck does he want?

"Where's my man?" he hollers as he bangs the door open.

Bill comes out of the kitchen, wiping his ham-sized hands on a dish towel. "How's it hanging?"

"It ain't hangin', bro. It ain't hanging at all." They laugh, hug, and backslap each other like brothers.

"You want a beer? The dinner crowd hasn't started yet. I can take ten."

Frank shakes his head. "Not this time. I'm here for my girl."

"What's the kid done now?" Bill asks, winking at me.

"Family time, Bill. You know how it is."

My spine stiffens. I don't want to go anywhere with him. This is supposed to be one of my safe places. He doesn't belong here—not during the day, not when I'm here. "I'm not off until six."

Frank grips Bill's shoulder. "You work her too much, Bill. A father needs to spend quality time with a daughter, keep her on the straight and narrow. Keep 'em from turning into their mothers. Am I right?"

Bill looks at me, a flash of concern in his dark eyes. "Well . . ."

"You said yourself it wasn't busy. Let's go, Sidney. Get your stuff."

I see the slightest shift in Bill's body, a slump in his shoulders. "I guess I can call in Jessie if I need to."

"Thatta boy! I'll see you Saturday. You're gonna wish you stayed home after I take your stash. Again. Tell Gonzales I'll be there by nine."

And there it is. Everyone capitulates to Frank. I think about refusing, but what's the point? Frank will get his way if he has to carry me out of there kicking and screaming. I hang up my apron, clock out, and grab my backpack and jacket.

"Kid—" Bill says. He's standing in the kitchen, a frown on his face.

I just look at him. "What?"

He hesitates. "Is everything . . . okay with you?"

"Everything's stupendous, Bill. Can't you see that?" I leave quickly so he doesn't see the dread etched across my face.

When I get to the truck, Aaron bobs his head out the window. "We're going gun fighting!"

"It's a gun range, stupid," Frankie says from the back seat. "You shoot at paper targets."

Frank's gun paraphernalia hogs the front seat, so I have to squeeze in the back with the boys.

Frankie's playing some kind of war game on a smartphone.

"Where'd you get that?" I ask him.

"Dad got it for me. Says I'm a man now."

I snort. And who's going to pay the monthly bill for service when Frank disappears again, and the money dries up? It's not gonna be me. There's no way I'm paying for a smartphone out of my precious escape money. I'm back to over $2,600 now. It feels real, substantial. "Enjoy it while you can."

"Stop trying to ruin everything!" Frankie never takes his gaze off the screen. "Just because you're a loser doesn't mean we all have to be as miserable as you."

It's immature and mean, and even though I know it, I can't help myself. I reach across Aaron and make a grab for Frankie's phone.

"Stop it!" Frankie squeals. He tries to smack me while Aaron shrinks into the center seat like he wants to disappear.

Frank slides into the driver's seat. "Shut the hell up."

We fall silent, my stomach like a brick. No one says a word during the twenty-minute drive to Frank's favorite gun range, Old Reggie's. It's basically an empty field with hay bales stacked into pyramids and paper targets of silhouetted humans tacked everywhere there's free space. There are wooden horses stacked with metal targets of varying sizes that spin when you hit them. To the left is a squat gray building with an inside range, but Frank never uses it. Old Reggie's never been one for rules and regulations, so he doesn't care if kids under twelve shoot, as long as there's an adult responsible for whatever happens.

I shrug on my jacket, then help Aaron slither his arms through his faded striped pullover. "School okay?" I ask him as we walk a little behind Frank. I've checked in with him at least once a week since I punched Jackson Cole.

He nods, a too-long curl tumbling into his eyes.

"Jackson still bothering you?"

"He calls me names."

"Names don't matter. Has he hit you again? Touched you?"

He smiles. "Not since you."

My heart swells up inside my chest. I pat his head. "Good."

"Sidney?"

"What?"

"At school, kids say you're a bully. And worser things, things I don't wanna say."

I sigh. I grab the collar of his pullover to stop him. "Listen to me. That's what the real bullies say to deflect attention from themselves. Me and you, we have every right to defend ourselves. You understand? You fight back; you give 'em a taste of what they'll get if they keep messing with you. That's not bullying. That's justice."

"Okay."

"And you say whatever you need to so they get off your back, you hear me?"

"I'm not allowed to say swears at school."

"Well, that's okay. There's lots of other awesome insults you could use. How about barf-breath or turd-brain?"

Aaron grins. "How about stupid-head?"

"Always a classic. Then there's blistering butthole or puss-filled pimple-head, if you want to get creative."

"Poop-brain."

"Stinky butt-muncher."

"Dumb-head."

"Good." I squeeze his arm. "How about smelly fart-eater?"

Aaron laughs, and the high, clear sound of it echoes all the way through me. He should laugh more. He's beautiful when he laughs.

We reach the trestle table where Frank is unpacking his collection of guns and laying them out.

Frankie's practically bouncing on his toes. "I want the Remington! With the sniper scope!"

"Put on your gear first." I hand the boys their protective eyewear and earmuffs, then put mine on. I give Aaron the pink Springfield 9mm XD-S Frank bought for Ma back when I was in elementary school. It's smaller than the Glock and easier for Aaron to hold. "Remember to plant your feet. Relax your knees. Use both hands. Place your fingers like this, with your thumb on the grip, your index finger pointed out. Remember, there's no safety, so you never put your finger on the trigger until you're ready to shoot. Then make sure you pull hard on the trigger. Got it?"

Aaron nods, his eyebrows scrunched in concentration. I point his body toward the closest target, guide the gun until it's level. "Pretend it's Jackson Cole," I whisper in his ear.

Aaron doesn't hit a target once, but Frank's too busy with Frankie to notice or yell at him.

Then it's my turn. I pick up Frank's Glock.

I curl the fingers of my right hand around the grip, straightening my pointer finger along the side of the frame, outside the trigger guard. I wrap my other hand around the other side of the grip, making sure my thumbs are parallel with my trigger finger. I get into my shooting stance, legs shoulder-width apart, knees slightly bent. I raise the muzzle and line up the shot, aiming through my sights for the closest paper target.

I love the gun in my hand, the weight of it, the power, the loud bang of the shot, even through the earmuffs. I feel the thrum of the bullet streaking through the air, punching into the hay bales, the satisfying kick of the gun. I imagine shooting all my demons. Every. Single. One. The bullet tearing into flesh, opening red gaping wounds.

Then he's hovering over my shoulder. "That's my girl," he says into the nape of my neck. Even through the earmuffs, I hear it. My body stiffens, goes cold.

"Widen your legs." With one hand, he reaches down and smacks my inner thigh. He leaves his hand there. No one else is close enough to see. It's so cold that most shooters are using the range inside. "I know you took off all night last weekend. I came to your room for a good-night kiss. Are you whoring around on me?"

I try to aim the gun, but my hands are shaking. He's talking to me like he talks to Ma, his tone laced with something sharp and possessive. I'm sick to my stomach, like I'm going to vomit right here, all over myself. "No."

He pinches the sensitive fat of my thigh, right over a healing cut. His stale, smoky breath is hot against my cheek. "Are you screwing around on me?"

"I'm—I'm not. I swear."

His voice changes, grows hoarse. "I need you. I know you need me, too."

I don't speak. I can't.

"Tell me you need me."

The words are stones in my throat. I open my mouth, but no sound comes out.

"Tell me you need me. Please."

"Dad!" Frankie yells. "Look at me! I hit the inner ring!"

Frank removes his hand from my leg. He strides over to Frankie and claps his shoulder. "That's my boy!"

Frankie nearly glows with satisfaction.

I watch them—father and son. The son happy, adoring. The father pleased, proud. How it should be. How it can never be for me again. My chest fills with a hard, heavy ache, with something like envy, but not quite. I turn my face away.

I don't hit the target again. Hell, I don't even hit the paper. My eyes are blurry, and I can't stop the trembling in my hands. My insides are twisted in iron knots.

Afterward, Frank takes us to Chili's for supper and Delia's Ice Cream Shoppe for dessert. He tells wild stories of football games and stupid high school stunts. He talks about some grand camping trip in Yellowstone he's planning for us next summer. I eat everything on my plate because I have to, I need to, but I don't taste any of it. The weight, the heaviness I've padded onto my body like armor, isn't working. He doesn't care what I look like.

I belong to him. He owns me. Like Ma. I bite my tongue until the coppery taste of blood seeps into my mouth.

By the time we get home, my nerves are frayed and jittery. I escape to my room as fast as I can. I slump at my desk and open my homework.

My vision blurs. Escape. Escape is the only thought keeping me tethered to this earth. I need to be gone. If I put in enough hours and don't have to withdraw any more funds, I can make my six thousand-dollar goal by summer.

It's so close I can taste it. My own apartment. My own car. College classes and a future, and best of all, it's a place that's not here.

I glance down at my textbook. Arianna's issues analysis outline on the electoral college stares at me accusingly. I crumple it up and hurl it into the trash can. An image of her drawn face flashes across my mind.

What does she expect from me? I didn't ask her to do what she did. I didn't ask her to try to save me. Why did she do it? She put herself on the line in a huge way for me, and I can't figure out why. Nobody does anything without wanting something in return. And I don't have anything worth giving.

I lean back in my desk chair and lift my shirt. The letters scrawled in permanent marker are gone now, the skin scrubbed raw. But I can still see it. I can still feel it. They picked the right word. I am dirty through and through, right down to my core. My skin is filthy with secrets, with the bad things I've done, with the bad thing I am.

The urge hits me, the buzzing need to cut, to hurt, to damage. But I don't pull out my stash. I think about the last line I wrote in the journal. *I cut because I don't have anything else.*

I stand in the center of my room with my arms at my sides, trembling from the desire to grab the razor, to use the pain to make everything go away. But nothing ever goes away.

I stare at the dozens of drawings taped on my walls: the White Admiral with the white bands across its dark wings, its hindwings speckled with a row of blue dashes. The Giant Swallowtail with pastel yellow thorax and its six-inch wingspan taking up almost the whole page, with those beautiful half-moon ridges marching up the outer margin of both wings. The tiny, azure Karner Blue and the mud-colored Mitchel's Satyr with yellow-ringed black spots that look like eyes staring out at me. They look so real, their colors so bright, like they could flap right off the paper and alight on my arms.

But they don't. They can't. They can only watch.

Why did Arianna help me? Why? Why did she bring me to her house and make me feel warm and safe and tell me things friends tell each other? And Lucas, too, with his goofy smile and kind eyes. Why did they make me remember all over again what it could be like?

To have someone. To not be alone. To not feel like you're dying slowly, like every day is taking something from you that you'll never get back.

What did Arianna see in me that made her think I was worth saving?

What did Lucas see?

What is there?

Maybe there's something. Maybe there's more. Maybe I could have friends. Real friends. Maybe I could be more than this, live for more than this. I could even be happy.

Arianna said we have choices. God gives us a choice. Every single one of us. We make choices for good or choices for evil. Choices for self-protection and survival or choices for something bigger, better, greater than ourselves. Even when it doesn't feel like a choice, it still is.

Maybe she's right. I have a choice.

I grab my dresser. I rock it from side to side and shove it in front of my closed bedroom door.

My heart leaps into my throat. Every nerve and skin cell is raw, exposed. I'm unraveling.

I stare at the scarred white dresser like it might leap out at me, but it doesn't move. I listen to the sound of my own harsh breathing. What now?

It stops.

I want to make it stop.

I choose for it to stop.

I curl my fingers into fists at my sides.

~

He comes at midnight.

The door opens, bumps into the dresser.

My eyes spring open.

Stay present. Stay here. The darkness presses down and my fingers are numb. I'm going numb, but I can't. I won't. Not this time.

Terror grips me. My heart pumps ice water into my arms and legs. Each thumping pulse forces blood through each tiny blood vessel, until my heart wants to explode like a blood-filled balloon.

There's a grunt as the door shoves in. The dresser groans and gives ground.

He slips into the room like a shadow.

The mattress creaks as he climbs in next to me, his skin hot, his breath sickly sweet.

Stay here, stay here, stay here. I'm usually gone by now, floating up past the ceiling, soaring out the window on jeweled wings. A Pale Spotted Swallowtail, black and shimmering, flapping free of the prison of my body, free of everything.

But not tonight.

He touches my skin beneath the blanket. Inside my skull, I'm screaming at myself to move, to stop him, to DO SOMETHING. I grab his arm. "No."

He flinches. No words have ever been spoken in here, in this dark cocoon that envelopes us. He shakes off my hand. Keeps going.

I shove him off me. "No!"

He encircles my wrist and slams it into the mattress. "Don't play games."

The words scrape against my throat. "No more."

"You want this. You've always wanted this."

"Get off me, you bastard!"

He slaps me so hard I taste blood. "Shut the hell up."

Still, I fight him. This is my choice. I decide. I knee his groin. He grunts and clamps his hand over my mouth. "Don't make me hurt you," he slurs into my ear.

I twist and try to wrench free of his grasp, to knock him off the bed somehow. But he's strong. So strong. He grips my shoulders and wrestles me onto my side, flips me onto my stomach. Now I'm even weaker. I scream. He shoves my face into my pillow, and there's barely a sound. My breath can't escape. I suck in fabric, not oxygen. I gasp and choke, ears ringing, head spinning. "Do you want them to hear you? Do you want them to know what a shitty whore their sister is?"

He releases my head just enough to allow me to turn my face to the side, his fist wrapped around my hair. My scalp burns. Hot tears of defeat sting my eyes.

He does what he does and he's rough and it hurts and I can't escape this time. I don't go numb or fly away. I feel it all. I feel everything.

My eyes are open and inside my skull I'm screaming, shrieking, my mouth open in a silent howl. There is no sound. No one would come even if I did, even if I could scream. I'm already the whore, the slut, the dirty girl who lets this happen, who didn't say no all those years ago.

And the boys—my brothers can't see this. I can't let them see this. I won't let them see this. I have to protect them.

The scream stays inside me, shattering my bones, liquefying my insides.

After he's gone, I curl into a ball on my bed, clutching my stomach. Shame washes over me. My heart jerks, bucking against my ribcage. *Bang bang bang.* Like gunshots. Like thunder, smashing through my skull.

After what seems like hours, the jerks and shudders reduce to a barely perceptible quiver. My heart recedes from the rest of my body, returning to its cavity beneath my ribs. My mouth feels caked with dust and grime, like I haven't had water in days.

I stare up at the woolly darkness above me. The ceiling is sucked up into the black vortex spiraling over my bed. My eyelids burn. The pain barrels into me and pounds my heart into dust.

I reach beneath my mattress and pull out the razor. I cut in the dark. Deep slashes. The warm blood wets my fingers.

But the soothing nothingness doesn't come. The still, the calm—it eludes me.

A low, cold terror seeps into my brain.

I throw the razor across the room.

NINETEEN

"We haven't broached this topic in a while," Dr. Yang drones the next day in our group counseling session. "I want to check in with both of you on your mental state. If you want to wait until our private sessions, we can do that. But you might learn something from each other if you're able to talk openly."

Arianna stares down at her hands folded on her lap. Her face is pale and there's a bluish tinge beneath her eyes. She called the cops on a party. She's a social pariah now, like me. Because of me.

The thought is uncomfortable, spearing me with guilt. I slouch lower in my seat, the hard metal chair digging into my back.

"What do you mean our mental states?" Arianna asks.

"Are you currently or have you recently entertained suicidal thoughts in the last month?"

I scratch at my stomach through my sweatshirt. "Define 'suicidal'?"

"Thoughts of death, of inflicting deadly harm on yourself."

I laugh; it comes out harsh and grating. "No. Of course not. I'm perfectly normal."

Dr. Yang flinches. He pulls his vibrating phone from his pants pocket and stares at it as if he's never seen it before. "I apologize, but this may be an emergency. I have to take it."

He leaves the room. The rain plinks against the window. The radiator hums. Everything inside me is hard and spiky. What happened last night in my room is a howling black hole sucking me under. I want to scratch my own skin off, claw out my own beating heart. But I can't.

I sit forward. The chair scrapes the floor. "With pills."

"Excuse me?" Arianna doesn't even glance up at me. She looks miserable.

A pang of sympathy pricks me. I fight it down. It makes me weak. I can't be weak. Not after last night. A helpless, defeated rage fills me. "You look like a pill person. You'd kill yourself with pills."

Arianna stiffens. "Why do you say that?"

I shrug. "Pills are for whiny girls who want attention."

She blinks, shocked and hurt. "You think I want attention?"

"Hell, yes. You play the flute in a band. You have a perfect house, perfect room, perfect everything. What is wrong with you people? You want to see what it's like on the other side or something? Your life is so perfect you got bored?"

She clenches her thin hands on her lap. "Stop talking, please."

But I can't. The monster inside me rears its ugly head. Tears burn the back of my throat. I want to hurt something, someone. I want to hurt her. She gave me a glimpse of something better, a promise that things might be different—but it was all a lie. The anger inside me is too huge, too ugly. I can't stop it. "Or maybe you'd slit your wrists. You'll soak in a big marble tub, probably your parents', until your skin is wrinkled and translucent and you can see the veins. Then you'll get a shard of glass or mirror or a broken CD or something, not a knife probably, and you'll practice a little bit, then you'll slice away. The wrong way, because you're a Beauty Queen with a capital B and who needs brains when you're rich and beautiful, but you'll get the job done."

Arianna grunts, gives a short shake of her head. "And how would you do it, *Sidney*?" She says my name like it's a curse word.

I force out the words even as I hate myself for saying them. "I've thought of several options. Mainly, it has to hurt, and it has to take a while. Maybe hanging. Or tying rocks to my legs and throwing myself in the river. Or being dragged to death behind a truck, but it would require a driver and I haven't found anyone with enough balls. You want to volunteer?"

Arianna blinks rapidly. Her face looks pinched, her lips bloodless. She grabs her backpack and swings it over her shoulders. "You don't have to be so mean."

Before I can say anything, she walks out of the classroom, the door banging closed behind her.

I blink moisture out of my eyes. It's better this way. I want it this way. This is what I want. I should feel smug and satisfied, but instead my gut is filled with jagged rocks.

Arianna is too good, too bright to look at. I'm the bad, ugly girl who pushed her away.

I shove out the door and slide into the stream of students. Arianna is already gone.

I feel eyes on me, gazes like shards of glass.

I lift my chin and walk into the crowd.

TWENTY

"You cut your hair," Dr. Yang says in surprise when I show up early for our individual session on Friday.

Instinctively, I reach up and touch the razored ends of my newly shorn hair. "You like?"

"It's different, but it suits you."

"Thanks. For real. I needed a change."

"Why did you chop it off?"

"I just—I wanted to be different. Like a transformation."

He steeples his fingers. "Like an outside manifestation of changes happening inside you, perhaps?"

"Perhaps," I allow. I don't think I could explain it even if I wanted to. That dark, twitchy feeling invading me, taking over my body as I stood in front of my bathroom mirror two nights ago. My scalp still burned from the strands of hair Frank ripped out. The thought of his hands on my hair—on any part of my body—sickened me.

I held the razor between my fingers. My emotions were a jumbling, jostling mess inside me. I had to get them out. I wanted to be anything or anyone other than the disgusting girl staring back at me in the mirror.

I took a hunk of my hair and sawed it off. Then I did it again and again, grabbing a handful and hacking through it. Long strands stuck to my T-shirt and drifted into the sink like dark, silky ribbons.

Now my hair falls in choppy layers around my ears, a fringe of bangs sweeping over my eyes. It's strange feeling the air on my neck. I don't really know or care how it looks. That's not why I did it.

Frank hates it, which gives me a dark, vicious sense of satisfaction. "You playing being queer?" he said when he first saw it. He came up behind me as I emptied the dishwasher. He grabbed at a chunk of hair, but it slipped between his fingers. The stale, smoky scent of cigarettes clung to his skin. He put his mouth right up against my ear. "We both know that's the furthest thing from the truth."

Ma waddled into the kitchen, holding her belly. "It's not that bad. It'll grow out," she said mildly.

For once, she stood up for me. Or maybe she liked that it made me less feminine and uglier in Frank's eyes. Either way, it confused and unsettled me.

Frank's phone buzzed, and he went out to the porch to make poker plans with one of his buddies. Ma leaned against the counter next to the sink. "Sidney? Is everything alright?" She peered at me from beneath her mop of freshly-washed hair. She looked almost normal.

My loneliness was a savage ache in my chest. I didn't say anything. Words were like nails in my throat.

She reached out her hand, grazed my cheek. Her fingers were dry and cool against my skin. "Are you okay?"

The push and pull inside me was so strong it threatened to yank my bones right out of their sockets, tear apart muscle and tendon and flesh. In that moment, I longed to fling myself into her arms, to cry against her softness and tell her everything, to let her promise me it would all be okay.

Then instinct took over. My hard, armored shell slipped into place. Ma wasn't genuine. She didn't really want to know. I flinched away from her touch.

Her face flattened, her eyes going hard and shiny. "You should get more sleep. You look awful."

The memory throbs painfully against the back of my skull. I'm done talking. I just want to get out of here.

Dr. Yang tries to ask me more questions, but even he can tell he won't get any more out of me today. He lets me out early.

I make it to Lit class with four minutes to spare before the bell rings. We've finished King Lear and started *The Scarlet Letter*. Which amuses the hell out of certain people.

"How's your scarlet letter today?" Margot whispers loudly as she bumps past my desk. A few people chortle. Several others shake their heads, turning away.

The memory jolts through me, churning my stomach. Anger and shame spark through me. I have to get her back. Some way, somehow, I'll make her pay for it. I clutch the edges of my desk with rigid fingers. Stay in control. I can't lose it, not now. "Did it take you all week to come up with that nugget? Be careful. Too much thinking at one time might cause your brain to explode."

Nyah stares at me, but she doesn't say anything. When I look back at her, she drops her gaze.

"What awful thing did you do to your hair?" Xavier asks.

"Lesbo," Margot coughs. "Carpet muncher."

I glare at her. "So what if I am? Who the hell cares?"

"So you're admitting it?" Margot's eyes widen.

I shake my head. "Did I say that? Sometimes I think you must have the IQ of a brick wall."

She looks like she's about to vomit more insults, but Miss Pierre walks in, shuffling a bunch of papers.

Lucas slides into the seat next to me. I feel his presence like static electricity. My mouth goes dry. We haven't spoken a whole lot in the last two weeks other than pleasantries. Every time he's tried to ask me how I'm doing, I've rebuffed him. It's my own damn fault.

And every day I feel him, sitting next to me, so close and so far away at the same time. It makes me guilty and sad and lonely.

I don't want to be this girl who's always afraid to trust, to live, to be happy. I want something different. But I don't know how to get it. The crap at home is worse than ever. And now I don't even have Arianna. When we pass each other in the hall, I can't even meet her gaze. I'm a coward. Worse than a coward.

I'm flailing in deep water, and if I don't do something soon, I'll drown.

I take a deep breath. "Hey."

He looks at me, a warm smile spreading across his face. "Hey, you. I like your hair."

I swallow hard. "I did it myself."

"It's very punk chic, or something. It makes your eyes look enormous."

My face flushes. I didn't do it for him, but part of me likes that he likes it. "Thanks."

"I go running after school sometimes." He hesitates. "Do you want to come with me? No pressure, no strings, no angle. I promise."

I remember the rhythmic pounding of my feet on the beach, timing my breaths with my stride, the cleansing ache in my side. I need that cold relief. I'm desperate for it. "I work at Bill's Bar every day after school."

His face falls. "Oh. Okay."

I pick up *The Scarlet Letter* and run my thumb over the pages. I want to choose. I can choose. I have to. I clear my throat. "I do have study hall last period."

His face breaks into a grin so wide and goofy, my heart squeezes a little. "I have woodworking. I can totally skip it."

Miss Pierre moves to the front of the room and claps her hands. "I hope everyone read chapter two last night. What did you guys think of Hester Prynne's public condemnation and humiliation on the scaffold? Pretty intense, right?"

Lucas slips me a folded piece of paper. I don't throw it away this time. *Meet me in the parking lot by the fence at 2:00. Bring your running shoes.*

I fold the note carefully and slip it between the pages of the book. I shouldn't meet with him. I'm taking too many risks. My already battered heart is getting too tangled up in dangerous emotions. *He's only going to hurt you,* my mind whispers. But I push the thought away.

I want to go. I want to be near this awkward, puppy-dog boy who's goofy but also smart and sensitive. I haven't felt this way since eighth grade. Before my life went completely toxic, where every breath I breathed was poison. It still is.

I want to breathe. I have to breathe. I have to do something, or I'm not going to make it. I need that cool, cleansing feeling to wash over me. I need it in ways I can't explain.

TWENTY-ONE

I'm already wearing tennis shoes, but I don't want to run in jeans again. I wait until ten minutes into the P.E. period and go in just to grab my sweatpants out of my locker. Everybody's running the track outside, but Coach Taylor's still in the gym, fiddling with one of the badminton nets.

"Shaw!" he yells when he sees me. "Get your lazy butt out there right now or I'll fail you!"

I shrug and keep walking. "You're already going to fail me. So what's the point?"

He growls something after me, but I don't stick around to hear it. I'm already gone.

But I'm not at the fence to meet Lucas at 2:00 p.m.

Instead, I'm in the bathroom, gripping the porcelain sink with both hands and staring into the mirror. My eyes—Frank's eyes—stare back at me. Intense, piercing, deep ocean blue, lost-at-sea blue.

I swallow, my heart rattling around in my chest. I've never given myself a pep talk before, and I'm not going to start now. I slap the mirror with my open palm. To hell with blue eyes. I'm going to run.

Outside, the sky is leached of color. The wind whips dead leaves into swirling eddies across the parking lot. The chill in the air nips at my exposed skin. I zip up my jacket.

Lucas jogs in place by the fence. "I was starting to think I must've written the time wrong. You ready?"

I try to smile at him, but it must come out as a grimace because he immediately asks me if something's wrong. I shake my head. "Let's do this."

"I like to run this overgrown path by the river. That cool with you?"

I nod, not trusting my voice. I'm glad I'm not the only one drawn to the river. I follow him when he turns left at the hole in the fence. He finds it quickly, a beaten dirt path wide enough for us to jog side by side.

Even though the forest has mostly lost its leaves, the brush is still untamed. Thorns snarl out and snag my clothes. Gnarled branches slap at my arms. The river rushes beside us, glittering in the sun.

Lucas pulls ahead of me. His stride is quick and smooth. He's so light on his feet, his sneakers look like they're barely touching the ground. He's like an antelope, leaping across the savannah, born to run.

In sharp contrast, I'm sloppy and uncoordinated, the proverbial bull in a china shop. After only a few labored minutes, I'm gasping for breath. I suck the freezing air right down into my lungs.

Lucas slows down, jogs beside me even though I'm in a flat-out run. "Sorry," he says.

"I feel like an idiot."

"Well, you are kind of flailing around like a drunken orangutan."

I choke out a laugh. "That bad, huh? Got any pointers?"

Lucas tells me how I should focus my energy toward forward propulsion while staying balanced. "Let your lower leg unfold beneath you. Don't reach too far in front. It should land nearly beneath your center of gravity." He shows me how to drive my legs through my hips, explains things like flexion and extension and knee kick-backs, his face flushed and his eyes shining.

We run the 1.5-mile trail and then walk back. My legs are shaking.

My side is in painful stitches, and a cold, clean whiteness invades my whole body.

"Can I ask you a question?" he asks, not even out of breath.

"I have a strange feeling you're gonna ask anyway."

"What happened with you and Arianna?"

I tense, instantly defensive. Why did he have to bring that up, of all things? "What do you mean? Nothing happened."

"It didn't seem that way. I mean—what she did for you? At the beach. That was a big thing for someone like her."

"Someone popular, you mean."

"The first thing I learned when I got here was not to cross Margot Hunter. You know, that whole insulting-the-alligator thing? Well, she did, and now none of those girls will talk to Arianna. She's more toxic than a nuclear warhead. Everyone's just waiting to see how Margot's going to get her revenge."

"I guess it sucks to be her."

"She did it for you."

"Yeah, you said that already." The white, clean feeling is fading fast.

"But now you're not talking to her either."

A growing headache pulses at the front of my skull. The poison seeps back in through the pores of my skin. "What does she want? For me to fling myself at her, declare my undying loyalty, and pledge myself to her for life? Or maybe carve out my pound of flesh that I owe her and present it to her on a bloody platter?"

"You're making about as much sense as a screen door on a submarine. She doesn't want anything. She's just sad."

"Did she tell you that? You two been chatting?" The words come out sharper than I intend. Why am I acting this way? My words sound terrible in my own ears, but I can't stop them.

"Yes, we have," Lucas says simply. "She did a brave thing. I respect that. And she cares about you."

I kick at a tree root in the path. "Nobody cares. Everybody's only out for themselves and what they can take from people, through manipulation or through force."

"That's a pessimistic view of things."

"Well, it's the correct view of things."

Lucas runs his hand through his unruly dark hair. "If you view every interaction through that filter, then yeah, it'll come true."

"Whatever. If I wanted a shrink, I'd pay for one. I already have Dr. Yang doing a bang-up job. He's even got me scribbling nonsense in a bright pink journal, so there's that."

Lucas frowns at me, but he doesn't back down. "Be all sarcastic if you want to, but that's what you're doing. You're pushing away everybody who cares about you."

Guilt washes over me in waves. "That's what you think?"

He stops in the middle of the trail and turns to face me. "Holy hell, Sidney! Just stop it, will you?"

I stare at him, stunned. He's upset. His jaw is clenched, that vein throbbing in his neck. "Of course, I think that. It's exactly what you're doing right now. You're pushing me away."

I lick my lips, trying to think of some defense. I don't have one. "I am not."

"Yes, you are. Not everyone is out to get you, okay?" His face goes still and serious. "Arianna is a good person. Don't push her away."

He's right. I know he is. She saved me at the beach and was perfectly decent to me, offering me friendship, that thing I both desperately want and am terrified of. And I treated her like crap. I haven't let Lucas in either.

Why? Because I always assume every interaction is a manipulation, a way to gain the upper hand. Because if I let myself trust again, care again, it'll open me up wide. And I can't bear the thought of another betrayal, another blade slipped between my ribs.

Because I'm scared. I'm a coward, just like Jasmine, who sacrificed anything and everything to be popular. Guilt and shame skewer me.

She doesn't deserve this. I've been terrible to her and she doesn't deserve it. I'm the one who's the coward now. I have to do something. I have to be better.

"Damn it all to hell." I stare at Lucas and he furrows his brow, like he knows what I'm thinking, like he can see straight into my heart. I take a deep breath. "Okay. I hear what you're saying. I do. I—I'll talk to her."

Lucas nods. "That's all I'm asking. You know, I would never have let that happen—what those girls did at the beach. I hope you know that. Eli either. Xavier was in on it. He sent me up to the house to get me out of the way. I'm generally a passive person, but holy hell, I wanted to punch his beautiful teeth out."

A laugh escapes my lips before I can clamp my mouth shut. "I thought his teeth were beautiful, too. The most beautiful part of him."

"The only beautiful part of him."

We stand looking at each other for a minute. We're already back to the trail leading to the hole in the fence, and the parking lot, and school, and Margot and Jasmine and work and Ma and Frank and my crazy, miserable life. Suddenly I don't want this to end. "There's a rock. Just a hundred or so yards further along the bank. There's no path, but no one goes there, either."

"Lead the way."

I push through the snarled underbrush. The slab of rock juts out into the river, the same as always. I sit down, hanging my legs over the edge. My feet dangle a few feet above the water. Out of the protection of the trees, the wind whips at my clothes. Lucas sits next to me. I sense the heat of his body, smell the faint odor of sweat-dried skin.

"This is amazing. So quiet," he says.

"I skip class to come here sometimes."

Lucas clears his throat. "Can I give you something?"

"No one's stopping you."

He presses something small and lumpy into my hand. It's some sort of carved wooden shape with two rounded sides curving into a V in the center. "What is this?"

The tops of his ears go red. "It's supposed to be a butterfly. I've seen all those wings and insects and stuff you draw on the edges of all your assignments. They're really good. Unlike this. I made it for you in woodworking class. The idea was much better than the execution, obviously."

"It looks sort of like a mangled heart."

One side of his mouth hitches into a goofy grin. "Well, I guess it works then. 'Cause my heart is mangled for you."

My fingers close over the wooden heart. "What did you just say?"

He clears his throat. "Sidney, I like you. I mean, when you're not acting like . . ."

"A royal pain in the ass?"

"Something like that. But yeah. There it is. I like you."

"Why?" The shiver starts in my skin and ripples clear through to my core. If he says something about my boobs, I'm going to push him straight into the water.

"That's easy. You're beautiful, but you're beautiful like the woods, the river. You've got to be still and really look, really let it sink into your whole self. You are your own person. You don't care what anybody else thinks. You're strong, and brave. You can be mean, but you don't have meanness in you—not like them."

I stare down at my legs, shaking my head.

"The first time I met you, you looked at me. I mean, you looked at me and saw me, not my skin. Everyone always just notices my face is a big zit. And that's all they can see. It felt like you didn't even care about that. Then the next time I saw you, you were verbally sparring with Margot and Jasmine, and you were so much smarter and quicker than they were. You said Jasmine was a 'loathsome toad.' I said to myself, 'Here's a girl. She's creative with her words, just like me.' And I just knew." He shrugs, grinning sheepishly.

My face heats up. For once, I can't think of a thing to say.

He leans in a little closer. "Also, you were nice to me."

"I was not," I say, offended.

"You warned me about my pink lighter."

"You were clearly lacking in common sense."

"Still." His smile widens for a moment, then he grows still, suddenly serious. "I told you I wouldn't touch you until you gave me permission. So, I'm asking. Can I kiss you?"

I try to stop it, but I can't help it. My body's betraying me again, but this time my veins tingle with a feeling so foreign, I don't even recognize it. I don't think my tongue can form words.

His fingers touch my chin and tilt my head up. I look at him, and his eyes are a rich, dark brown, a brown I can swim in, sink into. Not blue. Not like Frank's. Not like mine.

He kisses me. His lips are full and soft and send fizzing sparks shooting through my body. I'm dizzy, my stomach flipping in delicious somersaults.

His tongue gently pries open my lips, and then we are kissing harder, faster. I'm sinking, falling, free and loose and I don't know how I'll land, or if I will. It feels like flying and it feels like drowning, all at the same time.

Then his fingers slide along my scalp, into my hair, cradling my head. Like Frank. Frank's words slither through me. *Are you whoring around on me?*

I go cold. Shame floods me, and all the good feelings shrivel up like the dead and rotting leaves swirling in the river.

I shove him, hard.

"Ouch!" He looks at me in surprise.

"I can't," I gasp, wiping my mouth with the sleeve of my jacket.

"Wait. What are you—?"

I jump to my feet. "I have to go."

"I'll come with you."

"No!" I say with such force that he flinches. "Just—leave me alone. I'm not that girl. I'm not who you think I am."

I turn and flee, running as fast as I can through the bare trees, twigs slapping my arms, my face, and then I'm under the fence and across the parking lot to my car.

School's already out. I should be heading to my shift at Bill's. But I'm not. I can't. I want to go back to the solitude and safety of the rock—my rock—but I can't do that either. There's an intruder there. I led him there. And once again, it's my fault, my fault.

I peel out of the parking lot, but I don't know where to go. My head is wrecked. My skin is blistered from his touch. Wild thoughts flutter-flap through my head, panic on a Blue Morpho's iridescent wings.

I need to cut. I have to cut. Right now.

There's a foreclosed farm off of Briar Lane, only a mile from my house. I drive down the dirt road and pull off onto the weed-infested embankment. An old red barn stands amidst the barren, abandoned fields. The barn's paint is faded and peeling off in long swaths. Several of its wooden slats are gone, like missing teeth.

We used to go here, Jasmine and I, to stalk her butterflies. We captured them in nets and carefully maneuvered them into wide-mouthed glass jars. Jasmine used her tiny forceps to murder them without damaging their fragile wings. We pulled back two of the wooden slats of the barn and smoked cigarettes in the dusty shadows. And all of that is gone now. Dead memories.

I yank the plastic baggie out of the zippered pouch of my backpack and shake out the razor. It falls onto my lap, a sharp glint of metal.

A sigh escapes my lips. I lift my leg and balance it on the center console, my shoe pushing against the shifter. I roll my sweatpants to my kneecap and shove down my sock. I cut deep, inhaling sharply as the blade bites into the flesh below my ankle. Two sides of my skin open up like a mouth, pebbles of blood popping and trailing in slow trickles into my sock. I don't bother to wipe it up.

I make another cut, waiting for relief. But it doesn't come. I try again, and it still doesn't come.

Black fangs of despair sink into my brain. I can't do this. I can't.

I thought I could make it, power through until graduation, then flee and never look back. But I'm not strong enough. I'm not that girl Lucas sees. I'm not who Arianna thinks I am. I'm not strong. I'm weak and I'm dirty and my soul is a black shriek of fury.

I want to take the blade and gouge it deep into my own chest, scrape away the filth and the darkness, digging deep for something, anything, for any pearl or bone or scrap of the girl I used to be, the girl that sketched in a room surrounded by butterflies or the girl that crawled into bed with her frightened brothers or the smart-ass who doesn't care what anyone thinks. Or even the girl who Arianna trusted her secrets to or the one that Lucas saw and liked enough to want to kiss.

Where is that girl? Where is she?

There's only me. The freak who wants to cut her own skin off and beats up little kids and resents her own brothers, who pushes away any whiff of kindness because she doesn't deserve any of it, who hides her true self behind a shield of rage. The slut who thinks and does ugly, dirty, despicable things. The dirty little whore who lies still and silent for her own father.

Tears streak my face. I slash at my legs. Blood splatters my shoes, the seat, the console, the gear shift. I'm growling, gasping, hiccupping cries of outrage because it won't come. The cold calm, the sweet release, the honey soothing my raw, flayed insides—it's abandoned me as surely as everything and everyone else.

"No!" I sob. "No, no, no!" It's not enough. This isn't enough. I want more. I want more than this. I want to be more than this.

I want to claw out of my own skin and be someone—something, anything—else.

I pummel the steering wheel with my fists. I feel everything more than I've ever felt anything before. It's carving me open from the inside, slashing my gut, my lungs, my heart, my soul.

Everything hurts. Everything bleeds.

TWENTY-TWO

I miss another day of work. I've got a bunch of texts on my phone from Bill and Brianna, a few more from Lucas. I haven't even read them. There's a pile of unopened college brochures on my desk, an SAT study guide whose spine I have yet to crack. I skip group counseling, Lit, Government, and Phys Ed. I wouldn't have made it to school at all if what waited at home wasn't worse.

I feel hollowed out, like someone sucked up my insides with a straw. I am a corpse, skin covering white bone, nothing more. The darkness invading my head is so black, it obliterates everything.

I sit in the car in the driveway. It's the last week of October. Tomorrow is Halloween. Everything is brown; the roads are pitted and muddy. The sky is a sheet of gray metal. I stare at my bleak, dingy trailer. I want to drive away, but I'm ravenous, the pit in my belly aching to be filled. Payday's not until Friday, so I'm broke.

I'll grab some peanut butter and a spoon and a heavier sweater. Then I'll go to the river or the old barn again and just be gone, until midnight or one a.m., or however long it takes Frank to slump into a drunken stupor.

The boys clatter out the screen door and down the porch steps. They grab their scooters and take off down the driveway. Frankie doesn't even look my way. Aaron pauses next to my window. I roll it down. "I did a painting in art class, with pink glitter and everything. Wanna see?" His breath hits the glass in white puffs.

"Later. Go back inside and put a coat on. It's freezing."

"But Frankie's not wearing a coat!"

"Just do it. Go on." I roll the window back up and get out of the car.

"But I don't know where it is!"

"Didn't you wear it to school today?"

Aaron just stares at me with his huge brown eyes. "No."

"Why the hell not? Doesn't Ma know it's already down to twenty degrees in the mornings? You need your coat and your gloves. Every day. You'll catch pneumonia."

His gaze slides down to the ground. He kicks at the gravel.

"What? Spit it out."

"Ma had a headache. You got us ready today."

I close my eyes. A shiver runs down my spine. Now, suddenly, I remember Frank banging on my bedroom door. "Get the boys to school. I've got a wood-clearing gig in Niles with Tommy J." And me, jerked out of a fitful sleep, hastily cramming together peanut butter and pineapple sandwiches, tugging a comb through Aaron's hair, yelling at Frankie to brush his teeth, rushing them both out the door so they wouldn't be late, the frigid blast of cold, gray air. And Aaron, tugging on my sleeve, saying he was cold. I was so exhausted, I told him to shut up and stop whining.

I bite the inside of my cheeks, hard. It was me. I sent him to school without a coat. It wasn't Ma who failed him yet again. It was me.

Self-loathing overwhelms me. I can't do this. I'm barely holding my own crap together on a minute-to-minute basis, but they still need me. They still need me, and I have nothing left to give. Terror and shame fuse in my chest. What am I going to do?

I must have a horrified look on my face because Aaron throws himself at me, wrapping his little arms around my waist. "It's okay, Sidney. I wasn't even cold."

Because he's sweet, soft Aaron, he's already forgiven me. My heart crawls into my throat, and I can't speak. I press him against me, the warmth of his body seeping into mine. I want to say something, to tell him how much he means to me, to tell him something so wonderful his whole face will light up. But I can't.

"You're squeezing all my breath out," he says in a muffled voice.

I let him go. "Your coat is hanging on the backside of your door. Go get it."

I step over the backpacks and lunchboxes strewn on the porch steps and open the door. Aaron runs inside and comes back with his puffy white coat that makes him look like a midget version of the Michelin Man. "I'm hungry!"

"Are you asking for something?"

"Can you make a peanut-butter-string-cheese burrito? Pretty super-duper please?"

I'm so hungry, even that sounds good. I want to eat everything, anything. I let my backpack slide to the kitchen floor and open the fridge. "Okay, but then I've got to go. Where's Ma? Still sleeping it off?"

"I dunno. Nobody was here when we got home."

I spread a tortilla shell with a generous amount of peanut butter and wrap it around a string cheese. I pop it in the microwave for forty-five seconds, fold a paper towel around it so it's not too hot to hold, and hand it to Aaron. I glance at the calendar tacked to the wall with a thumbtack. Today's date is circled in red with "The Big Day" scrawled in Ma's scratchy handwriting.

My stomach clenches. She's at the second ultrasound, the one Frank paid extra for to get a better look at the baby's gender. He wants another boy. "Girls are only good for sex and cleaning," he said to me. "Too bad they can't do both at the same time." He laughed hard at that joke.

Just then, a truck roars into the driveway. A door slams. Damn it all to hell. I wanted to be gone already. I can't be here. I wipe my forehead with the sleeve of my sweatshirt. Don't panic. Think. I need to get out as fast as I can.

Frank stomps into the kitchen, a flask dangling from his right hand, a cigarette in the other. "It's cold as hell out there."

I finish wrapping my burrito around the cheese stick with fingers I can barely feel. I'm sluggish, numb.

"I just got the text from your mom. She's on her way home from the doc's office. We're all gonna get fancied up tonight. We're celebrating."

I keep my eyes on the table. "Celebrating what? Is it a boy?"

He steps closer, drops the flask on the table. He grabs my chin with his hand, forcing my head toward him. His gaze stabs into mine. I can smell the sickly stench of his breath, feel it tremble against my cheek.

"Go outside and play, Aaron," I say through clenched teeth.

"But I wanna celebrate too! I want cake!"

"Get out!"

I can't see Aaron because Frank's got an iron grip on my jaw, but I hear him scamper out, hear the bang of the screen door.

Frank blows a stream of smoke into my face. He stubs out the cigarette on my plate, flecks of ash landing on my burrito. He leans close, whispers into my hair, "It's a girl. I'm looking forward to it. If you won't put out, you know she will."

The image his words hurl into my head cracks my mind. My rage is an explosion. Fury blasts through me in white-hot pulses. No. No. No. I can't breathe, can't distinguish shapes or sounds. A curtain of red falls over my eyes. All I can see is blood. "Get away from me!"

"Just what do you think you're going to do about it?"

I gasp, heaving, but no oxygen can get to my lungs. My chest closes up like a vise. Everything is going black, then red, then black. I grab the bread knife covered in peanut butter and slash at his arm.

He releases my jaw with a curse. There's a long red scrape on the back of his hand. He comes at me fast. Grabs my wrist and backs me up until the ridge of the table bangs into the back of my thighs. He flips me and bends me over the table. My cheek smashes into the wood. The peanut butter jar sits inches from my nose.

"Just who do you think is in charge here? You nasty little whore.

Maybe your Ma is right. Maybe you need some sense knocked into you. I've been too easy on you kids. Look what good it did me."

I try to wriggle away, to kick out with my legs. He grinds his forearm into my spine, pinning me down. I hear the click and slide of his belt buckle. Then his hand, hot and urgent, scrabbling at my jeans. "Hold still! This is the only way you bitches ever learn."

Fury mixed with fear blazes through me. No. He's not going to do this. I won't let him. He grunts from the exertion of trying to yank down my zipper while keeping me pinned. I squirm and wriggle and jerk to the left. He loses his grip, and I roll off the table and fall hard to the floor.

I'm up and running for the door. Frank's right behind me. I knock a chair over. Frank stumbles over it, but regains his footing.

I grab the ugly ceramic rooster with both hands, turn, and hurl it at him. He throws up a hand to shield his face. The rooster crashes into him and shatters into a thousand pieces. Several small shards stick out of the skin of his hand.

His face goes savage.

Run! My brain shrieks, but my feet are rooted to the linoleum. I'm backed up against the counter. The only way to escape is outside, where the boys are. I can't let them see this.

My veins are threaded with frost, my legs made of lead. Terror zips up and down my spine.

He snatches at my hair, but it's too short. I duck away.

He comes at me again and grabs the neck of my sweatshirt. He jerks me stumbling and teetering through the kitchen, around the table, into the living room. My knee cracks against the coffee table. He doesn't slow down.

"Stop it! Stop! Let go!" I claw at his hand, his arm.

He drags me half-falling past the couch, down the hallway lined with family pictures. My flailing arms strike the framed embroidered purple vase with the flowers Ma made my eighth-grade summer. It crashes to the floor. I slip on a shard of glass.

He yanks me back up and wrestles me through his bedroom door. He throws me on the bed.

I roll, but he's on top of me. He slaps my face. Red and white stars explode across my vision. My eyes leak pain.

"Stop acting like you don't want it, like you aren't asking for it every miserable day of your life."

"Stop it!" I scream at him. I slap his hands away from my chest. "Get off me!"

He punches me in my stomach. My breath sucks itself right out of my lungs. I can't breathe. My vision blurs around the edges.

He pushes up my shirt, panting from exertion. "You know what the problem with you is? I waited too long."

When he reaches for the top button of his pants, I buck and knee him as hard as I can. I hurl myself to the right. This time, his body softens and gives way. I tumble off the side of the bed—Frank's side.

Awareness jolts through me. I know what to do now. I stick my hand beneath the mattress of the bed. My fingers close over the Glock. I stand up, holding the gun with trembling hands.

Frank scrambles off the bed and stands on the other side of the mattress. We stare at each other. "Just what do you think you're gonna do with that?"

I blink the stars and sweat out of my eyes. "I'm going to kill you."

He laughs a slow, silky laugh. "Give it here."

"Not a chance."

He makes a move to come around the bed. I point the gun right at his chest.

"Too bad it's not even loaded." His voice is full of razor blades. "Might as well have a water gun for how much good it'll do you."

I plant my feet. Focus. Keep the gun trained on his chest. Keep the barrel from shaking. "You messed up, Frank. The rest of your guns you keep in the gun cabinet in the closet. But this one's your baby. This one's clean and oiled and fully loaded. You thought it'd keep you safe when all the evil you've unleashed in the world finds its way back to you. Newsflash. It won't."

He licks his lips. Emotions flit in dark shadows across his face. He wants to dismiss me, but some little warning in the back of his brain niggles that he shouldn't. The survival instinct.

The tables have been turned.

He shakes his head and grunts in disgust, the moment lost. He wipes his bleeding hand on his shirt. He turns and walks toward the bedroom door. "Put that away when you're done playing with it."

I could leave now. I've got the gun. He'll let me walk right out of the house. But he won't forget this. He'll have to reassert his control, his dominance. It's not over.

It won't ever be over. And when I'm gone? It'll keep going. He'll keep going. Even if I manage to escape, even if I fly a thousand miles across the country and never return, he won't stop. He'll just hurt them instead of me.

He'll hurt her. My sister. The memory of his words, of the images he conjured up, scald my mind. The black cloud of my future falls away, and all of a sudden, I can see clearly. This is why college always seemed nebulous, hazy.

Somewhere deep inside me, I knew I could never leave with Frank still here.

Something dark slithers through me. I'll never let him hurt my sister like he hurt me. I'll never let him use the boys as punching bags. I can't leave without taking care of my family.

It's my responsibility to protect them. It always has been. "Stop."

He turns around. He sees my face, the coldness in my eyes. His eyes. He recognizes himself in me; he knows what I'm capable of. What I'm about to do.

He takes several steps back into the room, but he stays close to Ma's side of the bed. Slowly, he raises both his hands, palms out in a placating gesture. "Sidney. Baby girl. Let's talk about this. You want to shoot? I'll take you to the range. Maybe I've been too harsh. Your Ma always says it. Lighten up on them, Frank. You're pushing them too hard, Frank. Maybe she's right. Why don't you—"

I don't hesitate. I have no desire for answers, for apologies, for begging. That's my mother, the blubbering why, why, why's. I no longer care.

I aim the sights just a bit low and a hair to the left. I pull the trigger, and my arms hammer back into my chest. Even though I'm ready for the strength of the recoil, it's the noise of the shot, like a jackhammer inches from my ear, that shocks me.

There is no slow motion. Frank falls back against the wall, a startled look on his face, his mouth a red O. His right arm flails for something, anything, knocking against the lamp, his body slip-sliding down the wall.

My head rings. My ears are stuffed with cotton. Reality is jerky, like a hand-held movie. I take a breath. Focus.

I can't see him over the bed, so I walk around it on wooden legs, keeping the gun up, ready.

But my aim is true. He looks like some sort of disturbing doll, arms and legs kicked out in awkward directions. A spot of red blooms over his chest, a ring of scarlet water, no bigger than a silver dollar.

His eyes are open, still so blue, the color so rich and deep he cannot be dead. Dead people don't have eyes like this.

He's watching me, sucking out my soul with those eyes, eyes slowly losing their life, their vibrancy, until they're like marbles, shiny and smooth.

Empty.

TWENTY-THREE

I slump to my knees, the gun resting on my lap. It seems like hours but must only be minutes. Or seconds.

I blink, and it's like I'm waking up from a deep, dreamless sleep.

"Sidney?" My mother's voice, filtering through the fog.

Suddenly, Ma is pushing past me. Her scream smashes into me like a train. She falls onto the body, weeping. The noise thunders in my ears.

I stare at the wall, where there's a dime-sized hole in the drywall about chest high. The bullet went clean through.

Everything is numb. My legs are sloshy as water, and they won't hold me up. Fear takes hold again, thrumming through me.

I can't move. Can't think.

Ma lets out another anguished wail. "No, baby, no! Frank! Frank! Don't leave me!"

The sounds of her grief scrape me raw. "I'm—I'm sorry."

Ma looks back at me, her cheek slicked with blood like someone swiped it with a paintbrush. Her eyes are wet and red, her mouth slack. "What have you done?"

"He came after me, Ma," I choke out. "He was hurting me and—"

'Stop!" she growls suddenly. "Shut up!"

I flinch, speechless.

She scrubs her face with the back of her hand and stands up, one hand pressed to the hump of her belly. Her dress is smudged with blood. Her face is streaked with mascara, but she is no longer weeping. "Give me the gun."

I'm so shocked, I do what she says. Ma wipes it thoroughly with a clean section of her dress. "Check your clothes. If there's any blood, dump them somewhere. You need to be somewhere else. Anywhere else but here. You were never here."

"Ma—"

Her mouth contorts, emotions flickering across her face. Her eyes are clearer than they've been in years, hard and glittering and determined. "There's no time. Go."

I pull myself to my feet. My brain is so frayed I can't make sense of what's happening. "I need to—"

"Go!"

Like a robot, unfeeling, unthinking, I go. I pick up my backpack off the kitchen floor and wipe off slivers of ceramic rooster. I crunch across the floor.

When I get to the front door, Aaron is walking up the porch steps. Dark-bellied stratus clouds drape everything in sheets of gray. Far down the road, I can see the small red dot of Frankie riding his scooter.

The second gunshot startles us both.

Aaron's mouth falls open. He sees something in my face that must frighten him, because he starts to cry.

For a moment, I stand frozen, unable to move. Why would Ma shoot the gun? Did she shoot Frank again? He's already dead. I know he is. And even if he wasn't dead, why would she shoot him?

My thoughts are a swirling mess. Nothing makes sense.

I force myself to move. "Don't go inside." I grab the collar of Aaron's jacket. "You never went inside today, you hear me? It'll be easier for you."

"What'll be easier?" He gulps. "Sidney! What's wrong? Where's Ma? Where's Daddy?"

But I can't answer his questions. I can't comfort him.

Not now, when I'm teetering on the edge of a howling black hole. When my whole body is shuddering from shock. I just can't.

I brush past him. I get in the car and pull out of the driveway.

Aaron runs after me with confused tears streaking down his face. But I don't have to worry about leaving him anymore.

The monster in the house is dead.

TWENTY-FOUR

My hands tremble so badly on the steering wheel that I can barely keep the car on the road. My breath steams in jagged gasps in the cold air. The radio is playing but I can't hear anything but white noise.

Everything swells in and out of focus. Darkness hovers at the edges of my vision.

I'm driving. I don't know where. I need something. Anything. I can't be alone. I don't want to be alone. Things are disintegrating around the edges. What now? I can't think straight. I can't think at all. The gunshot echoes over and over, pulsing through my brain.

I blink my eyes. I've just driven over the meridian. I jerk the wheel, overcorrect back into my lane.

My heart slams against my throat, my chest, my skull. Somehow, I turn onto Thornberry Road, turn left at a nice tree-lined street with rows of stately brick colonials.

And there's her house. I don't even remember how I got here. Arianna's navy Nissan Altima is the only car parked in the driveway. I stagger up her sidewalk, punch at the doorbell with shaking fingers.

Arianna opens the door. She's wearing a lavender apron over a fuzzy cream sweater and dark leggings. Her black waves are piled in a bun on top of her head and she's swinging a spatula.

Her eyes widen.

"Can I come in?" I say, already pushing my way past her.

"Um. Hi?"

My legs give out then and I crumple to the floor. I lie on my back on the cool tile and watch the arched ceiling sway and fade above me, each breath ripped right out of my chest.

"Are you okay? What's going on?" Arianna stares down at me in alarm.

"I—I think I killed him."

"What? You killed something? I can't understand you."

"Someone. Frank. I killed Frank. I killed my father."

Arianna's face goes pale beneath her makeup. "Is this a joke?"

"Do I look like I'm joking?" I nearly scream.

She kneels down next to me, cradling the spatula. "Why—what happened—whatever did—how?"

"I don't know. I mean, I shot him."

"Like—with a gun?"

"No, with a camera." A jagged sob burns through my chest, punches through my lips.

Arianna stares at me blankly.

"Yes! Yes. With a gun. With a bullet. I pointed and squeezed the trigger and he . . .

"You pointed the gun at him? Like on purpose?"

I close my eyes. She's not getting it. This was a mistake. I shouldn't have come here. I try to sit up, but waves of dizziness surge through me. I start to fade.

"Whoa!" Arianna grabs me and helps me back to the floor. "Don't move. You look like a ghost. What in the world is going on? Should I call the police?"

"NO! I mean, no. Please. I need—I had nowhere else to go. I'm sorry. I shouldn't have come. I'll go."

"You're not going anywhere. You can stay right here as long as you need to. Do you want to move to the couch? My bedroom?"

I shake my head, and the ceiling tilts. I won't make it that far.

"Sidney, you need help. Let me help you. Talk to me."

The cold tiles press against my back. Hot tears prick my eyes. I cannot cry. The tears will drown me. I close my eyes.

I think of Ma, the way her eyes shuttered as she turned away from me, brushing me off. I remember Jasmine, how her mouth curled in satisfaction when she slurred the words, "emo cutter freak," how I'd wanted to tell her my secrets so badly that summer, how I started with the cuts, the least and weakest of my demons, how my weakness just gave her more fuel to hurt me.

You can't give any part of yourself to anyone. They'll just use it to break you. *You're already broken,* a voice whispers inside my head. *What more do you have to lose?*

It's now or never. Acid rises in my throat, and I can't stop the tears leaking down my face. I have to be brave. I choose to be brave. I take a deep, ragged breath. "Once upon a time, there was a little girl who lived in a small white house in the center of a field of corn. And in her house the walls yelled, and screamed, and banged and slapped and wept long tears. The little girl just thought it was normal. When the walls got really loud, the girl's little brothers came into her room in their PJs with their blankies and teddies, and she tucked them into her bed. Then she fell asleep with sweet baby breath on her cheek and a sharp elbow in her back, but it was safe in her room. Her room was the safest place in the whole house, in the whole universe.

"For a time, the little girl even believed she had magic in her fingers. She could fold her baby brothers into her arms and they would stop crying, they would stop being afraid. The little girl was never afraid—that's what gave her the magic.

"Then the little girl started to grow up. And her father went on journeys into the corn fields to find money while her mother fell under long spells where she wouldn't wake up. No matter how many times the girl touched her mother with her magic fingers, her mother wouldn't get up.

"And then—" My voice snags. Salty tears leak into my mouth. Every word tastes like vomit, scalds like poison. "The walls had shadows. When the night was darkest and the most still, the shadow stepped out of the wall and slid into the girl's room and it didn't make a sound. The walls didn't stop him. The magic didn't stop him.

"The things the shadow did weren't happy things. The girl didn't know what to do, so she didn't do anything. She lay still as a statue and her heartbeat slowed and her breath spiraled up past the ceiling and disappeared. Her skin turned papery and her bones grew brittle and broke right through her flesh. Up she drifted, like a butterfly, like the Pale Spotted Swallowtail, heavy black wings shimmering obsidian.

"There she could look down on her brothers, and make sure they were safe. There she could look down on her mother, alone in her bed. She could flutter through her window and explore the night sky. So whenever the shadow came, the girl broke out of her body and shed her skin and flapped up and away to somewhere else."

Arianna's warm, dry hand grabs mine. A soft moan escapes her lips.

I don't look at her. I can't. I stare at the ceiling, at a small crack in the corner shaped like a spider's web. My breath comes out harder, sharper. Pain scalds my throat, my tongue. But I don't quit. I won't. "So it went until the night shadows bled into the day. Even though she'd given the shadow everything he wanted, it still wasn't enough. He was still hungry. He wanted more. He snared her, tethered her down. He tore her wings so she couldn't fly away anymore.

"Now the girl knew whatever magic she thought she had was never really there. She just laid there and did nothing. She was just a coward, after all. And it was like everybody knew, like it was carved on her forehead. Like they could see the truth of what she really was. All the names they called her were true." I spit out the last few words like they're toxic.

"Oh, Sidney."

I force myself to turn my head, waiting for the judgment, the mockery, the contempt I know I deserve.

Only she doesn't say anything like that. Tears drip down her cheeks. Her eyes are deep wells of sadness. "I'm so, so sorry."

"I let him do—I let it happen. For four years."

"No. You can't think like that. He is responsible. You were just an innocent kid."

"Everything they say about me is true."

"No." Her voice goes hard. "No. What he did to you is not your fault."

"I just laid there, pretended it wasn't happening. I never *did* anything. I didn't—I didn't think I could. I didn't want to be this way—so ugly and filthy inside. I wanted it to stop. But I didn't know what to do. Then I met you and Lucas and all the therapy crap happened, and I decided to make him stop. But he wouldn't. I couldn't—I couldn't make him stop." *Until now.*

"I'm so sorry."

"My mother's pregnant." The words are bitter in my mouth. "With a girl."

Arianna squeezes my hand. I don't pull away. I'm too damn tired.

"That's why you did it."

I nod dully. My insides are hollowed out.

"When?"

"Just now. I don't know. Thirty, forty minutes ago."

Arianna's eyes widen. "You're sure he's . . . ?"

"He's dead. My mother checked."

"Your mother?"

"She came home right after. She was crying and screaming, then all of a sudden, she got quiet. She told me to leave. She wiped off the gun. I don't know what she's going to do. I don't know what to do."

Arianna's mouth presses into a thin line. Her face is drained of color. "You're shaking like a leaf. I'm going to get some blankets. You can lie on the couch. My parents won't be home for a couple of hours. You can stay here."

I take a deep, shuddering breath. "Thank you."

"We'll figure something out. It'll be okay."

Tears melt and crackle behind my eyelids. "No, it won't."

TWENTY-FIVE

For the next two hours, I lie on Arianna's couch, wrapped in her lacy lavender duvet. Arianna turns up the heat past 82 degrees, but I can't get warm. My body is wracked with tremors, and my teeth keep chattering.

I can't stop seeing his eyes. My eyes.

Arianna bakes me a fancy macaroni and cheese dish with gourmet cheeses like gruyere, asiago, and fontina, none of which I've ever tasted. I try to eat it, but I start heaving. Arianna puts it in the fridge for her parents.

She stalks back and forth in front of the couch. "What about Lucas? Should I call him?"

"No!"

She glances at me, surprised.

Shame engulfs me at the thought of Lucas finding out the truth about me. I barely survived telling Arianna. He won't want a thing to do with me after what happened at the rock anyway. "I mean, I can't, okay? Nobody else. Please."

"Okay, I promise." She nods and takes a breath. "What's next? What do we do? What are the options?"

Leave it to Arianna to already be making a plan. The truth is, I have no idea. I didn't plan any of this. "I don't know."

She starts pacing in front of the sofa, gnawing at her fingernails. "It's reasonable to assume your mom called the cops."

I manage a snort. "Ma doesn't really do reasonable, but in this case, yeah."

"So either you turn yourself in or wait for the cops to find you here. And then you claim self-defense."

"I can't do that."

She turns and faces me. "It was self-defense, wasn't it?"

I feel frozen, numb, like I'm talking about another Sidney, another murder that I didn't actually commit. "He stopped. He walked away. I shot him anyway. I knew what I was doing."

"But he—he hurt you."

Acid burns the back of my throat. "He wasn't trying to kill me. My life wasn't in danger. Not like that. Besides, how could I prove it? I can't."

"Okay," she says, nodding to herself. "Okay. Let me check something." She sinks into the couch next to me and fiddles with her phone. She sucks in a breath, the color draining from her bronze skin. "Oh, no. No, no, no."

"What?"

"I hope you don't mind. I just, I wanted to look it up and see if . . ."

"Spit it out."

"Patricide is the legal term for what you—what happened." Her voice is wobbly, unsure, like she thinks I'm going to leap up and bite her head off any second. "There are about three hundred cases a year in the U.S. In almost all cases, severe abuse of the child incited the incident . . ."

"Don't stop now. Just say it, whatever it is."

She rubs her temple. "The prosecutors decline to prosecute in only a minority of cases, in spite of known abuse and claims of self-defense. The average sentence is fifteen to twenty years."

I try to imagine prison. It can't be worse than the prison I've already endured. Still, my future claps shut like a steel trap. "Well, that's not awesome."

"It's not justice," Arianna growls. She slaps her phone down on the arm of the couch and lunges to her feet. She paces in front of the glass coffee table, faster now, biting at her fingernails like she's going to rip them off. She's angrier than I've ever seen her. "How is that fair? He subjected you to horrible—and then you go to prison for twenty years? Rapists get out in like seven years. Child molesters in four years. This is insane. I can't believe it. This can't be happening."

I just watch her pace and mutter. I'm separated from it all, distant, like I'm watching myself watching her. Arianna switches on a lamp, and we both notice the blue-tinged twilight through the windows at the same time.

Time is passing. Too much time. I can barely force out the words. "I should go back. I need to turn myself in. It's better if I do it that way, I think. Right?"

"You could run," Arianna says suddenly. "I have thirty thousand in the bank, for college. You can have some of it. As much as you need."

I consider it for half a second, then shake my head. "Where would I go? How would I get a job? I haven't even graduated high school. They would find me. It would just make things worse. Besides, I'm done with being a coward. Whatever happens next, I'll face it."

Arianna begins to cry, silent tears slipping down her cheeks. "I can't believe this is happening."

I pull myself to a sitting position. Waves of dizziness wash over me. I push aside the blankets and stand up. My legs hold me. Barely.

"You don't have a coat." Arianna goes to her coat closet near the front door. "You can borrow one of mine and give it back later."

Like there'll be a later. Like I won't be killing time for the next twenty years in a concrete prison cell. I shrug into a snug black leather jacket I can barely button.

Arianna's eyes are closed, her lips barely moving.

"What are you doing?"

She opens her eyes. "Praying."

I want to say I don't need her prayers, but I'm desperate. I'll take anything.

Arianna puts her hand on my shoulder. "You don't have to face this alone." She hesitates, a shadow passing over her features. "At least, not this part."

Part of me wants to tell her "thanks, but no thanks." But the other, bigger, part of me is utterly terrified. I have no idea what I'm going home to. "I—I can't ask you to do that."

"Nonsense," Arianna says briskly. Her shoulders are straight, her jaw set in determination. "I'm coming with you."

TWENTY-SIX

Several police cars and a forensic van are parked on the side of the road. Yellow tape cordons off the area around the trailer. I get out of the car. Arianna joins me and we walk up the driveway. Gravel crunches beneath my feet. The wind is sharp as a knife, slashing at my face, neck, and hands.

Dread scrabbles up my spine. My whole body is shaking. I want to run. I want to get as far away from this terrible place as I can. I want it to just stop. But it won't. The red lights flash across the yard and the front of the house. I hear muffled voices, the scratchy sound of radios.

This is real. This is happening. In a few minutes, they'll be closing the cuffs around my wrists. They'll be putting me in the back of the police car, behind the grate. Already in a cage. My legs start to give out and I stumble. Arianna holds me up.

A young cop in a starched blue uniform stops us. "You can't go in there, ma'am. This is a crime scene."

I can see uniformed bodies moving around the house, people in papery body suits and booties, collecting evidence. In my house. I imagine them ruffling through underwear drawers and examining soiled bedsheets and collecting dust, dirt, and dead cockroaches from underneath the beds.

I imagine Aaron, terrified, cowering in a corner while strangers clomp through his room. My stomach clenches. "Where's Ma? Where are my brothers?"

"What's your name, Miss?" the cop asks.

"Her name is Sidney Shaw," Arianna says. "This is her house."

The cop's radio crackles as he murmurs something into it.

"Where are my brothers?" I ask again, my voice rising. "Frankie! Aaron!"

"Please stay calm. The detectives are coming out to talk to you. Just stay calm."

Arianna's fingers grip my arm. Only her hand keeps me tethered to the here and now. I'm about to burst out of my skin.

Two people wearing regular clothes walk down the porch steps and duck beneath the yellow tape. The man is tall and lean, with a full beard and cold, dark eyes. The woman's auburn hair is pulled back into a tight ponytail. She's holding a notepad in her hand. "Hello. I'm Detective Henricksen, and this is Detective Okonjo. We've been waiting for you."

"Where's my mom? Where the hell are my brothers? I need to see them." My fingers curl into fists. My nails dig into the flesh of my palms. I have to see the boys before they take me away. I have to hug them both, wrap my arms around them and whisper all the things I've been afraid to say.

"Well, honey, we have some difficult news to tell you," Detective Okonjo says. "We've just taken your mother into custody."

Shock rolls over me. For a long moment, I can't even make out the meaning of their words. I play it again in my head. I take a step back, stunned. "What?"

The female detective's brow wrinkles in compassion. "Your mother spoke to the arriving officer on the scene. She confessed to murdering your father."

I'm drowning. Someone is holding my head underwater. I can't open my lungs to take in air. I'm going under.

Ma confessed? It doesn't make sense. She wouldn't do that. She's lazy and stupid and selfish, and every other insult Frank ever called her. She wouldn't. "There must be some mistake—"

Detective Henricksen shakes her head. "I'm sorry."

I can't think straight. I can barely follow the words the detectives are saying, let alone figure out what they mean. Broken, disjointed thoughts crash against my skull. My hands are shaking. I don't know what to do. I need my brothers. I have to see them. "Where are the boys?"

"A child advocate picked them up about ninety minutes ago. They're safe, don't worry."

"Foster care? You put my brothers in foster care?"

Detective Henricksen squints at me. "In an emergency placement, yes. How old are you?"

"Eighteen."

"I can put you in touch with the child advocate, or you can stay with friends or family members, if you wish. Is there a family member DHS could contact about taking the boys?"

I can barely focus. "Um, we have an aunt. Aunt Ellie. But she's out of state."

The detective nods kindly. "A DHS child advocate will contact your aunt to facilitate the process. Hopefully, your brothers will be out of the system soon. But you can't stay here tonight. This is a crime scene."

I look past the detectives at the flashing lights reflecting off the windows, the dilapidated siding, the sagging front porch. I've lived here my entire life.

In my mind's eye, I see everything like the forensic team would: the tired, sad little house with the cheap furniture and the peeling laminate counter tops and the dingy bedrooms with the tattered toys juxtaposed against the big screen TVs, the PlayStation, the shiny new iPhones. And the kitchen scattered with ceramic shards and the narrow hallway with the frame knocked off the wall and the bedroom sprayed with red.

How long until they see something, some piece of evidence pointing a bloody finger straight at me? And Frank—is his body still in there? Do his dead eyes scream an accusation? Does his dead mouth whisper, *I know who killed me?*

My knees buckle. Arianna's arm encircles my waist. Her shoulder leans into mine, holding me up. This is all real. Right now is really happening.

"I know this is a very difficult time for you," Detective Okonjo says, "but it would be very helpful if you could help us establish the timeline of events. Can you tell me what you did and when today? Did you attend school?"

Somehow, I manage to nod.

"And what did you do after school ended at three p.m.? Did you come home?" Detective Henricksen asks, her pen poised over her spiral-bound notepad.

This is the moment that changes everything. The moment to confess.

I feel numb all over. Why did Ma say she did it? Was she protecting me? Was that even possible? I can't let her take the fall. I don't know what's going on or what her reason is, but it's not right. No matter how terrible of a mother she's been, I can't let her do this. I'm the one who did this. I killed Frank.

I open my mouth, but nothing comes out.

Arianna speaks instead. She steps in close, her grip tightening on my waist. "She came to my house. She was with me."

TWENTY-SEVEN

The days after the shooting are a gray blur. Once again, Arianna saves me. I spend the next week at her house. I curl up on her floor in a pile of blankets and goose-down pillows. I can't stop shaking. I shake all day and all night long. The chill goes all the way down to my bones.

The bang of the gun keeps going off in my head, shattering my skull into shards, so impossibly loud, impossibly final. I drift in and out of consciousness, plagued with nightmares. I wake up trembling, drenched in sweat, my mouth clamping down over my screams.

I feel like I'm dying. The pressure is excruciating, like a hundred bricks placed one on top of the other on my chest, slowly crushing my rib cage. Everything's compressed, squashed, condensed into a heart-beat, pain shooting into every vein and artery.

Everything hurts.

I don't answer my texts or calls or look at my phone. I know most of them are from Lucas. But I just can't. I don't go to school. The thought of enduring all the questions, the pitying looks, the muffled whispers and averted gazes is too much to bear.

Dr. Yang gets my work from my teachers for me, which Arianna brings home to me in stacks. I haven't touched them. She says Lucas asks about me. Everyone asks about me, like they were ever concerned in the first place.

Arianna cooks me every meal. Authentic Colombian meals like canary bean and chorizo soup, yucca balls stuffed with cheese, and Columbian plantains with tomato and onion chutney. She makes me arugula salads with candied walnuts, dried cranberries, and crumbled feta cheese, hand-tossed flatbreads baked with a creamy white sauce, spinach, and oregano, and light, foamy custard that clings to my lips.

I eat, though I barely taste anything, because some distant part of me recognizes that this is a gift, one I cannot reject. Arianna watches me with concerned eyes. I tell her to eat, too. She takes careful, tiny bites. I thank her for saving me. Even in my shock, I know what she's done for me, how much it means.

When she's at school, the only thing I can do is draw. So I draw and draw and draw some more. I have a few charcoal pencils in my backpack, and the journal. Dr. Yang said it was for feelings, so I draw my grief in harsh, sweeping lines, sketching page after page of sandhill skippers and great coppers, northern cloudy-wings and western-tailed blues, pale swallowtails and mourning cloaks.

I draw my panic, my fear and guilt, the dread and the longing. I want my brothers. I want my mother, but the thought of her brings a tangled, muddled mess of emotions I don't know what to do with.

What is Ma doing right now? What is she feeling? Thinking? Is she sitting in a jail cell, scared and alone? Is she weeping over Frank, or is she thinking about me? Why did she take the fall for me? I don't understand it. I don't know how I'm supposed to feel—so I feel everything. It's overwhelming.

Even with Arianna right next to me, I'm more alone than I've ever felt. I'm like a little kid again, like what I want more than anything is for my mother to wrap me up in her safe, warm arms and tell me everything is okay now, everything will be fine. I yearn for something I can barely remember.

The days bleed together.

I keep waiting to wake up from this nightmare, but I never do.

TWENTY-EIGHT

For a few days, I have no idea what's going on.

I only know Ma was appointed a public defender, since we have no money. He never calls. Bill does, though. He leaves me three different messages, all saying the same thing: he's thinking of me, and I can take as long as I need before I go back to work. The job will be waiting for me. In spite of the hell I'm going through, Bill gives me a brief flash of hope. Maybe there will be some kind of life to build on when the dust has settled.

But first, I have to survive this.

It's the friend of the court child advocate lady, Michelle or Michaela or something, who calls me one afternoon on my cell to tell me my mother's been arraigned. The public defender argued for a low bail amount. I don't know if five hundred grand is low or not, but we couldn't put down one percent of that, let alone the insane amount a bail bond would require.

"So what happens next?" I ask the lady, twisting my rings over and over around my fingers. I'm sitting on a stool at Arianna's kitchen island, eating a handful of her mother's rice cake—only I've slathered them with an inch of peanut butter. My journal is open in front of me, a half-drawn cartoon of Ratty Bunny on one page. I'm making it for Aaron, for when he comes back home.

"Since your mother is pleading guilty, the lawyers will battle it out in a pretrial conference. They have to come to an agreement on the charges. Then it'll go before a judge. The defense requests a sentencing, and the prosecutor makes a recommendation. The judge decides on the final sentence."

"And then that's it?"

"Yes, honey. And then she will serve her term in prison, but she could get out earlier than her sentence for good behavior."

For a moment, I can't breathe. "Did—did she give a reason?"

"I'm afraid I don't have that information right now."

Guilt clamps down on my windpipe. "Is she okay? I mean, I know she's not, but she's pregnant and—"

"She's fine," the woman says kindly. "The pregnancy is fine. Don't you worry."

Like that could even be possible.

The woman clears her throat. "I called to tell you about your aunt. I got ahold of her. I gave her your number, so she may call you. She hasn't committed to anything yet, but I'm hopeful she'll take the boys and get them out of the system."

"When can I see them?" I've thought of them a million times every day. How scared they must be. Are they okay? Is anyone hurting them? I hate my helplessness. I hate the fact they're gone because of me.

"Soon, honey. I promise. Everything's a process. There's lots of red tape."

"Does Aaron have Ratty Bunny?"

"What?"

My voice cracks. "His stuffed rabbit. It's his favorite. He sleeps with it every night."

"I don't think so. I can get it for him once the house is no longer a crime scene. Hold tight, okay? We're taking care of them. I promise."

I hit the *end call* button and slump down at Arianna's kitchen table.

Pastor Torrès left a copy of the Cass County Gazette on the island. "Brokewater Woman Slays Former Football Star Husband, Confesses" reads the article third from the top.

Even in death, our family doesn't warrant a front-page headline. I push the newspaper off the island and watch it flutter to the tile floor.

TWENTY-NINE

Two days later, they tell me I can go back to the house.

Outside, the earth is a barren, frozen brown, the sky bloated with the thwarted promise of snow. The sun hasn't shown itself for days. The stalks of corn in the fields behind our house are withered, shriveled, and crushed into the dirt.

I enter the house and wander the rooms like a ghost. There are no lights or heat on. I wrap my arms tighter around myself. It's so cold I can see my breath.

The late afternoon shadows spill from every object, which now seem harsh and unfamiliar. It smells different. Everything about it is different.

I wander into the living room, take in the old coffee table, the big TV, the saggy couch. Frank will never slump in a drunken stupor on that couch again. Aaron and Frankie can watch cartoons without worrying about getting yelled at.

In the kitchen, my shoes crunch over the shards of the ceramic rooster. For a second, I see him at the table, hunched over his guns, his blue eyes at turns intense, laughing, and vicious. He'll never sit there again. It's my table now. Aaron can spread out his art supplies and glue and glitter to his heart's content.

I stare at my parents' closed bedroom door. There won't be any shouting and screaming from that room. Not anymore. I leave the door shut.

In my room, all the dresser drawers are hanging open, the contents spilled onto the carpet. Three of the drawers are cracked. The bedspread is pulled off the bed, all my books tossed out of the bookcase, the closet turned inside out.

I check beneath the mattress for my plastic baggie of razors and bandages. They even took that, too. It figures.

I kick around the pile of clothes on the floor next to my bed. The wooden heart Lucas carved for me is lying on top of a wrinkled pair of jeans. I pick it up, place it gently on the dresser. I can't think about him now, can't think about that kiss, the fire it ignited beneath my skin. He's called me a dozen times. I haven't called back.

I blink rapidly, staring at my familiar walls, the butterflies, their sleek bodies, their satiny colored wings. My gaze drifts to my bed. Frank will never come in here again. It's my room again, and only mine.

Frank is dead. We're all better for it. He'll never hurt me again. He'll never abuse Ma. He'll never hit or scream at the boys. And he'll never touch my unborn baby sister. Does it make me a terrible person that mixed in with the guilt and pain is relief? That things will be better, now that he's dead?

I'm the one that made this happen. I killed him. I killed my own father. Does that make me a monster?

I sense the darkness inside me. The monster is still there.

I leave my room and walk into the bedroom my brothers share. The beds are next to each other below the window, Frankie's bedspread covered with spiraling airplanes; Aaron's, Winnie the Pooh. Frankie's dresser is lined with dozens of googly-eyed rock people.

The new PlayStation is shoved into a corner on the floor, half covered by a pair of Aaron's Superman pajamas. Ratty Bunny sits on Aaron's bed, staring at me with his droopy button eyes.

This room looks almost untouched by the forensic team. Or maybe they were respectful in here and put everything back.

I pick up Ratty Bunny and hug him to my chest. He smells like Aaron's vanilla-scented shampoo. I pull open the top drawer of his nightstand. There are the unfolded sketch pages I've drawn for him over the years, scattered in piles next to a couple of Hot Wheels cars, a few crayons, a half-melted chocolate coin still wrapped in gold foil, and Aaron's favorite purple sparkly pen with the feather sticking out of the cap.

I go to the buffet in the hallway and jerk open the drawer. There's a slip of paper tucked into our spot. *My favorite sister* is scrawled in his awkward, slanty handwriting over a glued-on pink construction paper heart.

My heart cracks wide open.

I have to protect them. I have to save them. I have to do whatever it takes. They're suffering because of me, because of what I did.

I must get them back. And then I have to make this house a home. A real home. I have to be their parent now.

I took away Frank, and Ma went with him. Now they have no one but me. I have to be there for them. I think of the almost three grand sitting in my bank account. That money was meant to get me away from Frank. Now it has to be used to build something new. I don't know if college will happen. All I know is that I can't leave the boys now. My goal has changed.

They need stability. They need love. They need more than I have to give.

My arms tighten around Ratty Bunny. I gaze into his button eyes.

I have to change.

All the responsibility falls on me now. I cannot fall apart. I cannot close myself off and shut down. I can't half-ass recovery. I can't shove away my friends—and they are my friends, I know that now. Arianna saved me, risking her own skin to cover for me.

I have to be present, and strong, and brave.

I have to give this thing my all.

I cannot let the monster win anymore.

THIRTY

The doorbell rings, splintering the thick silence.

"Yoo hoo!" Arianna calls.

I open the door, blinking against the harsh daylight burning into my retinas.

"Holy cow! Sidney, it's freezing in here! Why are you in the dark? Can I turn some lights on?" She doesn't wait for me to nod before rushing in. She thrusts a giant-sized bag of Reese's Pieces in my hands, which nearly makes me cry with gratitude.

I turn and follow her as she bustles around the kitchen, flipping on any switch she sees. She turns up the thermostat, and the furnace rumbles to life. "Got any hot chocolate? You need to warm up."

"Top cupboard, next to the sink." I sit down at the table. I've been trapped one hundred feet underwater, and Arianna's bright, bustling presence is dragging me back to the surface. "How was school?"

"Fine. Boring. Busy."

I shake my head. "Tell me the truth."

She bites her nails and looks at me, like she's trying to gauge what she should say, like she's forcing herself to be happy, for me. It makes me feel horrible.

"You know what it's like. They just walk by me, like I'm not even there. Like I don't even exist anymore."

More guilt. So much guilt piling up on me, I can barely stand it. This is happening to her because of me. "No one talks to you?"

"Some do. Lucas. That girl who's always taking pictures for yearbook, Lena McKenna? My Bible study friends, actually. That sort of surprised me. At first it was really bad, but not so much anymore. A lot of people hate Margot. More than I thought." She shrugs. "It's different, being away from them. I think it will be okay."

Margot is like an irritating mosquito compared to the last week. My hand slips to my stomach. A mosquito I need to squash. But not today. "If Margot does anything to you, I'll make her regret it."

"I believe it." She slants her eyes at me. "How're you doing? Are you okay?"

"Spectacular. Never better."

"I know. Stupid question." She bangs through the cupboards and pulls out a container of powdered chocolate and two mugs. "Sidney, there's almost no food in this house. What are you eating?"

"I still have three jars of peanut butter."

Arianna shakes her head. "I would laugh, except you aren't joking." She pours water into the mugs, puts them in the microwave and sets the timer. "Lucas sent me a note for you. I have no idea why he doesn't just text you like a normal person." She pulls it out of her pocket and hands it to me.

There are no words, only a sketch of what looks like a mangled heart. His drawing skills are as lackluster as his woodworking skills. My cheeks redden, and I shove it into my pocket. "Thanks."

"Is there anything new with the case?"

"I don't know. That stupid public defender attorney won't return my call. There was an arraignment, she pled guilty, but I don't know what happens next." They have no reason to suspect anything happened other than exactly what my mother says happened, whatever that is. Only Aaron can say differently. A small shiver passes through my body.

I'm still holding Ratty Bunny. I tuck him into my lap, fold my arms on the table, and rest my head in my hands.

"Can you—I mean, can you visit your mom? In jail?"

I picture her slumped on a hard bench, dressed in orange or stripes or whatever prison garb she's forced to wear. I see her sad and alone and scared. Then I see her dull, glassy eyes, the way her face had looked carefully blank when she turned away from me that day I tried to tell her the truth. Acid burns the back of my throat. "I don't know."

Arianna is silent for a moment. The microwave drones. "But—don't you want to see your mother?"

"I don't know," I say again.

"Why?"

Irritation flares through me at the barrage of questions. For half a second, it feels like an intrusion. But I force myself to remember that this is what friends do. Arianna is concerned about me, that's all. I lift my head and meet her gaze. "Because she's a shitty mom, that's why."

"She's going to jail for you. She obviously loves you."

"Does she?" I can't keep the bitterness out of my voice. "It's about eighteen years too late."

A chair squeals against the linoleum as Arianna sits down. "Sidney . . . your mom . . . I'm sure if she had known, things would have been different."

I snort. "Maybe in your perfect life."

"It's just that . . . she didn't know. I mean . . . right?" *No mother would let that happen,* she doesn't say.

"I don't know," I whisper as the weight of the question that's gone unanswered for years presses my body into the floor. Because the truth is, I don't know.

The microwave beeps. Arianna gets the mugs, stirs in the packets, brings the mugs back to the table. Neither of us touch them. "Please forgive me for asking this, but did you ever tell her?"

"I tried." The words taste like death on my tongue. "I don't even know if she heard me. She just—she brushed me off like I didn't matter, and then . . . I couldn't try again after that. I just couldn't."

"Oh, Sidney."

Shame curdles inside me. "Don't say you're sorry for me. Don't you dare. I don't need your pity."

Arianna sighs. "It's not pity. It's called empathy. You know, caring about somebody."

I force myself to breathe. My fingers dig into Ratty Bunny's matted fur. She's right. I know she's right. I can trust her. Ever since the night of the beach party, she's proven it a hundred times over. She doesn't deserve all my sharp edges. "Okay, fine. Aren't you going to drink your hot chocolate?"

She grimaces, but takes a small sip.

There's a long silence.

"Then why this?" Arianna asks. "Why is she doing this huge thing for you?"

The what-ifs leap up out of the darkness to torment my mind. This is the thing I've been wrestling with for the past week. A monster lying in wait. There's a trick, a snare, a trap in there somewhere. I just don't know where it is. I can't figure it out. She's not a manipulator like Frank. So what's her end game?

"I don't know," I say. I almost stop there, but I remember my commitment to changing, to being different. Dr. Yang would tell me to keep trusting Arianna, even when it's hard. So I tell her everything. "Most of the time, I think there must be some selfish reason I'm not seeing. My whole life, she was a crappy mom. She was never there for me. Why would she start now? But then there's this tiny part of me that thinks she did this huge, noble thing for me, that she sacrificed for me. But if that's true . . . if she really loves me and I'm letting her go to prison for me . . . then that makes me the monster, doesn't it?"

Arianna has tears in her eyes. She presses her hand over mine. "You are not the monster in this story. And as far as your mom goes, there's only one way to find out."

I shake my head. The thought is terrifying. I both long to know and dread finding out the truth. There's only one thing for sure: I'm not strong enough to handle the answer.

My phone buzzes. We both jump.

I reach for the phone. "Hello?"

"Hello?" a throaty female voice says. "I'm trying to reach Sidney Shaw."

"What do you want?"

"Oh. Hello, Sidney. This is Ellen. Ellie. Your Aunt Ellie. Do you remember me?"

I blink. "I remember you, I think. Ma always talked about you."

"She did, did she? Well. That's good. How are you? Are you all right? I mean, never mind. Of course, you can't be all right. I've been meaning to call you since I heard . . ." She clears her throat.

I stare at Arianna. She raises her eyebrows, her eyes widening.

"Anyway," Aunt Ellie continues. "I know this must be uncomfortable for you. I know I haven't been around much, or at all, really. You don't know me, but I'm your aunt. The lady from family services called to tell me what happened. I'm just—it's awful. I want to help."

I don't speak. I don't know what to say.

"If you want me to come, I'll come. I can book a flight for Friday."

"You're flying here?"

"If that's okay with you. I realize you're eighteen, but Frankie and Aaron shouldn't be stuck with strangers. After what you've been through, you need to stay together. I can help. I want to help."

My brain's stuffed with confetti. The woman's saying so many words I can't follow what she means. "You—are you coming to stay?"

"I don't want to disrupt the boys from their school and friends. I'm self-employed, so I can work from anywhere, and I have no pressing concerns right now. But I don't have to come if it's not what you want."

I picture their empty bedroom, the ghost-silent house. I made a commitment to them. To do whatever it takes. "I want them home."

"Then it's settled. I'll see you Friday. Don't worry about picking me up. I'll take a—what's it called? One of those personal taxis. And I'll be in contact with a lawyer. We'll get those boys back in no time, I promise."

"Okay." I swallow. "Thank you."

"We'll talk more when I come."

I click off the phone with shaking fingers.

"This is a good thing," Arianna declares after I fill her in on the other half of the conversation.

"Are you sure?" I wrap my hands around the mug of hot chocolate. There are too many changes happening at once. Anxiety tugs at me, tightens my chest.

"You miss your brothers, right?"

I nod. I miss them like an unraveling in my bones. "Where's she been all these years? Where was she when we had no money? Mom always said she was loaded. Or when Frank was terrorizing our family? When my mother was too drunk to get out of bed?"

"You'll have to ask her."

I feel an anger I can't explain. "Trust me, I will."

"But she's coming now. And you need what she has to offer. She can get your brothers back."

This woman with the throaty voice has no face. I can't even recall a picture of her. My memories of those few family get-togethers are a blur. I was so young. Some ghost of a memory flits through my brain: blue smoke swirling in sunlight, thick strong fingers gripping my much smaller ones, spinning around and around and around. It doesn't make sense. That Aunt Ellen is a figment of my imagination, as much as Ma's Ellie coming to her rescue was a figment of hers. Now she's real, leaping out of a misty past straight into the chaos of my life.

"I've been praying for something to happen, so your brothers could come home," Arianna says. "This *is* a good thing."

I hope it is.

That night, I don't sleep in my room. I can't. I grab an extra blanket from the coat closet and curl up on Aaron's bed, breathing in the scent of his sheets, Ratty Bunny tucked in my arms.

I stare at the ceiling for hours, thoughts tumbling around in my head. By the time sleep finally comes, I've decided I've got to get out of this house. I need to be brave. It's time to go back to school.

THIRTY-ONE

The next day, I go to school. The hallway is crushed with students, all laughing and whooping and yelling. It's mid-November, a week before Thanksgiving, and the natives are restless.

But a path opens before me like the parting of the Red Sea. People are quieting, staring, their eyes like lasers boring into me. They all know Frank is dead. They all believe my mother shot him.

I lift my chin, look straight ahead, and walk through the crowd.

"Sorry about your family," several people murmur. No one calls me names. No one whispers insults. They stare at me like I'm some wounded deer that's just appeared in their midst. They have no idea what to do or how to act, like I'm made of glass and will shatter if they try to touch me.

I both hate it and feel an immense relief. They're leaving me alone. The oppressive disdain and ridicule that's dogged me for years has dissipated. I can breathe the air again.

In Classic Lit, the whole class is already there. Miss Pierre scrawls notes on themes of *The Scarlet Letter* in red marker on the whiteboard, her back turned. Everyone cranes their necks and whispers behind their hands when I walk in. I don't care. I pull out my book and stare at it until the lines of text blur.

"Hey," Eli says. "How are you doing? You okay?"

I ignore him. I have no interest in pity attention from people who haven't bothered to talk to me in four years. That familiar hard, spiky feeling rises inside me.

Lucas sits next to me. I can feel him staring at me, and his presence is much harder to ignore. My skin prickles. Sweat beads beneath my armpits. Finally, I snap the book shut. "What are you looking at?"

He cocks his head. "I'm really glad you're back."

"I'm here. Big whup."

He doesn't ask if I'm okay, not in a classroom full of eavesdroppers. I'm grateful for that."Do you want to go running with me?"

I remember his lips on mine, what it felt like to be touched. My cheeks redden.

I also remember pushing him and running away like some freak lunatic. My cheeks redden. "And why should I do that?"

His eyes are kind. "Because it helps. When your whole life sucks rocks, it helps."

He's right. I do want to run. I want to slam my legs against the pavement, beat the air with my fists, run until everything is erased except for the road ahead of me, the burning in my lungs.

"Welcome back, class." Miss Pierre catches sight of me and she falters a bit. "Well—hello, Sidney. We're glad to have you back. We're so sorry for what you're going through. But we're happy you're here. Please let me know if you need anything."

I slump further into my seat.

Lucas passes me one of his notes. *I really want to see you. Will you run with me? Please circle yes or no. Insert smiley face here.* I can't believe he still wants to talk to me after how I treated him.

I stare at the note for a long time. I'm different. I'm going to be different.

I circle yes.

When I hand him the paper, his fingers touch mine. A snap of electricity passes between us. "Sorry, not sorry," he says with a lopsided grin.

"I didn't even know you were coming," Arianna whispers as I slide into my seat in Government class. "Your phone has a text feature, you know."

I shrug. "Surprise. I'm here."

"I would have walked you to your classes."

"I'm not in need of a chaperone, thank you very much."

"Are you okay?"

"I'm fantastic."

"Are you sure? Did anyone say anything to you?"

Her questions are making me antsy again. "I said I'm fine!"

"Ladies, is there a problem?" Mr. Cross asks gruffly.

"No, sir," Arianna says.

"Sorry," I whisper as soon as Mr. Cross's back is turned. "Just grumpy."

"I'm glad you're here," she whispers back.

I pull out the bag of Reese's Pieces I picked up from the cafeteria vending machine and put a handful on her desk. She stares at them like they'll give her cancer. "You eat them one at a time," I say. "They're good, really. I think they even have vitamins in them."

She grimaces at me, but I get her to eat ten of them. She helps me through the review questions for the chapter on the federal judiciary court system I missed.

Halfway through class, the school secretary walks in. She scans the room until her gaze settles on me. "Miss Shaw, Dr. Yang wants to see you in his office." Her throaty whisper is loud enough for the whole class to hear.

Arianna rolls her eyes. We exchange grins, like old friends in on a joke. It feels comfortable. It feels good.

I gather my things and make my way to Dr. Yang's office. He'll want me to talk about my feelings. I don't think I could talk about them even if I wanted to.

I have no idea what I'm feeling. It changes from day to day, minute to minute. I'm full of anger, shame, and grief. Sometimes I'm numb; sometimes I'm so achingly sad it steals my breath away. But I'm also relieved. Frank is out of my life. And then I'm plagued with guilt.

I steel myself before I go in, making sure I've got my armor on.

I sit in the same blue chair I always do. He sits behind his desk like he always does. He's wearing a pea-green flannel suit that looks like a throwback from the eighties. There are dark circles beneath his eyes. "Good morning, Sidney."

"I hope you haven't been in mourning over me. I've gotta say it. You don't look so good, Doc."

"We're here to talk about you, Sidney. It's good to see you. I've missed you."

"I highly doubt it. Reese's?" I hold out a handful of the half-melted candy.

"No, thank you. How are you doing?"

I hate having to answer that awful question over and over. "I'm stupendous."

He frowns at me. "Sidney. Your mother killed your father. A huge bomb just exploded in the middle of your life."

I wince. "Yeah, I'm aware."

"How do you feel?"

Guilty as hell, but there's no way I can tell him that. "I'm devastated. I can barely get out of bed in the morning. Frank promised to fly me to Belize and buy me a Mercedes for my graduation. Now what am I going to do?"

He just raises his eyebrows at me.

"Wrong answer? I feel like somebody should throw a party. Preferably with little fruity drinks or a spiked punchbowl."

He steeples his fingers beneath his jaw. "Sidney, can you tell me how you're really feeling?"

I wish there was a window to look at. There's nothing but this horrid chair and Dr. Yang staring at me with his unsettling gaze.

I think about what Aunt Ellie told me yesterday after she got off the phone with the defense attorney. Ma's case is waiting on the presentence investigation report, which the judge will use to determine her sentence.

Defense counsel and the prosecution have already agreed on a charge—murder in the second. Ma refused to say a bad word about Frank, even when a battered wife syndrome defense might have lessened her prison time. Even if she had, it would've been a hard sell. Frank never broke any bones. Terror and humiliation were his favorite weapons, wounds that didn't leave visible scars.

I remember Aaron and Frankie. How I need to change, do better. And it's not going to happen if I keep making up crap. I take a deep breath. "Mostly, I'm relieved that he's gone."

"Tell me about that."

"He was a drunk. And mean. He was a lousy father."

"Some people would be pretty shocked by those statements," Dr. Yang says carefully.

"People think just because he had sticky fingers and could run like hell twenty years ago, that makes him a good guy. A hero. Or maybe they only know what they want to know, only see what they want to see."

"It sounds like that makes you angry."

I clench and unclench my fingers on my lap. "Yeah, it does."

"Is there a part of you that wishes he was still here? Do you miss him?"

"He's not here, so it's a moot point, isn't it?"

"You're not answering the question, Sidney."

"Yes," I say softly.

In some terrible, twisted way, I do. Before it all went to hell four years ago, there were some good memories nestled like small pearls in the darkness. My traitorous heart aches for the father who taught me poker, who told me every curse word when I was six and laughed his ass off when I repeated them in my little girl lisp, who told funny stories and brought crazy gifts whenever he returned from his trips, who took me to the range and taught me to shoot before I was nine, who bragged to his buddies about how clever and pretty I was when I was just a gangly, awkward kid, how I felt ten feet tall around him.

But all that came before. Before I grew breasts and hips and he saw something he wanted to own, to consume. Before he turned savage.

If I let myself think about those things, my heart becomes a black hole sucking me down to a nothingness I know I'll never escape from. "Can we talk about something else, now?"

"How do you feel about your mom?"

My mind shuts down. That I can't talk about, not with Dr. Yang, or I'll fall to pieces all over his nubby blue chair. She's the shadow that haunts my every waking moment, my dreams, and my nightmares. The same questions torment me, over and over. Why did she do what she did? Was she really sacrificing herself for me? Was it because she loved me, after all? Is it possible she really didn't know about Frank?

I swallow hard. "I meant a totally different topic, Doc. I just—I can't right now."

He nods in understanding. "Of course. How is the journal working for you?"

"I've been writing—er, drawing in it every night. Sorry."

"Art can be its own version of therapy. For this week, can you try to fit a few sentences in there?"

"About what?"

"How about some suggestions or thoughts on how to deal with emotions like grief and sadness constructively? Of course, if your inspiration takes you elsewhere, by all means, go with it."

I nod as the bell rings. "I'll try."

"I really am here to help, you know," he says as I pull myself out of the blue chair. He doesn't mention the apology letter. I figure I've gotten a free pass. "You can talk to me anytime."

"Thanks, Doc," I say. And I mean it this time.

THIRTY-TWO

I'm sitting at the kitchen table, scribbling chemistry formulas and eating handfuls of Reese's Pieces from the supersized bag Arianna brought me when the doorbell rings.

It's the woman from that night. I recognize her immediately. The female detective.

"Detective Henricksen." She's dressed in black slacks and a brown trench coat. Her skin is dry and cracked around her eyes. She smiles and half-lifts her badge from the front pocket of her coat. Behind her, the first flakes of snow bleed from the sky. "May I come in?"

I wipe my mouth and step back to allow the detective in. "You must be wondering why I'm here."

I stare at her, silent. The hairs on my neck prickle.

The detective clears her throat. "I wanted to check up on you. You've been through a rough time."

"Uh huh."

"I'm very sorry for your loss."

My fingers squeeze into fists. "Thank you."

She flashes me a kind, disarming smile. "I'm sorry to be a bother at such a difficult time. When a case is winding down, I usually go through the files one more time, just to tie up loose ends and such. I'm sure you understand."

What does it matter whether I understand or not? I nod stiffly.

"May I have a drink of water?"

I flush. "Of course." She follows me into the kitchen and sits down while I pour her a drink.

"Thank you." She sets down a pen and notepad and takes a sip. She looks directly at me. Her steady gaze is unnerving. It must be a cop thing. I know better than to look away. "Why don't you have a seat? I'm sure you'll be more comfortable."

I don't see any way to refuse without drawing suspicion, so I obey.

The detective smiles. "I was hoping you would be so kind as to clear up a few things for me."

My lips are so dry they feel like they're splitting open. "Sure."

"Your friend provided your alibi. Arianna Torrès?"

"She didn't lie, if that's what you're implying."

Detective Henricksen raises her eyebrows.

Damn it. *Stop talking.* I've watched enough TV to know my own words can weave the rope they'll use to hang me. I have to calm the hell down. I force a smile. "Yes, Arianna and I were together all afternoon, from after school until we came home and found the police cars."

Detective Henricksen shifts in her seat, leans forward a little. "When I was looking through the evidence, I reread some of the witness interviews. Your little brother. He changed his story a few times."

I struggle to keep my voice even and normal-sounding. "He's eight."

"So you're saying he's unreliable?"

"I'm saying he's eight. Maybe he was scared and got a little mixed up."

"Fair enough. When the officer interviewed him, Aaron said he was playing with his scooter outside, down the road. And you made him a 'peanut butter cheese wrap.'" She glances down at her notes. "Then he said no, he made it himself. When the officer asked him again, he again said he made it, you weren't home."

My gut clenches. "So what's the problem?"

"Every case has its . . . irregularities. Unlike Law & Order and CSI, not everything wraps up into a neat little bow."

"There you go."

"Can your eight-year-old brother make his own food?"

He never has. I always make his food for him. But I sidestep the question. "It's easy to make. Tortillas, cheese, and peanut butter, rolled up and stuck in the microwave."

She glances at her notes again. "Does he usually make his own food?"

Where is she going with this? "Not often."

"Well, see, here's the thing. Your brother also said he only heard one gunshot."

I don't move. I don't blink. "What does that mean?"

"I just wonder why Aaron only heard one gunshot, when your father was shot two times. Can you help me out with this?"

I clear my throat. I feel like I'm walking into a trap I can't see. "Um, I don't know. I wasn't there."

She taps her pen against her chin thoughtfully. "Unless . . . perhaps the timing was spread out. One gunshot earlier, while he's down the street playing. One killer. Then another gunshot, later. When he's closer to the house to hear it. Maybe a second perp. Maybe a cover-up?"

My heart hammers against my ribcage so loud the whole world must hear it. Heat flushes through me. I have to hold it together. I cannot fall apart, not here, not now. "Why would someone kill my dad and then cover it up?"

"I was hoping you had an idea."

I can barely force out the words. My throat is coated in acid. I'm going to vomit. "My mother confessed. You people already caught the killer." My voice snags on the word 'killer.'

Detective Henricksen nods. "You're right, of course." She tugs her auburn hair out of its bun and re-twists it, smoothing any stray hairs. "You know, a few of your father's friends we spoke with mentioned your father had a temper on him. And he had quite the beer habit."

"I guess so."

"Sometimes in a case, there are extenuating circumstances. Things a judge would be very sympathetic to."

What is she trying to say? "You could try talking to my mom."

The detective smiles. Her smile is kind, her expression warm. "We have. But right now, I'm talking with you. I think I can help you, if you're willing to talk to me."

"Thanks, but I'm okay."

She looks down at her notes again and frowns slightly, a line appearing between her brows. "Have you heard of GSR?"

"Gunshot residue."

"Of course, you have. You're a smart girl. So you also know that GSR leaves a fine, imperceptible film on everything near the location of the gunshot, but especially on the shooter's hands."

I try to keep my face from betraying anything. But I want to leap up and scrub my hands until they're red and raw.

As if she's reading my thoughts, she tilts her head and smiles ruefully. "Unfortunately for us, it only lasts for several hours. We did find GSR on your mother's hands, though."

"That makes sense, since she was the shooter."

Her kind expression never changes. "We also found another fingerprint on the gun. Yours."

Fear jolts through me. "I shot that gun all the time at the range. You can check with Reggie. He's seen me."

After a long second, she leans forward and speaks so quietly I almost can't hear her. "I wonder, if we'd tested your hands for GSR that night, would we have found something?"

I tremble from the effort of remaining sitting, of acting calm when I feel anything but. My thoughts flap around in my head, banging wildly against my skull.

"You can tell me the truth. It will feel better to get it off your chest. What happened? Did he get drunk and you were just protecting yourself? Was he going after your mom? Or maybe little Aaron?"

I need to think. And fast. Do I have the right to make her leave? Suddenly I wish I'd paid more attention during those Bill of Rights discussions in Government. I make myself sound confident, even though I'm about to throw up all over her trench coat. "I think it's time for you to go. My aunt will be here soon."

Detective Henricksen smiles benignly. "I truly want to help you, Sidney. If you work with me, I know any judge in the county would be sympathetic to you."

"Please," I force out, standing up.

She stands with me, gathers her things, and hands me a business card. "I hope you'll think about our discussion. I'll let myself out."

I shut the door behind her and sag against it. I cover my mouth with my hands, gagging, gasping, gulping in air that just won't come.

I see Frank's face, his cold marble eyes. I feel the gun, the heft of it, in my hands.

I crumple the card in my fist. But I don't throw it away. I can't. I am not innocent.

I am the guilty one, the one getting away with murder, the one letting someone else take the punishment. My own mother is in jail because of me.

Guilt and shame spike through me, pinning me to the floor like one of Jasmine's butterflies to their display boards.

THIRTY-THREE

I go to Arianna's house after school. She makes me sit at the island while she cooks. She flips through a box of recipes scrawled on old three-by-five cards.

"There's Pinterest for that," I say, blowing air into my frozen hands.

"These are family recipes dating back to my great-grandmother. My *abuelita* used to make the best flan. And *arepas*. But my mom? Not so much. Here we go." She pulls out a faded, dented card. *"Sudado de pollo.* You like chicken and rice? Oh, and *bananos calados*. Colombian-style fried bananas. Not nearly as exotic, but I guess it'll do."

"I don't even know what you just said. Other than it must be fancy. Don't make that for me."

"I'm making it for me. It reminds me of my *abuelita*. And it calms me. I basically cook all the family meals now. Not like we actually eat as a family."

"Are you eating? Like, actual food?" I ask pointedly. Her leggings look baggy.

She ignores me as she bangs through the cupboards and the fridge, pulling out ingredients. "I think we have everything we need here already."

"Can I help at least?"

She shakes her head. "No thanks. I love doing this." She chops up onions, red peppers, fresh garlic, and tomatoes. She pours some oil in a large pot and adds in the chopped veggies, salt and pepper. "Now tell me what's going on. Besides the obvious, I mean. Something else happened."

I give her a hard look. "You're terribly perceptive for a bobble-headed beauty queen."

She smiles grimly. "I'm multi-talented, too."

I tell her about the detective's visit, what she said. Her frown deepens the more I talk. She adds pink chicken legs, water, cumin powder, and something called Sazòn Goya spice to the pot and stands at the stove, stirring.

"What about Aaron?"

"He lied for me, but he didn't know there were two gunshots."

"Poor kid."

I stare at my hands, twirl my rings around my fingers. My thoughts are rolling around in my head like marbles. I can't get them into a straight line. "Maybe I should call her."

"Call who?"

"The detective."

Arianna puts down the wooden spoon and stares at me. "Are you crazy?"

"Maybe. I don't know. Maybe it's the right thing to do."

"Sidney Shaw? Wondering about the right thing to do?"

"I have my moments. I don't know. I hate making Aaron lie for me. I hate making you lie for me. I hate that my own mother is taking the punishment instead of me. Maybe the detective is right."

Arianna sets up a rice steamer and pours in two cups of dry white rice. "Or maybe she's just trying to get into your head."

My stomach cramps. My mother is going to prison. She is sitting in a jail cell, right now, surrounded by concrete walls. She is guilty of many things, but not this. What is she thinking? Why is she doing this? Why is she sacrificing herself for me? And can I really let her do that? How can I stay here, free, day after day, and do nothing? "It's working."

Arianna turns and faces me. Her hands press against her stomach, right over her scar. "Why did you do what you did?"

"To make it stop. To protect my family."

"Are you doing that? Are your brothers safe?"

"Yes, but—"

She chops the round yellow potatoes so hard the knife sticks in the wooden cutting board. She dumps the potatoes in the pot and turns toward me, her face wrinkled in concentration. "If you were sitting in a prison cell right now, would the boys be safe with your mom?"

I imagine the boys huddled in their rooms, scared and hungry. I imagine Frankie having to make the meals and clean up after Ma. Would he always remember to stub out her cigarettes? Would he be able to get to a grocery store without a car? Would he be strong enough to get her into bed when she passed out on the couch or the floor? "She barely remembers to feed herself, let alone them."

"So maybe this, right here, is the best possible outcome. The most just."

I shake my head, start to protest, but she interrupts me.

"Your mother chose to confess. Maybe you need to talk to her. To really know why, before you can find peace with this."

"I don't know if I can." Just the thought paralyzes me with guilt and terror. My muscles tense. Dark anxiety coils in the pit of my stomach.

"Just remember, whenever you start to doubt, you aren't sending her to prison. She chose to be there."

I let her words sink in. "This is awfully weird coming from you. I thought you'd be all gung-ho about God's justice and punishment for sins and honesty is the best policy."

"God is just," Arianna says simply. "And God's justice isn't always man's justice, either. Don't forget that. God isn't bound by man-made laws and judges and notions of punishment."

"What does that even mean?"

Arianna takes out bananas, butter, brown sugar, orange juice, and cinnamon. She peels and cuts four bananas in half, then lengthwise with quick, sure hands. She's frowning and chewing on her lower lip.

"In a better world, you never would've had to pull the trigger. Someone would have listened to you and stopped it. Or your father wouldn't have done what he did in the first place. We live in a world where girls are raped, but the rapist is a rockstar college athlete, so he gets thirty days in jail. That's not justice. But we'll all face God for the things we've done before it's all over. And He will mete out justice which is fair and true. And mercy, where mercy should be offered. That's all I know."

"You sound so sure."

"I am."

"You never doubt?"

"About this? No." She adds the bananas, brown sugar, and cinnamon to the skillet, stirring constantly. She adds the orange juice, and I watch the bananas darken in the pan. "You know," she says slowly, "Rahab lied to save the lives of the spies she had hidden in her attic. So the Israelites saved her, and she was praised in the Bible."

"Is that your whole plan in all of this? To get honor in heaven, more rubies on your crown?"

She laughs. "I wish."

"Why do you say it like that? You're like the most perfect person I know. Minus Lucas."

"Very funny. Do you not remember the depression, the cutting, and the eating disorder? All beneath a cheery Christian veneer? Oh, and to top it off, I preach love but I'm really a coward who watches her friends bully people relentlessly and doesn't do a thing about it."

"Former friends," I say.

"Former friends." The corners of her mouth lift, but it's more grimace than smile.

Suddenly I want to make things better for her, to do something to ease the pain behind her eyes. "You were that person. But you're not anymore. You made a choice to do something."

"I guess you're right."

"I'm always right."

She places both hands on the countertop, as if to steady herself.

"Are you okay? Are you dizzy?"

"It'll pass. It always does."

I watch her for a long moment. "Shouldn't God save you from this?"

"What do you mean?"

"This. Whatever's wrong with you. Isn't that the whole spiel? You give God your money and your faith, and He blesses you and takes away your problems."

She shakes her head. "I have faith in God because He loves me, in spite of all this. He never promises to take it away. Just to help you through. Until Heaven."

"Well, that sounds like a raw deal."

"It's not."

Arianna truly believes. However misguided, she is sincere. There is a kind of power in believing in something larger than yourself, I think. Maybe salvation.

She takes a deep breath and keeps moving. She puts the bananas on little dessert plates. "The ice cream will melt. We'll add it later." She spoons the rice on a plate, then adds the chicken and potato mixture. She adds a fork and pushes it across the island toward me. "Eat."

"You too." The whole time I was living at her house, she barely ate anything other than rice cakes, egg whites, carrot sticks, and Diet Coke. Only when I sat next to her would she eat a few small bites of whatever elaborate, authentic Colombian meal she'd created. Her parents never noticed or said anything. They were barely even home.

Just the smell makes my mouth water. And it tastes as delicious as it smells. "I've never had a better meal than this," I tell her around a mouthful of succulent chicken drenched in sauce. "Better than Bill's, and he makes the best mushroom burger on the planet."

She smiles wistfully. She scoops up a forkful of saucy rice, but doesn't take a bite. I can't imagine not eating, the will it must take to deny primal hunger.

"Do you want to die?" I ask her.

"What? No. Of course not."

"Are you punishing yourself because you don't think you're good enough? By starving yourself?"

She stares down at her plate. "I don't know. Maybe. Stupid, right?"

I know a thing or two about self-punishment. "Stupid, but understandable."

"It's easy to think how stupid it is in my head. To say it out loud. But not in my heart, deep down inside me."

I spear a chunk of potato, stare at it. "You think if you punish yourself enough, you can pay for your sins. Then the guilt will stop tormenting you."

"Something like that."

I think of the ladder of scars up and down my legs. "It doesn't work."

"I think I know that, too."

"It's something else. Something even harder than hurting your own body."

She looks at me, tears glistening in her thick eyelashes. "What?"

I shake my head. "I'm still working that out."

She just gazes down at her fork. She looks so sad, so tired and lost. It's hard to imagine now how I thought she was so perfect, so shallow and vain. Here in front of me, I can see all her broken places, all the hollowed-out parts of herself she's sacrificed for others.

Even now, she's sacrificing a part of herself for me. It makes me all warm inside, like a swig of hot apple cider melting me all the way down, but also guilty as hell. And scared for her. Like me, she doesn't have anything more to give away. I push my plate over to her. "Please eat something."

She cuts a slice of fried banana into tiny morsels. She looks at me, sees I'm still watching her, then gingerly lifts her fork to her mouth. I sit with her until she finishes the whole piece.

We sit, side by side. And for a while, at least, this is enough.

THIRTY-FOUR

The first week back at school, I have to stay after every day to take my make-up exams. Whether I actually did okay or my teachers took pity on me, I somehow manage to get mostly C's. Except for Badminton, which I'm failing. Figures.

I'm heading to the cafeteria to grab some Reese's Peanut Butter Cups before class when I hear the familiar buzz in the air, the hush and murmur and shuffle of bodies heading toward something interesting. Further down the hall, several people cluster around the end of the bank of lockers. The hairs on the back of my neck stand on end.

I elbow several people to get through. There's Margot, in black leggings and a tight, shimmery sweater dress, her arms folded over her chest. A catty, malicious smile plays across her cherry red lips. She's surrounded by her usual crew. Arianna shrinks against her locker, her face pale.

I shove past Nyah and Eli and stand next to Arianna. "What the hell?"

Arianna's eyes widen when she sees me. I can't tell if she's relieved or worried about what I might do next. Probably both.

Margot raises her eyebrows. "Look who it is."

My muscles tense. "What's your problem?"

Jasmine and Isabel stand to Margot's left. I look at Jasmine, and she shakes her head slightly, some sort of signal to me. I don't know how to interpret it. An apology? A warning? Or nothing at all?

Margot pulls lip gloss out of a pocket in her sweater dress and daubs it on her mouth. "We were explaining a few things about loyalty, trust, and the meaning of friendship, which some people don't seem to get at all. In fact, certain girls scurry around here like filthy little rats. Traitors. Repulsive, don't you think?"

"That's kind of pathetic, Margot," I say. "Now get out of our way."

Margot's lips twitch. "I just think it's so sweet how you two social pariahs have become little besties. Sweet or sickening. I can't decide."

"I don't care what you think. And neither does Arianna. Just leave us alone."

Margot cocks her head, as if studying me. "I've been wanting to offer my condolences to you and your family."

I know she's formulating some nasty insult, but I bite my tongue. "Then why don't you?"

"I was giving you your space, which you obviously need more of. Are you always this rude and sarcastic?"

"No. Sometimes I'm asleep."

A few people laugh.

Margot glowers at me. "Can't you even have a functional conversation like a human being?"

"Next time I have a conversation with an actual human being, I'll let you know."

Eli snorts. Then he says, "Margot."

There's a small crowd around us now. Margot tilts her head toward him but keeps her gaze lasered in on me. "What?"

"Leave her alone."

Her perfectly arched brows shoot up in surprise. "I'm simply offering her some friendly advice—"

"I think she's had enough advice," he says.

"What he said." I jerk my thumb back at Eli.

Margot's eyes narrow to slits. She jabs her finger against my chest.

"Don't think this is over. You're the same trashy skank you were before. Only, now we know where you get it. Your mother is a murderous, trailer-skank psycho."

The crowd gives an audible gasp. I take a step forward, until I'm inches from her face. Instinctively, she moves back. The monster is there, curled inside me, demanding to be let out. My pulse thuds in my throat, my hands balled into fists. I'm so hot my skin feels singed.

There's a shift in the air around me. This doesn't feel the same as before. People stare at Margot, not at me. I have their sympathy. I'm the ghost-girl, burdened by tragedy. Margot's bullying tactics finally reveal what she really is—ugly to her core.

My mouth fills with a dozen scathing cut-downs. I could slice her to pieces right here, without lifting a finger. The crowd is on my side. I never took my revenge for the beach. I could punch her, smash her pretty nose, yank out chunks of her hair, drag her to the ground.

Nobody would stop me.

If you stoop to their level, they win. That thing Lucas said at the beach echoes in my head. I have to be different. I can't keep doing this. I can't keep letting my anger control me, not even to give someone like Margot the thrashing she deserves.

Instead, I take a breath and step back. "Nah, I think I'll pass."

Margot's face darkens in fury. She looks like a fading, wild-eyed queen, desperate to hold on to her crown. "You little bitch."

She glances at Nyah to back her up, but Nyah doesn't say anything. Her mouth puckers like she's sucking on something sour.

Eli grabs her arm. "It's seriously time to go."

Arianna's beside me, anchoring me. I look at Jasmine again. Her eyes are rimmed with red. She seems miserable.

I imagine my legs, pounding to freedom. I imagine electric blue butterfly wings, glinting in sunlight. "See you around, Jasmine."

I grab Arianna's arm, and we walk through the crowd. As soon as we round the corner, Arianna hugs me.

"I can't even describe how much I love you right now." Her cheeks are bright, her eyes shining. "That was savage. You took her down like a boss. And you didn't even have to do anything."

Mr. Cross pokes his head out of the doorway. "Are you two planning on making it to class today, ladies? Because it seems like there's a party going on out here some of us are missing out on."

"Yes, sir," Arianna says between giggles.

"Good one, Mr. Cross," I say.

He rolls his eyes. "Just come to class, please."

Arianna and I exchange looks as we head into the classroom. She winks at me, and I smile back. A real smile, even in the midst of all the grief and chaos, like I haven't felt in days, or maybe even weeks. It feels better than I can say.

THIRTY-FIVE

In my nightmares, Frank comes for me. His eyes haunt me, stalking my dreams. Beautiful and cobalt blue, but flat and hard. Lifeless. Like marbles.

I wake up fast, sucking in air, drenched in sweat. My heart thuds against my rib cage. My fingers scratch the sheets into my fists. It's just a dream. I blink rapidly until the images fade away from the backs of my eyelids.

The bedroom is dark. The lights from a passing car arc across the far wall. Frankie's dresser, his bed, and the opened closet door shift and take indistinct shapes. Everything is draped in shadow.

There is no one here. I'm safe. My father is dead. He can't do anything to me anymore. Slowly, my fingers release the sheets. He's dead. Still, his eyes haunt me—his glassy, lifeless eyes. Eyes that never stop staring at me even when I close my eyelids.

My father's face swims in my mind's eye, and behind his floats my mother's. I ignore Frank, block his eyes from my mind.

Ma is harder. Susan Shaw has multiple faces: one blank and stupid, the mouth slack, eyes rolling back in her head from the alcohol and the pills; another face hard and sharp, eyes filled with scorn and jealousy.

And then her last face, the smile quick to appear, the eyes bright and cheerful.

Which one is my mother? Which one is real? Which one is sitting in jail, sacrificing her life for mine?

I'm done sleeping for tonight. I slip out of Aaron's bed and pad into the kitchen. The window over the sink gleams at me like a lidless black eye. I open the fridge and pour myself a glass of milk. My hands are still trembling.

The chair makes a scratching sound on the linoleum as I sit down at the new table Aunt Ellie bought yesterday. She arrived three days ago. She's nothing like I expected. She's a whirlwind spinning into my life, kicking up a flurry of dust and light in a house filled with secrets and darkness.

"Sidney?"

My gaze jerks up. "It's you."

Aunt Ellie flicks on the light switch. She steps into the kitchen as she pulls her silky sapphire blue kimono around her large midsection. Everything about Aunt Ellie is big—her height, her girth, her booming laugh, her commanding presence. Her burgundy hair, usually smoothed into a glossy helmet to her chin, is smushed on one side. Her long fingernails are painted a glossy plum purple. She wears billowy satin shirts with bold patterns and colorful slacks and skirts. She looks years younger than Ma, though she's five years older.

"Difficulty sleeping, dear?"

"Something like that." I'm still not used to this woman. She keeps up an exhausting storm of conversation and activities. It's like being dragged behind a truck.

In her first three days here, Aunt Ellie took me grocery shopping multiple times, buying more food than the cupboards can hold, until dozens of soup cans, bunches of fresh fruit, and boxes of pasta are crammed on the counters.

We spent two entire days picking out a brand-new table, new comforters for the boys, sheet sets for all the beds, and a new dresser for me to replace the one the cops broke. She's rearranged all the furniture in the house to "transform some of this depressing energy sapping the joy out of life."

I kept trying to pay for things, my anxiety rising every time she threw some expensive item into the cart. "Use your money for college," she told me finally, exasperated. "I'm a single woman with a shopping addiction. Let me shop!"

After a while, I stopped arguing with her.

Until she tried to take me clothes shopping after shuffling around in my closet, groaning in dismay. But I swore I'd never wear the frilly, flowery girly-clothes she picked out. I'm keeping my baggy jeans and oversized sweatshirts, thank you very much.

Aunt Ellie sighs excessively and passes her hand over her eyes whenever I come out in the morning. "You've got to look the way you want to feel, honey," she says. Whatever that's supposed to mean.

So far, our conversations have been about the weather, whether the couch should go in front of the living room window, what color best energizes an east-facing kitchen, what to do when the boys get back. In the evenings, she scrolls through eBay and Etsy, searching for more costume jewelry to add to her collection. Apparently, she makes, buys, and resells vintage costume jewelry. As a job.

When she's not shopping in person or online, she's on the phone with various court and DHS employees. She's filled out reams of paperwork. A worker came out to the house and asked a bunch of questions. We're just waiting for approval.

Sometimes I catch Aunt Ellie looking at me, her mouth pursed and her eyes hooded, like she wants to say something more important than lamenting over my fashion choices.

"Sorry if I woke you up," I say now.

"Oh, no worries, dear. I couldn't sleep either. Often happens. You mind company?"

My knee-jerk reaction is a resounding *no*. This woman is exhausting. But she's also family. She's dropped everything to come and stay for who-knows-how-long and help with the boys. I'm grateful, and I need to show it. "Make yourself at home. Literally."

Aunt Ellie opens the fridge and pours her own glass of milk. She gets a plate, a spoon, a jar of peanut butter, and a loaf of bread. "Ah. Now we're talking."

Even though she's fully clothed, she almost looks naked without her usual jewelry. I'm pretty sure half of her suitcase must've been packed full of vintage costume necklaces, earrings, bracelets, and brooches. Her earrings are giant dangling hoops inlaid with rubies and sapphires, emerald tear-drop pendants with tiny squares of frosted glass, or carved turquoise rimmed with filigree gold whorls.

She wears bracelets and bangles as thick as her wrist, inlaid with brilliant, peacock-feather colors in swirls, drops, and circles. She likes rings, like I do, but hers boast rubies as big as my knuckles. They're shimmery lemon-colored glass or carved amethyst cubes set in aged sterling, rose gold, and pewter. She told me she likes to mix the delicate, intricately designed Victorian style with large and chunky retro pieces and the geometric lines and bright colors of art nouveau. This woman is serious about her jewelry.

She hands me the spoon. "You like your peanut butter crunchy, right?"

I nod, surprised she's noticed me sneaking the jar into the boys' bedroom.

"I love my peanut butter, too, but I need something to go with it, or it clogs up my throat, you know what I'm saying?" She sits down opposite me and spreads peanut butter on two slices of bread. She passes the jar to me. She takes a bite, pauses, and gazes at me. Her lips are thin and pale without her smudged raspberry lipstick bleeding into the fine lines around her mouth. "Did you have a nightmare?"

"Yeah," I admit, though I don't elaborate.

Aunt Ellie laughs mirthlessly. "I absolutely despise nightmares. I haven't had one in ages. Oh, once in a while one might crop up, after I've let myself watch one of those gruesome criminal shows. No, my doctor says I have an active mind. Whatever that means. Kept my last husband up to all hours with my tossing and turning. Just a regular insomniac, I guess."

"Oh." I dig up a spoonful of peanut butter.

Aunt Ellie sighs and takes a swig of milk. She wipes away the white mustache with the back of her hand. "I suppose you probably have some questions for me. This seems as good a time as any, seeing as we both can't sleep and no malls are open."

The corner of my mouth twitches. "Was that what the shopping was for? A distraction?"

"Guilty as charged. I guess I just wasn't sure . . ." She folds her arms over her formidable bosom and gazes up at the ceiling. "Oh, hell. I was putting it off as long as I could. It's a trait of mine, you'll see."

I lick the spoon. Aunt Ellie talks enough for three people. Usually I just sit and listen, and at the end, she thinks we've had a conversation, either not realizing or not caring I've barely spoken a word.

"Last time I saw you, you were a little thing in pigtails. Aaron wasn't even born yet. You've grown up to be quite lovely, in spite of insisting on dressing like a boy. I've wanted to visit so many times . . . I can't count the number of times I've picked up the phone and stood there staring at it like a dummy, thinking of calling Susan and never doing it. Your mother made things complicated. She was never an easy person to love. And then, after Frank . . . Well, there it is."

"What do you mean?"

"He wouldn't let any family visit, or let Susan and you kids come see us. I thought you knew that."

"Mom said you disowned us. After she dropped out of college to run off with Frank. She made it sound romantic."

"No. Never. We never approved, that's true." She looks up again, as if she can see the story she's about to tell un-scrolling on the ceiling. "At first, he was just her newest boyfriend, albeit more handsome and charming than the rest. But she wouldn't call us, and then she dropped all of her classes and said she was moving to some hokey town to shack up with him. Your grandma and I didn't want her to quit. It was the only thing she had going for her . . . but Susan was a bit odd, even then.

"Sometimes she didn't leave her dorm room for days. Mom or I would bring her food. Other times she'd call us in the middle of the night blabbering on about something or other, and we could hardly understand her. She started saying we were bad for her, we were trying to hurt her. She'd lock the door when I came to visit.

"Then one day, she just wasn't there anymore. She left everything. Didn't even pack more than a suitcase. Just left with him. We didn't hear anything for over a year. Mom called the cops, but what could they do? Susan wrote us a letter saying she'd married Frank and there was nothing we could do to stop her. She said she was a mother now and we shouldn't try to find her. And I'm ashamed to say it, but we listened to her.

"She'd call sometimes, when Frank was away. Told us where she lived, sent a few photos of you and Frankie. We got her to visit once or twice, early on. I even came to visit, do you remember?"

I stare at Aunt Ellie, who is my family, my blood, but also a stranger. "I remember someone holding my hand, blue smoke, and spinning around in the sunshine. Was that you?"

She smiles, a tiny web of wrinkles crinkling around her eyes. "You remember that? I bought you a tire swing for the maple tree out front. Took forever to set it up, and when I came inside, Susan had drunk herself into a stupor. In the middle of the day. Things were stressful in the house. Frank didn't want me there. I came into her room, and you were tugging at your ma's nightgown, trying to get her up and out of bed. You were so tiny, so earnest, it about broke my heart. I grabbed your hand and took you outside the dark house, into the sunshine. I spun you on the tire swing for an hour, at least. My arms still get tired thinking about it. You laughed and laughed. Then Frank came back, and he was so angry I'd done something that made you happy. He kicked me out right then. Tore down the tire swing. I don't imagine you ever saw it again."

I shook my head. I don't remember the swing; only the spinning, the warmth of the sunlight dappling my skin, the blue smoke rippling like ribbons in the air.

"I bought you a ring, too. You were so taken with mine. Liked to wear them around the house, even though they were so big you could barely keep them on your itty-bitty fingers."

A memory skates around the edges of my mind. "The one with the blue plastic flower."

She smiles. "You remember. I didn't have money then, or I would've gotten you something better. I'm just tickled pink you still wear it."

The hairs on my arms prickle. I never thought about why I like wearing rings all the time. I never thought it might be because of an aunt I barely remember.

Aunt Ellie waves her hand. "I'm glad he didn't take that from you. He never liked me. I was trying to get her to leave him, and he knew it. I should have done more. But I didn't know how bad he was hurting Susan. He just took her away. That's all we knew. I—I was living my own life, and she said she wanted it this way.

"Susan . . . she only ever had eyes for the bad ones. Our father was a drunk. A mean one. Susan escaped by running straight into the arms of men just as bad as our daddy. I suppose she felt taken care of. She was used to being controlled. Instead of looking for something else, something better, she stuck with what she knew. It's a common enough story, I suspect."

I swallow the rest of my milk and stare into the bottom of the empty glass. It's hard to imagine Ma as a girl, just a bit older than me. She was nineteen when she ran off with Frank, me already in her belly.

I think about my mother, and Frank, and a lifetime of regret. The fact Ma's own father—my grandfather—was a mean drunk. She ran from him straight into the arms of the devil. Handsome and charming as hell, but a devil all the same. Generations of addiction and dysfunction, going how far back? To my grandparents, at least. Probably further. The thought is depressing as hell.

Aunt Ellie's gaze slides past me toward the window. The window over the sink is beginning to lighten, the earliest hints of morning threading through the night.

"Is it really that late? Or early, I should say." She touches my shoulder as she gets up. "Thanks for the talk, dear." Though I've hardly said anything at all.

THIRTY-SIX

On the Wednesday afternoon before Thanksgiving break, I'm on my way to Government when my phone rings. I tug it out of my backpack and stop in the middle of the hallway, staring at the unknown number as my classmates stream around me, laughing and shouting at each other.

For a second, I wonder if it's Bill. I haven't called him back or gone in to work since it happened. I want to work, but my escape plan has changed. The boys are my priority now. Besides, Bill was Frank's friend. The thought of looking into his eyes, of facing his grief and knowing I've caused it, sends dread swirling through me and ties my stomach in knots.

But it's not Bill. I wait for it to go to voicemail. The bell rings, the hallway clearing as people rush to their classrooms. When it gets quiet, I listen to the message.

"Hello, Sidney." The soft voice of Detective Henricksen sends a chill up and down my spine. "I just wanted to check in with you and see how you're doing. My offer is still open to talk. I want to help you in any way that I can. I do have a couple more questions, so I'm sure I'll be seeing you soon. Take care."

I click off my phone and shove it into my pocket like it's something toxic that might burn my hands. *You should tell her.* The thought flits through my mind. Sometimes, I feel like I would do anything to lift the shame that plagues me, to rid myself of the thoughts of my mother that haunt me.

The detective seems trustworthy, but it also feels like a trick. And yet, if I do nothing and they arrest me, how much worse will it be? Isn't it better to confess first? I don't know. But I don't think it's the right play. And neither does Arianna—which gives me confidence. I have to stay calm and wait it out, that's all.

A noise behind me makes me spin around, my heart thumping. It's Margot Hunter. She's hurrying down the hallway without her entourage, alone. I watch her, waiting for what she's going to do or say. We haven't seen much of each other since I confronted her at the lockers.

She catches my gaze for a moment. Her shoulders stiffen, her eyes narrowing. Then her gaze drops to her phone. She strides past me, her blonde ponytail flouncing behind her, suddenly intensely preoccupied. She doesn't say a word.

Good. At least that battle's over. I have plenty more on my plate already.

After school, I go for a long run by the river to burn away the anxiety over the case. It's cold outside but peaceful. A thin film of snow blankets the tree branches and the crunchy brown grass.

Lucas meets me there, and we run together. We don't say much, but we don't have to. I know we have to talk about how I abandoned him that day at the rock, but I'm not ready yet.

Lucas gives me my space. That's one of the things I appreciate about him. It's comforting just to have him around.

I run until the stress of the detective's phone call recedes into the background and all I can think about is my exhausted muscles, my burning lungs, and my aching sides.

When I walk into the house, my cheeks still stinging from the cold, I hear laughter. My heart leaps into my throat.

The boys are home.

Aaron sits at the table, pouring Honey Nut Cheerios into a bowl. Frankie sprawls with his chair scooted away from the table, his head flung back, his eyes closed. He's only wearing jeans. His skinny, preadolescent muscles ripple beneath his pale skin. They both look thinner.

Aaron's face cracks open in a huge grin. "Sidney!" He slides off his seat and runs to me. I wrap my arms around his small, soft body and squeeze him. His hair smells clean, like milk and lavender instead of vanilla.

"What took you so long?" Frankie says in his hard-edged voice. He barely opens his eyes.

I twist my blue plastic ring around my fingers. I want to hug him, too, but every inch of him radiates 'don't touch me' vibes. "It's nice to see you, too. Put some clothes on, Frankie. It's freezing out."

"I don't care."

"We're having breakfast for afternoon snack!" Aaron says. "Aunty Ellie says so!"

"Where is Aunt Ellie?"

"In the shower. She said she's gonna take us shopping for all new outfits!"

"Why does that not surprise me?"

"You want Chex and Cheese? I can make it all by myself," Aaron says proudly. Chex and Cheese is Aaron's breakfast and snack of choice: a slice of Kraft cheddar cheese melted over a bowl of Corn Chex. You don't even need milk.

"No thanks." I pull out the chair next to him. "Tell me everything that happened. Where were you?"

Aaron's eyes dart to Frankie. A shadow passes over his face. "In a big house with lots of other boys."

"Were they nice to you?"

Aaron gives a small shake of his head.

Frankie snorts. "What do you think?"

I turn on Frankie. "Did you protect him?"

"Why would I do that?"

"Because he's your brother, you idiot." My voice rises. "That's your job."

Frankie's eyes fly open. "Screw you, Sid-*ney*! You weren't even there. You got to stay at home and do nothing. Nobody dragged you away!"

I ignore him and turn to Aaron. Adrenaline mixed with anxiety pumps through my veins. I dread what he might say, but I have to know. "Did anybody hurt you? Like, really hurt you? Did someone touch you? You need to tell me. Right now."

Aaron's eyes are huge and watery, his face pale. "No-n-no," he stutters.

I sit back in my seat and take a relieved breath.

"Who died and made you the boss?" Frankie's eyes darken. He flinches at his own words.

Aaron sniffles.

"Don't be a baby," I say automatically. Guilt washes over me. This is not who I am. I am not Frank. I will not be him. I would rather die than hurt them ever again. I grab Aaron's hand. "I'm sorry. I didn't mean it. Okay?"

He nods and manages a wisp of a smile.

Aunt Ellie sashays into the kitchen, dressed in a white, embroidered peasant shirt and satin leggings. She's wearing giant baguette earrings with diamond-crusted curtains of individual strings, ropes of rose-colored pearls around her neck, and rings with amber jewels the size of nickels.

"Hurry up, boys! We've got shopping to do!" She fists her hands against her hips and surveys the counters. "I keep forgetting to buy a coffeemaker. I don't know how I've survived this long without my daily dose of caffeine. Let's add it to the list."

"We have hot chocolate," Aaron says.

Aunt Ellie smiles at him, her thick foundation crinkling around her eyes and mouth. Her cheeks and lips are rouged candy apple red. "Not enough caffeine, my dear. These days, I feel like I need it injected directly into a vein. Are you coming with us, Sidney?"

I'll be injecting something into my veins if I have to endure another shopping trip. "Too much homework. I've got to make up for everything I've missed."

Aunt Ellie nods. "We need to find an area rug. Maybe gray and blue stripes, maybe a white shag. I don't know yet. The energy in that bedroom still isn't right. We gotta make it look the way we want it to feel. Right, boys?"

My little brothers just stare at her like she's speaking another language.

But Aunt Ellie doesn't seem to notice. "And after that, Aaron, my dear, I thought we could pick up some things at Hobby Lobby so you could make something especially wonderful to take to your mom for her Christmas present."

"Like what?"

Aunt Ellie waves her hand. "Oh, the usual. Rubber shapes, stamps, stickers. Yarn."

"Colored foil?" he asks, his voice so full of hope it makes my heart hurt.

"Whatever your soul desires, my dear."

"Sounds gay to me," Frankie mumbles into his cereal bowl.

The muscles in Aaron's jaw contract. "Is not!"

"Of course, it's not. Mixed media collage is a well-respected form of art. Our dear Aaron has the talent to be a real artist, doesn't he, Sidney?"

"Yes, he does," I say, gritting my teeth. "And don't you ever use that word as an insult again, Frankie. Do you hear me?"

Frankie glowers. Aaron beams beneath the attention. "I'll make the best collage ever. I can't wait to give it to Ma!"

Aaron looks at me. His eyes hold a dark and uncanny perception I don't like. I break eye contact first. What does he remember? What did he say to the police? Does he suspect me? Does he know? I need to talk to him alone. As soon as possible.

"Are you sure you can't come with us, Sidney?" Aunt Ellie asks.

"No thanks. Like I said, homework. And I need to take a shower."

"You stink like dirty socks, Sid-*ney*."

I roll my eyes. "Just go get dressed so Aunt Ellie can take you shopping. It's quite the experience."

My muscles are tense, but I force myself to relax. This isn't how I wanted it to go our first day back together.

Things are going to be different this time. They have to be. I have to be better. I have to do better.

I took both of their parents away from them.

I owe them.

That night, I tuck Aaron in bed in his new Star Wars comforter and bring him Ratty Bunny. He clutches the stuffed animal to his chest and kisses its soft head. "I missed you more than everything," he whispers into its ear.

"Aaron, I need to talk to you." I run my fingers through his hair. "What did you say to the police? When they asked you questions?"

His eyes are huge in the lamp light. He looks so young. "I told them what you told me. You weren't there."

"You didn't say anything else? To anybody?"

He shakes his head.

"What about the detective lady with the reddish-brown hair?"

"I promise I didn't."

My body relaxes. I let out the breath I hadn't realized I was holding. Just the thought of the detective increases my heartrate. Whose side is she really on? She sounds so genuine, so trustworthy. But I should know better than anyone not to trust appearances.

"Sidney?"

"What?"

"Why'd I have to lie?"

"Because. You were helping to keep us safe. And together. So I can still watch over you. Okay?"

"Okay."

His simple little kid trust nearly shatters my heart. I lean close and kiss his forehead. His eyelids start to slide closed. He's tired. He probably hasn't felt safe in his bed since they took him away. But he's safe, now. Safe with me. "Good night, little man."

Later, I make him a message. I draw Ratty Bunny as a giant. He's squeezing Aaron, Frankie, and me in a great big bear hug, squishing us all so tight the air poofs out of our mouths and makes our cheeks bright red circles. "Oof!" stick-figure Aaron says, but he's smiling. I fold the paper into a triangle and tuck it into our message spot.

Now that the boys are home, I can't sleep in their room anymore. I go back to my room and stare at my bed. All the bad things happened there. Dark memories clot in my brain. I shake them out of my head. I won't sleep in that bed a single night more.

I open my closet doors. I push an old sleeping bag and two cardboard boxes of old clothes out into the room. I unroll the sleeping bag, drag in my blanket and pillow, and curl up on the closet floor.

I stare up at the rows of baggy T-shirts and sweatshirts. The one dress I own flutters like white moth's wings above my knees. It smells musty in here. Dust tickles my nose. But it's safer in here than out there.

It takes a long time to fall asleep. Nightmares stalk my dreams. My mother and father, trapped in a pit, look up at me with accusing eyes. They're both covered in blood. "You did this to us!" my mother screams, over and over. I try to run away, but each time the earth crumbles beneath me and I keep sliding into the pit with them.

Terror seizes me, and I wake up trembling and drenched in sweat.

The urge hits me. I want desperately to cut. But somehow I manage to keep myself from doing it. I think about Dr. Yang and pull out my journal. I draw the wings of a green hairstreak over and over, until the trembling stops and the frantic, scrabbling thoughts in my head slowly fade.

Still, I don't sleep for the rest of the night.

THIRTY-SEVEN

The same beige sedan keeps driving down our road. I've noticed it several times over the last week. I know who it is. Detective Henricksen. She hasn't forgotten me. She still wants me to confess.

Or maybe she's found fresh evidence and is just waiting for the arrest warrant to come through. Either way, it's unnerving as hell.

My stomach tightens, my mouth going dry. I watch through the window until the sedan rounds a bend in the road and disappears from sight.

There's a shriek from the living room.

I rush in to see Aunt Ellie bent over the coffee table, holding her cheek. Aaron sits on the couch, crying. Frankie stands with his arms crossed defiantly over his chest.

"What happened?"

Aunt Ellie straightens, her eyes bulging. "He hit me!"

Frankie's hands are balled into fists. "She tried to take away my PlayStation. For no reason! Dad got this for me, not you!"

Aunt Ellie shakes her head, her vintage chandelier earrings tinkling against her neck. "That disgusting game is not allowed in this house. Thugs shooting people in the streets, killing women? It's filth. I will not have it."

"This isn't your house! You don't make the rules!"

"I surely do, as long as I'm here—"

"Then leave!" Frankie screams.

Aaron cries harder.

Frankie's ruining it. He's going to drive her away and then what? The state will take the boys, and I'll have failed completely. "Frankie! Stop it!"

"You're grounded for a month!" Aunt Ellie is shaking, her voice rising to ear-splitting octaves. "No phone, no video games, no friends. You hear me, young man? That game goes in the trash."

"Go to hell!" he shrieks.

"That's it! You need your dirty mouth washed out with soap, young man."

I have to do something, right now. Before she can reach him, I step in front of her. I grab Frankie's narrow shoulders and shake him, hard. "Stop it! Just stop!"

"Leave me alone!"

His body goes rigid, his arm springing up so he can hit me, too. Anger sizzles up hot and fast. I grab his arm and twist it hard. "Stop it!"

He bleats in pain and smacks at me with his free hand.

Aunt Ellie stares at us like the strangers we are, like we're creatures she can't understand and never will. Her face blanches, her mouth working silently. We all freeze, waiting for her to scream at us or throw things, but she doesn't. She doesn't say anything either. She whirls and stomps into my parents' bedroom, slamming the door.

"She can't do this!" Frankie yells. "I hate her!"

"Just stop! We need her."

"We don't need anybody!"

"Yes, we do. We have to listen to her, or she'll leave, and you go back to foster care. Is that what you want?"

His face crumples. "No."

"Then stop! Stop acting like—"

"Like Dad?" he snaps, wetness glimmering in his eyes. "Why don't you?"

He shoves me away and runs into his room, slamming his own door.

I stand there, arms hanging limply at my sides. A sick feeling slithers into my gut. He's right. We're both like Frank. Frank is dead, but he's not gone, not completely. Frankie and I both have his monster living inside of us. We both turn hard, sharp with anger. I'm fighting it with all I have, but sometimes it feels like a losing battle, like it will never be enough.

Aaron lets out a sob. "Sidney!"

But I can't go to him. All the old, ugly emotions are swirling inside me and I'm afraid of what I might say, what I might do. I flee to my own room.

I despise this room, but with the boys back, I have nowhere else to go. It doesn't matter how many times Aunt Ellie scoots the furniture around. It's still both my sanctuary and my prison.

I slump at my desk and stare at my hands, the ridges of black charcoal beneath my fingernails. Hands that so easily resort to violence. I can't be him. I won't be him.

Pain roars in my head, the familiar biting urge rearing up inside me. I need to cut. I've moved the razor from my backpack to beneath my mattress. I find the baggie and pull it out, drop the razor into my hand.

I shimmy out of my sweatpants and stare at my legs, stunned.

I've cut my ankles a few times, attempting to get that cold calm, the sweet release, and failing every time. I only needed to tug down my socks for that. I've showered almost every day, but I haven't shaved. Haven't touched my legs. I've dressed and undressed a hundred times in the last weeks. But always in the dark, always without looking.

I didn't want to see what I did to myself that day on the side of the road, in the shadow of the old barn. Only a few days before I killed Frank.

I run my fingers over the thick red scabs. I slashed my legs from my ankles to my knees. Dozens of times. It looks brutal. It was brutal. I press against one of the scabs and wince.

I can't keep doing this. I don't want to do this.

I have to be better. Not just for the boys, but for me.

The razor slips from my fingers.

THIRTY-EIGHT

"Hey, you," Lucas says when I meet him in the parking lot after school the Monday before Thanksgiving. He's dressed in athletic gear and a light jacket.

I'm dressed like a polar bear. I wrap my scarf tightly around my throat and pull the blue wool hat Aunt Ellie bought me lower over my forehead. "Do you notice how n-no one else is stupid enough to be o-outside?" I say through chattering teeth.

The trees have lost all their leaves. Snow spirals down from the iron-bellied sky. But it's the wind that sears every inch of exposed skin that really does it. Everyone has already hurried to their cars. The parking lot is nearly empty.

Lucas gives me a crooked grin. "Stupid or incredibly brave. I prefer the latter. Besides, you'll warm up when we run."

"I think my muscles are frozen solid."

"It's all in your head."

The wind nearly whips my hat off. "Nope, it's definitely not."

"How's your mom's case doing?" Lucas asks as we shuffle toward the fence at the other end of the parking lot. The asphalt is slick with ice beneath the snow.

I stiffen but try not to let it show. "Her sentencing is scheduled for tomorrow. A judge decides. There's no jury because she—she pled guilty."

"Are you going to go?"

I shake my head. I'm not strong enough. How could I go and watch her get led off to prison for the crime I committed? Acid burns the back of my throat. "I don't think I can."

He nods in understanding, but he doesn't understand, not really.

"We should do something tomorrow, to take your mind off things. How about ice skating?"

I shiver as the cold wind snakes into a crevice between my scarf and my coat. That sounds horrible, but I just say, "Maybe."

Lucas starts to say something else, probably some lame joke, but my attention is drawn to a car rumbling into the parking lot. I turn and stare at it, my heart sinking. It's a beige sedan.

Detective Henricksen parks next to us and steps out of the car. Gusts of wind swirl around her trench coat. She's clutching a cup of coffee in one hand, her spiral notepad in the other.

"I was hoping I'd find you here," she says, grinning broadly.

"I'm not sure I can help you further," I say politely. A chill runs up my spine that has nothing to do with the weather.

"Are you okay?" Lucas asks under his breath.

"Sidney and I are well acquainted, aren't we?" she says. Her face is as warm and kind as I remember. "I'd appreciate just a few minutes of your time."

Part of me wants Lucas to stay, but I can't let him. I have no idea what the detective wants, and that makes her dangerous, no matter how benign she looks. "Why don't you wait in your car, Lucas? I'll get you as soon as we're done."

He nods and jogs over to his jeep. I turn back to Detective Henricksen. "Let's make this quick."

"Of course," she says sweetly. "I wanted to check on you, see if you've thought about my offer."

"That's funny. I don't recall any offer."

She's not wearing a hat. Her auburn hair is yanked back into a tight bun. Her fingers around her coffee cup are red, but she doesn't act cold. "I think you do. It's not too late, you know. I can still help you."

I shake my head.

Her eyes soften. "I know about guilt. I know how it eats you up inside."

The shame and guilt are there, right below the surface. I push it away. "What do you want?"

"I want the best for everyone. Think about your mom. Think about the baby."

I blink rapidly, trying to keep my emotions at bay. I can't show her anything. I can't

show her my weakness. "Maybe I am thinking about them."

The wind howls through the trees, shaking snow from the tree branches beyond the fence. They hit the ground with a soft thump.

"If Frank hurt you, I can help you. I can make it go easier for you."

I take a breath. The cold burns my throat. "I don't have anything to say."

Her smile falters for an instant. "You have an interesting history."

"What do you mean?"

She glances at her notebook. A few snowflakes catch in her eyelashes. "A history of out-of-control rage and impulsivity. A history of violence. You assaulted a child in September of this year, didn't you?"

My heart stops. "I didn't 'assault' him. He was hurting my brother and—"

She raises her eyebrows. "You seem willing to do anything to protect your brothers. That's commendable. The question is, how far would you go to protect them? Hit someone? Shoot them?"

I stare at her, unable to speak.

She hit a nerve, and she knows it. There's a flash in her eyes, the same predatory glint Frank got whenever he was playing you. When you were already ensnared in a trap you hadn't even seen coming.

She's not here for me. Of course not. She doesn't care what happens to Ma or the boys. Whatever guilt I'm feeling, whatever choices I might have to make, I'm not confessing to her.

She's after the glory, to win the game, to break the case everyone else thinks is a done deal. I'd rather freeze to death in my underwear than give her a thing. I glance across the parking lot. Lucas isn't waiting inside his heated vehicle; he's leaning against the hood of his jeep, ready to help if I need it. The sight fills me with warmth—and strength.

I straighten my shoulders and turn back to the detective. "Does your boss know you're out here harassing grieving witnesses? What about your partner? Where's he? Maybe I should give the precinct a call. Just to make sure you're on the up and up and all. You understand?"

The friendly officer act vanishes. Her gaze turns sharp. "I know it was you."

I don't break her stare. It's freezing, but my blood is hot. "Unless you have an arrest warrant tucked inside your bra, I'm leaving, and you can't stop me. Detective."

The flaps of her coat flutter in the wind. Her face hardens. But I see the shift in her eyes. She was bluffing, and she just lost.

No one else suspects a thing. It's only her. No matter how conflicted I feel about my own guilt, it feels good to beat her at her own game. I give her my sweetest smile.

She changes tactics. "I need to speak with your brother again. Verify his story. Wrap up these inconsistencies."

I fold my arms over my chest. I feel stronger now, braver. She can't hurt me. "That's not going to happen. Besides, it's too late. Ma's sentencing hearing is tomorrow."

Detective Henricksen sighs and moves toward her car, defeated.

I'm about to head for Lucas when she pauses and turns, as if she's just thought of something. Her mouth twists into a harsh smile. "Didn't your mother's lawyer call you? No? Those public defenders are lousy, aren't they? The sentencing was delayed. Your mother went into labor this morning."

THIRTY-NINE

The social worker finally calls the Friday after Thanksgiving. Aunt Ellie's face turns gray as she talks. She chews her smudged orange marmalade lipstick right off her lips.

Ma's baby was born five days ago. She came six weeks early. The pregnancy was high risk, so they brought her to a local hospital to give birth. There are problems.

When Aunt Ellie gets off the phone, she shakes her head. "Susan was drinking, wasn't she?"

I sit at the table, staring into the mouth of the peanut butter jar. My throat's thick and gunky. Slowly, I nod.

"And you didn't stop her?" she asks in a strangled voice.

A blade of guilt slides between my ribs. "I tried. She either insisted she'd only had one glass or denied she had any altogether. She had a secret stash. She'd always find more, even when I tried to dump it."

"How could she do that?"

I glance through the kitchen doorway to the living room, where Aaron's happily painting some ceramic Christmas ornament he and Aunt Ellie molded and baked in the oven yesterday.

Over Thanksgiving break, Aunt Ellie and the boys brought home a huge Christmas tree. We strung some sorry-looking lights around it, and Aunt Ellie and Aaron have been decorating it with homemade ornaments ever since.

Frankie's not interested in making construction-paper snowflakes or pipe-cleaner candy canes. He's in his room, playing Grand Theft Auto.

I've been drawing every day. I spent the morning shading in the black-and-white stripes of a Zebra Swallowtail butterfly with my charcoal sticks. My fingertips are smudged and blackened.

Two Christmases ago, Frank brought home a huge tree and decorated the whole house. He bought the big TV and joked and laughed while Ma baked gingerbread cookies. Last Christmas, Frank didn't even bother to come home, and Ma drank herself into a stupor.

I screw the lid back on the peanut butter jar. Abruptly, I'm not hungry at all. "I don't know."

Aunt Ellie passes her hand over her eyes. "I had no idea how bad off she was. I had no idea. I'm sorry, Sidney. You're right. You're not responsible for her drinking. She was. I just didn't realize—it's just too much."

"Too much what?"

She gazes up at the ceiling like some higher power is going to send her the fortitude she needs to get through this, to survive us. She fingers her tortoiseshell necklace. "I'm sorry, honey. I just—I need some time." She goes back into Ma's bedroom and shuts the door, where I can hear her pacing like a stressed-out house cat.

This, too, is up to me. After I make an appointment with the social worker, it's Arianna I call to come to the hospital with me. I don't say anything to the boys. They don't need to know yet. Arianna tells me to call Lucas.

The wooden heart he carved sits on my nightstand, gathering dust. "He won't want to. It's not going to be fun."

"You don't give him enough credit, Sidney. Try him."

I don't want to. But I do want to. I'm not sure I'm ready to have him see me this vulnerable. I have an internal debate with myself until I'm so annoyed I call him just to be done with it. He says yes immediately.

He's coming with us.

~

I watch the stark trees reaching for the gray, low-bellied sky with gnarled fingers. Sullen buildings heavy with snow slide past the car window. My hands are balled so tightly on my lap, the edges of my rings bite into my skin.

Lucas sits next to me. He chats easily with Arianna. He doesn't try to touch me, but I feel his presence like electricity crackling against my skin.

At the hospital, we check in at the nurses' station on the maternity ward. The counter is draped with twinkly Christmas lights. I want to crush every bulb with my bare hands.

We stand against the wall while we wait, listening to the sounds of nurses bustling in and out of rooms and babies crying. The hospital has that bleached, sharp antiseptic smell. I feel dazed, like I've just been in a car wreck, or am about to be.

A short woman with smooth brown skin walks up to us. She's dressed in a pinstripe pantsuit and shiny red heels. "I'm Michaela Davis. Please follow me."

The beads on the ends of her braids clack together as she walks. She leads us to a small room with rose-colored walls and fuchsia chairs. *God Rest Ye Merry Gentlemen* plays from a speaker on the desk.

Michaela Davis sits behind the desk, yanks a manila folder out of her briefcase, and stares at it for a moment. "I'm sorry to have to tell you this, but your sister has FASD, Fetal Alcohol Syndrome Disorder."

A steel band constricts my stomach. Images of deformed limbs and other monstrosities flare before my eyes. "Because my mother drank."

"Yes."

"How bad is it?" Arianna asks.

The social worker glances down at the still unopened folder. "She weighs just under five pounds, though she was full-term. She displays the classic signs: growth deficiencies in size, weight, and head circumference, facial abnormalities, tremors. It's likely she is at least moderately mentally disabled."

It's hard to breathe, to remember how to suck in air. Arianna takes my hand. On my other side, Lucas' shoulder presses into mine, holding me up. "What—what will happen to her?"

"We have some very good programs here. She may be cared for at the Children's Resource Center, which is where she'll be transferred after leaving the hospital. We also have several foster families who are trained to work with FAS children. There are also a few potential adoptive families already approved."

I never thought about what would happen after. Where the baby—my sister—would actually go. "So—so she's not coming home?"

"Your mother requested to terminate her parental rights."

I feel like I've been sucker-punched. "Can I see her?"

"Of course. First, I need to prepare you for what to expect. She has slight facial deformities, which include drooping eyelids, a thin upper lip, and a short nose. Also, please be aware that FAS infants are easily agitated. They don't like to be held or to make eye contact. They may have tremors."

"Screw this," I interrupt. "Just let me see her."

"Certainly. Please follow me." We follow her down another long, narrow hallway to the nursery. Several infants lay swaddled in their incubators, their fuzzy heads barely showing. They are the lucky ones, the ones born to good mothers.

"Here." Michaela Davis pauses at an incubator all the way in the back. Lucas takes my other hand as we look down at a newborn who appears almost normal. The baby's body is tiny, her head small and elongated. I can see the squat nose the social worker talked about, the shortened upper lip. But still, she looks like a baby.

It's her insides that are damaged, the tiny brain boiled in alcohol. It's in her glassy, unfocused eyes. Acid roils in my stomach. I taste it on my tongue.

"Are you all right?" Arianna asks me.

I just shake my head, unable to answer. I'm reeling. I'm heartbroken.

I'm so angry I want to destroy something, anything, smash it into a thousand million pieces.

I should have done more, could have done more to keep the alcohol away from my mother. I should have done something. Now this tiny thing with her stubby little fists and soft, downy skull and a mouth like a rose bud is the one who suffers.

Beside me, Arianna closes her eyes. Her mouth moves silently. I know she's praying for the baby, for my sister.

An Asian man in scrubs with spiky black hair and a mustache approaches us.

"This is nurse Jheon. He helped deliver your sister. I thought you might have some questions for him."

"Would you like to hold her?" he asks.

I blink rapidly. "Yes."

The baby screams as the nurse lifts her and places her tiny form in my arms.

I try to rock her, but her wails only intensify. Her gaze zags off to the side.

"Try holding her closer to your body."

I cradle her against my chest. She is so very, very small, wrapped up in a blanket like a burrito. Her webby veins show beneath her skin. I gaze at her tiny, shell-pink ear. This part of her, at least, is perfect. Her shrieks taper off into snotty whimpers, then huffy moan-gasps, as if she's too exhausted to cry any more.

The nurse crosses his arms. "She wouldn't stop crying for anybody else. You have a way with her."

I shrug, but warmth spreads through me. "What was my mother like?"

"The labor was long and hard. She wanted to see the infant right away. We could tell she had FASD. Your mom knew too. She'd been warned. She started crying. Your mother wouldn't calm down, so we gave her a sedative and took the baby away. When she was coherent again, she didn't ask for the baby, so we didn't bring her in. She sat in the hospital bed for twenty-four hours, staring at her arms, like she was holding something that wasn't there. They took her back to Huron Valley yesterday."

I touch my sister's soft, perfect ear. She needs a family that can take care of her right, can care for her needs in ways I could never do. It's a good thing Ma's giving up her rights. She gave up her right a long time ago.

But still, the pain radiating through me steals my breath away. I want to imprint my love on her somehow, to leave her with a sign, a stamp on her heart that will remind her. A promise she can carry into whatever future awaits her. Someone loved her. I love her.

"What's her name?" I choke out.

"Your mom didn't name her. Would you like to?"

My whole hand fits over her head. Her chocolate brown fuzz is soft as down. She needs a beautiful name, a strong name. "Zoe Rose."

"That's a lovely name," Arianna says, smiling.

"Can I see her? In foster care? Even after she's adopted?"

"It's possible something could be arranged. We could do an open adoption, where you get pictures and videos every so often." Michaela Davis tucks her briefcase beneath her arm. "I'll call your family next week."

We leave the hospital and head back to Arianna's car in silence. Snow sputters down from the slate-colored sky. My stomach roils. I'm sick. Sick to death of all of this. Most of all, I'm sick to death of myself.

I didn't try hard enough. I didn't stop Ma from drinking. I didn't save that beautiful baby—my own sister—in the incubator up in that hospital room. I could have done more. Should have. But I didn't do a damn thing.

"This isn't your fault," Arianna says like she can read my mind.

Lucas touches my arm.

I flinch. The monster inside me is moving, sliding through my veins like black sludge. "Just leave me alone."

"I'm not going anywhere." His voice is firm, unyielding.

I shake my head. I'm so full of shame I can barely look at him.

He steps closer, brushing my bangs out of my eyes. "Can I touch you?" he says softly so only I can hear.

Then he's holding me, wrapping his arms around me, tucking my head beneath his

chin. He's solid. Strong. Safe. I'm shivering, but my whole body fills with warmth all the way down to my toes.

After a moment, I wilt against him. "I'm sorry," I whisper. "I've been a big fat jerk to you."

"Maybe just a little bit," he says into my hair. "I know you don't mean it. You can't get rid of me that easily."

I want to say thank you to both of them, but the words stick in my throat. I don't know how.

Arianna rubs my shoulder. "It's going to be okay."

But I don't know if it will ever be okay. Not for Zoe Rose, and maybe not for me.

Lucas holds my hand the entire car ride home. It's like a thread, a cord connecting us to each other. I can feel it pulsing through his palm.

His fingers entwine through mine like a promise.

FORTY

The ride home is silent, but comforting. When we get back, Lucas gives me a long, fierce hug. I hug him back.

Arianna and I don't talk until we're in her bedroom, on the floor, leaning against her bed. We're wrapped in blankets with steaming mugs of hot chocolate by our sides. Her parents are at a prayer meeting, so we have the house to ourselves.

"I don't know the best way to say this," Arianna says softly, "but I'm worried about you. Even though Frank is gone, your eyes are still filled with shadows. It's like—it's like they still have power over you—your parents, and they aren't even here anymore."

That familiar spiky rage jabs through me. I open my mouth to say something sharp and ugly, then snap it shut. I can't do this. I can't hurt the people I care about just because I'm upset. Arianna and Lucas have already forgiven me so much. So has Aaron. If I don't get it together, I'll lose them all. And that would kill me.

"I know," I say instead. "I'm working on it. I'm sorry."

She gnaws on her pinkie fingernail. "Don't apologize for stuff you didn't do wrong. You sound like me."

I turn and look at her. Really look at her. She's still painfully thin. She's still not eating enough, even after all this time. I desperately want to help her. To reach for her hand the same way she reached for mine. "You can talk to me, you know. Believe it or not, I'm capable of listening, too."

She presses her hands against her belly, takes a breath. "I spent my whole life being perfect, doing everything everyone wanted me to—the grades, the flute, French, class secretary, the Bible studies, the bake sales. Everything. I didn't choose any of it.

"I'm tired of it. I'm tired of doing what my teachers and my parents and my youth group leader want. I'm sick and tired of worrying so much about what every single person thinks of me. Everyone, even guys I hate and my friends who aren't even my true friends.

"Before the beach, when I thought they were my friends, I had to talk like them and act like them and dress and do my hair like them. I only get their approval when I'm pretty—but not too pretty—and thin and subservient and meek. I hate it. I feel like a coward and a fraud *all the time*."

I stare at her. Her eyes look like they're drowning. My heart contracts. I force down the blackness inside me, beating it back to the edges of my mind. As much as I don't deserve it, this girl has given me parts of herself I never could've asked for. She risked so much for me, lied for me, abandoned her safe, popular existence for me, and she did it when I was nothing but a smart-mouthed jerk.

I owe her. More than that, I *want* to help her. Because she's my friend. Because I care about her. I can do this. I can be who she needs. "Keep talking. What else?"

"Sometimes I'm angry or I don't like something someone does, but I'm not supposed to say anything because then I'm the bitch, excuse my language. I'm so terrified someone's going to notice the mask is chipping and rip it off, and then people will know. I'm really nobody at all. And I'm losing it.

"That night at the beach? I was sitting and listening to a bunch of girls chatter about inane nonsense, and all I wanted was to get up and *leave*. Just walk away. But instead, I sat there. I sat there like a good girl, despite my insides practically screaming to do something else. I don't even listen to myself anymore. I don't even know if I should. That's messed up, right?"

"I guess so," I say, smiling grimly.

"It's like nobody sees me. I'm literally disappearing—and nobody even notices. My so-called former friends don't see me. My parents don't see me. Pretty soon I won't be able to see me either." She covers her mouth with her hands like she's just said something terrible. "I'm so sorry. I really am. You're going through all this stuff and listen to me blabber on about nothing."

"Stop apologizing. Seriously. It's driving me insane. You don't have to apologize for your existence."

"Sorry," she says automatically, then hiccups.

We exchange small, sad smiles. Her pain is as real as mine. She writes her pain on her body, like I do. "You have to eat something. You have to forgive yourself. You should know that better than anybody, with all your God and mercy and grace talk."

The muscles in her jaw twitch. She picks at her bitten fingernails. "You're right."

"Where is the grace for yourself? If God forgives you, then who are you to reject forgiveness?"

She hesitates for a long moment. She rocks gently back and forth, her shoulders hunched. "You're right."

My throat tightens. It's hard to speak the words, but I have to. "I can't do this by myself."

"You have Lucas."

I shake my head. "No. He's important. But I need you."

Tears shimmer in her eyes. "I remember when I first saw you. I would watch you in class, in the halls, being you, loud and snarky and fierce and not caring at all what other people thought, even when they hated you. I admired you. I wanted to know how you did it. I wanted to *be* you."

I laugh in spite of the seriousness of the conversation.

After a moment, she laughs, too. "Just being around you makes me want to be stronger."

"You're like the Viceroy."

"The what?"

"The Viceroy has the same orange, brown, and white colors and patterns of the Monarch butterfly." I smile as I say the words, remembering how avidly Jasmine would tell me every little fact about each of her specimens. "Monarchs eat milkweed, which makes them taste bad to birds and other predators. Viceroys feed on willows and poplar, not milkweed. So by looking like the Monarch, the Viceroy is protected because the birds think he'll taste terrible. He's a mimic."

"Okay, yeah. I can see that. Fake it 'til you make it, right?" She nods, nibbling at her fingernails. "I never pegged you for a butterfly girl. Like, at all."

"I'm full of surprises." I give her shoulder a little shove. "You're strong. You've already proven it. It's time to surprise yourself."

She hesitates, then lifts the hot chocolate and takes a drink. A regular, normal drink. Then another one. Her face is pale, but she keeps drinking. "Okay. Okay, I will."

"And what else?"

"What else?"

"Yeah. What else do you want for yourself that you've given up for someone else?"

She's quiet for a long time. I'm starting to think she's not going to answer when she finally speaks. "I don't want to go to college."

"Seriously? For real?"

"Not like my parents want me to. I don't want to go to med school. I have zero interest in being a doctor. I want to be a sous chef or a pastry chef, like at a chic outdoor, lakefront restaurant. I've been researching all these great culinary schools in Chicago."

"That sounds perfect for you."

She shakes her head. "That's basically like throwing away my future, according to my parents. My mom would totally flip out."

"She'll live. And so will you."

"That's debatable." She looks up at me, her eyes suddenly bright. "You could go to the Art Institute of Chicago. You're so good I'm sure you'd get in. We could rent the tiniest studio apartment on Michigan Avenue, like where the bedroom is also the living room and the bathroom is the size of a phone booth? We could room together."

And just like that, a future unfurls in front of me I can almost see and feel. It could actually be real. It is luminous, brilliant, nearly too shiny to look at.

Arianna takes several small sips of the hot chocolate. "There. I drank half of it. That's—that's all I can do right now." Her hand trembles when she puts her mug down on the carpet.

"Good enough, for now. You feel okay?"

She nods, pressing her hands against her stomach. "Yeah. I do."

I take a deep breath. Chicago isn't that far away. I could come home every weekend, check on the boys, make sure they're okay. "The big city idea of yours. It isn't the worst thing I've ever heard."

Her face breaks into a smile. "Let's do it." She hesitates, tilting her head as she looks at me. "But you can't stay like this. It's like your anger is burning you up inside."

"Deep words, Beauty Queen." But we both know she's right.

I want the light Lucas cracked open and the warmth Arianna brings with her calm, steady, dependable, gentle self. I want light, and life, and laughter. And something like love.

I want the future Arianna painted for me, of art school in a big city with the skyscrapers arcing above me and lights and sounds and the studio apartment with someone to come back to, someone to share it all with, someone who knows all my dark places and likes me anyway. I want a future where I forge a new me, a new life, but my ties to home, to my brothers, are still strong as steel. I want it all. I need these things like oxygen after nearly drowning.

Arianna leans in close. I see the cracks in her makeup, the smudged hollows beneath her eyes. "You're the strongest person I know. You didn't come this far to falter now."

"What's that even supposed to mean? You sound like an afterschool Lifetime movie special."

"You know exactly what it means. You need to find whatever answers are there to find, even if they're the ones you fear the most."

My breath hitches in my throat. "Then what?"

"And then, you move on. You find a way to forgive."

"I don't know—I don't know if I can do that. I mean, I know it's part of your religion and everything. It's just not for me. How can I possibly do that? After everything?" How can a bright, shiny word like forgiveness fit into all this darkness?

"Forgiveness isn't about letting the person who hurt you off the hook. It doesn't mean there aren't consequences or that you even have to talk to them ever again. It's about letting it go, setting yourself free. So you can live your life with peace instead of bitterness, hatred, and resentment, all those toxic things that destroy us."

"Letting go," I echo.

She fingers the lacy edge of her comforter. "It's about forgiving ourselves, too."

I roll my eyes. "You sure you don't want to be a pastor like your dad? 'Cause you sure sound like you're preaching."

Still, I hear every word she says.

It's like daylight is pressing against the skin of my eyelids. All I need to do is open my eyes.

I just have to remember how.

FORTY-ONE

"I'm sorry," Aunt Ellie says. She's standing in the doorway to my room, staring at me with hooded eyes.

My heart tightens in my chest. It's hard to breathe. It's the first Monday of Christmas break. The boys are in their room on the PlayStation. I sit on my bed, staring at my wall of butterfly art until my eyes burn. "What happened?"

Aunt Ellie just returned from the circuit courthouse for Ma's sentencing hearing. "She wouldn't say a bad word against Frank, not a thing. There wasn't much the defense could do."

"Just tell me." My voice sounds raw in my own ears.

"The judge gave her thirty years."

My gaze lands on an iron-hued butterfly from the U.K., the Large Blue. I remember what Jasmine told me about it. As a grub-like caterpillar, it excretes the addictive scent of honeydew from its glands to attract worker ants. The worker ants carry the caterpillar to their colony and deposit it directly into their nest of ant larvae.

The caterpillar secretes the sugary honeydew the adult ants crave, while devouring the ant eggs and larvae for its own food. In some cases, the caterpillar consumes so many ant babies, the entire colony collapses.

The ants sacrifice their young to the point of their own destruction.

I stare at the picture until my vision blurs. Frank did this to me. So did Ma. They did it together. My own parents. I was a child, and their hurt was intentional, driven by their own arrogance and self-interest. Their own needs stunting, warping, and twisting them until they were withered husks of want. Always howling for more. Always taking, taking, taking.

Except Ma went into that courtroom and accepted the blame. She's going to prison instead of me. She gave up her life for me.

And this is something I don't know what to do with.

I can't reconcile it with the mother I knew. It doesn't make sense to me. *Maybe it's real,* my mind whispers. Maybe some small part of her still loves me. In that moment she hunched over Frank's body, maybe she realized how awful she'd been, and in one fell stroke, offered the next thirty years of her life to make up for it.

Or maybe I'm being set up for the largest disappointment of my life. One I won't be able to recover from.

"It's not all bad," Aunt Ellie says quietly. "The lawyer said she could be out in twenty, with good behavior. I'm so sorry, Sidney."

I don't speak. There's absolutely nothing to say.

"Susan will be transferred to the Women's Huron Valley Correctional Facility in Ypsilanti. It's almost two and a half hours away."

I blink back the tears. The pain inside me is a living thing, burrowing deep.

"I filled out visitation application forms," Aunt Ellie says. "You just need to sign yours, and then you can go see her. They have some crazy rules up in that prison. You can't wear hoodies, or holes in your jeans, or clothing too loose or too tight.

"And get this, no underwire bras. Can you believe it? Every underthing I own is from Victoria's Secret. I'll have to go bra shopping just so I can visit my own sister." She coughs, like she's trying to mask a sob.

"Okay."

She stands in my doorway, hesitating. "You know you can talk to me, right? If there's ever anything you need to say. If there's anything you want to tell me. I'm here."

"Thanks, Aunt Ellie." But I don't say anything. I can't.

Not now, when the awful reality of my mother's future settles on my shoulders like ash.

FORTY-TWO

For the next four days, a massive snowstorm covers all of southwest Michigan. Brokewater is like a little village trapped in a constantly shaking snow globe. Great buckets of snow spiral relentlessly from the iron-bellied sky. The storm knocks out the power, traps cars in driveways. Snow drowns everything, swallowing up mailboxes, powerlines, cars. The drifts pile up taller than my bedroom window.

On Christmas Eve, I tell the boys we're having a sleepover. For once, Frankie decides to act halfway decent. We drag the boys' mattresses into the living room and push the presents and the tree out of the way. Frankie helps me pull in the kitchen chairs, and we build a fort over the mattresses with sheets. Frankie and Aaron burrow beneath the makeshift tent and make shapes and shadows with their flashlights, cupping the flashlights beneath their chins and whispering about ghosts and witches.

I ask the boys what they want for supper. "Marshmallow delight!" Frankie shouts. Aaron dissolves into a fit of giggles. This is another treat I've been making them since Aaron was a toddler: two pieces of peanut-butter-covered bread stuffed with several big marshmallows.

Later, they fall asleep wrapped up in blankets, marshmallow fluff scabbing their lips, their winter hats pressed over their ears. I wear two sweatshirts and my coat, and still I'm shivering. We're making new memories, building a new family. It's a good thing.

The storm breaks early on Christmas morning. After breakfast, we open presents. I used funds from my bank account to buy everyone gifts. I get Aaron his first watercolor paint set. I get Frankie some cool decals for his skateboard and scooter. I bought Aunt Ellie a pair of funky garland earrings I found on eBay.

I open the smallest present last. Inside a velvet box is a white-gold ring studded with tiny, glittering diamonds. The center is a fiery blue sapphire shaped like a heart. I pull off one of the plastic rings on my left hand and slip it on. It fits perfectly. It must have cost . . . I don't even know how much.

My stomach knots up. It's too beautiful to look at. "I can't take this."

"Of course you can. Look how you want to feel, darling." Aunt Ellie raises a pretend glass. "To family. And new beginnings."

I imagine my mother sitting silent and still, her limp arms forming a baby-shaped space. She should be here, sharing this moment with us. She should be sitting here, surrounded by shredded wrapping paper and opened boxes, the lights from the tree twinkling in her eyes.

I took that away from her.

~

The rest of Christmas break passes in a blur. I see Arianna a couple of times, but mostly I text Lucas, who's visiting his mom in Florida, and write final essays about the role of women in classic literature and the literary uses of mental illness in Shakespeare.

Twice Aunt Ellie takes the boys the two and a half hours to see Ma. She asks me to come. Both times, my body goes numb and my mind fills with a black cloud of shame.

The shadows always flit at the corner of my mind. The guilt, the anger, the dread—they're always here, just below the surface, taunting me.

The question is, what am I going to do about it?

I know I have to go. I have to face her. I have to know the truth—if the mother I've always resented actually loves me after all. If she truly did this noble, sacrificial thing for me.

But I'm not ready. I'm just starting to rebuild all the broken parts inside me. I'm still terrified that the truth will shatter me, that I'll never be able to pick up all the pieces.

That this time, I'll be destroyed for good.

FORTY-THREE

On Sunday morning, Aaron and I look through the cupboards, searching for some strange food combination to try. We scoop SpaghettiOs out of the can with a spoon. I get out the whipped cream, and the boys alternate bites of lukewarm tomato pasta rings with mouthfuls of sugary foam.

Lucas is texting me about somewhere he wants to take me when everything goes sideways. Again. Aaron starts in with his high-pitched whining, and Frankie pushes him out of his chair. Aunt Ellie yells at him over Aaron's shrieks of wounded outrage.

"You're out of control, young man. I've had quite enough!"

Frankie stares up at her scornfully. "Oh, yeah? What're you gonna do about it?"

Aunt Ellie lifts her hand, carved jade and garnet rings flashing, like she's about to backhand him. Frankie's eyes go wide. Aaron hiccups and watches silently from the floor.

My heart hammers against my ribs. "Aunt Ellie," I say in the calmest voice I can muster.

She drops her hand, a mortified expression on her face. "I'm so sorry." She flicks her gaze to the ceiling like something up there is going to rescue her from the steaming pile of crap she's stepped into. "I can't believe—I wouldn't have done it."

Frankie just glares at her.

"I would never . . ." Her voice wavers. "I didn't mean it. I'm so sorry." She flees to her room, shutting the door with an ominous bang.

I turn to my brother. "Frankie."

"What, Sid-*ney*?" But some of the fight has left his voice. "We don't need her here. We don't want her."

Aaron's lower lip trembles. Fat tears slide down his cheek. "I want Ma."

Frankie stares down at his feet. "I want Dad."

I shrug helplessly. "You can't have them. And why do you want them, anyway? They were terrible people. Both of them."

Frankie's eyes go dark. "That's not true!"

Hot sparks flare beneath my skin. "Frank was gone all the time, who knows where, and when he was here, he was a ticking time bomb waiting to go off!"

"Only because of you! You made him mad all the time!"

My jaw clenches. I try to rein in my words even as they bolt out of my mouth. "Frank treated Ma and the rest of us like garbage stuck to the bottom of his shoe."

Frankie's face reddens. "You're a liar!"

Aaron's gaze bounces from Frankie to me and back again.

I stride across the kitchen and grab Frankie's shirt with both hands. "Stop it! Just stop. Or I'll—"

Frankie stares at me, blinking furiously. Wetness glimmers at the corners of his eyes. "Or what? You'll hit me?"

His words hit me. Hard. I uncurl my fingers from his shirt, stumble back. "No. I won't hit you. How could you think that?"

He shakes his head, screwing up his face like he's either going to scream or burst into tears. Instead, he sprints to his room and slams the door.

I go to the bedroom door but don't try to push my way in. "I'm sorry, Frankie. Okay? I'm sorry."

"Go away!" His voice is muffled through the door.

I lean my forehead against the wood. This is so hard. Harder than I thought possible. But I can't give up on him. I think of Arianna, how she never gave up on me, even when I was sharp and spiky and ugly. "I will never hit you, because I'm not Frank. And neither are you. We both get to decide who we want to be."

Silence.

"We're a family, Frankie."

"No, we're not," he snarls, tears in his voice.

"Yes, we are, and we don't hurt each other. It's not going to be that way for us. Not anymore."

He doesn't answer, but I know he heard me.

It hits me then, why Frankie and Aaron defend our parents so fiercely. Because I taught them how to be small and silent, how to disappear into their room when the fighting started, how to recognize the warning signs, the inflection in Frank's voice, the dark gleam in his eyes.

They never saw the rest, the worst things. I protected them from that.

Aaron comes up beside me, twines his fingers with mine. "I like not being scared." His voice is small and soft.

They don't know. They don't know how bad it was. I protected them. They'll remember Frank and Ma during the good times. They'll have their memories, distorted, as if seen through a murky glass. I won't take that from them.

I will let them have this. I'm strong enough to bear the truth for them. I'm strong enough to fight for us, for this family.

I squeeze his hand.

FORTY-FOUR

After school on Wednesday, I go see Bill for the first time since it happened. It's already mid-January. I can't put it off any longer. There's no way I have a job waiting for me after all this time, but I want to say something to Bill, to say goodbye and thanks in a way that's real.

When I walk in a little after four, the place is nearly dead. There's a sad tabletop tinsel-covered tree on top of the bar, leftover holiday cheer. A family with three tow-headed toddlers sit in a booth in the back, and a couple of truckers sip coffee over newspapers. Brianna gives me a wave.

I head straight for the kitchen. I breathe in the familiar, comforting smell of grease and oil, fries and onions. Bill's flipping a burger that doesn't look like a burger. It's a round piece of cardboard, or maybe dogfood mashed into a hamburger shape.

Bill's face stretches into a wide grin when he sees me. His dreads fall loose around his shoulders, and he's shaved his beard. "Look what this place's come to. We added a veggie burger to the menu to please all the crazy vegans. Veggie burger. That's an oxymoron if I ever heard one." He puts down his spatula and wraps me in an awkward shoulder hug.

"It looks disgusting."

"I'm sure it is. Been too revolted to actually try it yet. Just the smell turns my appetite."

"I know I haven't been in to work in, like, months."

He waves his arm. "It hasn't been too busy, unfortunately. We can use you whenever you're ready. But if you're not, we'll wait."

My mouth falls open. "Really?"

"Really. I've missed you, kid."

"I seriously doubt that."

"Always with the sarcasm. How's your Ma?"

"They sentenced her to thirty years," I say, my voice raw. Speaking the words out loud makes my stomach twist with guilt. My stomach hurts all the time, now. "Her lawyer says she'll get out sooner, but who knows."

He shakes his head. "Such a shame. Do you have a minute? I wanted to talk to you, after your dad—after what happened. It didn't seem right over the phone."

"Okay."

He glances around, makes sure we're alone in the back. "I've always had a soft spot for you, kid. I hope you know that. I've always felt like I could look out for you, if you worked here. But I fear I've failed."

My throat tightens. "What are you talking about?"

"I don't know what you think about what happened. I hope you don't hate your mother for it. Frank has—had—this charming, gregarious personality when he was out in public. I used to be envious of how good he was with the ladies. It was no effort for him.

"But there was another side to him, a side most people never saw. I never really saw it myself, either. It was like hints of something, some darkness in him, but it would pass so quickly I would wonder if I'd imagined the whole thing. He got in fights, could turn on a frat brother or a player on the field in a flash. Are you following me? Do you want me to stop?"

I spin my rings on my fingers. Anxiety prickles the hairs on my neck. "I'm following you."

"I just—I have a suspicion you know this about him more than anybody. When we were at MSU sophomore year, something happened. What'd he tell you about getting expelled?"

"What he told everybody else, I guess. He partied too much and let his grades slide. Lost his football scholarship and got kicked out of school. It was his one shot to glory and happiness forever, blah blah blah."

There's tension in his face. "He could've gotten a tutor for his grades; the university would have worked around it. It was something else. There was a massive party just before Christmas at our fraternity house. It was packed with players and girls. Some high school girls squeezed in. Everyone was partying hard, dancing, drinking, drugs, you name it. We knew those girls were high schoolers, if that. Freshman or sophomores. Young. They were damn babies all dressed up in mini-skirts and their mama's makeup."

My heart jams into my throat.

"Frank singled one out. He was dancing with her hard. He was with your mom by then, but she wasn't there. Had the flu or something. I told him, 'Hands off, dude; that merchandise isn't for sale.' He just laughed at me. I was young and stupid, too, half-drunk, and I didn't see him take her upstairs. Long story short, the girl spilled the beans when she went home and got caught by her parents. Her parents called the cops."

I try to breathe, but my brain isn't getting enough oxygen. "What happened?"

"She was fourteen. But she was also drunk off her ass and dressed like . . . that shouldn't have mattered, but it does, you know? It wouldn't have been a slam-dunk case in court. It would've been ugly every step of the way. The school settled with the family out of court. Frank got off without a record, but one of the stipulations was that MSU expel your father. Which they did. No school would touch him after that."

I count back the years in my head. Frank would have been a sophomore at MSU in 1998. My mother, a freshman. In March of 1998, she would have been eight weeks pregnant with me. "Did my mom know?"

"She did. She supported your father 100%. Blamed the girl for throwing herself at him." Bill shakes his head. "Frank never spent a minute with a girl that didn't see him as a god. Comes with the territory of being a star running-back, I guess. That's why it's so strange your mom went and shot him."

My skin feels shredded. I'm about to unravel, thin threads of myself rippling off and floating away. "Why are you telling me this?"

"I always wondered if it shouldn't have gone the other way. If there should have been a trial." He looks at me. His eyes are tired and heavy with regret. "I don't know what went on behind closed doors, and I don't need to know. But ever since I found out what your mom did, I've had this feeling I can't get rid of. This feeling that I let you down. That I wasn't watching close enough."

He stares at me, his head cocked, like he wants to say more. It's like he's examining me, studying my insides, like he can see much more than I'm willing to show.

I feel exposed. I also feel a deep sadness. Bill is a good guy. He would have helped me, I think, if I'd had the courage to tell him the truth.

Guilt spears me again. I need to change the subject. "What about Frank's parents?"

"Frank's dad—your granddaddy—took off when Frank was just a toddler. He was a drinker, a gambler. He probably drank himself to death a decade ago. But you know already, don't you?"

I shake my head. Neither of my parents ever talked about their childhood. I remember visiting a grandmother in the nursing home. She was thin and pale and severe, with zero interest in her grandchildren. She died when I was nine. "My family keeps a lot of secrets."

Bill looks at me again, like he's not surprised. "Your grandmother coddled your father, gave him whatever he desired, even though they didn't come from money. He could do no wrong. She depended on him for everything, companionship, money, attention. She didn't care for your mother. None, that's for sure. That's all I know. We all have our crosses to bear, kid."

For a long moment, we just stare at each other.

"I just wanted to stop by," I say, my words dropping into the silence like stones.

He nods, a short quick jerk of his chin, and turns back to the grill. "Crap on a stick!" he mutters, pushing at the blackened veggie burger with his spatula. "You think they'll even notice?"

I pat the naked woman tattoo on his arm. "I doubt it. I'll call you. When I'm ready."

"Merry belated Christmas, kid. I hope it was a good one. Take home some Choco-Butter Pie, will you?"

He knows Choco-Butter Pie is my favorite, which is an unfortunate name for a delectable swirl of dark chocolate mousse, creamy peanut butter, and whipped cream on top of a gooey sugar cookie crust.

Brianna puts an entire pie into a white cardboard box and hands it to me. She pops her gum. "It's boring without you. I hope you come back soon."

I start to roll my eyes and say something snarky, but then I stop. She's just trying to be nice. "Thanks," I say.

Outside, the sky is nearly black. The wind whips my hair and drives wet snowflakes into my face. I head back to the car with the pie box heavy in my hands, my head spinning.

I barely see the road. Fat snowflakes dart from the night sky and slap against the windshield. My fingers grip the frozen steering wheel. There is only darkness beyond the twin beams of my headlights.

The girl. She was fourteen. The same age I was when my father chose to take what I didn't have to give. She pre-dated me. Frank turned his twisted gaze on her long before I was around.

He was the damaged one. Not me.

I was a child. Innocent. He was the one who was warped, sick, dirty. I am not those things. I never was.

Not me.

FORTY-FIVE

When I get home from Bill's, my mind is still buzzing from everything I've learned. I nearly crash into Aunt Ellie, who's lugging her worn leather suitcase into the kitchen. She's wearing her coat and gloves.

My stomach drops, my brain instantly going into high alert. "What's going on?"

"I'm sorry, Sidney. I really am." Her gaze connects with mine and then darts away. "It's too much. I thought—it doesn't matter what I thought. It's too late. There's no saving that one. He's just like his father. I just can't stand around and watch it happen."

"Wait. What's happening?" But even before she speaks, I know. It's written all over her face. She thought she'd whoosh in like our knight in shining armor. She thought she'd rescue us like you rescue a litter of puppies at the animal shelter. But we aren't soft, adorable puppies.

We're broken. That makes us hard in some places, sharp as splintered glass. If you want to get close to us, if you dare, you'll get cut. You'll bleed. She doesn't want to bleed.

"You're leaving." The light in my chest snuffs out like a candle flame.

"I'm going home. I called a taxi. I'll wait outside. I'm sorry. Just—

sorry." She strides past me and bangs out the door, her bracelets clinking on her wrists, her purple paisley scarf fluttering behind her.

I wheel and stare at the boys who've crowded into the kitchen and crouched behind the table. Like they can hide from me. "What happened?"

"Frankie spit on her."

"What?!"

I expect Frankie to start yelling denials, but he doesn't. "She started saying stuff about Dad again." The oversized X-Men T-shirt he's wearing makes him look younger, fragile. His eyes are scared. His fingers grip the back of the kitchen chair. "I got so angry I couldn't help it."

Aaron starts to cry. "Are they gonna take us away again?"

I fight down the panic rising up my throat like acid. What now? What are we going to do? Aunt Ellie is too much like her sister. Where was she all those years when we needed her? Nowhere.

We let her in. We trusted her. And now she's just fleeing, abandoning us as surely as everyone else who's come before her.

Frankie's face is white as a sheet of paper. "They're going to put us in that place again."

Aaron stares at me, pleading. "Don't let them take us away."

"Please, Sidney. I won't be bad anymore. Please." Frankie's voice is full of dread, his eyes wide and scared. The tough veneer is gone. Frankie is just a terrified kid. And he needs me.

Who protected them, all these years? Kept them safe? Kept us together? I did. It's always been up to me. And they're looking to me now, desperate for me to save them. I have to save them. "That's not going to happen. Not if I can help it."

I spin on my heels and march outside. The cold blasts into me, but I barely feel it. The feeble porchlight casts the sky in bruised shadows. Fat snowflakes drift through the air.

Aunt Ellie is hunched on the bottom step of the porch, her suitcase on the ground beside her, her phone in her hands. I hurry down the steps and turn to face her. "You aren't leaving."

"I can't do this. I'm so sorry."

I shiver, stomping my feet. I feel expanded and compressed at the same time, my lungs like balloons about to burst from a tremendous, crushing pressure. "There's no one else. You go, and those boys in there are gone. They'll be lost to the system. Do you understand? There's no one else. You came in here and you promised me. You promised."

The creases in her skin are sharp in the gritty glow from the porch-light. Her eyes are wells I cannot penetrate. "I tried."

"Trying isn't good enough!"

"Sidney, I'm sorry." She tugs on her left earring, a vintage pewter heart with a dangling pinecone-shaped purple jewel. Her gaze wheels up toward the sky. But there's just the snow and the dark—no easy answers or solutions to divine from the stars. Not here. Not for us. "Whatever you think—whatever this looks like to you—I do care. I hope you know that."

The snow melts into my socks. My feet are freezing. White vapor puffs from my mouth with every breath. "Everybody says that, but they don't mean it. Because when the real shit hits the fan, they're nowhere to be found."

A pair of headlights sways down the road and swings into our drive-way. Snow streaks the halos of light. Aunt Ellie stands up. She grabs the handle of her suitcase and starts walking.

My eyelashes crust with frost. I'm shivering so hard it's difficult to speak clearly. "Ma gave up," I say to her back. "She gave up every damn day. Whenever it was hard, she just gave up."

She stops. "I—I don't have a choice."

"That's where you're wrong. You always have a choice."

"I don't know how to do this."

"Frankie's got some sharp edges, I know." My words tumble over themselves, tripping up my tongue. I can't get them out fast enough. "He can be a pain in the ass. But he's just a kid, and he's hurting like the rest of us. He needs you. We need you." My lungs burn for air. I will literally do anything to keep her here, to keep the boys safe. "Please."

Finally, she turns back around. "You don't understand. I always run.

I ran out on three husbands. Would've run on the fourth, if he hadn't gotten himself killed in a car accident. I thought I could be different. I thought this was a chance to make up for—" She stops, shakes her head. "I run. That's what I do."

"Not anymore. You left your whole life to come here and be with us. That's not nothing. It's huge. To us, to those boys in there. It's everything."

"I know that," she says in a soft voice. She glances at the waiting taxi. "I know."

"We need you." My heart slams against my ribs. Everything is cracking open—my skull, my skeleton, my organs, my chest collapsing in on itself. I have to be strong. I have to be brave. I have to let her in. "There are things I need to tell you. Things you should know. Why I—why I can't see Mom."

She looks at me through the falling snow.

"I'm ready, now. But I need help. I can't do it all alone. I need you."

"You do?"

"Yes," I say without a moment's hesitation. "I know I don't always act like it, but I do. You're family."

Shadows pass across her face, warring emotions I mostly recognize, like regret, fear, shame. Then others, grief tangled with something else, something I don't yet dare to believe. "We need to talk," she says slowly.

"Yes. We need to talk. I know that. I'm ready."

"Okay."

"Okay?" I echo. *Please, please,* I pray to whatever entity is up there.

Aunt Ellie sighs heavily as she wipes snowflakes from her eyelashes. "You can be very convincing, you know that?"

I barely dare to breathe. "So I've been told. It must be my sweet and amiable demeanor."

She snorts. One corner of her mouth twitches.

"I'm also freezing my ass off."

"Language, missy."

I take a shaky breath. "Please come back inside."

Finally, she nods. "We're making ground rules. And everybody goes to therapy. Even me."

Relief flushes through me. My whole body is weak with it. "Yes, ma'am."

"And that trailer? It's got to go."

Now that's something we can both agree on.

Aunt Ellie pays the taxi, and we go back inside. The boys are silent. They follow me to the couch and we sit down and look up at Aunt Ellie, waiting for whatever's going to happen. Her gaze sweeps toward the ceiling. She takes a breath. "I'm no good at this," she begins slowly.

And so we talk. Frankie sits next to me. I know better than to grab his hand, but I press my shoulder into his, like Lucas did with me at the hospital. After a minute, Frankie's taut body softens.

I think he gets it, finally. We all have to change. We all have to make concessions, to conform to the shape our new lives have taken. This, right here, all of us together in this room, this is a good thing.

This is family. This is what we fight for.

This is what I'm fighting for.

And that's why I have to confront Ma.

Soon.

FORTY-SIX

"I can't believe you're forcing me to wear this . . . *thing*," I grumble to Arianna. I'm squeezed into a too-tight purple tube dress Arianna and Aunt Ellie somehow convinced me to buy after dragging me to the mall and forcing me to try on twenty different fluffy, swirly, flowery dresses. My stomach is all squashed, and wires poke me in several sensitive areas. I can barely breathe. "How am I supposed to actually eat in this?"

Arianna just smiles. "It looks lovely on you."

"Ha. I feel like a horse in a corset."

Butter bubbles and spits in the skillet. Arianna adds the clams and covers the skillet with a lid. Her hair is piled in sleek ringlets on top of her head, and her dress is a sparkly gray the color of storm clouds. She looks like a movie star ready for the Oscars, but she's acting like a star chef in full control of her kitchen.

Arianna worked up the courage to tell her parents she's not going to college, and she asked me to be with her. She's spent the last two hours cooking. She set out the good china and showed me how to do the napkins. She promptly redid them, so now they're precisely folded and propped like burgundy pyramids beside each plate.

She tugs on a pair of mitts and pulls the spinach-and-artichoke lasagna dish out of the oven, then places it on the counter, next to the chicken alfredo and the baked ziti with mushrooms.

I stare at all the food. "Are you feeding a small army here? Maybe all of Jesus' disciples at the Last Supper?"

She rubs her forehead with the back of her arm. "I just want it to be perfect, okay? Can you check on the clams?"

I clomp over to the stove, nearly falling in the three-inch heels Arianna lent me. I lean down and rub my ankles. "These are horrible contraptions. Invented by a man, I'm sure."

"Think of this as practice for the prom."

"No way. I'd rather boil myself—"

"—In a vat of oil. Yeah, yeah. I know. But don't tell me you'll be able to say no to Lucas."

I adjust the strapless bra Aunt Ellie made me get, which must be some kind of instrument of torture. "I can say no to anything. Saying no is not my problem."

Arianna raises one eyebrow. "Just like you said no to me?"

"I wanted to do this. Obviously."

She laughs. "Have it your way, but you'll have to dress up for graduation, too."

"Ugh. All that pomp and circumstance . . . billowy gowns, marching around like clowns, sitting ramrod straight for three hours trying not to snore while the principal misreads two hundred names? And for what? A piece of paper?"

Arianna drops the clams into the pot of soup bubbling on the stove. "I'm working very hard for that piece of paper, thank you very much."

"At least it's still two months away." The whole house smells of oregano and toasted cheese. My stomach growls. "If I have to stare at all this food for much longer, I'm gonna hurt someone. Namely, the chef."

"My parents should be here any minute. I told them six-thirty."

It's already almost seven. Pastor Torrès is at some Bible study/bowling night thing I don't really understand. Mrs. Torrès is working late, per usual.

As the minutes pass, the lines around her mouth tighten a little more. We split a breadstick without speaking. Arianna rips up her half in teeny, tiny pieces.

At 7:30 p.m., she takes out the custard she made for dessert and dusts the puffy, golden top with confectioner's sugar and nutmeg. At 7:45, her parents finally show up.

"*Hola*, girls," Mrs. Torrès says. "Oh, darling, how sweet. But I already ate. Your father didn't tell me you'd be making anything."

Arianna and I stand side by side next to the dining table. Her hands press against her stomach. Her voice is calm, but there's a ragged edge to it. "Actually, I told you both about this dinner last week. You can have a little bit, can't you?"

Mrs. Torrès hangs her tan trench coat in the coat closet. "I don't know. You know I don't eat after six. This isn't my normal schedule. I still have patient files to finish tonight."

"It's important. Where's Papà?"

"Spreading salt on the sidewalk. Really, Ari, I've had a difficult day. Can't this wait until tomorrow?"

Pastor Torrès strides in with a red bowling ball bag in one hand and a Bible in the other, his head and shoulders dusted with snow. "Sorry we're late, *Mija*. Bible study went over." He winks at us.

"The food's probably cold, but please, have a seat." Arianna gestures with one hand.

"You two look *muchas bonitas*. No one told me this was a party," Pastor Torrès says as we sit down. Arianna says a prayer over our food and pours sparkling apple cider into the wine glasses.

Mrs. Torrès' lips form a straight, bloodless line. "Really, Ari? Could you have made a meal with more carbs?"

I take a huge bite of lasagna. "This is awesome sauce."

Pastor Torrès nods. "I have to agree. This is fantastic, *Mija*. Tastes a little . . . I can't even describe it."

Arianna smiles. "It's the caramelized onion and blue cheese."

"And the expertise of the chef," I say.

Mrs. Torrès puts a tiny piece of ziti on her fork. She literally winces as she puts it in her mouth. She catches me looking at her. Her gaze travels over me, like I'm a pig being appraised for my meat at a 4H fair. "Sidney dear, have you lost weight?"

I stiffen. I know I've been running a lot lately, but I'm sure as hell not doing it to get skinny. I have enough issues with all the crap going on inside my head to worry about my weight. The only thing I think about calories right now is how to get more of them into Arianna. "Have I?"

Mrs. Torrès beams at me. "You have. I can tell. That's wonderful. Please tell us your secret. Arianna's been getting a little thick in the waist lately."

Beside me, Arianna goes rigid.

My blood pounds in my ears. It's all I can do not to stab something living with my fork. Right then, I have an epic realization. Not all anger is bad. Because the anger I feel right now on Arianna's behalf feels pretty damn righteous.

"I call it the bread and pasta diet," I say, and spear all the ziti, lasagna, and alfredo I can and cram it all into my mouth. I chew several times with my mouth open, bits of spinach and cheesy sauce spilling down my chin. "It's hard, but I'm willing to sacrifice for my figure."

Mrs. Torrès' face blanches. She fingers her gold cross. "There's no need to be rude."

"Hey, now," Pastor Torrès says quickly. "Sidney was just joking around."

"No, I wasn't. Haven't you heard? Beauty comes in all shapes and sizes."

"You should give more consideration to your health," Mrs. Torrès snaps.

"And you should give more consideration to the well-being of your daughter."

"What's that supposed to mean?"

This is going sideways fast. I want to leap up from my seat and scream some sense into these people. I want to yell, "Arianna's not going to your stupid college to be a stupid doctor. How you like them apples?" But this is Arianna's show. I've got to let her do this her way. I grit my teeth and try to breathe with this terrible dress constricting my ribs.

"I have something to say," Arianna says softly.

"I'd rather hear what your friend has to say for herself." Mrs. Torrès' voice is sharp.

"Just drop it, Paola."

"I see no reason—"

"I said I have something to say." Arianna speaks louder, her eyes flashing. "I'm not going to college."

Her parents freeze, both of them, like they've been choreographed. Pastor Torrès holds a fork dripping with tomato sauce in midair. Mrs. Torrès' hand clenches around her sparkling cider glass. Her eyebrows nearly touch her hairline. "What did you say?"

Arianna's trembling. "I don't want to be a doctor. I hate the sight of blood, and the thought of med school literally makes me sick. I want to be a chef. I love to cook."

Mrs. Torrès stares at Arianna, her mouth slack.

"But college is the key to your future." Pastor Torrès looks confused.

"No. No, it's not. I'm not going to college. I'm going to culinary school. I've applied to the Culinary Arts Institute in Chicago."

Mrs. Torrès scowls. Her fingers tighten around her cross necklace, like she can force the good Lord to put a stop to this hot mess. "This is unacceptable."

"I will never be as smart or as thin as you think I should be, Mamà. I tried, and it nearly killed me. I'm tired of living my life based on how other people think I should act. I'm tired of being forced into things when I should have the choice." Arianna sucks in her breath. "But what I want never seems to matter to you. I'm sorry if you're upset, but I'm not going to change my mind."

Mrs. Torrès stands up, dropping her napkin on top of her barely-touched food. "*¡Nanay cucas!* Your grandparents didn't sacrifice everything to come to this country for their granddaughter to become a—a *cook*." She says the word like it's a slur. "That's what my mother did when she came here. She cooked and cleaned for rich, lazy women who couldn't be bothered to do it themselves. Do you understand?"

"I do," Arianna says in a firm voice. "But this is different. I want to choose my own future."

"You are a foolish child!"

Pastor Torrès places his hand on his wife's arm.

She shakes him off. "This is not the proper time or place to have this discussion. You've obviously exposed yourself to certain . . . negative influences. You have no idea how disappointed I am right now, Arianna."

We watch her huff out of the dining room. Arianna gnaws on her fingernails. Her eyes glisten in the candlelight. I want to chase down Mrs. Torrès and shake her bony body until her eyeballs bounce out of their sockets.

"What the hell was that? Pardon my language, sir."

Pastor Torrès stands up and comes around the table. His face is red, like he's embarrassed. He should be. He squeezes Arianna's shoulder. "I apologize for your mother, Ari. You're right. We've put too much pressure on you. Let me talk to your mom. She's just really upset right now. She wants the best for you, *mi amor*. We'll figure something out."

I have my doubts about that, but at least she has one parent who's not a psycho.

Arianna squeezes his hand. "Thanks, Papà."

He gives me a rueful smile. "Please don't judge us based on tonight, okay? Ari's mother really loves her, and so do I. I guess we haven't realized how quickly she's growing up."

I feel a small stab of envy, but also relief. Arianna's father loves her. She is safe with him.

Pastor Torrès rubs his belly. "Please excuse me, ladies. I have a men's ministries meeting early tomorrow morning. I hope we see you in church soon, Sidney."

"I'm not making any promises."

"We'll wear you down eventually." Pastor Torrès grins. "In case Ari hasn't told you, I play to win!"

Arianna rolls her eyes. We say goodnight, and he goes upstairs. We finish our food. I eat everything on my plate. Arianna manages to finish her serving of lasagna. She smiles, her lower lip quivering. "Well, I survived it, anyway. The pasta and my parents."

"Sometimes, that's the most you can hope for. You did good."

"It was pretty epic, wasn't it? Did you see the look on my mom's face?"

"Like she was choking on a piece of kale."

We both laugh.

We clean up the table and dish all of the excess food into Tupperware containers. I start the dishes, and Arianna wipes off the island. "I feel better, you know," she says, "even with everything in my life that's still the same, like my mom. I mean, it's still hard. It still hurts. But every time I make myself take a bite of food, it's like I'm fighting for myself. Each time, it makes me just a little bit stronger. Does that make sense?"

It does. Sudden tears scratch the back of my throat. There's so many things I want to say, but I don't know how. I hope she knows. I want her to know.

Later, when we're done mopping the floor, we go back to Arianna's room. We put on comfy sweatpants and sit on Arianna's bed. I pull out my sketch pad and charcoal and draw Arianna in profile. I sketch in the shape of her head, the arch of her eyebrows and bow of her upper lip, the curve of her eyelashes and sweep of her hair. I add the light, dark, and mid-tones, blending the subtle shadows with my shading stump and picking out highlights with the kneaded eraser.

Arianna peers over my shoulder. "Holy cow! I mean—you're amazing. This is amazing. It's like, that's me, but it's more than me. There's this sadness in my face, but there's . . . strength, too. It's—it's beautiful." Her voice goes hoarse. And I know she gets it.

I have this. I have her.

I know her broken places and she knows mine.

I hold it inside me, a reminder of how a broken thing can be remade into something beautiful, something new and astonishing, something good.

FORTY-SEVEN

On Thursday after school, Lucas convinces me to go on a date with him. He wants to blindfold me, but I won't let him. We bundle into his car, and while he drives, we talk about books and music and running. His pink rhinestone lighter rattles in the plastic cup holder.

I pick it up, flick on the flame and watch it shimmer. "How's your mom?"

"Not good. The doctors say she has less than a month, probably. My dad says she's not eating. She only talks to me on the phone, won't Facetime anymore. She doesn't want me to see her, what the cancer's doing to her body." His voice cracks, the skin around his mouth stretched taut.

Guilt spears me. He always seems so damn serene and cheery that it's easy to forget I'm not the only one who watched my life implode around me.

I click the silver lid shut. "Do you wish you were there?"

"Sometimes, yeah. Sometimes, not so much. Sometimes I feel like a crappy son for being happy here, when she's suffering so much. Dad says he's going to fly me down when it's close to the end. So I can—so I'm there."

This is one of those what-the-hell-do-I-say moments I'm terrible at. I keep flicking the lid open and shut. Click. Click. Click. I want to reach out and touch him. I want to ease the pain I see behind his eyes. But I don't know how. I don't know what to do. I don't know what normal people are supposed to do. I'm only me. And I pretty much suck at all of this.

Lucas keeps talking. "I think she'll find peace now, though. She wasn't a happy person. You know how some people wear their heart on their sleeve? She wears her disappointment with life on her sleeve."

I imagine his mother in a hospital bed, barely breathing beneath thin blue sheets. I've never seen a picture of her, but I imagine an older version of Lucas with softened features and long, sleek black hair.

"That sounds depressing."

"It was. She was—is, I mean. I'm not one for wasting time complaining about my life, but yeah. Sometimes it really sucks. As a little kid, you want to make your parents happy, you know? You think it's your fault if they aren't. You think you're the cause of their disappointment."

I know a little bit about that. "What do you do? When things are bad?"

"I run. And think. Or I play my guitar."

"You play the guitar?"

"I play. Badly, mind you. Like epically, terribly, makes-your-ears bleed awful. But I play for me. Just like I run for me, not for competing or winning or anything like that, much to my mom's chagrin. I mean, don't get me wrong. I like to win. I like a trophy as much as the next guy. But it's more for me. Running helps me work through all those bad feelings. I just let myself feel it, you know?"

I click the lighter. Open, closed, open. Stare at the little flame until my eyes blur. I don't really know. The bad feelings are exactly what I'm trying to run away from. The guilt, the fear, the memories—I don't want to feel any of it. "What do you mean?"

"From my experience, going through it is the only way. You try to run away from it or go around it. It just stalks you, holds on tighter. So I use music to feel what I need to, to feel my way through something, to grieve."

"So you cry? Like, on purpose?"

Lucas snorts. "You make it sound so terrible. There's nothing wrong with crying. Tears are healing. They help you drain out the sorrow and anguish, so you can start filling yourself with more positive emotions, when you're ready."

"You're so Zen about it. Like Yoda."

"I'll take that as a compliment. 'Do or do not. There is no try.'"

He brakes for a stoplight, looks to the left twice before turning on the deserted road. He's so careful and deliberate about everything. He hasn't gone a mile over the speed limit the whole way here, wherever here is.

"You should play for me some time."

"You mean my guitar? I'd love to. But I left it back home."

My jaw clenches at the word 'home', reminding me yet again his home isn't here in Brokewater. And when his mom dies, he's going to be gone. Poof. Out of my life. The thought jolts through me. I don't want him to leave. I grip the lighter so tightly my knuckles turn white. "Are you going to stay in Florida after the funeral?"

He shakes his head. "My aunt and uncle are letting me stay until graduation, since it's my senior year. I need continuity, or something."

Relief floods me. I let out my breath. "Do you want to stay here?"

He smiles without turning his head. "Of course."

"That's good. I mean, not that I care much, really. I mean, I do. Gah. I'm an idiot, is what I mean."

"You couldn't be an idiot if you tried."

"You'd be surprised." I gaze out the window. "Hey, Lucas?"

"Yeah."

"What's wrong with you? You seem too perfect. I'm starting to suspect you must be a closet serial killer or something. Like, do you secretly eat neighborhood pets, or are you planning to join Boko Haram and blow up a library?"

He smiles, but it doesn't quite reach his eyes. "Nope. I'm not planning any axe murders and I love the library. Satisfied?"

"Nope. Not even a little."

"We're here," he says as we pull into a vast, empty parking lot. The sign says Silver Beach Parking.

"I hate to break it to you, but we're a bit off season."

His face is smooth again, cheerful and overly pleased with himself. He takes my hand. "Just wait and see. Bring your gloves. It's cold enough out here to freeze the brass balls off a monkey."

The wind snarls our hair and bites our cheeks, but the winter sky is a sharp, cloudless blue. Our boots crunch through clean, white snow. The beach is deep in hibernation beneath us. It's hard to imagine flip flops and bikinis, sun screen and sand castles.

Once we reach the shoreline, I see why Lucas brought me here. Lake Michigan is frozen. Last week's storms whipped the water into a boil, the surge and swell of the waves busting up the ice fields, jamming slabs of solid, foot-thick ice straight up into the air. Some stand five feet tall, others ten feet, still others fifteen or more. They thrust upward from the lake's frozen surface like gleaming, jagged teeth.

"Let's go out there."

"It's dangerous. The ice floes can settle, shift suddenly. We could fall in and freeze to death. We could get smashed between massive blocks of ice."

"Details, shmetails."

"I thought you might say that," Lucas says dryly.

I pull him out onto the wind-scoured ice. We walk out one hundred, two hundred feet, until we're surrounded on every side, lost in a labyrinth. The structures look like the splintered shards of a giant pane of glass hurled to the ground with great force. They're blade-shaped, knife-edged, brutal in their beauty.

The ice is sleek, translucent blue, frost laced in filigree eddies and elaborate whirling spiders' webs. Some are glossy, shimmering marble, others bristling with crystals, the scabs of crusted snow.

My breath snags in my throat. I'm walking across Lake Michigan.

I'm an explorer discovering an otherworldly, snow-dazzled planet, an alien terrain of the strange, the astonishing, the absurd. My chest expands, filling with sharp shards of light. My fingers twitch. I want to draw this, paint it, consume it, fit it within my body somehow, bind it to my bones.

Lucas sees it in my face. His crooked grin spreads wide. He doesn't say anything. He doesn't need to.

"Do you believe in God?" I ask him.

"I think so. Right here, right now, I really want to."

"Me too."

Lucas takes my hand again. He leads me through the jumbled maze of ice until we come out to an open space. The pier is a diminishing black line stretching back to the distant shoreline.

We're nearly parallel with the lighthouse at the end of the pier. Only it no longer looks like a lighthouse at all. It's draped in layer upon layer of icicles, every inch of it. It looks frosted, dripping with pearled icing, glimmering like an ice palace out of a fairy tale.

"I've lived here all my life. How have I never seen this?"

"It takes the perfect conditions. The water around the pier can't be frozen yet. A cold front with strong winds needs to blow in for a long period of time, for hours and hours. Every time the waves crash against the lighthouse, a few droplets of the spray freeze. It happens again, and again, and again. Slowly, and then all at once. Until there's this."

I shake my head, bewildered, speechless. "How do you know all that?"

He shrugs and grins sheepishly. "Confession: I wanted to impress you, so I looked it up on Google."

"I'm still impressed. Kind of."

"I'll take it."

I kneel and brush snow from the mantle of ice skinning the lake's surface. This ice is a murky brownish-green, thick and opaque. I imagine the deep water swirling below: cold, black, silent.

The white sun drifts down the sky. Blue shadows lengthen. The wind picks up, scraping over the great hunks of ice, gusting around their angles and slanted edges, spraying our exposed faces with pellets of snow.

The ice shudders and groans.

The slab looming above me shifts with a grinding, popping sound. A small fissure splits open beneath me. It gapes wider, large enough to fit my hand through, then my foot.

Lucas grabs my arm. "Run!"

We run, slip sliding across the ice. I stumble, jerk myself up, keep running, the sharp, brittle air searing my lungs. We hit the shore, falling, laughing, collapsing into the snow in reckless relief.

Lucas pulls me up and we race to his Jeep. He turns the heat up as high as it will go. Our cheeks and ears ache; our fingers and toes are numb.

"Can I touch you?"

When I nod, Lucas pulls the gloves off my fingers and rubs them between his own. Slowly, we thaw. The windows steam up. Soon we tug off our coats, discard our hats, unwind our scarves. Lucas pulls off his hat, his black hair sticking up all over like he stuck his toe in a socket.

I look at him, at his kind, earnest eyes and shy, crooked smile. My heart is filled to bursting with wanting. It's a foreign feeling, terrifying but exhilarating. It would be safer to shut down, withdraw, to make damn sure nobody cracks me open again.

But I think of the beauty that can come from a breaking, a shattering of a thing that was whole, then broken, then reshaped into something else entirely. The memory of the ice, still pressed against the backs of my eyelids, shivers and sparks inside me.

It's safer to stay off the ice.

To hell with safe.

Before I can think better of it, I wrap my fingers around the back of Lucas's neck and kiss him, hard, on the lips.

"You're amazing," Lucas whispers.

I kiss him. I kiss him, and I kiss him again. He kisses me back. Champagne bubbles pop and fizz in my blood. My stomach explodes in a flurry of wings—sherbet yellow sulphurs, metallic blues, taffy orange hairstreaks. I lean into him. He wraps his arms around me. His warm hands rub my back, my arms, nuzzle my cheeks. They aren't anything like Frank's hands. This is something entirely different. This is something good.

I run my own hands through his soft tufts of hair. He touches my ear, the hollow of my throat. We're kissing and I'm cracking open, little spider cracks smashing into jagged fissures of light, light pouring through and drenching everything.

We kiss for a long time. His mouth fits with mine. I tuck perfectly into his arms. Everything's warm, safe, right. My skin tingles and my heart skitters and I want to pull him closer, kiss him harder. I want him to hold me forever and ever.

His fingers trace circles like rings of fire down my back. His hands slip beneath my shirt.

My whole body goes cold like I'm back out on the ice, only this time it cracks wide open, gaping like a mouth. I plunge through into the black depths.

I jerk away from him and scramble across the seat, fold myself against the door. I'm trembling, my pulse jittering in my throat. Images cascade over me, searing the insides of my eyelids. Frank's eyes, piercing into me. Frank's arrogant, predatory smile. Frank's greedy hands, taking from me what I didn't want to give. Frank's words, scouring my flesh. *Slut. Skank. Are you whoring around on me? I need you. You're mine. Only mine.*

"I can't." My voice is raw. My insides feel hollowed out with a spoon. Suddenly all the old feelings come prowling back. Everything is dirty. Everything is tainted. I'm filthy, ugly, damaged.

"Sidney? What's wrong? Did I do something?"

My cheek presses against the steamed window. It's wet with condensation. If I could flee, I would already be gone, but I'm trapped here. Outside, the air is freezing, the wind whipping swirls of snow around the car.

I need to call Arianna to come and get me. My phone is somewhere under the coats, scarves, and other discarded clothing items. I start searching, my fingers shaking. "I can't do that. What you want—what they all want. I can't. Despite what you may have read scrawled on the bathroom walls. I can't. Find a different girl. A better one. One that's not . . . me."

"But I want you."

I shake my head, back and forth, harder and harder. This was a mistake. I screwed it all up again. I have no idea how to do this. No clue how to be a regular teenager with a regular life. "No, you don't."

He reaches across the seat and takes my hand. I try to jerk it away, but he's strong when he wants to be. He doesn't let go. "Will you listen to me? I don't care what's scrawled on a bathroom wall. That's not why I'm here. I don't want a different girl. I want the one in the car with me, the one I'm head over heels for. If you aren't ready, you aren't ready. That's okay. I'll wait."

He says it so simply, like things could ever be that easy. "Yeah, right. The males of the species generally get what they want. If the socially acceptable, PC charade of getting the girl's permission first doesn't work out in their favor, they take it by force."

"I'm not like that. I thought you'd know that by now. I mean what I say. I'll wait."

Tears leak down my cheeks, betraying me yet again. I can barely speak, but I force myself to say the words. "You don't understand. I may never be ready. I might not ever be able to do that stuff."

"Okay."

"You aren't hearing me."

"Yes, I am."

"I'm not—I'm not good. I can't be who you want."

He tilts his head and stares at me in silence for a long moment. "I think I understand. I have a cousin who went through—I mean, one time her camp counselor—"

My eyes must go wild, because he stops. My frantic heart is about to pound right out of my skin. I shake so hard my arm bangs against the plastic armrest.

I can't have this conversation. Whatever he's about to say, I just can't hear it. My own fear is a dull roaring in my ears.

I can't believe I'm doing this, spazzing out right in front of him. The familiar self-hatred wells up. I just want to make it stop, make everything go away.

"Can I sing to you?"

"What?"

"Can I sing you a song? I write some of my own stuff when I play my guitar. It's mostly awful. Seriously, my singing is on par with a monkey's, but it relaxes me, makes me still inside."

He takes my silence as the answer he wants to hear. His voice is a little too high and off-key, but his rhythm is good. The song is about loving someone who's already gone, how you don't stop loving someone after they're dead, how love carries a person through the darkest times. It has a haunting, lilting quality to it that seems amplified in the car, drifting over the hum of the engine and the soft hiss of the heater.

I close my eyes and let the song sink into me. My heartbeat slows. I try to breathe again.

At the end, he hits a note really off-key, and his voice squeaks and cracks almost at the same time. He starts laughing. After a moment, I can laugh with him.

I rub my eyes with my free hand. "That wasn't the worst thing I've ever heard. I mean, I wasn't clawing my eardrums out or anything."

"Thank you very much. I accept flowers, copious applause, and gift cards to Dick's Sporting Goods and GuitarHeaven.com." He's still holding my hand so tightly my fingers are losing sensation. "Will you please come here?"

I shake my head. I can't.

He comes to me instead. He unfolds his lanky body and crawls awkwardly across the seat. He gathers me into a hug. At first, I stiffen.

"I think you're amazing," he says into my hair.

"I'm getting snot on your shirt," I mumble back.

He laughs. I feel it rumbling through his chest. He is safe, I tell myself. And I am stronger than I was before. I am brave. I can do this. I allow myself to melt into his embrace.

We lay like this for a long time, warm and safe in each other's arms. The feeling settling over me is something new and bright and scary as hell. It's almost too fragile to look at, too delicate to touch.

It's like waking up from a long and difficult sleep or a deep thaw—coming back to the world. It happens slowly, one numb limb at a time.

FORTY-EIGHT

I wake up sweating, gasping, my fingers clutching at my sleeping bag. Another bad dream. I stare up at the inky darkness above me. The urge to cut rears up, but I resist it. I take long, slow, steady breaths.

I'm changing. I want the change, this shifting, nebulous idea in my head of who I could be, someone different, better than who I am now, something transformed. I want it. I need it. I need it so much it hums in my blood, thrums through my skin, calcifies my bones.

Every day I am stronger. Braver. Better. Every day I feel myself coming back to life.

But part of me is still stuck. There are shadows, that black thing gnawing inside me. I need to know. I have to know.

I have to know what to do with this black guilt, the rage and sorrow choking my throat. And the question that swirls at the very center of me: am I just as guilty as they are?

After all, I am free. My mother is locked away for my sake, a truth that fills me with shame. Is it possible my mother doesn't know the truth about Frank? That she didn't protect me all those years because she didn't know? Does she love me after all? She's in prison because of me. Should I be where she is? Don't those shackles belong on my wrists, not hers?

My skin's blistered, every nerve frayed. All this time, I didn't think I could handle the truth—that either way, it would destroy me. But I was wrong.

I've made friends. I've protected my brothers. I've built a family. And I'm starting to build a life—a real life, a good life.

I am strong enough, now. Brave enough.

I'm in the chrysalis.

The caterpillar who inches along the ground, plagued by shadows and predators, who can't even see the sky—does she still imagine being in it? Does she dream of flying, of sunlight flashing off iridescent wings?

Does she feel that primal urge within her cells, a flickering deep within her DNA, like a whisper—that she wasn't made for this? That there's more, so much more—but she'll have to destroy herself to reach it.

It will be her destruction or her salvation. She doesn't know which.

She spins her own coffin anyway.

FORTY-NINE

With its benign brown brick façade, the Women's Huron Valley Correctional Facility looks like it could be a library from the front, or even a school. That is, if you can ignore the perimeter fences and the guard towers looming threateningly over the yard. I undergo the check-in and frisk procedures and clip the plastic visitor badge to my sweatshirt, obediently holding out my hand for the black light stamp.

I sit in the cold metal chair, my knee juddering as I watch the other female prisoners with their families. To my left, a mother holds a chubby baby on her lap, reading aloud to him from a battered children's book. In one corner, a correctional officer stands like a sentry, keeping watch.

The electronic double doors buzz open. The inmates' sneakers squeak against the concrete floor as they shuffle in. At first, my gaze falls right past her. The woman standing in front of me is a stranger. She's wearing a navy-blue shirt and pants set striped with a bar of bright orange. She's at least thirty pounds thinner, with short brown hair cut in a bob just below her ears.

"Sidney."

I blink up at her. Everything I've prepared to say is gone. My mind goes blank, empty, numb.

Ma moves toward me like she's going to hug me. I flinch. A shadow flits across her face. She retreats, sitting down opposite me. "We can hug when we come in and when we leave," she says in a hurt voice.

I want her to hug me, even as I push her away. At the same time, I don't want to hug her. I don't want to touch her at all.

"I'm so glad you came. How are you doing?" She smells clean, like soap. She folds her hands on her lap. Her fingernails are trimmed close to the skin. She's still wearing her wedding ring.

"Okay." The English language has all but abandoned me. My tongue feels like a block of clay.

"It's been a long time."

"Uh huh."

"I've missed you so much."

My mother circles me with words, traps me with longing. It's not fair. I've spent all my life despising and wanting this woman, loathing and loving, scorning and desiring. Everything I wanted and needed her to be, she wasn't. My emotions are a tangled knot in the pit of my stomach.

"How's Ellie and the boys? They come to visit every week, like clockwork."

"They're fine."

"They're growing so fast. Too fast."

Across the room, a child laughs. I feel the pull of this new Susan Shaw, this bright and shiny mother. Who is this woman? "Yep."

"Did you get a prepaid card?" She gestures at the vending machines lining the far wall. "I'm starving. Ellie always brings in a card so we can fill up on snacks. The boys love it."

I shake my head.

She huffs a breath. "Remember it next time, okay? How's Zoe? I heard you named her. I suppose it's nice, though it's not what I would've chosen."

My hands clench into fists on the table, all my old anger and resentment rushing back. How dare she ask about Zoe? I hate the sound of her name on Ma's lips. "She's sick, thanks to you."

"Sidney, honey, why do you have to be like this? Why can't we have a nice, pleasant visit?"

"I'm not here for a nice, pleasant visit," I force out.

She frowns, disappointed. "Please don't ruin this. This is the first time I've seen you in months. Do you know how long I've been looking forward to this?"

Shame strikes me right in the center of my chest. All the old wounds open up, my heart red and vulnerable and pulsing with pain. I came here to answer that haunting question "why", but now that I'm face-to-face with her, my resolve is crumbling.

"I take classes here, do counseling," she says brightly. "They've got a substance abuse program. And other classes, like school. I can sign up for auto mechanics. Can you imagine? Me fixing up cars, up to my elbows in black grease? They've even got a garden. I used to like gardening."

I stare down at my fingernails, pick at a stray flag of skin. "I'm not here to talk about gardens, Ma."

Ma lifts her hand. It hovers over mine, hesitating.

I pull my hand away. I can't. It's too much.

Ma's hand drops onto her lap. She sighs. "I have an illness, Sidney. They call it major depressive disorder and cyclothymia, which they said is like bipolar, kind of. They diagnosed me here. I was—well, you know what it was like. I don't even remember—" Her voice catches. "I suffered so much. My illness made things difficult for me."

My fingers curl up into my palms, nails burrowing into my skin. More laughter from across the room. My soul crumples, and I am nine again, bathing my sick, drunken mother because Ma's forgotten how to wash herself, hasn't done it in days.

It was the first time Frank took off. He was gone for two weeks, and every single day felt like Ma was descending further into a black hole, dragging us after her. I can still feel the slippery bar of soap in my hands, the sudsy water, my mother's slick, rubbery skin. I stared at the milk-white stalk of her neck while I scrubbed.

A strange and shameful feeling washed over me when I stole a glance at Ma's body, her drooping breasts and splayed legs, her wet nakedness exposed in a swirl of pubic hair. Even at nine, I knew. Even at nine, mothering a grown woman, I knew this wasn't how things should be. "*You* made things difficult for us, your kids. I never even had a childhood."

"There were good times," Ma says wistfully, hopefully, almost begging.

I sit frozen, hardly able to move, to breathe.

"I used to sing to you. I taught you to draw and paint. I helped you knit a scarf in third grade, remember? You always followed me around like a little puppy, helping me clean up after the boys. We put soapy wash clothes under our feet and danced around the kitchen to mop it. Do you remember that?"

I do. Longing snakes through me, coiling around my heart, squeezing so hard it hurts. "That was a long time ago."

"Not so long ago. It seems like yesterday."

I can't help it. Anger is burning me up inside and I can't contain it. "And all those times you passed out in your room for days? All the times I had to feed and bathe and dress the boys, do the dishes and clean the floors and scrub the toilet, staying up late, too exhausted to finish my homework? All those times I had to check on you, to make sure you were still breathing, to snatch the cigarette out of your fingers so the whole damn house didn't burn down. How long ago was that?"

She closes her eyes. "I don't like to think about that."

"Neither do I. Only you took that choice away from me."

"You're always so difficult, so angry. This isn't easy for me, you know." She sighs. "The doctors make me talk about things and help me see all the reasons why I had to drown out my problems with alcohol. I was so lonely when Frank was gone. If you must know, you kids were too much. I was overwhelmed."

I keep shaking my head. I don't want to hear this. She's just spouting more excuses. Still passing the blame. Everything inside me is sharp and jagged as broken glass. "Did you know?"

"What?"

"Did you know what was really happening?"

"I don't know what you're talking about."

"That summer after eighth grade. I tried to tell you the truth about—"

"Oh, Sidney, the past is in the past. Can't we both forgive and forget and move on? Can't we just have a nice visit? I've missed you so much."

"I need to know."

"I don't want to talk about this." Her gaze slides away from my face. "It's upsetting me."

The words are gravel in my throat. "I need to know if you knew what Frank was doing to me. That he was coming in my room at night. That he was—"

"Stop that." Something changes in her face, some emotion I can't read flickering across her hardened features. "There you go. Starting in on your lies again."

"We're done here." I stand up quickly, my legs trembling.

Her face blanches. She reaches for me. "Wait. Sit back down."

I just stare at her.

"Sit down, please."

"Tell me the truth, or I'm gone."

She folds her hands on her lap. She nods to herself, like she's deciding something. She meets my eyes. "Have it your way."

I sit.

"You need to understand," she says slowly, her voice flat. "You were always a selfish little liar."

I go still. "What?"

"You lied all the time, trying to make me look bad every chance you got, trying to get between Frank and me." It's like a flip has been switched inside her. Her gaze is suddenly cold, the lines around her mouth sharp. Gone is the soft, sweet Ma from only a few minutes ago. My mother, the chameleon. "You were dressing skanky, itching for attention from a man, any man. I recognized the look in your eyes, the swing of your hips. It was dripping off you. Frank's just a man, like any other. He'll take what's offered."

Outwardly, I don't even flinch. I'm made of stone. My heart is carved in marble. "I was his daughter."

"What Frank and me had—it was primal. It was eternal. We loved each other more than we'd loved anybody else. I would've done anything for him. Anything. And he always came back to me. Do you understand? Most people don't get it. Most people never experience real love. They wouldn't know it if it slapped them in the face. Sure, he wandered. He disappeared sometimes. He enjoyed himself. He's a man. He's entitled to that. But he always, always came home. To me, to my arms. I was his."

"You always chose him. Over your own kids."

She nods. "Aren't you supposed to love your husband more than your kids? He came first."

"No, you aren't."

"Well, I did. I do. I've never apologized for that, and I'm not starting now."

"I don't understand."

Ma's voice is sharp-edged as a knife. "You came to me that summer to brag."

I'm so shocked, my heart skips a beat. "What?"

"You know how Frank was. He was enamored by young flesh. You wanted to shove it in my face, to show you were better than me, that you'd won. He wanted you, not me. My own daughter."

I shake my head, stunned to silence by her words. By what this means. She knew. All along, all these years, she's known what he was doing. And she never did a thing to stop it.

Ma rubs her eyes with her fists. Her mouth is pressed into a tight, bloodless line. "Every chance you got, you threw it in my face."

"I was fourteen."

"Old enough. Like that other girl. She was plenty willing until he didn't want her anymore. Then she called rape. Typical slut."

My breath stills in my chest. "You mean the girl at the fraternity party. When you were pregnant with me."

Ma's eyebrows pinch together. "You've been talking to Bill."

"He said he told you, tried to warn you."

She gives a short, hard bark of laughter. "He did. Frank already told me himself. That girl wasn't special. She wasn't the first, and she was far from the last. Your daddy didn't love any of 'em. They were trash, shiny toys to play with and throw away."

"She was just a kid."

Ma shrugs, like that doesn't even matter. "He loved me. He always came home to me."

"If you loved him so much, then why are you here?" I ask the question, the one that matters most, my heart in my throat. "Why did you do this for me?" I spread my hands out, gesturing at us, the concrete walls, the guards, Ma's drab prison garb, everything.

Ma sniffs and leans back in her chair. "Him being gone nearly killed me. But something happened—I don't know. Something clicked in my head. I thought I wanted to die, too. I wanted to lie there next to him and put a bullet in my head. I thought I couldn't breathe without him, couldn't survive the days without him with me. 'Til death do us part."

I blink. My vision blurs. "That's why you told me to get out."

Ma doesn't even have the decency to blush. "At first. I didn't want you between us, in the way even in death. It should've been him and me, always and forever. So I told you to leave. I sank to my knees and put the gun to my head.

"But I couldn't do it. I kept seeing your face in front of me. And I knew what you'd say, what everybody would say, when they arrested you."

"What?" I whisper.

"It would all come out. The whole bloody, ugly mess. They'd call me a terrible mother. They'd call him worse things. I knew how it'd look. How the whole world would judge us. All those ugly, despicable secrets, mine and Frank's and yours, splashed on the front page for everyone to see.

"I couldn't bear it. I couldn't bear to see Frank destroyed like that. His name dragged through the mud in death, when he couldn't even defend himself. I would do anything for him, do you understand? Anything. And there was still something I could do. I could still protect him. How could I not?

"I shot him again, for GSR and forensics and everything. I've watched enough TV to know how it goes."

I stare at her, stunned. Finally, we're getting down to the bottom of it, the lies unspooling themselves around the cold, hard nugget of truth. "You did this for yourself?"

"For all of us. Do you want it out there? Plastered on every newspaper, website, and evening news show? Tarnishing Frank's good name?"

"His good name? Are you insane?"

"Five minutes," the correctional officer warns.

She crosses her arms. "Frank would want it this way. His reputation was always so important to him. It's the last thing I can do for him. It's not so bad in here. I still get to watch my favorite soaps. I get my cigarettes."

I stare at her. The snarl of feelings, the resentment and the longing, the anger and the love, the moments of happiness and the years of bitterness—they clump into a knot at the base of my throat.

I have my answer. Even in death, Frank wins when it comes to my mother.

She sacrificed to save him, not me. She didn't sacrifice anything, ever, for me.

And in a strange, complicated way I can't explain, that frees me. The truth I thought would destroy me hasn't broken me. I am strong enough, brave enough, to realize this. My mother does not love me. But not because of anything I've done.

She is incapable of real love. That is not my fault. It is hers. In her own way, she is a monster, just like Frank.

"I've tried to hate you my whole life," I say.

"Tried?" Ma raises her eyebrows.

"I can't. I've tried, and I can't." I don't know if a daughter can ever completely hate her mother, no matter what she's done. There is too much between us. The hollow ache in my heart tells me I still love her. Some small, lost, and lonely part of me will always love her, or at least, the idea of her, what she should have been.

She gives me a slow, satisfied smile. "You gonna come see me again, then?"

I shake my head. I stare at her, at the hard angles of her face, the shift of her eyes, her darting gaze never landing on my face, never looking at me straight. Never really seeing me at all.

I feel something, like the whisper of a breath on the back of my neck. The universe is expanding, growing larger around me, encompassing something more, something higher and bigger and better than myself. I think of Arianna's God, of the concept of grace, of love, of mercy and faith and all the things I thought I had lost but can find again.

But I won't find them here. I won't find them with her.

"No, Ma. I'm not going to visit you."

"What?" Her face contorts. "After everything I've done for you?"

I shake my head.

"You did this to me," she hisses, leaning close. "I'm in here suffering because of you!"

I take a deep breath. "If I've learned anything, it's this: you don't apologize to or for the monsters in your house."

"What the hell's that supposed to mean?"

My fingers uncurl on my lap. I think the words through before I say them. I've seen the consequences of what people do when they're controlled by their brokenness. They break other people.

I don't want to break anymore. I don't want to break Aaron or Frankie or Zoe Rose. I want this to end, the generations of hurt and pain and abuse. I want it to end with me. "You don't have any power over me. Not anymore."

She stares at me, uncomprehending.

Even now, she is still blind. I look at her and I see a future path I will not take. What I feel for her suddenly isn't hate or anger. It's pity. She is her own punishment. The four walls surrounding her are a prison of her own making.

The electronic doors buzz open. Two dozen women in blue and orange disentangle themselves from their families.

"Sidney!" Ma cries.

But I don't answer. I don't need to.

The prisoners shuffle back through the double doors yawning open like a mouth, my mother with them. I watch her go.

I leave the prison an orphan, yet somehow lighter than I've ever felt.

FIFTY

Every day, I run. Sometimes with Lucas. Sometimes by myself. I run the river path. I run the track at school. I run the dirt road to the old red barn.

It's been two weeks since I went to the prison. Two weeks since I walked away an orphan. I know I'm free, but I'm not sure I really believe it yet. When the bad thoughts come prowling in, I outrun them. I run until my mind is scoured clean. My feet slap the wet dirt in tune with my heartbeat. The world is snow and ice and mud. I am galloping through it, a part of everything.

At school, Margot leaves us alone. If she sees us, she snorts, tosses her hair, and pretends she needs to turn and walk in the opposite direction. She and Eli break up. I don't know why, and I don't care.

Last week, Aunt Ellie went back to Ohio to clear out her apartment, see old friends, and take care of whatever she needs to before she can start her new life here. She put her belongings in storage until we find a house that isn't this one. All of her jewelry comes back with her, stuffed inside two giant suitcases.

Most evenings after supper, I pull out my drawing pad. I use my Prismacolor pencils and a thick sheet of watercolor paper. I use my greens, yellows, and whites to color the rich shades of the Luna Moth. I take my time, putting down layers of waxy pigment on the thick, textured paper. I burnish everything to blend and smooth the colors, regularly wiping my hands to keep them from smudging the paper. I concentrate on my work, hatching and crosshatching each layer of color for the brilliant, pale green wings.

The focus keeps me centered. I feel calm, still. I can give myself to the page, to the white paper and the smudgy charcoal and the rich, inky pastels in a way I couldn't with cutting, when my canvas was my own skin, my own self.

When you give yourself to the razor, it takes pieces of you. But art is different. Art gives you back to yourself.

Sometimes Aaron sits next to me with his construction paper and sparkly neon crayons. When I'm finished with my own work, I draw him Ratty Bunny sleeping on his very own bed in his very own room, Ratty Bunny jumping on a trampoline, Ratty Bunny enjoying a rabbit-sized Jacuzzi.

Aaron starts giggling.

"What?" I ask him as I sketch a floppy ear.

"Ratty Bunny's farting up all those bubbles."

"Is he?" I pencil in bigger bubbles popping around Ratty Bunny's submerged tail. I give him a smug, satisfied grin beneath his whiskers.

Aaron leans into me, his warm body shaking as he laughs harder. "More farting bubbles!"

So I do. Later, after I folded his drawings into triangles and he tucked them into the pocket of his sweatshirt, I take out my pastels and show him the parts of the butterfly. How she uses her proboscis like a straw to suck up flower nectar. How her leg is five-jointed, and how her foot, the tarsus, can actually taste each flower petal she lands on. How her brilliant colors are from both pigment and structure, the tiny scales shingling her wings like the roof of a house. How the iridescent flashes of her wings are like the tints reflected in a glass prism, the spectrum of a rainbow, the refractory blue of the sky, the pearly sheen of oil on water. How exquisite she is, and she doesn't even know it.

He listens, his face rapt. He smells like Cheetos and crayon wax, like the vanilla-scented shampoo he never quite gets all the way washed out of his hair. We even get Frankie to come over and draw his own version of Ratty Bunny.

I make a joke, and he laughs. My heart squeezes in my chest. What I feel for them swells up inside me. Pride, fierce protectiveness, and love —so much love.

Frankie's thin, wiry body presses against mine. I put my arm around his shoulders, and for once, he doesn't pull away. I think of the darkness inside both of us. The monster with sharp teeth ripping and tearing at our insides. The monster that makes us lash out at everyone who could help us.

No one but me can fight my monster. No one but Frankie can fight his. But I can still be there for him. I can let him know he's not alone. I can tell him it's worth fighting the darkness coiled inside him. That he has to, or it will eat him alive. I will tell him. Over and over again.

Until he finally believes it. Until we both do.

FIFTY-ONE

I'm right on time for my session with Dr. Yang. I put the folded apology letter on his desk. I finally finished it last night. "A little late, but better than never, right?"

He only raises his eyebrows at me.

"I am sorry that I hit Jackson Cole," I say slowly. "I let my anger get the best of me and I acted impulsively. He's no angel, but he was twelve years old. Frankie's age. Just a kid. I should have treated him with more compassion. I should have talked to someone first, instead of taking things into my own hands. Anger isn't bad, but I should have handled it better."

Dr. Yang leans back in his chair and gives me a broad smile. "Bravo."

I shrug. "No medals needed. It only took me like seven months."

"You clearly put thought and effort into it, Sidney. That's more than enough."

I sit in the La-Z-Boy, but instead of slumping, I lean forward, my elbows on my knees. "Why did you put me and Arianna together for counseling?"

He steeples his fingers beneath his chin. "It was a hunch. I saw something in your eyes, both of you. There are different ways we harm ourselves, close ourselves off from the world. I felt like you could help each other, and it didn't feel right to add other students into the group. It would be you and Arianna or it wouldn't be anyone at all. It worked out, didn't it?"

I don't know what he expected, but he looks a bit surprised when I say yes. "Very good. I hope these sessions have made a difference for you this year. I hope there's some good starting to shine through in your life."

"Doc, that's a pretty poetic line. Are you moonlighting as a beatbox poet?"

"Not at this time, no. I think the students here keep me busy enough. Do you have weekend plans? Filling out college applications, perhaps? There are still some colleges with open enrollment."

"No. But not for the reason you think." I fill him in on our new lives with Aunt Ellie, our house-hunting excursions, our visit with Zoe Rose, who is doing well, considering. Michaela Davis told us a family in Niles is interested in adopting her. They've worked with FASD children before. They know how to help her. And they want Zoe to grow up knowing us, her siblings. This thought is like a bubble I keep cupped in my hands, still so fragile I'm afraid to let it out into the light.

Aunt Ellie's put the boys in counseling. I hope talking to someone who's an expert on feelings can help Frankie sort through his. I'm seeing a new counselor, too. My first appointment is next week, but that doesn't mean I'll stop visiting Dr. Yang. I have a grudging affection for this chair.

He takes off his glasses and rubs his eyes with the sleeve of his shirt.

"Wait—Doc, are you crying?"

He smiles at me with watery eyes. "Just allergies."

"In February? Come on."

"Sidney, I cannot tell you how proud I am of you these past several months. You are incredibly strong."

"Or stupid."

He shakes his head. "Certainly not stupid. Please tell me you're planning on going to college."

"Yes, sir."

Dr. Yang grabs his chest and mock-falls like he's having a heart attack. "Sir? Really? I didn't realize you even knew that word."

I shrug. "I'm trying it out."

"It suits you. You thinking about a possible major?"

"Yep. Interpretive dance. Does that suit me, too?"

"Not even a little. How about for real?"

"Okay, for real. Art education, maybe. It would be fun to teach little kids how to paint and draw and stuff."

"That sounds excellent. As long as you refrain from punching anyone in the face."

I grin. "Attempting to spice up therapy with a little comedy routine, Doc?"

He smiles. "We are all capable of change, Sidney. At any age, and no matter what we're up against."

I spin my rings. I take off the blue sapphire one from Aunt Ellie and press it between my fingers. I shape the words in my mouth with my tongue, smoothing them like stones. "Did you really mean what you said, about wanting to help me?"

"Are you kidding me?"

I wonder how it might have been different if I was brave enough before, if I'd been able to open my mouth and let those ugly, secret words out into this room. If I'd allowed myself to trust him.

Would Ma still be serving out her sentence in prison? Were there other ways I could have helped her, saved us all, if I hadn't been such a coward? If I'd known then how people can surprise you, if you find the right ones, the ones who are broken but also strong. The ones whose broken pieces fit like puzzle pieces inside you. But you have to keep looking for them. You have to keep risking parts of yourself in order to find them, to help them find you. You have to keep risking. Every day.

Dr. Yang is one of them, one of the good ones who opens up spaces for other people, who helps them see how to let the light in.

"I wrote some things down in my journal. If you, ah, want to hear them."

He smiles. "If you are willing to share with me, then yes, I would love to hear it."

My fingers tighten around the journal in my lap. Most of the pages are filled with the butterflies I drew over and over, but in the margins, in the spaces between the wings, I've been writing. Every night, I write.

The words are sticky in my throat, but I know I need to say them. "My dad was a bad guy. He did some really bad things. He hit me sometimes. He did worse things. I tried to protect my brothers. I had to take care of them because my mom was drunk all the time and out of it. But she wasn't always like that, so I—I both hated her and loved her at the same time."

I still miss her with a fierce ache. I miss the mother she should have been. But I don't feel shame anymore. Like Arianna said, you don't apologize to or for the monsters in your house.

"Thank you for telling me," Dr. Yang says. Now he really looks like he might cry.

I keep talking. He keeps listening. I tell him the story I told Arianna, about the broken girl with broken wings. It's hard, and I'm scared the whole time, but he doesn't take his eyes off me. He never looks bored or angry or judgmental.

By the time the bell rings, we've both got copious amounts of wetness in our eyes.

"You need to keep doing this, keep writing. Keep talking," he says. "Over and over again. Not just once."

I shake my head. I feel sad and uncomfortable and drained. But I'm also lighter, and cleaner, somehow, like after a hard run. "I don't think I'm brave enough."

"Do you remember the mountain I talked about during the first group counseling session? How it's scary and seems so overwhelming when you start at the bottom? But you are doing something brave and amazing with each and every step, no matter how small it is. How when you keep going, day after day, you can finally turn around and discover how far you've traveled, higher than you ever thought possible. And the view is breathtaking."

"Doc, you're doing that poet thing again." But his words sink all the way down into the core of me. "It's hard. Everything you're talking about."

He smiles, and he doesn't look tired anymore. "If you remember anything from these sessions, Sidney, I hope you remember this: Anything worthwhile is hard as hell. Sometimes the most difficult things are the most important, and the most rewarding."

When the bell rings, I grab my backpack and head for the door. "Dr. Yang," I say, pausing in the doorway. "You are. Making a difference for me, I mean."

Then I'm gone, out into the rush and crush of students impatient to rush to the next class, the next thing, the next moment, the next, the next, the next.

FIFTY-TWO

The next day, I'm headed to Chemistry when there's a tug on my arm. It's Jasmine, standing by herself, her arms crossed over her chest. Her face is pale beneath her makeup. There's a cluster of pimples around her mouth. "Can I talk to you?"

"Aren't you already?"

She hesitates. "I'm not sure what to say."

I still. "Try me."

"We got your apology letter to Jackson. It was really good. Thank you. You were right. My little brother is kind of a dick."

I raise my eyebrows. "I shouldn't have hit him, though."

A hint of a smile graces her lips. "No, probably not." Her expression darkens. She's quiet while a few people pass us in the hallway. "I didn't know. I didn't know how bad it was for you. I understand now. Why you cut. Why you were so angry all the time."

She might as well have punched me in the gut. My stomach contracts.

I flash back to all those lazy summers sprawled on her bed, my fingernails blackened with charcoal, my skin sun-kissed, hair damp from the pool, my mind drowsy and entranced as I listened to her.

I hear the bray of her laugh, the melodic sound of her voice, at turns serious or excited, lecturing me on the life cycle of one of her larvae like she'd lecture an undergraduate class of future scientists. I listened like her words were a lifeline, like if I internalized them enough, I could bind them inside myself. I could know how to fly away on those butterfly wings of hers, like Icarus before he dared the heat of the sun.

"That was a long time ago," I say softly.

"Not that long." Her brow furrows. "I was a crappy friend."

At last, we both agree on something. I stop the sharp words before they come out of my mouth. I don't have to be a jerk. I nod, hearing her out.

"I'm sorry for all the stuff we—I—did to you. You were trying to tell me something, back then. And I didn't listen. Whatever it was, I didn't listen."

I don't say anything. How can I? She's finally saying what I so desperately needed her to say four years ago. I bite my lip, trying to keep it together.

"I didn't know what they—what Margot—was going to do at the beach. I'm sorry for that." She shifts her feet from side to side. She grips her phone with whitened knuckles.

The bell rings. We just stare at each other. She looks uncomfortable as hell, but she's not walking away.

"Okay," I say finally.

"I just—I'm sorry. I've wanted to talk to you for months, but I just—I flaked out. I couldn't do it, not after everything I'd done to you. You probably don't want to forgive me, but I'm asking for a truce."

I twist my rings on my fingers. What might have been doesn't matter anymore. The enmity between us—the betrayals, the treachery, the fighting and the animosity—it doesn't matter.

I can let it all go—the anger, the spite, the pain. I can let go of the bitterness without letting go of everything, without letting go of her. She's a huge part of my past, a thousand bittersweet memories tacked to a display board.

I smile at her. People can change. They can make mistakes and decide to be different, to be better. Forgiveness is part of that. Holding on to the good things, letting go of the bad. Dr. Yang would be proud. "Do you still have them?"

"What?"

"Your butterflies. The ones on your walls. Do you still have them?"

Her face contorts. Suddenly she looks forlorn, almost bereft. Like she's just realized she's lost something important. "Not the caterpillar jars. The display plaques are stuffed in cardboard boxes on the top shelf of my mom's closet."

"My favorite was always the Blue Morpho butterfly, with those iridescent, sapphire wings."

She looks down at her boots. "Mine, too."

"I'll see you around, Jasmine."

Her lip trembles ever so slightly as she grins back at me. "Not if I see you first."

I turn and walk into Chemistry, a small smile still on my face. The next time I see Jasmine in the hallways or the cafeteria, I'll nod at her. She'll say hello back.

It's a start.

FIFTY-THREE

I wake up in the dark, sweating, trembling, my heart jittering in my chest. I feel the need, the wanting, so strong it's overpowering. I stare up at the darkness above me and I force myself to breathe in, breathe out, breathe in.

Sometimes the loneliness and the sorrow and the sense of loss strikes me like a crater in my chest. It's a black hole drilling through my ribs, my heart.

The wanting for things I can't have will never leave me. The pain of my past, the bad things I've done and the bad things done to me, they will not go away.

I fumble for the razor I tucked into an old shoe on my closet floor. The process is so familiar I can do it in complete darkness. I slide the blade across my ankle. The sweet, hot pain slices through me, cutting through the tangle of guilt and sorrow. I close my eyes, waiting for the relief that comes with the pain.

But there's something else, a little pulsing ember of hope. I'm stronger than this. I can be better than this. I deserve better than this.

I deserved to be loved. I deserve love.

I think about the things Dr. Yang says. And Lucas. And Arianna. We have to go through our fear, our pain. Not under or around it or behind it, but through it.

I put down the razor. I stop seeking relief, seeking numbness. I let myself feel it. The emotions hit me like a flood, a tsunami of sadness. Anger. Sorrow. Regret. Rage. Grief. I let in each feeling as it comes.

I don't push it away. I don't grind it into rage. I don't slice it into bloody ribbons.

It comes. It roars through me. It comes again. The tears stream down my face and I am sobbing, gasping, weeping. The pain radiates through every inch of me.

I was hurt by the people who were supposed to love me the most. It wasn't fair, or just, or right. It wasn't my fault—it isn't my fault.

I am motherless. I am fatherless. Yet, I am still me. I am who I am in spite of them.

I still have this darkness inside of me.

But I am also strong. And brave. And good.

I have to fight the darkness.

Every day, I fight it.

FIFTY-FOUR

I spend as much time with Arianna and Lucas as I can. Lucas comes over and meets Aunt Ellie and the boys. He wins them over completely with his easy-going charm.

We take the boys to see Zoe Rose, to cuddle and cradle her and wrap her up in as much love as we can soak into her little body.

Lucas drives us all the way out to the indoor roller skating rink in Grand Rapids. We slip and fall all over the place, laughing at each other until our sides ache.

One day after school, Lucas takes me to Delia's Ice Cream Shoppe. It's still cold out, but Delia's has gourmet coffees, cappuccinos, espressos, etcetera, etcetera. The booths are lime-green with pink Formica table tops. A toy electric train runs continuously around a track hanging from the ceiling.

We share a booth in the back, around the corner from the noisy kids. I drink a peanut butter chocolate swirl shake, while Lucas sips a mocha latte, extra mocha. Our legs press against each other.

Lucas pulls out his mom's pink lighter and taps it on the Formica table top. The skin around his mouth tightens.

I press my shoulder against his. "What's wrong?"

"I lied, before."

I tense. "What do you mean?"

"I told you I made peace with my mom's death. I acted like it didn't bother me, but it does. Sometimes, I feel like a horrible person. I'm out here, living my life—falling in love, even—" My heart jerks at his words, but he stumbles on. "I spent so much of my childhood trying to make her happy, trying to be funny and goofy and never add to her sadness. It kind of worked, for a while. Then she got sick. And I—I resent her. How terrible is that?" He flicks the lighter on and off, on and off. "That's killer, right? Resenting someone who's dying, who's leaving me forever?"

I shove my leg harder against his, trying to beam all the warmth and comfort I can straight into his sadness-infused body. "That sucks."

"I don't run for fun. I run to get away from the bad feelings I don't like inside myself."

"I think that's a pretty normal feeling."

"Is it?" His gaze flickers over my face, searching for something.

"It is." I finally feel like I can see him. And I want to know more. I want to see everything. Because I know he understands, at least a little, that quicksand of shame—how fast it takes you down, how deep it goes.

"Half the time, I desperately miss her. Half the time, I'm already grieving for her death. And half the time, I'm furious with her. That probably makes no sense at all."

"Only the parts where I question what kind of math they're teaching you down in Florida. Three halves?"

He snorts, then laughs, then does this sort of gasping-sob thing.

I entwine my fingers through his. "Remember what you told me? You feel your way through it."

He scrubs his arm across his eyes.

"You're not alone. I'm here."

He squeezes my hand. We sit like that for a long time, our drinks melting, forgotten.

It's so ordinary, I think, to break and be broken. It's so much more extraordinary to put in the hard, agonizing work of rebuilding yourself, piece by piece, shard by shard.

My heart tightens. I need to show him parts of myself he might not want to see. I don't know much about relationships, but I know this: I need to share myself with him, the way he's shared himself with me. I need him to see into me the way I see into him.

I lick my lips, inhale a shaky breath.

"You okay?" Lucas puts his arm around my shoulders. I sink into him, smell the clean, woodsy scent of his sweatshirt.

Will he hate me once I've told him? Will he be disgusted and turn away, like Jasmine, like Ma? I don't know, but I need to do this anyway. For me.

I start with the least of my secrets, but even this is enough to make most guys run for the hills. I know that much. "I have scars."

"Most of us do."

"No. Real scars. Ugly scars. All over my legs."

"From an accident?"

My throat is dry and scratchy. "No. I—I did it to myself."

"Will you show me?" His voice is gentle.

I pull away and lift my leg up on the booth. With trembling fingers, I roll up my pants to my shin, revealing the crosshatched scars and cuts. My skin looks like a battleground.

Now is when he turns away, his face contorted in revulsion.

Only he doesn't. He reaches out and touches the lumpy scar tissue above my ankle. "Sidney, I'm so sorry."

"It's worse in other places."

"What made you need to hurt yourself like that?"

I blink rapidly. "I—things happened at home. Bad things."

A shadow passes over his face. His lips tighten. "Who hurt you?"

"I want to tell you. I want to tell you everything. And I will. But—I need a little more time."

"If someone's hurting you—"

I shake my head. "No. Not anymore. I just—I can't yet. But I will. Can you understand that?"

"As long as you promise me you're safe."

I nod.

"Are you still . . . hurting yourself?"

"I'm working really hard not to. I promise."

His expression softens. He draws me in close. I go to him, let him wrap both his arms around me. I nestle into his chest. His strong, steady heartbeat thuds against my ear. I wind my fingers through his and hold on tight.

"Scars make you strong," he says into my hair. "They mean you're a survivor. And that makes them beautiful. You're beautiful."

"I have scars nobody can see," I say, my voice weak.

His arms tighten around me. "You can show me when you're ready. I'm here. Okay? I'm right here."

I close my eyes. Something opens up inside me—a deep, rich warmth, a beautiful tenderness, like sunlight, like star shine on silver waves, like the flutter of iridescent wings.

It expands inside me, filling up the hollow places in my heart.

FIFTY-FIVE

It is a day in late March that feels like spring, if you close your eyes and manage not to see the soggy brown earth, the rapidly melting pelts of snow. The sun kisses my cheeks. The breeze lifts the dark fringe of my hair. Shadows from gravestones elongate across the matted grass.

This is how I feel. I am afraid. But I know now I am stronger than my fear. I don't know what's coming next. I don't know the direction the road turns ahead, or the places it may go. I only know the way behind me is closed.

I am still. Everything inside me is still.

I stare at the name engraved on the stone. This is the first and last time I will ever visit my father's grave. I'm not entirely sure why I've come, but it seems right. It's another form of letting go. Frank's been dead for months, but only now does he seem really, truly gone.

The nightmares may never go away. But I will survive them.

I feel a deep ache, a hollowed-out feeling like something precious and elemental has been torn right out of my chest. I think of how the nurse described my mother after they took Zoe Rose away from her in the hospital, how her arms continued to cradle nothing, empty air.

I will always have this. The ache of emptiness where a father's love should be. The stone-shaped pain of my mother, who was here, then not here, whose absence is a jagged wound barely scabbed over.

But these wounds are not fatal.

I breathe deeply. It is so natural, so right, to breathe. To live. It is right to experience sorrow, regret, guilt, passion, rage, pleasure, joy, pain, love. It is right to wake up every day and keep going, to force your way through, to fight for the good things. When they come, you have to grab on and not let go. You have to take risks and be vulnerable and let the good things in. It's scary as hell, but you do it anyway.

If you're lucky, you have a true friend or maybe two to support you, to brush you off and help you get up when you fall. But ultimately, it's up to you.

You are your own chrysalis.

You choose whether to let it all go, everything you knew, everything you thought kept you safe, kept you in control. You choose whether to believe in something bigger than yourself. If you know in your heart of hearts that there's more than this, more than the muck of the ground. There's a blue sky up there, beckoning for you to stretch your wings and fly.

I do not touch the stone or whisper any final words. I rise and walk back through the gravestones toward the car, where Lucas and Arianna wait for me.

The sun is in my eyes. I squint but do not look away.

The Beginning

AUTHOR'S NOTE

While *Beneath the Skin* is entirely fiction, the issues explored inside this book are not. Sidney's story weighed on my heart for over a decade before I wrote this book. I personally struggled with cutting, depression, and eating disorders from the age of thirteen until my early twenties. Much of Sidney and Arianna's pain is my own.

While I have not experienced the hell Sidney lived through, her darkest struggles reflect my mother's story. My mother suffered horrific sexual abuse at the hands of her father, my biological grandfather. I remember being twelve years old, hunched over a chicken sandwich at a restaurant much like Bill's Bar and Grill. My bare legs stuck to the hard, yellow booth. My Mom sat across from me, her face taut and pale. She didn't touch the fries on her plate.

That day, she told me her story. She told me of the abuse she suffered and explained why I'd never met my grandfather. My mother protected me. She saved me from a fate that befalls far too many innocent children. As of the publication of this book, my biological grandfather is in prison for the third time for the sexual assault of a minor.

My mother didn't have to kill anyone, like Sidney feels she must. When my mother was fourteen, a concerned teacher expressed an interest in her and asked her pointed questions about her home life.

Mom took this as her sign. Slowly, painfully, the truth came out. That teacher believed her and helped my mother escape her situation.

Words have power. We must speak our truth if anyone is to hear us. If they don't listen, speak louder. Yell. Scream. Go to someone else.

Telling someone was the first step in my mom's arduous journey toward healing. She still had to choose hope. She had to choose life, trust, and faith. She refused to perpetuate the cycle of abuse.

My mother is a cycle-breaker, much like Sidney. It takes tremendous courage to break the chains that trap and ensnare generations of families. You can do this, too.

You are stronger than you know.

You are beautiful and smart and talented and important. You matter.

If you or someone you love struggles with cutting, depression, eating disorders, or abuse, there is help. If you're being abused or were abused in the past, it's not your fault. Please tell someone. If they don't believe you, tell someone else. Speak for yourself. You're worth it.

Please use the following list of resources for help.

SEXUAL ABUSE

- **National Sexual Assault Hotline**: A national hotline operated by **RAINN** which serves people affected by sexual violence. It automatically routes the caller to their nearest sexual assault service provider. You can also search your local center at www.Rainn.org. Hotline: 800.656.HOPE.
- **National Child Abuse Hotline**: They can provide local referrals for services. A centralized call center provides the caller with the option of talking to a counselor. They are also connected to a language line that can provide service in over 140 languages. Hotline: 800.4.A.CHILD (422.2253).
- **Darkness to Light**: They provide crisis intervention and referral services to children or people affected by sexual abuse of children. Hotline calls are automatically routed to a local center. Helpline: 866.FOR.LIGHT (367.5444).

- **Cyber Tipline**: This tipline is operated by the **National Center for Missing and Exploited Children**. It can be used to communicate information to the authorities about child pornography or child sex trafficking. Hotline: 800.THE.LOST (843.5678).
- **National Children's Alliance**: This organization represents the national network of Child Advocacy Centers (CAC). CACs are a multi-disciplinary team of law enforcement, mental and physical health practitioners who investigate instances of child physical and sexual abuse. Their website explains the process and has a directory according to geographic location. www.nationalchildren'salliance.org.
- **Stop It Now**: Provides information to victims and parents/relatives/friends of child sexual abuse. The site also has resources for offender treatment as well as information on recognizing the signs of child sexual abuse. www.stopitnow.org. Hotline: 888-PREVENT (773.8368).
- **Justice for Children**: Provides a full range of advocacy services for abused and neglected children. www.justiceforchildren.org.

SELF-HARM

- **To Write Love On Her Arms**: A non-profit movement dedicated to presenting hope and finding help for people struggling with depression, addiction, self-injury, and suicide. www.TWLOHA.com.
- **1-800-SUICIDE**: A hotline for people contemplating suicide.
- **1-800-273-TALK**: A 24-hour crisis hotline if you're about to self-harm or are in an emergency situation.
- **S.A.F.E. Alternatives**: A professional network and educational resource base committed to helping you and others achieve an end to self-injurious behavior. www.selfinjury.com.

EATING DISORDERS

- **National Eating Disorder Association (NEDA)**: The largest non-profit organization in the United States working to promote awareness and prevention of eating disorders. NEDA also provides treatment referrals, support networks, and resources for those struggling and their loved ones. For crisis situations, **text "NEDA" to 741741** to be connected with a trained volunteer at Crisis Text Line. Helpline: 1-800-931-2237. www.nationaleatingdisorders.org.

- **Project HEAL**: Project HEAL is a non-profit organization that fundraises to provide grants to individuals who cannot otherwise afford eating disorder treatment. www.projectheal.org
- **Crisis Call Center**: 800-273-8255 or text ANSWER to 839863. Twenty-four hours a day, seven days a week. http://crisiscallcenter.org/crisis-services.

ACKNOWLEDGMENTS

First and foremost, I want to express my gratitude to my amazing readers. This book is for you. I hope you loved reading it as much as I loved writing it.

Many thanks to my fantastic group of beta readers who read this manuscript in its early stages and offered invaluable advice. Without you, this book wouldn't be what it is. I want to personally thank Janice Marden, Becca Cross, Kieren W. Moseng, Kathy Sanocki, Jeremy Steinkraus, Lena Hillbrand, Marjorie Frakes, Nidhi Upadhyaya, Rotceh Cova, Maranda Russell, Jazmin Cybulski, Tami Austin, Kelley Cantrell, Miranda Navarro, September Horton and her daughter Elizabeth. A huge thank you especially to Mallory Burgey and Leslie Spurrier for going above and beyond in their thoughtful critiques.

Thank you to Cody Mauro for a fantastic developmental edit. You saw the forest through the trees and helped me take Sidney's story to the next level. To Eliza Enriquez for her excellent proofreader's eye. And to Michelle Browne, a fantastic beta reader, editor, and really cool human being.

Thank you from the bottom of my heart to my good friend and fellow author Sarah McDugal, who took many hours out of her hectic schedule to read this manuscript and offer feedback.

To my cover designer, Clarissa Yeo, you are simply the best. You captured the essence of Sidney and her journey in a single image, creating a cover that still makes my heart leap every time I look at it.

Thank you to my parents, who supported my dreams way back when I was still telling stories into a tape recorder. And to my husband, who never doubted my ability and always believed in me. Thank you for your constant encouragement and support.

ABOUT THE AUTHOR

Kyla Stone is an emerging author of YA and women's fiction. She lives in Georgia with her family and two very spoiled cats. She loves reading, photography, board games, traveling, and dark chocolate. This is Kyla's debut novel.

Visit her at:

www.Facebook.com/KylaStoneBooks

www.Amazon.com/author/KylaStone

38626607R00195

Printed in Great Britain
by Amazon